BITE OF
THE BLACK WIDOW

JACK GANNON
CYNDI WILLIAMS-BARNIER

For Permission requests, write to:

YBR Publishing
PO Box 4904
Beaufort SC 29903-4904
contact@ybrpub.com
843-900-0859

ISBN-13: 978-1-7349515-4-7

Cover art by Chris Kapp
https://christopherkapp.myportfolio.com/contact
Cover design by Jack Gannon

YBR PUBLISHING, LLC

Jack Gannon – Co-Founder, Production Manager
Cyndi Williams-Barnier – Co-Founder, Production Editor
Bill Barnier – Senior Editor
Loreen Ridge-Husum – Art Director

"Will you walk into my parlour?"
said the Spider to the Fly,
"'Tis the prettiest little parlour
that ever you did spy;
The way into my parlour
is up a winding stair,
And I've a many curious things to show
when you are there."

~Mary Howitt

AUTHORS' NOTE

Part of Chapter 15 runs concurrent with "Trail of The Talon", book 3 in the Task Force Series, also by the authors.

ALSO BY THE AUTHORS

The Task Force Series
2s and 3s (formerly Murder in Twos and Threes)
The Task Force That Saved Christmas (includes the previous-published
Silent Night Murder Night and Reel to Real Murder)
Trail of The Talon
Trail of The Hunter

The InSpectre Series
Dawn of The Living Ghost
Tears of Destiny

Others
Tales on The Yellow Brick Road
I Walked in Santa's Boots: Lowcountry Christmas Memories

CHAPTER 1

ITSY BITSY SPIDER
MANY YEARS AGO

"COME ON, CHRYSIE, I'M BORED! Let's go outside and play!"

"Jeffrey, quit calling me 'Chrysie'. Besides, you're still getting over a summer cold. You shouldn't be outside." The two children sat on the hardwood living room floor of the old, shabby house, playing jacks. "My *name* is Chrystal, it's a proper lady's name. I'm a southern lady. We do things like sew clothes. Like ours, that mom made. See the paisley curtains up there?" Pointing at the living room windows, she emphasized, "She made those. *That's* what women do."

Five-year-old Jeffrey Leigh rolled on the floor, laughing at his older sister. Crusted mucus lined his nose and upper lip. Skinny legs showed scabs from too many rough and rowdy falls. "You ain't no lady, Chrysie, you're only ten." Dangling his legs in the air, he noticed one of his tennis shoes was untied, so he tied it in mid-air. "When you get knobbies like Mommy, *then* you'll be a lady."

Chrystal narrowed her eyes and looked down at her chest. "Oh yeah, *Jeffy*, well I *do* have knobbies, they're just little right now," Chrystal retorted. She bent her upper body backwards to show off the small breasts under her t-shirt. "Anytime now momma's gonna take me to get my first bra. Ladies wear bras!"

"Ha-Ha!" Jeffrey taunted, extending his chest dramatically, mocking his older sister. Chrystal scrambled forward, pinning Jeffery to the floor, starting a game of "tickle."

The two children rolled around, Chrystal tickling Jeffrey until he hurt from laughing, sending him into a coughing frenzy. Chrystal's ponytail came loose, and long brown hair covered Jeffrey's face. The squeals and giggles brought their mother from the kitchen to investigate, in time to watch a candy dish fly off the coffee table and little chocolate candies roll in all directions, mostly underneath the tattered couch. "Dammit, you two, you've been at this all day! I need some quiet while I make dinner!" she snapped. "Oh, good Lord, go play outside, it's a nice summer day, get out of here!"

The children raced to the front door. "Wait!" Jeffrey exclaimed as a thought flashed in his mind. "The ruler, we haven't done the ruler thing since a long time! Can we do it? I bet I'm bigger!"

Their mother grabbed a lock of Chrystal's hair and tugged. "You two are getting on my last nerve. Go outside and stay there. I got things to do before your daddy gets home, probably irritated as usual." She tugged Chrystal's hair again, "Got it, little girl?"

Chrystal grimaced and whined, "Momma, you're hurting me!" She pulled her hair free from her mother's grasp. "Yeah, I got it." Chrystal's face was scrunched, her feelings hurt. It hadn't been the first time her mother pulled her hair; or punished both children with a too-firm hand.

Chrystal retrieved the rubber band from the floor and pulled her hair back into a ponytail. "OK, Jeff, go get the ruler and I'll meet you out back." Chrystal felt dejected. She ran through the kitchen, bounded out the side door, and hopped down the pocked cement steps. Jeffrey ran full speed to his bedroom to retrieve the ruler and pencil. Their mother lit a cigarette and leaned against the refrigerator. Her jet-black hair was pulled into a bun, and she wore an apron atop a colorful, homemade housedress.

Jeffrey thundered down the hall full of youthful energy, pushed open the screened kitchen door, and ran into the yard. "Bye, Mommy, gotta hurry."

"Close the damn—" she began to say, but his departure cut her sentence short. "Dammit, kids. I thought I'd raised you better." She flicked her cigarette outside, slammed the door, and patted her neck with a dishtowel. Beads of sweat trickled down her back. She adjusted the window air conditioner a notch lower on her way to clean up the spilled candy.

"OK, my turn first, like always!" Jeffrey stood against the side of the house under the previous measuring marks.

"Jeffy, quit. *Ladies* are supposed to go first anyway, that's the rule! And get off your tippy toes, that's cheating."

Jeffrey lowered himself, sullen. Pieces of old gray paint chipped off the wood siding. "You're not a lady yet," he pouted.

"Fine, whatever." Chrystal placed the ruler atop his head and drew a little line on the side of the house. "There. Wow, Jeffy, you grew a *lot* since last month." She didn't want to hurt his feelings, knowing the line had barely moved.

"Mark it, mark it! My name and today's date!"

"Got it, Jeffy," she said as she glared down at him. "We've only been doing this for how long now?"

"Hey, Jeffy's a baby-name, don't call me that." He crossed his arms and scowled.

"OK, let's make a deal. You don't call me Chrysie or Chrysti or those other stupid names. And no more talk about *knobbies*! I'll let you call me Chrys and you'll be Jeff, no more baby names. But only *you* get to call me Chrys, no one else, *ever*. Deal?"

Jeffrey squinted, and the ninety-five-degree heat bore down on them. "Deal, and a pinky shake." Jeffrey uncrossed his arms, happy with the amends. They intertwined pinky fingers.

"My turn now." Chrystal stood against the house. She too, fought the competitive urge to stand taller.

"Man, Chrys, you've grown way taller. I can barely reach." Jeffrey's little forehead crinkled at the thought of being outdone by his big sister. "No fair."

"Here, I'll hold the ruler and you make the mark. Besides, girls grow faster than boys. Since I'm five years older, I'm gonna be bigger." She turned to check the mark, realizing she'd grown about an inch. "Na, 'bout the same again. You're catching up," she said, trying to spare his feelings once more. "Come on, let's go sit in the shade. It's hot, but we can't go in. Mama's tired of us bein' in her hair."

Jeffrey snickered, envisioning little fingers tangled in their mother's hair. They sat on the ground under a crape myrtle tree in full pink bloom, near the small crawl space door under the house. The rusty, metal door had bars to let air flow easily through the crawl space.

Jeffrey sat on the top concrete step, staring at the blackness inside. A cool breeze flowed from within. "Wonder what's under there, Chrys? Could be monsters! Maybe that's the bumping under the floor at night!" His eyes grew wide, thinking he'd finally uncovered the mystery of the nightly bumps and thumps.

"No, Jeff, daddy says that's the water pipes under the house, remember? He said they're old and groan to be repaired."

Jeffrey snorted, "Yeah, he says Mommy's pipes are old, too, whatever that means. Sounds funny." He poked at a few rocks with the ruler, which made a little black widow scurry to find new shelter. "Look! A black Spidey!" His high-pitched voice cracked, excited at the prospect of playing with an insect. "It came from under that big rock!"

"No, Jeff, leave the spider alone. Don't play with bugs like that one, they could be deadly. Quit poking, it could hurt you!"

"I'm not touching it, Chrys, the ruler is. Now it's goin' under the house. There might be a Spidey family in a big web, let's go look!" He looked at Chrystal, hoping she'd go along with the idea. Instead, her lips tightened, and she crossed her arms in defiance.

"Okay, Chrys, I get it. Then, how 'bout do the 'Itsy Bitsy Spider' song, with our fingers."

"Alright, just once, then I wanna go swing."

The two sat in the grass, singing the old nursery rhyme, mimicking the thumb and forefinger movements of a spider climbing a waterspout. Each time they messed up, they would giggle and start over. "Come on, Jeff. Let's go play on the swing set."

Jeffrey looked back at the crawlspace door. "No, Chrys, I wanna find the spider!"

"*No*, Jeff, I wanna go swing, come on. Leave it alone."

"You're not my boss! Go swing by yourself. I never get to do what I wanna do. I'm gonna go find the Spidey family."

"Fine, I hope you find the whole spider family and they bite you. They have eight eyes, so they'll see you really good!"

"Eight eyes? Na-uh. No one has eight eyes, stupid." Jeffrey squatted and tried to open the barred door. He couldn't find the opening, however. It wasn't a normal door, and for a small boy, was large and heavy. He shook, pushed, and pulled on the bars.

Discovering that by lifting it straight up two metal pins ascended into the top frame, allowing the two bottom pins to exit the holes at the base. He pulled it toward him, and the whole door came loose, sending him falling backward. "Ow, shit!"

"Jeff! You're not allowed to say that word."

"Uh-huh, mommy says it all the time! Especially when she and daddy fight. Get this thing off me, Chrys!"

Chrystal lifted the door and set it aside. "Fine, you go on! I don't need to play with you anyway." Walking away, she noticed her friend Jesse across the street on her swing set.

"Hey, Chrystal! Come over and swing with me!"

Chrystal's demeanor changed in an instant, happy to see her friend. Looking back, she watched her brother wriggling on hands and knees into the crawlspace. "Idiot," she said aloud. *I'll teach him a lesson, so he'll do what I say from now on*, she thought. Once Jeffrey was inside, Chrystal quietly put the door back in place. He crawled along, oblivious to anything other than the underside of the house. *There, that'll scare him enough; if he can't get out, then he'll do what I say next time.*

Chrystal ran across the street to her friend Jesse Lexington. "What were you doing to your brother under the house?" Jesse asked.

"Ah, just gonna teach him a lesson for a few minutes, that's all."

Jeffrey crawled on hands and knees in the four-foot-tall space. The sand was soft and chilly to the touch. He wondered why someone put sand under the house rather than dirt. He contemplated getting his toy dump trucks but was too busy investigating.

Air vents with metal bars lined the base of the house every few feet. Streaks of sunlight crept in, breaking the darkness; specs of dust sparkled in the light rays. *It's so quiet down here*, he thought.

The muted light aided Jeffrey in his quest to explore further. To the left was a row of support piers, preventing him from seeing the entire underneath of the house. To the right, he spotted the shiny black spider crawling in front of him. "There you are. Come here, I wanna play with you." He placed the ruler in front of the spider. "Go on, get on the ruler so I can see you better."

The insect rolled on its back, exposing the red hourglass shape on its abdomen. "Wow, that's cool!" he squealed. The black widow caught hold of the ruler and climbed on. "All aboard, ye maties," the boy muttered, recalling the phrase from a TV show. "You're really pretty, all shiny with a big fat butt." He giggled at the words *fat butt*, because it was the same thing his daddy said when he smacked his mother's bottom and said, "Love that fat butt, Alice." Jeffrey smiled when he said, "Alice, I'll name you Alice, yeah, because you got a fat butt like mommy."

The spider inched up the ruler, moving closer to the boy's hand. He sat and watched, intrigued with its long black legs, wanting to see the odd red spot on its underside again.

His eyes widened when it climbed onto his hand, tickling him with its legs. He dropped the ruler and flinched as he giggled. Instinctively, the spider bit the boy's hand. Jeffrey flicked his hand in pain. "Ow, shit! That hurt!" The spider landed in the sand and scurried away.

"Bad spider. You should die for that!" Jeffrey got back on his hands and knees, wanting to forget about Alice and ignore the growing pain to explore the rest of the crawl space. "This looks like a cave, maybe there's buried treasure under here."

Jeffrey noticed more spiders in disheveled webs. He wondered why their webs weren't round. "You guys are messy. Why can't you have pretty webs anyway?" Jeffrey began to feel sick, and mucus dribbled from his nose. Muscle cramps began, and his stomach hurt. He began to sweat even more than what the summer heat caused. He thought about turning back to leave, but wanted to explore more.

Halfway around the circle, Jeffrey grew weaker and began to shake. With his eyes squeezed closed, he sat and wrapped his arms around his stomach. "Mommy, I'm sick!" He breathed heavily, pain radiating throughout his back and shoulders. *"Mommy! Come get me!"* His abdomen rumbled and convulsed; he vomited onto his shirt, shorts, and into the sand. Jeffrey heaved repeatedly until nothing was left and began to cry. Instinct and panic took over. Continuing around the circle, he was no longer interested in the surroundings but instead wanted to get to his mommy. The dizziness and his burning chest confused him.

Fear turned to terror. His heart pounded and he tried to suck more air into his lungs, but it was as though the worst of his cold had suddenly returned with a vengeance. On the last turn toward the opening, he buckled face first into the sand. He shook his head to get the sand out of his mouth, nose, and eyes.

Finally seeing the light streaming in from the opening, he pulled himself by elbows only, his legs too cramped to move. Finally reaching the opening, he didn't understand why the door was back in place.

Jeffrey tried to push the door up and pull it toward him as he'd done earlier. It seemed heavier than before, his strength ebbing. *I did it before...pull up, pull toward me, door comes off.* He tried again, not understanding that from under the house he had to push *out* instead of *in* to remove the door. His insides were on fire. "Mommy, Chrys, help!" he pleaded in a scratchy whisper.

A few minutes seemed like an eternity for Jeffrey. Dim black spots blurred his vision, and he could no longer draw a breath. With strength fading rapidly, he squeezed an arm through the bars, reaching for his sister, waving to catch her attention. Darkness engulfed him. The last thing Jeffrey was aware of was his sister happily swinging with her friend across the street.

His little body finally sagged. One small hand clung to the bars, the other frozen in an eternal outreach for help...his face pressed in between.

A lone black widow climbed onto his face, probed tentatively with its forelegs, then continued on her voyage into the shadows under the house…

CHAPTER 2

A FATE WORSE THAN DEATH

"I'M GOIN' TO MY HOUSE. Gonna find out what time dinner is. Wanna come over and eat with us?" Chrystal asked her friend Jesse. "I think we're having spaghetti. Just ignore my irritating little brother; he'll keep staring at your chest."

Jesse held her long hair back with both hands, looking down at the front of her t-shirt, then over at Chrystal's shirt. Jesse was advancing into her own stages of puberty but was ahead of Chrystal. She'd developed the habit of slouching to hide her early curves from boys. "I'll ask mom and dad if I can come."

Chrystal jumped off the swing, slipped her dirty feet into her old flip-flops, and began walking back to the kitchen door.

She noticed that Jeffrey wasn't outside, and, at first, she thought he may have gone inside. Then she remembered. "Oh, my God, I forgot!" she screeched. He'd been under the house for at least half an hour. She knew he would be crying. She also knew she would be in trouble with her mom.

As she ran home fast, the crawl space door came into view. Tiny fingers were wrapped around a bar, one arm stuck out, not moving. "Jeffrey! I'm sorry! I'm so—," her apology stopped short. His pale face was pressed against the bars, eyes closed, mouth open, and his lips were a strange blue color. "Jeff?" she asked in a small whisper. *"Jeffrey!"* Frantically she pulled at the bars, forgetting how to remove the door. *"Momma! Help, Momma!"*

Jesse heard Chrystal screaming and abruptly dug her feet into the sand to stop the swing. She ran to her friend, her own blond hair flapping behind her. At the same time, Chrystal's mother rushed out of the house in a panic and screamed when she saw Jeffrey's motionless body behind the access door.

"Go home, Jesse! Have your mommy call 911!"

Jesse stood still, her hands over her mouth.

"Dammit, girl, listen to me! Go home and call 911, something's happened to Jeffrey!"

Alice shoved Chrystal aside and yanked the door loose while working his arm from between the bars. Jeffrey slumped forward, his head landing on the sand in front of her. *"Jeffrey, wake up, Jeffrey!"* She shook him frantically, pulled his small body out of the crawl space, and placed him prone on the grass. She realized his skin was pale and cold to the touch. He wasn't breathing. *"Oh, my God, Jeffrey! Chrystal, what the hell happened?"*

Chrystal stood off to the side, crying. "Momma," she said, her voice cracking, "I-I don't know. He was just in there a few minutes. He was fine, and we were only playing a game!" Jesse ran back from her house, grabbing her friend in a tight hug.

Alice began CPR, though she didn't remember exactly what to do. She never dreamed she'd have to actually perform it on one of her children. "Jesse, did your mother call for help?"

"Mommy's calling now, and Daddy's coming over."

The heart, gotta get the heart beating again, she thought, trying to remember the process. She pushed on his little chest, hoping the compressions would work. *Breathe, Jeffrey. Breathe!* She blew several breaths into his mouth, praying the entire time. After six or seven breaths, she yelled out, *"Jeffrey! Honey, wake up, please, you can't go away, my baby!"* She heard someone running behind her.

"Alice, move aside." Jesse's father, a navy corpsman, knelt before the boy's still body. He began CPR, though he recognized it was too late. He said a silent prayer as he worked, hoping for a miracle.

Within a minute, a siren shrieked in the distance. Chrystal put her hand on her mother's shoulder. "Mama, the ambulance people are coming, it's gonna be okay." She was sure the medical people would give her little brother a miracle medicine, and he'd be alright. It didn't matter if she were in trouble, as long as Jeffrey woke up.

Alice took Chrystal's hand and forced her to the ground next to her. "Chrystal Leigh, what did you do to him? How did he get locked under there? *You did this; he couldn't have locked himself under there!*"

Chrystal stared at her mother's face, wet with streaked mascara. "Momma, your fingernails are hurting me! We were just p-playing, I swear."

The sound of the ambulance siren grew louder. It rounded its way onto their block and stopped in the grass opposite where everyone was gathered. Three men jumped out, retrieved a stretcher, medical bags, and IV equipment. While the paramedics worked, Alice's husband arrived home from work, pulling his car into the driveway. John Leigh panicked, seeing the ambulance and his son on the grass. He bolted out of the car, leaving the door open and engine running. "Alice, my God! What's going—Jeffrey?" He cut his sentence short, watching as the paramedics worked on his son. He grabbed his wife and held her against him. His forehead wrinkled, not wanting to believe what he was seeing. Full of dread, he shouted, *"Alice, what happened?"*

"I don't know! Chrystal did something to him. She locked him under the house. I came out and found him not breathing, tried doing CPR, and told Jesse to call nine-one-one."

"I dunno, I think it's been too long. Let's get him in and hurry," said one of the paramedics, who then turned to John and Alice. "You can meet us at the ER, we gotta hurry." They quickly loaded Jeffrey into the ambulance, and headed off at breakneck speed, siren wailing.

John grabbed Crystal by her arms and squeezed, leaving instant red marks. Her head and ponytail bobbled back and forth as he shook her. "What did you do to him, Chrystal? *By God, if something happens to him—*" John's anger increased, thinking that his son might already be dead. "Get your ass in the car; we need to get to the ER."

Chrystal sobbed; her arms hurt where he'd squeezed them.

"It'll be okay," Jesse said. "They'll fix him up and everyone will come home just fine."

Chrystal looked into her friend's eyes, wanting to believe her. "No," she replied. Chrystal shook her head. "No, it won't. This is the worst day of my life." Chrystal crawled into the back seat, staring at Jesse as they drove away—sad, forlorn, and very afraid...

CHAPTER 3

I KILLED HIM

THE LEIGH FAMILY ARRIVED AT THE HOSPITAL SHORTLY AFTER THE AMBULANCE. John ran to the emergency room double doors inside the lobby and yanked on them. They were locked, so he shook them even harder.

"Sir! Sir! You can't go in there, I'm sorry. You have to check in here first." The woman occupied a small room, near the ER doors. She was standing as she spoke to John through a small round opening in the glass window.

John and Alice desperately tried to explain the situation, but the clerk held her hands up in a *stop* gesture. "Yes, sir, ma'am. I understand. I'm not allowed to let anyone back without a doctor's authorization. Give me your insurance information. When we're done with the paperwork you can have a seat over there." She pointed at orange plastic chairs in the lobby. "The doctor will talk with you as soon as he can."

John slammed his fist on the counter, his anger rising from fear and frustration. "Dammit, woman, our son is back there, probably dying!" He pointed a finger at the ER doors. "We don't know what's wrong or what happened. We don't have the information you want; we just need to see our child. *Now!*"

She glared at John over the top of her glasses. Her voice was stern, unsympathetic. "Sir, if you don't calm down, provide me with the information and be seated, I'll call security and have you escorted out, or arrested. The choice is yours."

John glared at the woman. "What? My son's dying, and you want us to fill out a damned form?" John's face and neck reddened. "OK, call your security—I'm going in, now!"

Despite Alice's pleas, afraid he'd be arrested, John pulled and kicked at the ER doors. The attendant in the small room called for security when John stood back and kicked the locked doors one last time in desperation. The lock gave way, and they both charged down the ER hallway. Chrystal shyly followed behind, both hands covering her mouth. In anguish, they searched each room for Jeffrey. Finally, in the last room, they found him surrounded by doctors and nurses. They had cut away his shirt. A tracheal tube protruded from his throat. He was unresponsive; wires and tubes were jabbed into his small body. The heart monitor on the wall showed a straight red line, and trilled a long, sad tone, one that everyone recognized.

"You're the parents?" one of the doctors asked when he saw John and Alice.

Alice wailed pitifully, ignoring the doctor's question, realizing her son was dead. Two nurses moved aside to let her come to his side. Carefully picking up his small, cold hand, she put it to her cheek. She laid her head on her child's chest and wept.

Compassionately, the doctor spoke again, "Mr. and Mrs. Leigh, I'm so sorry. We tried to resuscitate him, but he was, well, too far gone when they brought him to us. Take a few minutes, and we'll talk next door in the conference room. We think we understand what happened."

John stood at the foot of the bed, silently sobbing. He covered his mouth with one hand and held onto his stomach with the other, fighting a sudden queasiness. Guilt flooded his head, remembering the day Jeffrey was born. He wasn't able to stay long after his birth. He'd had to rush back to work. He realized he was never home to spend time with the kids, and the remorse ate away at his gut. "My boy," he whispered.

Seized by fear, Chrystal stood in the doorway. "I killed him," she mumbled softly, wide-eyed. The hospital staff stared at her. She crossed both arms tightly against her chest, shaking uncontrollably, shielding herself from an invisible doom. She watched her parents, both broken-hearted, crying. Chrystal wanted to cry but was perplexed when she couldn't. She knew she was the guilty one who acted irresponsibly.

The bright lights turned into dozens of minuscule spots, and darkness took over. Chrystal fell to the floor in a small heap…

CHAPTER 4

DAWN OF THE BLACK WIDOW
2017

Lᴀᴄʏ ʙᴀᴄᴋᴇᴅ ʜᴇʀ ᴄᴀʀ ɪɴᴛᴏ ᴀ sᴘᴏᴛ ᴀᴡᴀʏ ғʀᴏᴍ ᴛʜᴇ ʙᴜsɪɴᴇss' ғʀᴏɴᴛ ᴅᴏᴏʀ, not wanting anyone to see her or her car.

She placed one high-heeled shoe onto the graveled parking lot of the Drop Inn Bar and Motel, off Interstate 95 south of the Virginia/North Carolina state line. She discovered his hangout several days earlier, and what would soon be the place where she would begin her quest for justice.

Lacy had chosen a particular outfit for the evening: black stilettos, a tight one-piece black long-sleeved dress, and thigh-high black stockings. *Man-hunting clothes*, she mused to herself, smiling at the thought.

A yellow flickering bug light overhead offered a dismal glow in the darkness. It lit her reflection in the car window, and she stopped to take in the view. *Okay, you do indeed look hot,* Lacy thought. *Long, silky red hair, short dress to show off the legs, lotsa cleavage. How can he say no? A killer night for sure.* Her stomach flipped at the word *killer*, more from anticipation than anxiety. She checked her purse for the third time since leaving home. The auto-injector remained nestled securely in the bottom.

Lacy strolled to the bar's front door, contemplating her plan. A middle-aged couple stumbled out, laughing, and clinging to each other, smelling of beer and stale cigarettes.

"Hey, sorry 'bout—oh, hey!" the man said, trying to stand straight, but wobbled on his feet, nevertheless. "Ooo-wee, you're lookin' damn sexy there, babe!"

His date elbowed him in the ribs, annoyed.

The grin left his face. "Dammit, I was just lookin', hon! Come on, let's go get us a room. But damn, we gotta get you shoes like hers. I wanna watch you doin' me wearin' those."

Lacy scowled, silent as the two staggered through the dim parking lot to the motel. Country western music pounded a bass reverberation against the windows of the bar. She abhorred nightclubs as a rule but was seduced by the prospect of beginning the end of a lifetime of suffering.

She yanked the door open with resolve and stepped in. The abruptness of dim lights, loud voices, noisy music, and pungent smells played havoc with her nervous stomach. The jukebox belted out "Goodbye Earl" by The Dixie Chicks. *How apropos*, she thought, searching the bar through squinted eyes. A sly grin formed on her face, but she pushed it back. *Just like a good movie murder scene, the perfect background music.*

Men overwhelmed the club: *young, old, obnoxious, loud, quiet, every flavor of cruelty, gathered in one place,* she thought. She took a seat on a barstool, aware that her dress inched upwards, revealing long sensual legs. The hem of her stockings came into view, to the delight of many. A game of pool started at the back of the room, and Lacy watched sparsely dressed women dote over the men.

A deep voice spoke from behind the bar, "Ma'am, getcha drink?"

The bartender caught Lacy by surprise. "Ah, yeah. Sure." She forced a smile at the pudgy, gawking man. "I'll have—" she started to say, clutching tightly at her purse, amused with her coming reply "—a Black Widow, if you don't mind."

The bartender raised his eyebrows and leaned his elbows onto the beer-and-cigarette-stained counter. "Ma'am, if you're lookin' for one of them fancy foo-foo drinks, we don't do those here. Its beer or liquor, that's it, no mixin' stuff, 'less you want rum and coke. I can do somethin' like that." He was unshaven, with fowl breath and yellow teeth. Sweat stained the armpits of his blue t-shirt.

Lacy feigned a pout. "Vodka, straight up, not much ice. Make it a double, please."

"Now *that* I understand, Miss Prim and Proper," the bartender said with a wink. He shuffled off to make the drink.

"Moron," she whispered to herself.

Lacy watched a woman bend over a pool table to take a shot. Her short skirt crept up, revealing red thong panties tucked in the crack of her supple round butt. Lacy experienced a strange pleasure at the sight. It was an unusual urge, befuddling her senses.

"Here ya go. Vodka, double, not much ice, just like the lady asked."

Caught off-guard for the second time, Lacy narrowed her eyes, offering a polite grin. "Here's thirty bucks. Keep the change." She offered the currency, holding it close to her face. He reached forward, unhurried, smiling as he reached for the bills. Their fingers brushed for an instant, and his smile grew larger as he withdrew his hand holding the paper money. The happy bartender sauntered away.

Lacy sipped her drink, her eyes hunting for the quarry in the room.

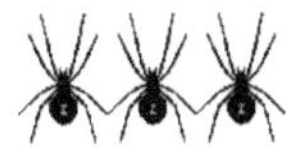

Lacy sat for the next half hour, waiting, and watching. She was growing impatient. *Come on, you're here. I've seen you come in here every Friday night; at least I think it's you. I'm waiting for you, you son-of-a-bitch.*

Then, as if wishing could make it so, he appeared.

A tall, thin man entered from an adjacent room, strolled to the far end of the bar, and ordered a whiskey. He sipped his drink, taking in the club's action while he leaned against the jukebox. He was dressed in a typical outfit befitting the honkytonk bar: a dark Stetson hat, pointed-toed boots, checkered shirt, and blue jeans. He almost choked on his drink when he spotted the red-haired woman in black sitting at the bar. *Sexy—no, she's damned gorgeous! Gotta meet her*, he thought.

Straightening his posture, he adjusted his hat, took one more drink, and headed toward her end of the bar. Courteously he tipped the bill of his hat. "Mind if I sit here, ma'am? Shame for a pretty girl like you to be sittin' alone," he said in a deep southern drawl.

Lacy's elbow rested on the bar, chin in hand, an amused expression on her face. She eyed the man, her head never moving. A small smile appeared on her face. *It's about time, you lazy ass. Stupid outfit, impudent pickup line. If those boots were any pointier, they'd look like a pair of Louboutin's.* "Well, by all means, please." She waved at the stool next to her. "I was hoping for some company this evening. Have a seat, handsome." *He's already so wasted he doesn't even recognize me. Excellent!*

The man took a seat beside her, setting his hat on the bar, smoothing back his hair. He was excited that she took an interest in him so quickly. "Hey, it's just not right for you to be drinkin' by yourself. Looked like you could use some company."

"Well, thank you. You're quite astute, aren't you?"

"Ass-what?" he said, his eyebrows furled in confusion.

She chuckled slightly. "Sorry. Observant. Most people don't really pay attention to me. I'm not much of a social butterfly." She gave a small nervous laugh. "I don't get out much."

He guffawed and slapped the counter. "Girl, you don't know how pretty you are! Damn, you're hotter'n Taylor Swift! Shit, but she ain't got nothin' on you. Hey, bartender. Gimme another whiskey and whatever the hottie's drinkin'.'"

"I'm having a—" she paused for emphasis. "Black Widow," she said, when the bartender was out of earshot. She smiled again thinking about the name of the drink.

An evening of drinking with little food was beginning to take its toll on him. "A black what? Widow, like the spider? Damn, girl. That's kinda kinky."

"Yeah. Guess I can get a bit, ah, twisted, every now and again." She cocked her head sideways and gave a sensual smile. *Jake,* she thought his name to herself.

He took a deep breath, trying to bring his tipsy fog under control. "Sorry, I didn't even get your name. I'm Jake. Jake Collins. Sometimes I come on too strong when I've been drinkin'. What's your name?"

"Lacy. My name's Lacy." She smiled and took a sip of her drink. "Enjoy your drink, Jake, the evening's still young." Lacy sat back, observing him, and giving him a better view of her body. Anger burned inside her brain, but she controlled it. She crossed her legs; he watched intently. "See something you like?"

"Yes'm. Must say, you have gorgeous legs, if I can say?"

She reached out and lightly touched his hand. "Well, yes Jake, you may say. See anything else you like, or are my legs the only thing?" She raised her other hand to her neck and gently traced her fingers along her throat to her collarbone and hovered just above her exposed cleavage. His eyes followed her hand.

He pulled in closer, tilting his head to the side, "Lacy, hon. Y'know, we can take this somewhere quiet, kinda romantic, if you want. We'll take a whole bottle of whiskey with us; bartender will put it on my tab. Don't let this place make you think bad of me. I'll be a fine gentleman to a lady like yourself, I promise."

Lacy studied his face. "Sounds like a lovely idea, cowboy. You got a private place in mind where you can be 'a fine gentleman'?" She took the last swig of her drink, stood, lightly dragging her hand on his shoulders. "Come on, Jake Collins, let's go take a stroll…"

Her hurriedly devised plan was to hide her venom-filled injector under a pillow when he went into the bathroom. She planned to straddle him in the bed, retrieve the injector as he ejaculated, and shoot the deadly venom into his hip.

She patted the edge of the bed. "Come on over, Jake, I've got something for you." The two kissed and fondled each other for the next few minutes. Lacy eventually ended up sitting atop him as planned. He had other ideas, however. He flipped her over and held her face down onto the mattress. Overpowering Lacy, he basically raped her. Memories flooded her head, remembering what he'd done to her years before. She sensed his thighs tighten as he climaxed; Lacy grabbed the injector from under the pillow and swung her arm back without being able to aim. The needle entered at an odd angle, stabbing him in the upper leg. He howled more in surprise than pain. The jab stung despite all the alcohol he'd had.

"What the hell'd you stick me with, bitch?" he demanded, rolling off her. Lacy hopped off the bed, backing away from him.

"I stuck you with a lifetime of shame and fear, you piece of shit! You raped me! And I don't mean what you did just now!" He looked at her, confused and in pain. "Don't you remember, *Jake*? Don't you remember that day at school when you and your pals beat me up, ripped off my clothes, stuffed pillows under my hips, and raped me? You were having *such* a wonderful time."

Jake fought with his body, trying to get to his feet, but the signals from his brain refused to work. Lacy moved from the dresser and sat on the edge of the bed, her naked body inches from his. A surge of pleasure shot through her, seeing him writhe in pain.

Lacy stood. "You had a great time. You never considered how you hurt me, degraded me, and ruined my life! All four of you, you used and raped me and got away with it." Her voice quivered and anger seethed inside. "You scared me to death, threatening to kill me and my family if I ever said anything." Her face reddened, and she leaned in closer. "All of you, so big and strong and in control, no way a little girl like me could have resisted. Well, I've been waiting for the right time, Jake! *I'm* in control now, *I'm* the strong one. You can't hurt me this time—because I'm the one hurting you! And tonight's your lucky night. You get to be the first one to pay for what you did to me."

Jake gave a vociferous moan, clutching his midsection, and curled into a fetal position near the edge of the bed. "Damn you, bitch, wha'd ya do to me?" He screamed out in agony. His body involuntarily curled up tighter, his knees nearly touching his chin. The pain in his stomach felt as if he'd been stabbed with a knife. The nausea was too much; he rolled off the bed, knocking the whiskey bottle off the nightstand as he fell. Landing on his back, he managed to turn over and pull himself along on cramped fingers and toes. He barely made it to the bathroom door when his insides heaved, vomiting violently. He dragged himself forward through the puddle of soured liquor, throwing up more once he reached the toilet.

Lacy was pleased, subconsciously stroking her bare stomach while watching Jake's torment. She finally stepped to her clothes on the floor and began to dress.

Jake's body twitched and jerked on the bathroom floor; he tried using the tub to raise himself, but his muscles and nerves were on fire. The serum rapidly coursed through his alcohol laden blood stream, invading his internal organs. One last fierce spasm rolled him across the floor, his body letting loose urine, feces, and more vomit at the same time.

Lacy stood in the doorway, then sat on the edge of the bathtub looking at the naked man. She took great satisfaction at the dying Jake wallowing in his own waste, the proof of her venom's effectiveness. She stood, smiling, and turned to leave. But her mind changed gears. Turning again, she abruptly kicked the man in the abdomen with a bare foot, hard, nearly slipping in the sludge herself. The blow made him recoil, sending his body into another uncontrolled spasm. The serum was working faster than she calculated. She wanted him to suffer more.

She never thought of herself as violent or aggressive, but the first kick was pleasing. She struck him again and again with her bare feet, owning the moment, taking great pleasure in his pain. Her long-desired revenge had finally come to fruition, with unexpected joy and brutality; it was better than she ever imagined.

She continued her attack, cursing at Jake all the while. He gasped, "Stop it—dammit, stop!" She stopped, and he looked up. The pain in his eyes was as great as the pain in his stomach. "Wh-who are you?" he demanded. His respirations were turning into a choking, gagging struggle and his face reddened to a beet-red color. His fading vision changed the way Lacy looked. "You? It's *you!*" he rasped. "I remember now. We-we was just havin' fun is all!"

"Well, it appears my serum was a little slow in aiding your memory," Lacy said, frowning. "Hurry up and die, you piece of shit. I've had enough of you now. I need to see you get what you deserve." She got into the tub, rinsed off her legs and feet, then jumped the short distance from the edge of the tub to the carpet just outside the open door. She gathered her stockings and stuffed them in her purse, hopped on one foot and then the other struggling to get her shoes onto her wet feet. She gave up, knowing the stilettos would only slow her down. She decided to carry them instead. Checking the room once more, she made sure she had her belongings. She wanted no physical evidence left behind.

Jake grasped the edge of the bathtub, pushed himself up with his arms, and fell forward into the tub. He clutched the shower curtain to raise himself, but instead the curtain tore loose and fell over his prone body. He gasped a final breath, closing his eyes in painful resignation.

Lacy set her bag and shoes on the floor and pulled the sheets off the bed. From the bathroom door, she stretched forward and flung open the white sheets so they would spread out over Jake's still form. "Nity, nite, Jake, in your little cocoon. Your friends will be joining you soon, don't you worry."

She grabbed tissues, wiped the doorknobs, then closed and locked the bathroom door. Still holding the tissues, she turned off the lights and backed out of the room. "Jake, I think I made a couple of mistakes tonight, nothing I can't fix for the next one. Don't you worry, sweetheart. The other three—well, I'll handle them much better than you got tonight. Sleep well in hell, big man…"

CHAPTER 5

DEAD MEN TELL "HO" TALES

GAIL REALIZED HOW MUCH SHE DISLIKED HER LIFE WITH EACH PASSING DAY. If not for the baby on the way, she would easily give up on everything. She knew, however, that her situation was her own fault.

Months prior, the petite, fair-haired college dropout secured a job as the housekeeper at a local adult motel, a pay-by-the-hour establishment. It was the only job she could find after Gail's parents forced her out of the family home following her confession that she had gotten pregnant. She had sex for the first time following her prom, and that one night of passion was successful in producing a baby. Her boyfriend disavowed Gail, and denied he'd ever touched her. She didn't have the money to force a paternity test to confirm he was the father, and her parents didn't care.

The motel owner, also the owner of the bar adjacent to the motel, was a balding, overweight man in his mid-fifties with a severe case of rosacea on his face. Feeling sorry for the girl, he agreed to let her live in one of the motel rooms after begging for a place to stay. He approved upon the condition that she'd work as the housekeeper and be on hand day and night to answer customers' needs. He liked the idea of no more telephone interruptions at his house during the night. Gail painfully reminded him of his own daughter: young, pregnant, and unmarried.

"Drop Inn Bar and Motel," she'd muttered after she was hired. *What a freakin' impression that's gonna make on a resume. If anyone would even look at my resume now. At least we have a home, such as it is*, she thought as she stroked her stomach.

Nonetheless, the mother-to-be was determined to create a place for them. Gail's young life eventually would become a world of cloth diapers, baby bottles, and undertaking whatever it took to keep them both safe and content within the seedy motel. She received no money as compensation, just a room for herself and the baby. When she was hired, the owner told her she could keep any money, items, or things of particular interest she found in the rooms. "People leave crap behind all the time. Most times they can't remember where they'd been the night before anyway!" he said, laughing. "You bring the stuff to me first, though, let me hold it a few days, and if no one comes back to get their shit, then everything is yours."

Gail readily agreed, and decided she liked the owner. He didn't have to help her, but greatly appreciated that he did. "When my baby is born, would it be okay to take her around with me while I clean the rooms? She won't get in the way, I promise. It's a girl. My doctor at the clinic did the ultrasound. I'm gonna name her Virginia."

"Baby girl, huh? Bet she'll be just as cute as you." The man sat back in his chair and crossed his fingers together over his large belly. "Hell, what could it hurt? Not like anyone 'round here's gonna complain, huh? Sure."

A few months later, when Virginia was born, he kept his word and allowed Gail to tote the baby around during her daily cleaning and service calls.

The working women at the motel were aware Gail was unhappy and disheartened. She had a job but no income, a new baby, parents that disowned her, and to top it off, she was living in a rattrap motel. If the women were able to work the night before, they'd leave some money on the rooms' TV stands for Gail to try to help with expenses.

The women came to like her and eventually made a pact not to bother Gail during the nights if possible, so the young mother could have some quiet time. If anyone caused trouble or created a big mess, the ladies tried to handle it without having to call her.

Even though the working girls did their best to make her job easier, Gail still cleaned each room during the day; the stains on the sheets were a constant reminder of the one night that changed her life forever. But then a glance at her little girl replaced that regret with a young mother's deep love.

Gail checked all the cleaning supplies on her cart, then strapped in baby Virginia. After making sure she was comfortably tucked in her baby seat, on the middle shelf, she reviewed the list of rooms that were rented the night before. "OK, Ginny, looks like we got a light day today. Guess porkin' around wasn't in much demand last night." Four-month-old Virginia giggled at her mother's voice.

Many of the working women had their own rooms reserved, day or night. The rest of the rooms were open for the public and the one-night couples who needed a place for a quick getaway.

Gail checked her list. Room number twenty-three was one of the one-night rooms. The name on the list simply read *Lacy*.

"'Lacy'?" Gail questioned the woman's name. "Who do you suppose 'Lacy' is, Ginny?" she asked her baby. "Maybe we got a new girl in the group, ya think?"

Gail unlocked the door, her nose assaulted by a horrid smell. The odor was a combination of vomit, feces, urine, and cheap whiskey. "Holy shit," Gail said, holding her arm over her nose. She backed away from the open door, searching for fresh air.

"Ginny, I'm gonna freshen that room before I take you in, sweetie! Whoever this Lacy chick is, her room probably looks just as bad as it smells."

She removed a can of air freshener from her cart, stuck her arm into the open doorway, and sprayed in for at least thirty seconds. Satisfied that the smell was almost tolerable, she rolled her cleaning cart into the room.

"Aw, shit, Virginia, look at this place! Sorry, Mommy shouldn't teach you to cuss. Okay, Ginny, ready to start. Just do me a favor, and don't add to the problem right now, ok?" Baby Virginia gave an uncomprehending, toothless smile in reply.

Gail detached the vacuum cleaner from the opposite end of her cart, uncoiled the cord, and plugged it into the wall socket next to the TV. She saw a wallet on the floor behind the foldable luggage rack and picked it up. The wallet contained a driver's license for a man named Jake Collins, credit cards, and over a hundred dollars in cash. She glanced out the open motel room door. Finding no one around, she slipped part of the money in her apron before putting the wallet in her Lost and Found bowl on the cart's bottom shelf. A black cowboy hat, clothing and an overturned bottle of whiskey lay on the floor. Curiously, the bed sheets were missing, and spots of fresh blood dotted the mattress.

The bathroom door was closed. Gail noticed a semi-moist splatter of vomit on the carpet edge next to the door. "Puked up their booze again, looks like." The bathroom door was locked. "Great, they only lock the door when they've stopped up the plumbing." She unlocked the door with a master key. After she opened the door she screamed, "Oh my God!" Gail backed away, horrified at the sight. Cold shivers ran up her spine.

Gail noticed the shower curtain pulled off its rings and dumped in the tub, topped by the two missing bed sheets. The toilet was full of more vomit. The floor was covered in body fluids. "Damn! Pee, shit, barf, it's all over the floor!" Gail exclaimed. "Worst damn mess I've ever seen! Why the hell did they do that? Well, I'll be here a while for sure, Ginny!"

She pulled on latex gloves and stepped carefully onto a clean spot on the floor and reached for the tub.

Gail lifted the edge of the sheets and curtain. "What the hell?" She grasped the curtain and the sheets to lift them out of the tub…

…and touched something unexpectedly solid underneath.

Her brow furrowed in confusion when she pulled the sheets toward her…

…revealing a body with a pasty face and lifeless eyes staring into space.

Gail screamed again, this time in terror as she skidded backwards on the slippery floor. Virginia jumped at the sound and screamed in unison…

CHAPTER 6

MCCALL OF THE WILD

"**D**ISPATCH, ONE-ZERO-THREE."

"Go ahead, one-zero-three."

"Get the Coroner down here. Call the Sheriff, he's gonna want to see this. And yeah, it's early, just wake him up. Find the lead detective, we need forensics, too. And call the next county over to see if we can borrow their dog and handler for a while."

"Ten-four, one-zero-three. Want some chow down there?"

"Yes, ma'am. Find a deputy to bring food and bottled water out later, looks like we're gonna be here a while."

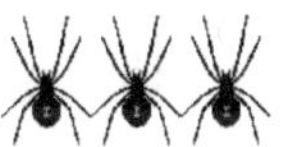

Three Sheriff's Department cars, one ambulance, and one first responder fire truck was parked outside the Drop Inn Bar and Motel. Crime scene tape flapped in the morning wind. No one was allowed to come in or leave, including the working ladies, their customers, or anyone else who had spent the night at the motel. Protocol dictated that everyone needed to be questioned. A panorama of emergency lights flashed and gleamed in the early morning fog. Garbled voices crackled from police radios in and around the small motel.

"John, what the hell is goin' on here?" the sheriff growled. He didn't give the lieutenant time to answer, nor did he expect one. "We gotta keep this quiet," he said through gritted teeth. "Why the hell've you got paramedics and fire people out here for a freakin' dead guy? He's dead, for God's sake! Been dead all night. He's just another stiff. Not like they can resurrect him. We need to keep this crap low-key."

"Sheriff, it's protocol. First responder stuff. I didn't do it; Dispatch was just doin' their job. Housekeeper called it in without notifying Jim first. It was all over the radios faster'n shit hittin' the fan. Everyone jumps at a chance for a little excitement. *This time* I couldn't do anything." Angered, the Lieutenant's ears turned a light shade of pink.

Sheriff McCall was a short, gray-haired man in his fifties. He huffed and grumbled, eyes glued to the ground, contemplating the situation. He rubbed at his smartly clipped graying mustache, irritated at the crowd gathering in the parking lot. All were gawking at the open door to room twenty-three. He kicked at the gravel with his boot; a cloud of white dust puffed and floated away.

Detectives and a forensics team came and went from the room, performing their normal duties. Evidence bags were marked, sealed, and boxed. Camera flashes could be seen through the open door. The sheriff keyed his radio mic clipped to his epaulette and barked, "Dispatch, one-hundred."

"Go ahead, Sheriff McCall."

"These fire and EMS people, get them the hell outta here. We don't need 'em." The sheriff's free arm flung about while he spoke, exasperated.

"Yes, sir, we'll tell them to disregard and return to base."

"And call off that dog and handler, too. We don't need 'em now. Evidence trail's too cold. No signs of exterior evidence anyway. Copy?"

"Ten-four, sir, calling now."

"Sir," the lieutenant interrupted as he walked toward the sheriff, "We really should follow this by the book. The dog could still pick up a trail and—"

"Shut the hell up, John. I got command of the scene now," he blasted, his face reddening. "And I said no damn dog. It was a random passerby in the night and they're long gone, got it? No trail, see?" The Sheriff extended both arms, motioning that nothing was there. "Won't be no damn pertinent evidence, neither. *You got that?*"

Lieutenant Summers lifted an eyebrow and his lips tightened. "Yes, sir, got it. I always got it. Where do you want the detectives to set up the *interviews,* sir?"

The Sheriff pointed a thumb at the building behind him. "Over there, at the bar. My brother Jim, he's got that little motel manager's office of his, just have 'em set up in there. And tell Jim that I wanna see his ass when he gets here. And, John, I gotta talk to him before the detectives do, you make sure of that. Gotta see what he knows about this dead guy. Wanna see my brother Alex, too, see what he'd been serving this guy last night before he croaked."

Irritated, John walked away, knowing it was going to be another cover up he was forced to be part of. Sheriff Max McCall, Jim McCall, and Alex McCall were brothers, all in on everything. The Sheriff and his staff ignored the bar and motel when prostitutes began hanging around. It brought in money for his brothers and some to spread around to the deputies as Christmas bonuses to insure their cooperation. There usually weren't any problems other than an occasional bar fight. This time an unforeseen player changed all the rules…

CHAPTER 7

"WHAT'S UP, DOC?"

"**W**HAT'CHA THINK, DOC? There's no blood. Not from him anyway it seems, there's a bit on the bed though. Probably from the other guy." The detective placed his hands on his knees, bent forward to speak to the coroner who was examining the man in the tub. "Maybe he offed himself, drank himself to death." Both the coroner and detective wore disposable Tyvek coveralls, nitrile gloves, and polypropylene covers for their shoes.

"No, my friend," the aging coroner spoke softly. "I think we got ourselves a good old-fashioned murder of some type. Can't tell for sure till I get 'em back to the shop and let 'em cut him open. Based on rigor and temp, looks like he died 'round midnight. Appears this was where he died, curled up in a fetal position, doesn't look like he was moved from somewhere else. But I'm seeing some pre-mortem scratches on his back and severe bruising in the abdominal area. May even have some cracked ribs by the feel of it. I found petechial hemorrhaging in and around his eyes. There's no ligature marks on his neck, so no one choked him to death."

"Petec-what?" the detective interrupted.

"He may have died from anaphylaxis, an allergic reaction to something. That could explain all the vomit and feces. Anaphylaxis is most often caused from, what, let's say allergens in foods, drugs, or insect venom. I don't see a swarm of hornets anywhere, nor much food. Mostly whiskey. He could have popped a bunch of drugs and his airway constricted 'til he couldn't breathe anymore. It's all speculation for now. And the bruising and scratches don't add up with the anaphylaxis."

"So, for him to have crapped, pissed, and puked all over the place, that's a whole 'nother story, doc? That tells me something else is going on here, not just a fight." The detective pointed at the tub. "And looks like someone took the time to tuck him in nice and cozy. Looks like he tried to climb out by grabbing the shower curtain and pulled it down, sort of wrapping him up. I suspect someone else covered him with the bed sheets, but I got no idea why. Then they locked the bathroom door before leaving. That part don't make sense, either. I just don't have this one figured out yet," the detective said.

"Think back to your psych training, son," the coroner said, struggling to stand. The arthritis in his knees popped and cracked. "Ask yourself why someone would literally want to wrap up death and lock it away." The two men stood facing each other, eye to eye, outside of the bathroom. The seriousness of the moment was palpable. "I think you may have one damn sicko on your hands. I'd bet money on finding something even more strange with this murder, once we're done with the autopsy. I've seen lots of bizarre homicides in my career, and I have a hunch about this one."

"Yep. And the only evidence *I* have is a trail of barf. Hopefully, someone around here saw or heard something," the detective replied.

"Come on, let's get the gurney, and help me get this guy into the van." The coroner shook a gloved finger at the detective and spoke. "I'll find you something, boy, I always do…"

CHAPTER 8

THE RIGHT BROTHERS

WHEN THE SHERIFF'S TWO BROTHERS ARRIVED, he waved them toward the front door of the bar. "Alex, Jim, come on in. We gotta talk."

The three brothers were a few years apart, the Sheriff being the oldest. Each was short, overweight, graying, and all bore an uncanny resemblance to each other. Jim built the bar and motel and hired his brother Alex to tend bar for him. Together they ran the business as best as they could, and Sheriff McCall tried to keep his department away because of the call girl side-business.

"Y'all sit down at the bar and let's talk. See here, Jim, I've done my damned best to look the other way around this place so you can make some money. Hell, even a couple of my deputies come up here to visit those—those whores.

Insulting the women irritated Jim. "They're just trying to make a living, Max!" His neck and cheeks reddened.

"Shut up, Jim," Alex piped in. "Max is trying to get us out of hot water. Go on, Max."

Sheriff McCall set his worn, tan Stetson on the counter and continued. "Alex, did you know this guy? What did he drink, who was he with? Was he acting hinky or mixed up in drugs? I need some info before our detectives start gnawing on you."

"Naw, that's Jake, he's in here every Friday. He's just some skinny punk, comes in, drinks whiskey, plays the jukebox, and tries hard as hell to get laid. Hell, even an ugly squirrel gets a nut now and again. Normally ends up going over to the motel. I gave him a bottle of whiskey, and the son-of-a-bitch still has, well had, a high tab. I'll never get paid now. He had a hot temper, too. Could be he got in a fight over that girl he was with last night."

"What girl?" Jim piped in.

"Pretty little thing. Wasn't like the other skanks and 'tards that hang around here. She was classy, had manners. Sexy lookin' with red hair. Not one of our regulars, if you get what I mean. Wanted some funny drink though, one of those mixed ones with a weird name, can't remember what it was. Gave her Vodka instead. Men kept hittin' on her, then old Jake comes strollin' over and I'll be damned if she didn't hook up with him. That's the *last* kind of guy I'd think *she'd* want to go out with. Talked for a while. He asked me for a bottle and off they went to the motel. Think she killed him, Max?"

"If she did, I don't see how. It's a nasty, stinkin' mess over there. Puke and shit all over the bathroom. Looks like a big old brawl took place, nothin' like a little lady could do, I don't think."

"Great, just great," Jim started. "My little cleanin' lady's gonna love this. She'll either quit or ask for money to clean it. And talk of this is probably all over town by now."

"You're cleaning lady is the one who found 'em, Jim. She called 9-1-1. Had a baby with her. You lettin' a woman work here and tote a baby around with her? You lost your mind, man? Social Services finds out, you'll be in deeper shit than Jake is dead," the sheriff scorned.

"Come on now. Don't drag that poor girl into this."

"She's already over in your office, detectives interviewing her," the sheriff said. "She's pretty shook up."

"Thing is," said Alex, "We need to get this quiet, quick as we can, Max. We gotta keep this place on the down low, protect the women who work here, keep all this off the radar. We're makin' good money. Hell, half the money we take in is cash for the rooms; we don't report that to the IRS. You're not gonna open an investigation, are you? I mean, announce it out on the air? TV and newspapers? There's a couple reporters already outside lined up at the crime scene tape!"

"Calm down, both of ya. Of course, I gotta open an investigation, idiots. But there's gonna be no evidence, forensics ain't gonna find anything, there's no blood on him, hell there's no fingerprints. Someone cleaned up good when they left. It's obvious he'd been in a fight, got scratches, bruises and busted ribs. Probably did get in a fight over that woman. My bet is he died of internal injuries. The detectives got orders from me to keep this quiet. No BOLOs, nothing going in NCIC, no talking to reporters, nothin'. We find his family, let 'em bury him, mourn, then everyone will forget all about it, okay? You two don't talk to nobody but me and the detectives, and even keep that vague, got it?"

The two brothers nodded in unison.

"Keep a tight watch on this place for a while," the sheriff said. "Make sure all is quiet and handle troubles on your own. We don't want this to come back and bite us in the ass…"

CHAPTER 9

A HAPPY WIDOW

"LACY, WHERE'VE YOU BEEN?" SAID THE FEMALE from the other end of the phone. "I've been worried sick about you! I go outta town for one night, I call and you're not there and you don't answer your cell phone? Tell me you *did not* go out with someone!"

Lacy yawned and stretched in her bed. "Lexi, I've never been better in my life."

"Tell me you didn't *sleep* with some guy!"

"Lexi, honey, listen, I did it. I finally did it! We've talked about this for so long. You went out of town, but then I found him by accident. Well, one of them. I just had to go, with or without you. You were in the middle of that conference and didn't answer either. I couldn't wait and take a chance he'd get away. I dressed up like we said. Hell, he didn't even recognize me at first. I got him in the motel room and did it, just like we planned, or almost planned."

"What do you mean *almost*, Lacy?"

"Well, it didn't go as smoothly as we thought it would, but I'm okay. It was *so* good. He paid, too. I got him back. It felt great! Lexi, I *liked* killing him." Sitting up in bed, Lacy put her phone on speaker. Straight-faced, and more poignant about the issue, she continued, "It's like for years, you think on something, hope for it, wait for it, think about it all the time, plan for it, then suddenly it's here. I had to jump at the chance, I just *had* to."

"Which one was it? How did you find him? I'm not real happy with this, I was supposed to go along to protect you."

"It was a total fluke. Here, in *our* town of all places! What are the chances? I saw him at a gas station a few weeks back, in a truck. I did a double take and followed him. He pulled into this little bar. I've been seeing his truck there every Friday afternoon since. I didn't want to tell you just yet, 'til I was sure. And yesterday, like after five, I got all dressed up, got up my nerve, and hoped he'd still be there. It was Jake, Lexi. Jake! The main one!"

"Oh, God, Lacy! Are you sure it was him? I'm upset, okay? But I'm glad at the same time, I guess, I dunno. I'm on my way home and we're gonna talk about this. A sincere talk. We're gonna sit down, and plan this out better if you're really serious about doing this shit. Obviously, you are, you took care of one last night. You get caught, you go to jail! You say it didn't go smoothly, and that worries me. No more little Podunk bars, it's too dangerous. I have something else in mind…"

On the local TV news, the anchor read, "And in other local news today, a mysterious death at the Drop Inn Bar and Motel near Henderson, North Carolina. Authorities have not released the name of the deceased pending notification of the family, or the cause of death, but information from the scene indicates a possible homicide. More information as it becomes available…"

CHAPTER 10

PROTOCOL PYTHAGORAS

Tom MICHELSON WRAPPED UP ANOTHER LONG day in the Task Force Division administrative building. Ever since his beloved cat, Frank Sinatra, passed away a few years earlier, he purposely worked longer days, lingering in his bland, quiet office. While he enjoyed the challenge of removing malevolence in the world, he still missed Frank, his only companion for years. A small, framed photo of the Siamese rested on the right side of his desk. The cat's large blue eyes stared upward, almost appearing to smile at Tom. It was a comforting, daily reminder of his feline best friend.

Arthritis had taken hold of the 64-year-old retired Marine, so keeping his office at a higher-than-normal temperature brought comfort during his work hours. He speculated the ailment stemmed from years-old battlefield wounds and was a constant reminder of the choices he'd made to make other lives better.

Tom was proud of the work he'd done as the Task Force Director. He lost only a few field agents during that time, compared to losing as many Marines in just one engagement in the Mid-East in the 1990s.

Mark Jason was a superlative Task Force leader. Granted, Mark was only the second person to hold the position of Field Team

Leader. Under the first field leader, Marshall Gray, an agent was lost every few months; none, however, were lost since Mark took command of the team. He had an analytical mind for command, operations and groundwork that impressed Tom. *He may be the one who needs to take over the whole operation soon,* he thought.

A knock on his doorframe shook him from his reverie. "Another retirement daydream, Tom?" asked the Navy admiral at the open door.

With a wave, Tom said, "Bill, come on in, old friend." Bill Sutton was one of the top admirals in the Pentagon. Tom stood and shook hands with the older gentleman. "To what do I owe this honor?" Tom asked. "Please, have a seat."

"Well, this one is your idea." He handed Tom a manila folder. "When your department came up with the Alpha Omega Spatial Exam, you told our top testers it would never be solved. But we made it a standard test in the NIS recruit challenges anyway, knowing no one would ever pass it."

"So, tell me something I don't know," said Tom. "It's not designed to find the solution."

"Well, Tom, after a dozen years of testing our crewmen, we had a JG solve it. And it only took thirty seconds."

Tom's mouth fell open to speak, but nothing came out. In near shock, he slapped his hands on the desk. "Solved? In *thirty seconds?* That's impossible! It was guaranteed unsolvable, like calculating pi to the last decimal, because the problem itself does not contain all the variables to the equation to allow for completing the answer. It's only a test of aptitude."

"Nevertheless, it happened." Bill sat back, intertwining his fingers, waiting for Tom to open the file. "This sailor calculated the missing part of the equation in her head, apparently, and then completed the entire answer."

Tom read the name, then looked at the admiral. Tom's forehead wrinkled, and eyes squinted. "Oh—my—God. You're shittin' me, right?"

"Nope. This is the candidate you said could never exist."

Tom retrieved his reading glasses from the desk drawer. He read the lieutenant junior grade's profile page, test score, and test monitor's notes. He keyed in a command on his computer to bring up the encrypted test session video of the lieutenant. The view was to monitor the person keying from the second it activated until thirty seconds later, when the answer was complete, and the test ended. He entered a command dividing his screen into four images. Each showed a different view of the person taking the test, with one zoomed in on the test on the desktop. Tom couldn't keep up with the keystrokes. The lieutenant was too fast on the keyboard. "Son of a bitch," Tom said. He looked at Bill and asked, "How?"

"We checked the computer database; the sailors' testing stations were selected at random by numbers on slips of paper. No computer manipulation possible. Every precaution taken as standard. It was solved. End of story."

"Never thought I'd see the day." Tom rose from his desk, closed, and locked his office door. He returned and picked up his desk phone receiver and pressed the one button he never expected to touch: the blue button below the keypad. Once the clicking in the receiver stopped, he simply said, "Protocol Pythagoras is activated…"

CHAPTER 11

JUST LIKE GRAMPA

"LIEUTENANT JUNIOR GRADE ANGELA JASON reporting for duty, sir!"

"At ease, lieutenant."

Angela smiled and stepped toward her father, Mark Jason, giving him a warm and always-welcome hug.

"Well, come on into the office. Let me take a close look at you." Placing his hands on her shoulders, he looked her over from head to toe. His voice was full of pride at the sight of his only daughter wearing Navy whites. Her black hair was pulled up in a tight bun.

"How much has it grown back?"

Angela reached for her hair in reflex. "It's mostly grown back. I hated that they made me cut it short."

"Just the way the Jurgens boy likes it, remember?"

"Oh my God, Dad! Will you and Mom ever let up?" she said, laughing.

"Not until you get married."

She ran her fingers through his beard and the hair along his temples. "Got some white lines growing in there, 'Pops'. Haven't you ever heard of Grecian Formula?"

"I'm giving you incentive to get us some grandkids."

"Oh Lord!"

He picked up a framed picture off his desk. The image was of young Mark in his Navy dress white uniform, about the same age as was Angela now, with his father Zachary in the same office. "This picture was from the first time I visited your grandpa in here, all dressed up and on leave." He cast an eye toward his assistant's door and called, "Hey, Ellie!"

Eleanor Worthington strolled in, carrying a digital camera. Mark shook his head. He'd long given up figuring out *how* she knew what he needed before he needed it.

A sweet, but formal, English accent rolled off Eleanor's tongue as she politely commanded, "Okay, Jason's, by the desk, like Zachary's pose." Mark and Angela stood in front of the desk, much like the photo of Mark in his Navy uniform with his father when the elder Jason ran the company. Eleanor took photos from numerous angles. Pleased with the results, she turned to leave. "I'll have a photo added to your desk as soon as possible, sir. And nice to see you again, Angela, welcome home."

"Now, in about twenty years, when your own child joins the Navy, you'll take a picture like these to add to your old man's and grandpa's."

"And who said I was going to have a child anyway, Dad? Maybe I'll stay single and become an old spinster Navy sand crab."

Mark smiled and walked over to his office bar. He opened two decanters, pouring bourbon into a tumbler for himself and Pinot Grigio into a wine glass for his daughter. Mark chuckled as he poured. "'Sand crab'. I haven't heard that old term in quite a while. No, honey, the world is yours, and I sure would like a grandbaby at some point. Come on, let's sit and talk." Angela placed her cover on the coffee table and sat next to him on the overstuffed couch. "So, how's NIS?" he asked, referring to the Naval Intelligence Service.

Angela looked at him and smiled. "Yes, it's a beautiful day out."

Mark chuckled again. He already knew she couldn't answer, just like he wasn't supposed to answer questions about his Task Force missions. "I can tell we're going to have many personal conversations in the future."

She sipped her wine. "I'm really enjoying my posting, Dad. It's a great challenge, and I can make a difference there."

"Yeah, I was like that too, when I was doing SEAL missions."

"I never worried about you coming home. Mom worried about your long overseas deployments, but I never doubted you'd come back safe and sound, every time."

"I know," said Mark. "You've always been secure and self-confident, to a fault. I don't think I've seen you cry once, well, at least not since kindergarten."

"Hey, what can I say? I've got the best parents in the world. You two made sure I never had to deal with stupid stuff so I could concentrate on being my best. I always wanted to be, well, perfect for you, Dad." She took another sip. "You gave me a great start and I couldn't let you down."

Mark sat forward, holding his glass in his hands. He looked deep into his daughter's eyes. He felt a profound love and joy in her. He knew he'd been blessed when she was born. "Yeah, sometimes that special perfectionist aptitude tends to get in the way. Just be careful with it. But, hey, you didn't say you were coming home on leave, Angel."

"Actually, I was ordered to report here."

"Richmond? There's no naval base in Richmond. The closest is in Norfolk and Portsmouth."

"No, Dad, here. Your office." She opened her black military case, pulled out some papers, and handed them to her father.

At first glance, he thought it looked like military deployment orders. He began to read.

There was a quick knock on the hallway door, and Tom Michelson entered before Mark could answer. Closing the door behind him, Tom said, "Lieutenant Jason, greetings! Haven't seen you since Marshall's memorial service after the Biblical Bomber affair. Sorry, bad associative memories there. But look at you! The Navy service suits you."

She stood and extended her right hand. "Thank you, Colonel Michelson, sir."

Smiling, he waved at her to sit. "I'm retired now, lieutenant. You can just call me, 'sir.'"

"Yes, sir."

"Want a drink, Tom? We're sitting here having some chit-chat."

"No, no, but thank you, Mark."

"So," said Mark, "what happened that got you out of the Division offices?"

"What happened is why I had Angela ordered here, Mark." He looked at Angela, then Mark. "Why didn't you tell me she was a prodigious savant…?"

CHAPTER 12

TOO LATE TO MAKE A DATE

"Well, you never asked, that's why."

Tom sat in an overstuffed armchair adjacent to the couch where Mark and Angela sat, gently nodding at Mark's answer. "You're absolutely correct, I didn't ask."

"And," Mark continued, "her talent was none of your business, said with all due respect, sir."

"Yep, you're always blunt and to the point, Mark. Actually, it is now. This just became official business." Tom opened his briefcase and removed a thick folder with papers. "When did you first discover her ability for three-dimensional spatial logic?"

Mark looked at Angela. "Oh, early on in grade school. But in fifth grade, when her math teacher started introducing fractions and ratios, she tended to blurt out the answers before the teacher finished writing the questions on the blackboard."

Angela sat forward on the couch; her fingers interlocked. "Whiteboard, Dad. Blackboards were back in your day."

Mark smiled at his daughter. "And she demonstrated a near-perfect eidetic memory by eighth grade."

"Very interesting," said Tom. "Angela, why didn't you make straight A's through school?"

Angela shrugged her shoulders. "I sort of played it down, sir. Intentionally answered some test questions wrong so I wouldn't always get A's. I didn't want to be labeled a geek or nerd," she replied, "nor did I want to be seen as standoffish because of it. And I joined the navy because I wanted to be just like my daddy. Get my time in, study business, then take his place here. That's why I didn't apply for the test until after I had a few years in."

"Kind of a family tradition, actually," said Mark. "After Dad graduated college, he took out a loan and invested in Wall Street while he made an extraordinarily strong company here. I never attended traditional college. Although I took correspondence courses while in the navy, I've managed to turn this company into an international powerhouse, and also joined Task Force at your invitation." He pointed to his desk, specifically at the wood block on the left corner with the large gold key on top. "And one day, that will be her desk and her name will be on the door to this office. But first she'll be busting her ass to get here, just like I did."

"Well, I can't help but applaud your family and company. Jason Enterprises is a major supplier, and many times is a sole source for military weapons and specialty items used by the Task Force Division. I'm amazed at some of the weapons, gadgets, and what-nots that your company comes up with. They often exceed other companies, hell, even the military research and development."

Mark's eyes narrowed. "But, this doesn't answer the one big question of the day." Mark lifted Angela's orders. "Why in the world was Angela ordered to report to *this* office? Not exactly a standard duty station, twenty stories in the Richmond sky."

Tom quietly pointed to the room behind Mark's desk. It was formerly the CEO's private balcony at Jason Enterprises. A couple years earlier it was retrofitted into a soundproof, bulletproof alcove, serving as a covert office for Mark and his Task Force's operations and duties. Without a word, Mark rose, went to the pocket door, and placed his hand on a wall panel, disguised to be a small, framed painting. The surface turned a pale blue beneath his palm and flashed a bright yellow before returning to its normal color. The door slid into the wall with a quiet rush, revealing an office far more technologically advanced than Mark's public one. He stepped in and waited for Tom and Angela to follow.

Once the three were inside, the stainless-steel door automatically slid closed and locked with an almost-imperceptible metallic click. Angela took note of a strange humming noise coming from a miniature cubicle at the end of the small room. To her astonishment, a small, white, fiberglass robot rolled out and advanced toward Angela, stopping directly in front of her.

"Dad! Is this the final product?"

Before she continued with the questions, the four-foot-tall robot circled its way around her body. It scanned her from head to toe with a horizontal red laser line, cataloging height, weight, uniform, hair, eye, and skin color. It came to a stop in front of her again, and spoke in a pleasant female voice, "Angela Jason: United States Navy, Naval Intelligence, Rank, Lieutenant, Junior Grade. Daughter of Mark and Jan Jason, President and Executive Vice President of Jason Enterprises. Current duty assignment: Classified, Security Level, Eyes-Only-As-Needed. Welcome back, Lieutenant Junior Grade Jason." The robot lifted its right arm to its head, giving a mechanical salute, something Mark instructed R&D to program into it whenever military personnel visited, mostly to show off its capabilities.

"It's cute!" Angela squealed, bending down to see eye-to-eye with the machine. "It's got a regular human voice, not like a robot at all! Whose voice did you emulate?"

Tom smacked a hand over both eyes, an exaggerated reaction to Angela's girly response, not the soldier-like response he'd hoped from her, especially this day. "Mark, for God's sake, man, can we get back on task sometime soon?"

Mark stood in place, silently snickering at his daughter's sudden innocence and at Tom's frustration.

"A present for you from your father," the robot said, extending its left arm and presenting Angela with a USB/Wi-Fi pen created by JE.

"The robot's JPR30," Mark stated. "Thirtieth and final model—well, nothing's really final around here actually. But, we finished all the prototype testers and they'll be buzzing all over this building by the first of the month. Finally got 'em all programmed to do better than average problem solving. Open and close things without instruction, built-in GPS. The military units are bullet resistant, and over the top with their own weaponry and gadgets. This little lady can even cross the street, go next door to fetch a Cappuccino, lay the cards on the table and play poker with you, and play three-dimensional chess, Angela."

At the word "chess" Angela stood. "Dad? Chess! Really? Way awesome!" She crossed her arms. "Do you think this OS can actually beat me?" she asked.

"Hito gives it a 50/50 chance, and he'll revise after you play your first game against it. Okay, everyone, we're in here for a reason! Tom has business to attend to apparently. Let's get a move-on before the good colonel has a stroke."

All three took seats in front of individual touch-screen computers, and Tom began. "When the Task Force was founded after 9/11, the initial design by the Joint Chiefs, under orders from the president, was to have a specialized field team of four former military officers, each with unique unequalled skills."

"I already know that much," said Mark. "Mind getting to the answer pretty quick?"

Tom chuckled. "Again, that's one trait I love about you, Mark. You hate beating around the bush. Well, here's one thing you never read in the Task Force charter." He reached into his briefcase and removed a folded set of papers and handed them to Mark.

"About a year later I gathered the seven top mathematicians in the world to create a test, an exam of sorts. The goal was to find intelligence candidates who had the mental wherewithal to interpret computer code from terrorist organizations, enemy governments— well, super cryptologist types, to give the best possible advantages for the United States. This code was designed to be unsolvable, with each of the designers keeping only parts of the algorithm with them across the world. The best scores by candidates might have hit up to forty percent after about thirty minutes. It really wasn't meant to be solved, just to see how close they actually came to solving it, and how long they took. Imagine the eyebrows that hit the ceiling when your little girl not only solved the equation but did it in half a minute."

Mark crossed his arms and leaned back in his chair. He looked over at Angela. "Why'd you take so long?"

"I really wasn't in a hurry."

"Makes sense."

Tom gave the two a longer than brief, narrow-eyed, frustrated look. "Anyway, a fifth position was created in the field team, in hopes it would one day be filled, but with no great expectations of finding anyone."

Angela still contemplated the robot in the back of her mind, reveling in all its own special operation algorithms. She would have loved to help program the rolling computer, had she not chosen naval service instead. She whispered, "Dad, how much will you sell it for?"

Mark leaned toward her, "Open market, one mil. The software will be only rudimentary; we'll get the big bucks with the specialized per-customer programming and regular upgrades."

Tom grinned. "And no doubt our wise politicians in Congress will find some way to pay ten times that amount. As much as I support capitalism, can we get serious now?" Tom turned to his computer and pressed the screen in the bottom-left corner, activating the thumbprint reader.

The screen rippled into a new image of the Task Force Division logo, and the screen read:

STAND BY FOR OPTICAL CONFIRMATION

The computer camera flashed, and twin blue beams focused on both his eyes. The screen then flashed:

CONFIRMED, ENTER ACCESS

After entering his access authority, the screen went black with six words appearing in white block letters, one at a time:

PROTOCOL PYTHAGORAS
MISSION AND AGENT NAME: ORACLE

Below the words was a starburst symbol. "Good afternoon, Director Michelson," the monitor said in a male voice. "Please confirm Agent Oracle."

"I like the robot's voice better," Angela said.

"Angel, you do know what Pythagoras stands for don't you?"

"Of course, Daddy. He was from Rome, 570 BC. Great mathematician and scientist. Best known for the Pythagorean Theorem. I studied that in grammar school, don't you remember?"

"Sounds like the name of a dinosaur with a lisp," Mark chuckled.

"Agent Oracle confirmed," the computer said, then Tom entered a command code known only to him. Tom rotated in his chair, glaring at the two. Mark immediately understood, first scowling at Tom and then softening his expression turning his gaze to his daughter.

Angela saw both men looking at her. "Oh, well, I suppose now's not a good time to finally say 'yes' to the Jurgens boy..."

CHAPTER 13

IN FOR A PENNY, IN FOR A BILLION

JAN JASON SAT IN HER HUSBAND'S CHAIR, reading a contract in a binder, twirling a lock of her long red hair in her right hand. Facing the wall containing the hidden office, she looked up completely unsurprised when the secret door opened. Jan closed the binder when Mark, Angela, and Tom stepped out.

"Jan, so very good to see you again." Tom extended his hand in greeting.

She returned the gesture and smiled politely. "Tom. How are you?"

"I'm well, thank you,"

Jan looked at the trio. "Why do I have a gut feeling I'm not going to like the answer to my question? What's going on? By the way, hi, Angel..."

After hearing the explanation for Tom's meeting with Mark and Angela, Jan shook her head and pinched the bridge of her nose with her fingers. She shook a finger at Tom. "Tom. No. I really don't think so. It's enough that I agreed with letting Mark join your Task

Force in the first place." She pointed a finger at her daughter. "But, Angel, for you to join is asking way more than a wife and mother should be asked to endure."

"It's a chance to be part of something bigger, something important," Angela spoke calmly. "I'll still have my Naval career, Mom."

"Uh, huh. Mark, you better fix me something strong before I have voluntary PMS."

Mark smiled and moved to the wet bar. He returned with a tumbler, bent forward, hovering just in front of her face, and placed a light gentle kiss on her lips, then a second for good measure.

"Damn, you still make my toes tingle when you do that," she whispered.

"Tequila works every time. But, it's not like we didn't see this possibility way in advance, Jan."

"She'll be a great asset—" Tom began.

"Don't go there, Tom," Jan interrupted. "You give me that spiel of her being a major asset to the United States because of her great mental abilities. I just may kick your butt out a window right now, and it's a damn fast way down twenty floors. I don't need to be given political speeches. Lord knows I hear enough of that garbage on the news every evening. Sorry, this is the overprotective mother speaking here."

Tom held his hands up in surrender. He saw Mark wink at him, acknowledging his wise decision.

"Tom, you'll excuse us for just a few minutes while I tend to some business first? Just a few minutes. I wasn't expecting this visit and we have a timeline to meet on a few issues," Jan said as she silently glared at him. Mark did his best to hide his smile at the grizzled retired marine withering under the stare of the forty-two-year-old redhead. Tom stepped to the bar area, poured himself a glass of bourbon, then took a seat at his place on the couch.

Satisfied she had control of the executive office for the time, she swiveled in Mark's chair. "I've just completed negotiations with the ASI, and we not only have the contract for their next communications satellite, which needs our signatures right away, but also a private meeting confirmed with His Holiness."

"The Pope?" asked Tom from across the room, looking up from flipping through a newspaper. Jan stared at him again. He returned his gaze to the newspaper. He realized after all; he was addressing the second most powerful person in the international company.

Jan continued, "We just put a quarter-billion-dollar contract in our coffers, with over one hundred million going into the local Italian economy. The R&D will take place downstairs, with additional work done in the Venice branch. Had a nice chat with our friend Father Saul and negotiated an additional module to the satellite construction for improved international signal feed for the Vatican to reach parishioners worldwide. Well, I made that a gift from Jason Enterprises, actually."

Angela listened carefully to the conversation while pouring a second glass of wine at the bar. "Which will make for a potential eight to nine-billion-dollar profit for Jason Enterprises. And only at an additional four million dollars cost. But, using part of it as a gift, or rather donation, should help with taxes of course, securing an even higher profit margin."

Mark shrugged his shoulders and stopped Jan from replying by saying, "It's too late to tell her not to do that. Tom already figured it out."

"Accounting predicted 8.7 million within six months. Very good, Angel!"

Angela corrected her mother as she turned around and leaned against the bar, "Four months."

Tom opened his mouth to comment on the exchange, then thought better of it and said nothing, turning to another page in the newspaper.

Hours later, Mark, Jan, Angela, and Tom were still in Mark's office. Once the lunch hour had come and gone, Eleanor realized they all were probably hungry and decided to order in a dinner for the four. Not realizing the time, or that they were actually hungry, they were grateful for the break.

The daytime shift was packing up to leave and was being replaced by the smaller evening shift. The heated conversation in the office was still in full swing. Eleanor remained at her desk in the outer office, continuing her own work but always ready for Mark's summons.

Jan was on her third small glass of tequila. She felt comfortable, and far from intoxicated. Angela stopped after her second glass of wine and simply watched the rest of the day as the older generation talked about her future.

"—never mind if you put her in one of your uniforms, the Jurgens boy will probably have a heart attack the first time he sees her in that. It's too racy."

"Racy? Seriously, Jan? Since when does sexual attributes have anything to do with Task Force uniforms?" Tom asked.

"You obviously haven't seen Mark in his uniform the way I see him in his uniform."

Tom looked at Mark. "Why are you modeling your uniform for your wife?"

"Hey, it was a terrific Halloween party," Mark said, smiling. "And she made a great Lady Godiva."

"Mom!" Angela shouted in surprise. "Really? TMI!"

"Of course, not! Your dad's kidding. He didn't really wear the uniform, and I didn't go as Lady Godiva, at least not until after the guests left."

"Oh, yuck, don't tell me anymore," Angela pleaded.

"Again, she won't be in the field," Tom tried to reassure Jan. "She will never be anywhere except in the analysis offices."

"Look, Tom, you work for the government, right?"

"Of course."

"That's why I don't believe you."

"Jan, really," said Tom, a puzzled look on his face. "Okay, you have a point. But, Jan, that has nothing to do with Angela's mission, and—"

"So why should I believe you when everyone else in Washington lies so boldly?"

Tom looked at Mark. "Are you going to help? I can't get in a word edgewise."

"She's doing fine," Mark answered. "Frankly, you're crashing and burning quite well all by yourself."

"Gee, thanks."

Jan simply stared at everyone defiantly, holding her ground on all topics at hand.

"Jan, it's as simple as this—I'm *not* like everyone else in Washington, okay?"

That was all Angela could take. She stood, obviously miffed. "Well, we've been here for hours. There's one thing that wasn't asked."

"What's that, Angel?" Mark asked.

"If I even want this job." She placed her hands behind her back in standard military parade-rest. "I did say that it'd be a great opportunity, to be part of something bigger than myself. Respectfully, Colonel, you never offered me the position, all you said was I was who you were looking for to do this special job. Task Force isn't a part of Naval Intelligence or even the military, and I really can't be *ordered* to join." She stepped over to her parents and hugged each of them. "Mom, Dad, I appreciate you looking out for me. But I'm twenty-four years old, and in Naval Intelligence for nearly all of them—where the keyword is 'intelligence'. I think I can make my own decisions at this point." She turned smartly and faced Tom, standing at attention before the retired marine.

Tom stood. He was a few inches shorter than the tall young woman, but she looked straight ahead at her own eye-level. Tom spoke with admiration and confidence, but with formality. "Lieutenant JG Jason, you've been given the description of the duties for which you have been approached. This is a voluntary position. Whether you accept or decline, all information discussed today remains in this room and with the individuals present. The Task Force Division, a department of the Federal Government, charged with protecting the United States, offers you the position of Agent Oracle. Do you accept or decline?"

Mark and Jan both stood.

"Sir," Angela answered in a strong voice, "I accept, sir."

Tom smiled at her parents before he continued. He reached into his jacket pocket and removed an envelope. Handing it to her, he said, "You are ordered to remain in Richmond, Virginia, until your classification has been modified within Naval Operations. Your official status is 'on leave pending reassignment'. Your superiors at NIS will be notified of your transfer. You may take the next few days to return to rest up and relax before you are placed at your new station. From this moment on, your work is classified 'Eyes Only' and you may not discuss your work with anyone." He looked at Mark. "Well, present company excepted, of course."

"Yes, sir." She saluted, and Tom returned the salute.

"At ease, young lady. Mark, Jan. It's been a fun visit. Thanks for putting up with me today."

Jan said, "Not exactly how I planned my day, but I'm glad I got to have my say." She wrapped an arm around Angela's shoulder.

"You keep my little girl safe, Tom, or you'll find out who's scarier than your Agent Spy here." She gave Tom a big hug.

"Sir?" Angela interrupted.

Tom looked up at Angela; her face had a serious look. "Yes?"

"Request permission to hug the Colonel, sir."

Tom chuckled loudly. "Come here, you rascal. That's totally out of protocol, but I've known you long enough. You better get over here and hug your old friend while it's not fraternization!"

Angela's face beamed with a giant smile, and she hugged Tom, almost like a little schoolgirl.

"Mark, I'll see you at the next Task Force meeting." Tom shook Mark's hand and left via Eleanor's office, rather than Mark's hall door.

Without looking up from the computer, Eleanor spoke, "Have a good evening, Mr. Michelson."

"Good night, Eleanor."

Jan put her hands on her hips and looked at Angela. "My daughter, the secret agent. What else can happen today?"

Angela smiled and winked at her parents, "I supposed I can call the Jurgens boy; finally ask him out for drinks and see if he wants me to play Lady Godiva..."

CHAPTER 14

THE SARGE AND DODGER SHOW

No ONE IN HIS RIGHT MIND EVER MESSED WITH "SARGE" BRUNSON, especially on a Friday night, when he and his best friend, Roger "Dodger" Ahrens, were having their weekly shot contest. Sarge and Dodger, both in their mid-50s, had been the Mutt and Jeff of their squad from boot camp to the front lines in Iraq. Sarge was 250 pounds of near-solid muscle, 6-foot-5 and pudgy around the middle. Dodger was 5-foot-11 and never weighed more than 180 pounds his entire adult life. Together they had been an unbeatable duo of death and destruction when taking down Al-Qaida forces. Their forced medical retirement, mostly due to enemy gunshot wounds, may have taken them out of uniform, but their popular Friday night bourbon competition continued unabated, with only rare exception.

The Recovery Room bar was a popular watering hole for veterans and former military (retired or otherwise) in the Richmond area. The walls were lined with military memorabilia donated by patrons over the years. Friday night found the bar always full, thanks to the boisterous Sarge and Dodger.

Al, the barkeep, was a slightly heavy middle-aged man who ran his bar like a navy ship: tight and controlled. The wait staff, all younger women, shifted from table to table like a well-oiled machine. They topped off glasses without waiting for calls from customers and made sure snack bowls were filled, moving like quicksilver keeping the customers satisfied but out of the reach of a fast-playful grab.

TJ, whose full name was Tamra Jason, was Mark Jason's cousin, and served as the bar's bouncer. Almost as tall as her 6-foot-tall cousin, she was an expert in several martial arts, giving credit to her cousin as her Sensei. Any troublemakers were surprised when the lithe, athletic woman easily tossed them out onto the sidewalk, usually followed by applause from the other customers.

No one except Al was aware, however, that Mark Jason, under his authority as Agent Spy of Task Force Division, had turned The Recovery Room into one of his covert operation locations.

"So, them commies still wanna reduce our retirement pay while they jack up their own," said Dodger. "How many of 'em ever shot a freekin' Qaida?"

"You're kidding," said Sarge, downing another drink. They'd long lost count and drank just to drink. "Tell me any public servant in Washington who actually did anythin' to protect the U S of A today. They're a buncha cuckin' fommunists."

"That's what I said," said Dodger. "Hey, that kinda talk get you fired from that Jason guy?"

"Nah, he's good. We're on the same page mos'a the time."

Dodger gently placed his empty glass on the bar as soon as he found the countertop. "Speakin' o' pages," he said, trying his best to concentrate. "I got shit to tell ya, pal. You ain't gonna like it."

"What?" Sarge growled.

"I got it, buddy," Dodger said. "I freekin' got the big C."

Sarge stopped his arm in mid-raise, then gently set his shot glass on the bar. It was as though he'd never had a drop, now fully alert and attentive. Sarge lowered his head a bit and looked Dodger in the eyes. In a whisper he spoke, "Dodger, no. You're shittin' me."

Sarge gave a small nervous chuckle. "Come on man, you just messin' with my head, right?"

"Ain't that some crap? I start chemo on Monday."

"Why didn't you tell me before?" Sarge demanded, now louder, irritated. He was annoyed that Dodger had kept the news from him, but more so that he was so calm about it.

Dodger looked at the quantity of empty shot glasses on the bar. "Man, I wanted to tell you when I found out. We been through hell together, you'n'me. We kicked lotsa ass over the years, we killed 'em, man. We killed everyone who threatened us, we blew the shit outa all those 'Qaida's and we came home. How'm I supposed to tell ya that some mutant cell is doing what those ragheads couldn't? There's no one for me to shoot or blow up, dammit, Sarge!" Tears welled up in his eyes.

"Son of a bitch," Sarge growled. He put his massive, muscled arm around his best friend's shoulder. "You tell me what you need, Dodger, I don't care what it is, you tell me, and I'll get it for you. You're not in this alone, buddy. We're gonna kick this shit together." He turned to everyone in the bar, knowing that their conversation was overheard. It was, after all, Friday evening, and the Sarge/Dodger show was the draw. The two men weren't surprised by the silence in the bar. "Hey, all you flyboys, boaters and pounders," said Sarge. "We take care of each other, and Dodger here needs all of us. Right?"

Everyone in the bar lifted their glasses in response.

"We got your back, pal, count on it." Sarge clapped his hand on Dodger's back again.

Sandra Freeman, chief Internet Technician and International Security Liaison at Jason Enterprises, entered the bar as Sarge was placing a hand on Dodgers back. The five-foot-six short-haired brunette looked around, taking in the military paraphernalia adorning every wall. She noted the missing-in-action table set for the soldier who would never come home. The waitresses all wore snug red tank-tops and blue denim short-shorts. She noticed the black-haired woman with the incredible figure behind the counter, and the slightly plump and balding bartender beside her. Sarge and his friend were sitting at the bar.

"Whatcha grinnin' at, Sarge? See something you like?"

"What? No! I jus' never thought I'd see her here. Let's just go back to drinkin'. Whose turn is it?"

Freeman took a cleansing breath and stepped to the barstool on Sarge's right. "Hi, Sarge. Kinda needed some company after work. Wondered where you'd run off to, then I remembered your Friday night tradition. Okay if I sit here?"

Sarge patted the barstool beside him. "Pull up a stool, Freeman. We were getting' some things off our minds."

She noticed the eight empty shot glasses on the counter between Sarge and the other man, and she motioned toward the brunette. "I'll take whatever they've had, ah, TJ," Freeman said after noticing the bar assistant's name tag.

"One top-shelf bourbon, coming up." TJ turned and reached for the shot glass shelf behind the bar.

"Two things, Freeman. She's duh bouncer, an' she's your boss's cousin."

Freeman looked at Sarge and raised her eyebrows in surprise. "She's Mark Jason's cousin?"

Sarge bumped Dodger in the shoulder with his own. "Hey, Dodger, Freeman here hadn't had one yet and she's already thinking amnesty—conflict of interest—wrong place wrong time. Aw, hell, she won't care after a few shots."

Dodger leaned forward onto the bar and looked past Sarge. "Freeman? You're *his* Freeman?"

She ran a hand through her hair in indignation. "No, sir, I am not *his* Freeman, I only work with the man," she said politely.

"I ain't no 'sir'," Dodger said calmly, "just like ol' Brunson here."

"So, that's where you get it," Freeman said to Sarge.

"Where I get what?"

"'I ain't no 'sir'"," Freeman repeated.

Freeman straightened her white blouse, rolling her sleeves at the cuffs before picking up the shot glass and held it up, as a toast. "Here's mud in your eye." Sarge watched her kick it back without any reaction. Just as calmly, she set the empty glass on the bar and asked TJ for another. "You've been talking for months about how you do this every Friday with Mr. Dodger here. So, I decided to come join you and see what it was all about." She drank the second shot down as fast as the first.

People began to pay closer attention to the three.

Dodger noticed her lack of response to the strong drink. She rested her forearms on the bar and looked over at the two ogling men. "Bourbon's not usually my drink of choice, but this isn't too bad." TJ filled her glass again. She raised the third glass halfway to her mouth, stopped and raised it toward the two men.

Sarge leaned into her slightly and said in a low grumble, "What da hell you tryin' to do, Freeman? Make me look bad in frunna everyone?"

"No, sir," she said with a straight face. "Only wanting to catch up and get in the right frame of mind to enjoy the evening with you two fine gentlemen."

Dodger burst out laughing. "Hear that, Sarge? She called us *fine gennamen*! Boy, you need glasses, baby!"

"I'm not a baby."

"Not with that pretty figure, you're definitely not a baby," Dodger agreed. He smiled when he saw Freeman blush. He leaned over to Sarge and whispered, "That's how ya do it if'n you want her."

"Ah, shut yer ass," Sarge whispered back. "TJ! 'Nother roun'!"

"Right away." She winked at him. *"Sir."*

"You're not going to correct her?" asked Freeman mockingly.

"There're only two women who've ever put me on my back without the intention of screwing my brains out, you and her. I have no desire to be sucker-dropped again, *ma'am.*" That drew laughter from the nearest patrons. Everyone was fully tuned in for the Friday Night Show.

"Well, if you'd been paying attention to what you were doing, I wouldn't't've had to take you down."

More laughter came from the crowd.

Dodger, Sarge, and Freeman lifted their glasses in toast. With heavy lidded eyes, Sarge spoke, "To Old Glory," Freeman and Dodger added, "Hear, hear!" In unison, they drank their shots and set the empty glasses on the counter, Dodger's coming down a little harder than anticipated.

TJ refilled their empty glasses. Al, the bartender, and owner of The Recovery Room, said, "This round's on me, lady and gents!"

Freeman smiled at the bar owner. "Well, sum-bitch," said Sarge. "Tha's the first time I've seen you smile, Freeman. You got a nice smile there."

"Thank you, sir,"

Sarge did a John-Wayne swagger from the waist up as he drank his number-seven shot, then slammed the glass on the bar. "I am not no dog-gammed 'sir'! How many times I gotta tell you? How many was 'at, anyways?"

"How many of those glasses are yours?" Freeman asked, detecting the effect of a lot of bourbon in a short period. "Five or six?" Her head felt foggy, and her vision was in and out of focus. She looked at TJ behind the bar. "My God, you're gorgeous," Freeman said almost imperceptibly.

"Sorry?" TJ asked.

Freeman's eyes widened. "Um, sorry, think the bourbon's starting to get to me."

"What a rook," Sarge taunted as he raised his glass carefully. The last thing he saw was arms reaching for him.

Freeman caught the much-heavier retired army sergeant as he fell to the floor, keeping his head from landing first. But her effort also sent her to the floor with him. Fortunately, his massive bulk cushioned her fall.

She took a deep breath, stood up, and tried to balance the best she could.

TJ was at her side, guiding her back onto the barstool. She held out her hand to Freeman. "Car keys," TJ said.

Freeman closed her eyes, concentrating to focus. "I took a cab; I don't own a car."

"You're the first smart drunk I've ever met, besides these two every Friday," TJ said, smiling. "I actually see there's a cab parked out front now," said TJ.

"I'll take Sarge home, it's on the way to mine, if you'll get someone to take his friend home."

"Already done, we always have him covered. He's on our way home, too." said TJ. "You be careful now. Can you manage him ok?"

"Yeah," she said. Freeman reached down, grabbed Sarge's massive right arm across her shoulder, and slapped him in the face with her free hand. "Wake up, 'sir'."

Sarge's eyes opened slightly, and he could barely scowl at her. "I ain't no—whatever you said," he said, trying but failing to growl.

"Let's get you home, big boy," Freeman said, balancing herself in her kitten-style shoes.

"Where we goin'?"

"Home."

"Home? Okay. Commin' wit' me?"

The taxi waited outside the bar. She helped him into the back seat, closed the door, held onto the taxi's trunk as best she could, and walked around to the other back door. Before the taxi began rolling, he slid sideways and laid his head in her lap.

"Hey, Freeman, y'know whuh?"

"What, Sarge?" she asked as she closed her eyes and rested her head.

"You got some nice titties." He suddenly snored.

The taxi driver crinkled his eyebrows and took a quick peek in the rearview mirror.

Absentmindedly she gently stroked his crew-cut hair trying to stay awake until the taxi stopped at Sarge's home.

Freeman woke with a start. Her head pounded, and her closed eyes felt like sandpaper. *Migraine pills, coffee, water, long hot shower,* bringing her thoughts together. She stretched her arms, and the sheets slide off her naked breasts.

Startled, she brought her hands up to cover them. Then one hand slowly traveled down her torso under the sheet. "Where are my pajamas?" She couldn't remember getting into bed the night before. She steadied herself, then realized the bed she was in was not hers. "Where the hell am I?" she said aloud.

She noticed the unusual lumps in the bed between herself and the door; large lumps that glistened in a reflected night light's glow. She rolled out of bed away from the form, turned on the nightstand light, and gasped.

Sarge Brunson's broad naked chest rose and fell in deep breaths.

Without thinking, Freeman reached one hand to her groin area and discovered the signs of a good time she could not remember.

"Oh, shit..."

CHAPTER 15

THE CEO, THE SEEKER, AND THE SECRET

MARK STOPPED HIS CAR AT THE GUARD'S STATION when he pulled into the company parking garage. "Good morning, Phillip," Mark said to the parking attendant. "How are you this fine morning?"

"I'm well as always, Mr. Jason! But it looks like rain; you may want to retrieve your umbrella from the car if you're going in the front today."

"Nah, no need. I'm waterproof, I won't melt in the rain, but I'm taking the private up."

"Very good, sir, have a wonderful day." The attendant slid behind the wheel of Mark's car to park it in the Jason family section of the garage. Mark took his private elevator to the twentieth floor—jokingly dubbed as "The 20th" or "Executive Row" by the employees.

Coffee mug in one hand and briefcase in the other, Mark stepped out of the elevator and strolled unhurriedly to his office. He entered through the adjoining office wid his assistant, Eleanor Worthington who greeted him in her distinguished English accent, "Good morning, Mr. Jason."

"Good morning, Ellie."

Eleanor took his nearly empty coffee mug and presented him with the Wall Street Journal and a fresh mug of coffee with the Jason Enterprises logo on it. He never asked her to do the daily ritual for him, she had simply done it on her first day on the job and continued for all the years since.

She followed him into his expansive office and proceeded to the wet bar while he placed the paper in the center of his desk. He took a sip of his coffee and his brow furrowed as he processed the taste. "El Injerto, Ellie?" He stared into the cup.

She gave an imperceptive nod. "The crop was especially good this season," she said. He recognized a minuscule hint of pride on her face and in her voice. He was happy with Navy coffee, but it had become a matter of respect for Ellie that he learned about the wonders of coffees from around the world.

"So, what's on today's agenda?" he asked.

"You probably want to take a seat first, sir. There's quite a bit on the list." She lifted her glasses from the gold chain on her neck, rested them on her nose, and read the calendar entries on her tablet screen. "First, you have a conference with our vice-presidents at nine; a meeting with Mr. Takinoma at ten; Mrs. Nehring at eleven; lunch at the Rappahannock with a new client at noon; a meeting with Annette from R and D at two-thirty, after which you go home for dinner with the governor and his wife."

"The governor?" Mark nearly choked on his coffee. "When did this come up?"

Eleanor pressed the appointment on the screen to highlight the details. "You called me from overseas last month to set it up, sir."

"I did?"

"I believe you were trying not to get your, ahem, ass shot off at the time, sir." Mark lowered his head and gave a small chuckle. "You've been leading a double-life as a secret agent for years now; too many blows to the head starting to cause amnesia, sir? Speaking of your night life career, Mr. Geffers is waiting on your secure line," she said, handing him a cell phone from her jacket pocket. Mark's secret life as the Federal Task Force field leader made his life challenging and bringing Eleanor into his circle of confidants was one of his best decisions. She kept his busy life more organized, especially with his circle of bureaucrats, executives, government *powers-that-be* at the Pentagon, and the White House constantly demanding his attention. Her subtle command authority left little room for discussion or opposition.

Mark looked up; his expression immediately switched from comfortable to serious. "That'll be all, Ellie. Thank you." He watched the tall blonde leave his office, closing the door on her way out. He stood, shoved one hand in his pants pocket, and pressed the unmute button on the cell phone with the other hand. "Go, Seeker."

"Boss, I'm in pursuit of The Talon," Task Force Agent Seeker's voice boomed from the phone.

"Are you serious? How the hell did you get his location?" Mark moved from behind his desk and began to pace the floor as the two talked.

"It's a long story, boss, I'll catch you up when I have time."

Mark nodded to himself. "Sounds good. Big capture if you can make it. Keep me up to date on your progress. And be careful!"

"Don't I always, boss?"

Mark smiled. "You really want me to bring up Belize again?"

"Point taken. Seeker out." The connection went dead.

Mark put the cell phone in his jacket pocket, walked back to his desk, and pressed the voice command shortcut on his keyboard. "Open access to Task Force Division." He waited for his computer to open the secure connection to his network in Washington, D.C.

The computer announced, "Confirm identification."

"Jason, Marcus. Commander, United States Navy Reserve, TFAS2FT1. Connection requested, research level."

The computer screen flashed CONNECTION COMPLETE. "Access records on The Talon," Mark ordered. As the remote computer connection worked, he sat back in his chair. "So much for a quiet day at the office…"

Mark looked up from the financial reports on his desktop computer. Eleanor entered from the adjoining office, knocking first, but proceeding without waiting. Only Mark's wife Jan, and Eleanor could enter unbidden. She came to a stop at his desk and stood smartly with a portfolio crossed in her arms. "Yes, Ellie?" he asked.

"The report from Program 12-AC79 on the 14th floor," she replied calmly.

"Save me the time," Mark said, leaning back in his executive chair and crossing his arms. "Pass or fail?"

She removed her glasses and let them dangle on her chest by their chain. Eleanor gave one of her rare emotional responses; she closed her eyes and lowered her jaw slightly. "Fail, sir, I'm afraid. The J167 module crashed on the final test." Eleanor hated reporting bad news to Mark; it ate away at her perfectionist demeanor.

Mark removed his reading glasses and rubbed his cheeks in frustration, the posture making his heavily muscled arms tighten the fabric of his suit coat around his biceps. "OK, this has to be fixed. Call Hito and tell him to shorten his vacation. We're already pushing the deadline on this new laser infrared guidance system, and the Joint Chiefs want this in the new rockets for fighting ISIS. If Hito can get this fixed within the week, I'll make sure he gets double time off at Christmas."

"I already called him with that offer, sir, and he'll be in the office tomorrow morning."

Mark looked up at her stoic face. "Should I be surprised that I've become that predictable, Ellie?"

"Not predictable, sir, it was the only logical next step to keep the admiral off you're, ah, ass."

"Indeed," his eyebrows rose in response to her forward answer. Mark leaned forward and retrieved the portfolio from her. He took a moment to glance through the summary before initialing the bottom of the front page. "Well, my ass and I thank you for your consideration of this plight. If the admiral calls—"

Eleanor interrupted in a low slow monotone, "You are unavailable while you're figuring out his pain in your ass."

"I do like your official terminology," Mark said with a smile.

"By the way sir, your 2:30 review is here."

"Ah, yes, our intern with the happy supervisor," Mark said, glancing at the flashing reminder on his computer terminal. "Send them in, please, Ellie."

"Yes, sir." Eleanor turned on her heel, opened the interoffice door, and bid the two women enter.

Both women wore white lab coats over their civilian attire: formal, bland skirts, and flat shoes. The supervisor, Annette Penning, was slightly overweight and prematurely gray but still attractive, and only a couple inches shorter than the six-foot-four company president. Her intern, Chrystal Leigh, was five-foot-two with dark brown hair pulled back in a loose ponytail and wore dark-frame Franklin-style glasses. Mark couldn't help but form a small grin, thinking the two appeared almost *too* scientific, *too* nerdy.

Mark rose from his chair and extended his hand to Annette first. "Good to see you again, Annette." He then greeted young Chrystal. "Pleased to see you again, too, Chrystal, I've been hearing good things about you."

"It's a great honor to meet you again, Mr. Jason," Chrystal said, accepting his hand and giving a nervous smile. For a moment, she felt self-conscious and lowered her eyes to the floor.

"Please have a seat, ladies." Mark waved at the two chairs across from him in invitation. Annette handed a binder to Mark as she sat. He put his reading glasses back on, opened the cover, speed-reading the first page, and then reclined back as he turned to page two and then three.

Annette sat in comfortable silence while Mark read the report. She was used to such meetings and the long waits while Mark perused through files. Chrystal, however, was quite uncomfortable in the extended silence, not yet accustomed to the corporate etiquette or protocols at Jason Enterprises. She jumped in her seat when Mark suddenly whistled. He sat forward in his chair, leaning hard against the desk and stared at the intern intently over the top of his glasses. "*You* developed this?" he asked, more demanding than he intended.

Chrystal's eyes searched the room for an answer. Blushing, she nervously answered, "Yes, sir."

"Has this been tested?" Mark asked Annette.

"First-level, Mr. Jason. One hundred percent results in the cultures. We normally need a long permit process from the FDA, the CDC and the World Health Organization to go to the second level. But we've never had a hundred percent affirmation in the first-level tests before. It's unheard of. Chrystal here did quite a job on this, sir."

More silence filled the office suite as Mark adjusted his glasses and read deeper into the report.

You designed this anti-toxin *yourself*?" he asked Chrystal again, without looking up.

"Yes, sir," she answered, her voice still quivering. She couldn't help but feel in awe of sitting in front of one of the most powerful men in Richmond, Virginia. By reputation he was a man who could break the will of any politician in Washington, D.C. "It's been a study of mine since I was a young girl—"

Mark held up a hand, interrupting her answer. "I wasn't ready for the personal history just yet," he said, the kindness in his voice in total opposition to the words. "That's a couple questions down the review process here."

"Yes, sir," Chrystal replied and nodded, shoving her hands between her knees. She wasn't sure if she should be embarrassed or feel complimented. He was exactly like his reputation, firm but always courteous.

"How long has she been assigned to this?" Mark asked Annette.

"This was not on her assigned duties. She did this entirely on her own time, Mr. Jason."

Mark turned his gaze to Chrystal, this time with a more probing stare and mouth half open. "This anti-toxin design, its years ahead of even current military study and testing. Using a cross-species convergence of venom within a single genus, and then a universal toxin with no side-effects? Now, this is the personal question, Chrystal. You came up with this on your own time, why?"

Chrystal dropped her head momentarily, then looked up to answer. "Someone in my family said—".

Mark's cell phone abruptly rang in a dual-beep tone. Agitated, Mark motioned with his hand, and momentarily closed his eyes while he reached into his inside jacket pocket. He recognized the phone number on the digital display and realized the importance of the call. "My apologies, ladies," he said as he stood. "Please remain seated, this should only take a moment." He walked several steps over to the conversation area of his office, opened the flip phone and said softly, "Go."

Agent Seeker was on the other end of the line. "Hope this isn't a bad time, boss," said the strong male voice.

"I always like being interrupted in the middle of an important break-through, Agent," Mark whispered. "Update, and it needs to be the news I was waiting to hear."

"I've followed The Talon to Buenos Aires. Checked in with the embassy, so if I kill anyone no one will get pissed off any more than necessary. Helluva vacation, boss."

"Always helps to be in the right place at the right time." Mark stood with his back to the women, his hand on his hip as he spoke. "Wait, what did you say? *Buenos Aires?* I don't remember signing a requisition for a Task Force jet to Buenos Aires for a four-thousand-mile trip!" Mark's whisper turned into a growl, louder than he intended. Both women turned their heads in his direction.

"No boss, my personal jet, the 747."

"Oh, yeah, your home with wings. So, if you're off chasing our extortionist in some foreign country, what happened to the girl he kidnapped?"

"Got her, sir, just in time, too. She's fine and back with her parents. Talon just slipped away. Hunter and the other agents forwarded intel that showed he fled to Buenos Aires, his home away from home."

Mark took a moment to process the information. He'd read the criminal files when the mission began, recalling what little was known of the international extortionist who was given the name *The Talon.*

Mark heard an unexpected female voice in the background. "Where the hell is my damn bra this time?" she shouted in an angry tone.

Mark lowered his head. "Do I want to know what that's all about, Seeker?"

"Um, probably not, sir. I'll fill in all the details in my mission brief when I get back. I'd really like to get this guy, boss. And frankly he's pissed off Stephanie, too."

Mark stared at the wall. "Stephanie? As in FBI Special Agent Stephanie Anderson?"

"Um," the voice on the phone hesitated in reply. "Well, you could kinda say she got pulled into the case. Like I said, I was on vacation."

Her voice interrupted from the background again. "I'm *not* wearing my thong on the hunt; I want my regular undies. Where did we unpack them, Seeker? I can't remember, can you?"

"Steph, shush. I'm on a call with the boss!"

Mark closed his eyes. "Please, just don't let her make an international incident. And I definitely want regular reports on what's going on down there, no clothing items included, please."

"Yes, sir," Seeker said, and the line went dead.

Mark tucked the phone back in his pocket, took a deep breath, and returned to his desk chair. "My apologies," Mark said with a half-hearted smile. "Just another one of those little international matters this company has to deal with on a regular basis. So, where were we? Ah, yes, Chrystal. Give me a little more detail about how you arrived at this, um, formula."

Mark listened to the impressive young intern while she gave her formulaic dissertation of her findings, introspection, hypothesis, and final proven conclusions to her experiments.

He shuffled the papers into the folder and straightened them. "Well, you've been an intern with us right at six months now. I've read every single lab experiment you've worked on, talked with your supervisor here," he said, pointing at Annette, "and now this." He held up the folder. "I've never seen the likes of you, young lady. Psychological testing, high IQ, the highest GPA possible, what can I say? You're damned near perfect. Someday, I hope to have you on my staff permanently. For now, I'm increasing your intern status to level nine. Trust me, you can go far with this company." Mark scribbled something on a notepad and passed it to Chrystal. "And here's your new salary for the extent of your internship here while you're working on your PhD."

A large grin confirmed her delight, and Chrystal's face turned a bright pink.

"Mr. Jason, I—I don't know what to say. Thank you!"

"No, thank *you*, Chrystal. You may not realize what you've just done here in this particular experiment. The next thing we have to do is call some very important people. Then make calls to the US Patent and Trademark Office, and a few more people, right, Eleanor?

Eleanor stopped at Mark's desk and opened the binder to a specific page. Mark looked at the page, then up into her eyes. "Thank you, Ellie. Chrystal, please follow Miss Worthington to Legal. The next step in your future has just begun."

Jan entered as Eleanor led the scientists out. "Did I miss anything important?"

Mark rose and hugged his wife. "Well, I think you're gonna need a bigger purse, 'cause our stock value is about to skyrocket..."

CHAPTER 16

DEATH BY BLACK WIDOW

Detective Flores stood near the door in the pathologist's lab. He wasn't fond of autopsies in the least, and leaned on the wall, one hand pinching his nose. "Come on, Doc, find anything? I need to get outta here 'fore I barf."

The pathologist leaned over the body, bifocals hovered at the end of his nose, and a thick gray mustache covered his entire top lip. He chuckled at the detective. "I get a kick out of you tough cops. Shoot 'em up, beat 'em up, blood everywhere, their heads half blown off, and you're all studly and macho. But get you in the lab with a body on the table, chest cut clean open, you're nothin' but big pussies."

"Meow," the detective mocked. "Hey, it's the smell in here, OK? That formaldehyde stuff or whatever it is—makes your stomach turn. And the sound of that saw, it's just creepy. How come coroners don't do the autopsies anyway?"

"They're not pathologists, son, at least not usually. Gotta be a doctor for this. Vicks on the counter, if you wanna stick some up your nose. It helps."

"No. I'll be fine, I think."

"Suit yourself, Mister Flores, I really don't care. Just don't barf on this clean floor. Whatever killed this guy was somethin' real nasty. He suffered badly before he died. Internal organs, nerves, muscles, brain—they all, well, let's just say they got all effed-up real quick and looks like he had pain like you can't imagine. Seems to have died of asphyxiation, all this puke in his airway. Whoever did this is one sick bastard. The *only* thing I can see externally, out of place, is some sort of prick mark on his right hip. It's reddened and swollen. Could be from a needle or auto-injector of some sort. There's perimortem bruises on his face, throat, and abdomen. Someone was pissed off and let him have it hard, I imagine. You've got a real sicko on your hands; better look into this guy's past really good, see if he ticked off anyone who'd want revenge. Got the lab double checking everything now—may take a few more hours, maybe even days."

"Okay. Chief's in a hurry on this. Told me to come down and get an answer quick-like."

The Doctor eyeballed the detective. "You tell your chief, if he's a better expert in forensics than me, he can come down and do it himself. Otherwise, I'm runnin' the show right now. Lemme get my work done. I'll call you as soon as we've checked this guy inside and out. Got all his organs out to be studied. I'm gonna sew him back up now, unless you care to stay and help?"

The young detective didn't answer, bolting out of the door instead. "Yeah," the doctor chuckled. "Didn't think you had time to stay."

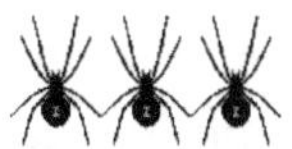

"What? Are you messin' with my head?" said the coroner. "A little spider, even the most venomous ones, couldn't have done this."

The laboratory experts' report detailed that they'd extensively examined the victim's blood, finally proving a toxin had indeed killed the man.

A forensic pathologist who delivered the report replied, "Yes, sir." The pathologist was young, but well-educated. He had black hair, wore black horn-rimmed glasses, and his white lab coat gave him a stereotypical geeky appearance. But his voice and command of the subject was the total opposite of his outward look. "We tested vial after vial of blood. Under the microscope, it was obvious. Gas chromatograph also confirmed its spider venom for sure, specifically of the Latrodectus genus, sir. And the amount in his system, well, it would have taken numerous spiders to do this. A single widow bite is fifteen times more venomous than one rattlesnake bite. That should tell you something. He didn't just fall into a web of spiders, sir."

"Latro-what?" the coroner balked, squinting his eyes, trying to recall the word. "Latro—dectus? It sounds familiar, but I'm too freekin' old to remember."

"Oh, yes, sir. I understand. It's of the black widow genus, with thirty-two recognized species throughout the world. Well, the venom has a neurotoxin called latrotoxin, and the female black widow has unusually large venom glands and her bite can be particularly harmful to humans." The pathologist stood as he spoke and waved a hand at the hallway. "Come down to the lab, take a look for yourself, in the microscope, you'll get a better idea of what's going on."

"It's been years since I've practiced medicine, or even worked in a lab, but hell, yeah, I wanna take a look."

Minutes later, in the lab, the coroner looked up at the young man, skeptical, then down into the magnified lenses of the microscope again. "Holy shit!" he proclaimed as he studied the sample. Still bent over, he looked up at the pathologist. "We have someone deranged as hell," the coroner said. "But the concentration in the bloodstream, that's only possible if someone was milking these arachnids."

"Not only that, "said the lab expert. "It's from a species that's not found in America."

"What?"

"This particular one, we've concluded, is from Madagascar. Halfway across the world. Very peculiar. Someone's stolen, obtained, whatever, venom from some lab, probably in the United States, and used it on this victim. He condensed it, put it in something like a common injection needle, like an EpiPen, and stabbed the victim in the hip."

The coroner stood straight, contemplating the situation. "Except for one fact."

"What's that, sir?"

"The overwhelming DNA found on scene and on the victim, was from a female. Our killer's a woman…"

CHAPTER 17

SECRETS AT JASON ENTERPRISES
ONE MONTH LATER

Mark AND JAN SAT IN THE COMFORTABLE LIVING room area of his office. An 85-inch smart television was mounted on the wall. As usual, the screen showed a continuous scrolling banner of stock updates, news feeds, weather reports, and congressional actions.

They were reviewing a contract proposal when Eleanor stepped in. "Mr. Brunson and Miss Freeman are here, Mr. Jason."

Sarge and Freeman arrived together and stood slightly inside Eleanor's office door. "Is there a problem?" Eleanor asked them quietly.

Sarge and Freeman looked at each other.

"Don't say a word," Eleanor said as she extended her hand to stop any response. She closed the door to Mark's office then closed her office door to the hallway. "Yes, I know all about it. Are you going to tell him?" she asked.

"Tell him what?" asked Freeman, shyly.

"You *do* realize the company policy on employees dating."

"There's no dating, or anything else."

Eleanor tilted her head backward, looking down her nose at them. "But there *is* the matter of the 'anything else'."

Sarge looked at Freeman, clearing his throat. Before he could speak, Freeman said, "It's better that you don't ask how she knows, Sarge." Freeman turned to Eleanor and continued, "It was an accident, a mistake…a long mistake."

Eleanor raised one eyebrow. "Ah. Just remember to decline the bourbon if he offers it, Miss Freeman. Stick to the rum." She returned to Mark's office door. "And don't sit next to each other." She opened the door, awaiting Mark's signal that he was ready to meet with his employees.

"He's ready to see you now."

Mark was at his desk. Sarge and Freeman took the outer two seats in front of the desk. Jan eyed the two, then took a seat in the middle. "Good morning, Sarge, Ms. Freeman."

"Good morning, sir, ma'am," they replied in unison.

"One moment folks, we're waiting for one more for today's brief." Eleanor looked to her right and waved someone in. "Everyone, this is Chrystal Leigh, an intern in R and D. Chrystal, you've met Sarge Brunson, Chief of Security. This is Sandra Freeman, who runs our international IT division. And, my wife, Jan of course.

"E-excuse me," Chrystal said, crossing in front of Sarge to sit between them. "Thank you, Mr. Jason."

"Niceties are over for now," Mark began in his business-like voice. "We've taken on not one but two new contracts. But as fortune would have it, they overlap each other." Chrystal began to ask a question, but Mark stopped her. "Not question time yet. We have an off-book contract to develop a new lethal liquid toxin in the fight against ISIS. As far as everyone else in this building, and across the country is concerned, this project does not exist. This is a 14th Floor project only, got it? Sarge, make the security arrangements, and I want a full security test of all building systems.

Freeman, I will give you the new protocols for the Triple-Z team to program and monitor, standard procedures. Sarge, get Hito to run an entire security check of all intranet and internet network connections. All employee passwords go to twenty-four-hour lifespans and replace all employee keycards with new ones programmed with a new rotation matrix. All employees must undergo a new optical scan programming with concurrent handprint scan to enter the building. I want new encryption on all smartphones and other devices with network access. Yes, it'll be a pain in the ass, but we have some critical assignments before us, international at that." He interlaced his fingers and took a deep breath. "We're gonna be creating a chemical that can kill, in defiance of all international treaties. Chrystal will be part of the team in creating this. But, these terrorists must be eradicated, and I am in full agreement with whatever measures are necessary to achieve that goal. "Chrystal, you're the newest employee here. Are you up for this?"

She realized everyone was staring at her. Slightly demure in her response, "Oh, yes, sir, I am whatever you say I am, sir. I'm up for whatever task you give me. Just give the word."

"The word is hereby given," said Mark. Jan will notify all our satellite offices. All supervisors will be contacting you, Ms. Freeman, for a briefing and orders. Sarge, you have your orders. Lock this company down tighter than Fort Knox."

"Yes, sir,"

"Oh, and Sarge. Ah, you should probably take a little hiatus from the Recovery Room for a while." Mark winked at Freeman as he spoke to him. "Rumors get started that way."

Sarge gave Mark a puzzled but knowing look, wondering how Mark had found out so soon. He wasn't surprised, however. "Ah, yes, sir," he said, leaving the room, casting one last glance at Mark as he left. Freeman hurriedly left the room, hoping that Mark wouldn't try to single her out as well.

"Chrystal," Mark began, "your off-the-clock studies have already garnered a lot of interest. You're getting immediate reassignment to the 14th."

"'The 14th', Sir?"

Jan picked up several folders from her desktop and stood next to Chrystal. "If Jason Enterprises is like Fort Knox, then the 14th floor of this building is like the Pentagon. Along with the new chemical we just talked about, your job now is to refine your antivenin. The FDA and CDC want more information on your compound process. There is so much potential for your serum, I want you to perfect, document and process it in excruciating detail. I'm not sure you fully understand the complexity of this situation, but it will be clear to you soon. We have to fast-track this. As soon as you have the documentation and research procedures we'll copyright and trademark them, in your name."

"M-my name?"

Jan picked up. "Well, technically, you will hold the copyright, since you developed it on your own. You have an exclusive agreement with Jason Enterprises, and JE will trademark it and handle all the commercial distribution once it's tested and approved for full use. Of course, we'll cover all the costs in testing and verification with the FDA and CDC and WHO and all other necessary government departments. Dear, in less than two years, you should be a very wealthy woman."

Mark added, "In simple exchange, you will sign a binding agreement with this company wherein you will work here for the next ten years exclusively. However, you will only work on projects assigned to you, no new independent work without supervisory consent. Do you understand, Chrystal? It's a lot to take in right now. Any new discoveries you make from here forward will be the property of Jason Enterprises, but you will be compensated handsomely. Your technology is high market, and you're quite marketable. We want to keep you, and compensate you as deserved.

Frankly, no one in the world can do what you're doing right now. Sound like something you'd be interested in?"

"Absolutely!" Chrystal said.

"There is one little rule, though. You cannot tell anyone about what you're exposed to on the 14th Floor. As a matter of fact, the 14th floor does not exist."

"Not even my roommate?"

"No, not even your roommate. A breach of 14th Floor security could be punishable in ways you can't even imagine. We will explain this in better detail, but this just became a matter of national security." He stood and motioned at Jan. "Mrs. Jason will escort you down to your new workstation, and your personal effects from R and D will be brought to you. Consequently, your entire life has just changed in a matter of a few minutes, including your personal life."

"Th-thank you, sir! Mrs. Jason, thank you!"

"Come along, Chrystal," said Jan. Her long red hair flowed like a silk cape and Chrystal couldn't help but watch her hair as she followed.

Mark pressed the intercom connection to his assistant. "Ellie, ask Hito to update Chrystal Leigh's security access again. This time it's Code 14-1…"

CHAPTER 18

GRADUATION DAY
10 YEARS EARLIER

Chrystal and Jesse stood together in the senior class procession lines, surrounded by over three thousand fellow students graduating from Virginia State University in Richmond, Virginia. Best friends since childhood, they relished that their last names were close enough alphabetically and were able to sit together on their final day in college.

"Whatcha think, girly?" Jesse asked Chrystal. "Who's supposed to be our guest speaker?"

"Dunno," Chrystal replied. "That's our college president for ya, always has to have one last surprise before sending off the grads into the cold cruel world."

"Oh, come on, it ain't that cold and cruel."

"No? We're at war with terrorists. We're always on security alerts. Ya know?"

"That's just the government. We're not going into government, we're gonna be normal people, together like always!" She took Chrystal's hand in hers.

"A girl couldn't ask for a better friend," Chrystal said as she squeezed back. "Oh, look, we're starting!" She smiled at Jesse pointing toward the front of the line. "Not a rehearsal this time."

The seniors filed to their seats to the sound of "Pomp and Circumstance", with the athletic arena's seating area filled with thousands of family, friends, and lower classmates. The line of black gowns and caps stood out against the scarlet aisles as they flowed into the matching scarlet folding chairs arranged in rows on the auditorium floor.

Once all the seniors were standing at their seats, the local Reverend DeVeaux, began. "Oh, Great and Dear Lord, we gather today to send forth these young minds fresh with the knowledge they have received these past few years. May they succeed and prosper in their future endeavors, for these are the heralds of changes in the future of our great nation. May they all be prophets of your positive change to lead us to a better world, Amen." A gentle "Amen" echoed throughout the stadium.

The Master of Ceremonies then introduced the university president, alumni chairman, special alumni, and acknowledged other guests on the stage who didn't have a speaking part. "Finally, it gives me great pleasure to introduce our own local hero. He doesn't like being called a hero, but he is. As a Navy SEAL, he fought our country's enemies all across the world. Here in Richmond, he continues to fight for those who work for him and their families by providing resources used by our militaries to keep us safe. He remains a Lieutenant Commander in the Navy Reserves. He has a beautiful wife, Jan, and a brilliant daughter, Angela, whom we expect to see here as a student after high school. In the three years since he took over his father's company, he made a name for himself with his political and business successes and social commitments throughout the world. Graduating seniors, ladies and gentlemen, it gives me great pleasure to introduce the president of our city's premiere industrial powerhouse Jason Enterprises, Mark

Jason!" The auditorium's occupants gave Mark a great round of applause as he approached the dais.

"He's kinda cute, for an old guy," said Jesse tugging on Chrystal's sleeve.

Chrystal smiled back. "Yeah, if you're into that kinda guy."

Mark stood behind the podium, waiting for the reception to settle. The applause wouldn't stop, and he grinned, his manicured box beard edged his smile like a dark brown picture frame. "If you don't stop, I'll be late for dinner, and Jan doesn't like me to miss dinner when she's cooking beef bourguignon!" That only caused more applause accompanied by laughter, which soon quieted.

"Wow," he began, his voice echoing deep and loud through speakers throughout the building. "That definitely out-does the reception I got when Dad handed me the gold key to Jason Enterprises." There was a smattering of laughter. "I hope there's champagne to follow," he said to the president seated behind him.

"Only Dom Perignon," the president yelled loud enough to be heard by the microphone.

"He's got taste," Mark said, still smiling, facing the audience. "And that's what I'd like to talk to you about today: *taste*."

He removed the wireless microphone from the podium so he could walk back and forth across the stage as he spoke. "What is 'taste', anyway? Besides the scientific definition of how your body perceives the food you eat or liquids you drink. There are other tastes: a taste for adventure, or a taste for danger, or business, or a taste for life, and so on. But what does that mean, anyway?

"You've all tasted sugar. You like it. And because of that, your brain rewired itself to always enjoy the taste of something sweet. When you have a taste for something, you want it more than anything else. I'm not talking about an obsession, where you'd do anything to satisfy that taste, like drugs, for example." There were "whoops" from the students. Mark pointed toward the source of the sound. "There ya go! No, I'm talking about something you love to do so much you could do it for the rest of your life and never tire of it.

"I have a taste for sky diving. My wife has a taste for the family together at dinner every night. So, I enjoy the memories of my years in the Navy when I was being paid to jump out of perfectly good airplanes. Now, when we fly, she makes sure I'm as far away from the cabin door as possible, just in case."

Laughter came from the audience.

"My father had the taste for business. He started our company with a huge bank loan and an idea to provide unique goods and resources which others needed. When he learned of people with new expertise, like so many of you here today, he went after them before other companies could. And his voracious appetite for the best is what allowed him to build Jason Enterprises into a strong national company in its first ten years. His taste never wavered or settled, it got stronger. He went after private and public contracts like a shark until he turned the company into an international leader, while earning the unwavering loyalty and respect of his work family.

"Unfortunately, he didn't have the taste of self, and didn't take care of himself as he should. I was called out of the Navy after ten years to take over this company when my Dad became too ill to continue working.

"But I had my own tastes to satisfy. The taste to help others. If I told you what I did in the Navy, well, they would tell me I'd have to kill you, as the old saying goes." Laughter again. "There is one I can kinda talk about, though. There was one old fellow I met in China, when I was on an assignment, who was being roughed up by some unsavory types. Now, while I should have kept my vision on my mission, my taste to help was stronger, and I deviated to help him. The details aren't important. But the old man and I were on our life paths." There were scattered cheers from the audience. "He asked what I wanted in return. I said nothing because helping was the right thing to do. We parted with a promise of an open home should either of us ever need one.

"A few months later I was on leave in Hong Kong, and who do I meet in a restaurant? That same old man! He recognized me at once, and said he wanted to give me the true secret of pleasure in life. You know what he gave me?" Mark listened as the answer "no" came from the seniors and audience. "He was visiting family when I came upon him being attacked. He worked for a detergent manufacturer in the States. All he wanted to give me was an Ancient Chinese Secret. Now I have a lifetime supply of 'Calgon bath products." The adults burst into raucous laughter, remembering the old TV commercial. Many of the younger students didn't get it completely.

"My point though, is if you don't have a taste for something, you likely will not succeed. But you seniors have shown through your hard studies that you have the taste to succeed. Some of you even hunger for it. By that I mean, for a select few of you, your taste for success is passionate, powerful, unwavering!

"My father was a graduate from here back before there was electricity." More laughter. "Never mind all the electronic conveniences we enjoy today. When he died a little over a year ago, one of his requests was for Jason Enterprises to begin a scholarship reward program at his Alma Mater. That's why I'm here today." Mark waved toward the side of the stage, and his wife Jan approached carrying a plaque and an envelope. She gave him a quick kiss at her arrival, eliciting emotional "ahhs" and chuckles from the audience. She stepped behind him to his right as he returned to the podium and replaced the microphone. "For over a year I've been working with the university's president and administration to set up this award. It will be given to one student each year who demonstrates unwavering devotion and dedication to study, together with an exceptional record of advanced application in their field. We received numerous recommendations from the university, and everyone was reviewed thoroughly. The names of the finalists were given to me for selection.

"This," Mark said, raising the plaque, "goes to the first recipient of the Zachary Jason Scholarship and Endowment. This person will go to a master's program in their field, at the college or university of their choice. Upon completion, they will come to work at Jason Enterprises as an intern, with financial coverage for a doctoral study." A single, shrill whistle came from a graduate near the back row. The enthusiasm started a round of applause until Mark held up his hand for quiet. He raised an envelope. "This is a check for $100,000 for the recipient to use to help pay off college loans and pay living expenses while continuing their education in preparation for a new life as a Jason Enterprise paid intern and eventually a fully-vested employee. Whoever you are, don't blow it all on the tables in Las Vegas when you go on summer vacation. We'll be watching closely."

Laughter rolled through the arena with light conversations on who was the winner of the rich prize. An awkward silence fell while Mark stood behind the podium, viewing the gathering from left to right. "OK, that's enough dramatic pause. How 'bout we announce the first winner of this award, shall we?" Jan stepped forward to Mark's side and took the envelope from him. She opened it and leaned toward the microphone to say, "The winner of the first annual Zachary Jason Scholarship and Endowment is—"

She handed Mark the card and he announced, "CHRYSTAL LEIGH!…"

CHAPTER 19

CELEBRATION DAY
TODAY

T HE DAY HAD BEEN LONG, BUT ENDED spectacularly. Chrystal looked forward to a relaxing evening at home. She parked her old Mercury sedan in the four-story apartment building's parking lot, gathered her groceries and purse, and locked the doors. She paused in the main foyer to check her mailbox. She mumbled to herself while checking the mail. "Great, two bills, four useless ads, grocery coupons. They expire next Saturday, maybe I can use these. Oh, Lord, a letter from Mom, just what I needed, another lecture." When the elevator doors opened, she entered and hit the third-floor button with a free thumb. *Wonder what Mom wants now; can't be good, never is.*

Once inside the small apartment she shared with her life-long best friend, Jesse, she set her keys and purse on a side table, kicked off her shoes, and took the groceries to the kitchen/dining area. She peered down a short hallway to the right, "Sweetie, you home?" There was no response.

She and Jesse had been friends since childhood. They'd gone to the same schools and both graduated from the same college. Chrystal earned her master's degree while Jesse endeavored to open her own auto mechanic shop. Working as a mechanic wasn't a normal career move for most women, but Jesse loved the work, and her shop was incredibly popular. She even took evening courses in advanced engineering and eventually earned her own master's degree.

The award dollars from Jason Enterprises helped at first, but with the cost of living, repayment of school debts, and trying to pay off two cars, expenses were tight. Both women worked hard to make ends meet. They'd picked out the low-rent, one-bath, one-bedroom apartment together. Larger models were available, but the two weren't financially sound enough to afford anything else. Besides, they loved the tiny apartment and that was all that mattered to them.

The two best friends were inseparable. They slept in the same queen-sized bed and spent long hours talking and sharing, reminiscing the good times as well as the bad. They weren't romantically involved, but would seem so to anyone watching them in public when they strolled arm in arm, or snuggled close at a restaurant booth. To them, it was just *girl-stuff.*

She retrieved a two-pack of T-bone steaks from the freezer, wishing now she'd thawed them earlier. "But, hey," Chrystal spoke out loud, "that's why modern science gave us microwaves, right?"

After a quick defrost cycle in the microwave, she put the seasoned steaks in a cast iron skillet. A few minutes later she flipped over the steaks and turned off the heat, ensuring all the juices inside the meat stayed intact. She poured some black olives in a bowl and began to make two small salads.

There was a sound from the foyer. The front door opened, then gently shut, followed by the sound of keys dropping on the foyer table. Though Jesse wore steel-toed boots, her footsteps were gentle, as if a child or a trotting dog were heading into the apartment.

Jesse stepped into the kitchen in her shop uniform and boots. She wrapped both arms around Chrystal's shoulders from behind and hugged tight. "Oh, my, someone had a good day if we're having steak! And they smell great, I'm starving. What's the special occasion, girl?"

Chrystal turned inside Jesse's embrace, both about the same height; they faced each other eye to eye. Chrystal returned the hug and kissed Jesse on the cheek. "Look at you, all greasy and dirty. There isn't a spot on you that's clean! It's gotta go, baby."

"Ah, hey, it's my job." Jesse reached over and popped a couple of olives in her mouth. "I love my shop; it makes me happy." Jesse smiled.

"Okay, Miss Mechanic, get those boots out of this kitchen, do something with your face, and open the champagne. We have stuff to celebrate."

"Stuff? What kind of stuff?" Hopping on one foot down the hallway, trying to remove a boot, and mumbling with olives in her mouth, Jesse said, "Champagne? You got champagne? And dinner? We can't afford all that! What's up? I like it, but what are we celebrating?" She'd managed to extract a foot from one boot, then sat on the floor to remove the other.

"Wait until dinner! I'll tell you all about it then. Get cleaned up and set the table, okay?"

"Okay, right back." Jesse popped into the bathroom and unzipped her dirty coveralls, dropping them on the floor atop her boots. She pulled her hair back in a ponytail, washed her face, and returned just wearing a sports bra and panties.

"Okay, bubbly first, where's it hiding?" she asked excitedly. She poked her head into the freezer, knowing Chrystal would have put it there for a good chill.

"Girl, set the table!"

"I got it! Can't get in the mood for celebrating unless I got bubbly first." She popped the cork and poured a drink for each of them, handing Chrystal a flute, holding hers in the air. "So, what are we toasting?"

Chrystal savored the moment, looking at Jesse's smiling face. "Let's just say it's a new beginning." They clinked glasses together and took a sip.

"Well, since you won't start, I'll tell you 'bout my day first," Jesse said, setting the table as she spoke. She sat in her chair at the small kitchenette table, settling in to tell her story. Without regard to manners, she plunked her hot, swollen socked feet atop another chair. "We got in this *sweet*, red Mercedes SL roadster convertible for repair today. I'd just finished servicing a CLS and this beauty rolls in, and I was the only mechanic open! Cool huh?" Jesse gulped her champagne, her face beamed when she talked about automobiles.

Chrystal opened the oven and inserted both stakes, still on the iron pan, to slowly finish cooking.

"What's a CLS? What's an SL? Speak English, anyway?"

Jesse giggled at Chrystal's lack of knowledge about cars, and champagne bubbles snorted up her nose. She righted herself and sat forward, giving a little cough to clear the sinuses. "It's another model of the Mercedes, just a lot newer. This SL was a 1959 model, mint condition. Girl, I'd give anything to own that!"

Chrystal smiled. "I always thought you'd be a great mechanic. Ever since that day I saw you put together your new swing set by yourself, before your daddy woke up from his nap, it was done."

"Yeah. That was fun. I didn't want him to do it anyway. So, what about your news?"

After they were both seated, Chrystal lifted her glass and Jesse followed suit. "Here's to both our good days," Chrystal toasted. They clinked glasses together again then began with their salad.

"So," said Jesse, "come on already!"

Chrystal smiled recalling Mark's statement to her. "Well, there's good news and maybe some not so good news," she began.

"The good news is that I got a promotion today with a nice pay raise, according to my new supervisor."

"That's fantastic!" Jesse got up and gave Chrystal a tight hug. "So, if you moved out of R and D, what did you move into?"

"That's the bad news, well part of it. I had to sign a non-disclosure agreement. If I say a word about my new job I could probably be arrested. Probably even executed, the way they went on about it. And if I tell anyone else, they may get their head chopped off, too, it seems. And, I got a letter from *my mother* today. I couldn't bring myself to open yet."

The expression on Jesse's face was not what Chrystal expected. Jesse smiled big. "That's so freakin' cool! It's like, *yeah, I can tell ya, but I'd have to kill ya*! Big old Secret Squirrel stuff. Didn't your boss say something like that at college graduation?"

It was Chrystal's turn to snort champagne out through her nose when she laughed. "No, not a secret agent, or squirrel, or anything like that. Just super hush-hush work. But, it's definitely exciting and mentally challenging. I do love a challenge."

"After this marvelous dinner," said Jesse, savoring a light pink piece of steak, "why don't we go get more champagne and put a great chick-flick in the DVD? And don't you worry about that letter from your mother. Chunk it in the pile with the others. Together, we'll open them, sometime down the road, and maybe laugh together and burn them in the fireplace."

Chrystal raised her glass again. "Sounds like a wonderful idea!..."

CHAPTER 20

PYTHAGORAS ARRIVES

"Come on, Angela, I've been waiting to show you around this place," Tom said.

"Don't you mean show off the employees and their specialties, Colonel?"

Tom smiled knowing she was right. Angela was beginning to learn the complexities of the Task Force team, realizing it could be quite daunting.

"Angela, in a place like this, expect the unexpected is probably the best piece of advice I'll ever give you. Sure, we're gonna show off everyone and show what their passions are. But consider it cross training for you. Not that you'll be trained to do their jobs, but to be aware of their particular expertise, their capabilities. Because someday you may need to know their strengths, so you'll know who to depend on. This division has been together so long under your dad's leadership that everyone intuitively knows what the other will do next, or what they need in the heat of a battle. You shouldn't ever have to go out as a field agent, but always—"

"Expect the unexpected," Angela finished the sentence.

"You got it, kiddo." Tom smiled.

While they walked down the long Task Force corridor, Angela noticed each office displayed nameplates with the agent's code names and a different geometric symbol engraved on the plate. "Well, Colonel, I have questions already."

"And what would they be, Angela?"

"Well, I see nameplates on the doors for Proteus, Hunter, Seeker, and straight on at the end of the hall is Dad's—I mean, Agent Spy. Silly name to give himself, don't know why he did that." She gave a small grin, realizing she'd have to call him *Spy* instead of *Dad* when in the facility. "So, why's Spy's plate gold, and the others' silver?"

Tom stopped and crossed his arms. "OK, Angela, take your years of studying and learning, and your navy training, and put on your Freud hat for just a minute. Why don't *you* think it through and tell *me* why they're different colors?"

Angela crossed her arms as well, accepting the challenge. She focused on the four door plates, glancing from one to the other. "They're both precious metals and valuable commodities, a reflection of the personalities behind each door. Each metal has its own advantages and disadvantages, but work well together, as in jewelry. Gold is more expensive, per ounce. Gold can be stretched and bent without losing its structural integrity, unlike silver. It's steadfast, just like the man behind the door." She walked to her father's office door. "Whereas silver requires polishing, but gains character with use, just as the people behind the silver doors require constant training. And gold is the denser of the two metals, which Dad can be when he's fixated on a problem."

"Very good, Angela, and your conclusion?"

"Spy's been there, done that, got the gold key. The others are just as good, but they need a bit more polishing with time."

"Bravo, young lady." Tom clapped his hands, proud of her analogy.

"But wait, Colonel, there's one more nameplate on the other side of the hall, past Spy's office." She stepped to it and read aloud the name, "Oracle. My office?" She studied the symbol on the plate: a circle in a square in an equilateral triangle in another circle. "The symbol of Hephaestus?"

"You recognize it?" Tom asked. "You're Mark Jason's daughter, of course you recognize it. I've seen the library in your family home."

He pressed his supervisor's code into the optical reader beside the door and said, "Look into the scanner."

Angela crinkled her eyes at the Colonel, but did as ordered and placed her face in front of the panel. Horizontal red-light beams scanned her eyes, followed by matching vertical beams. Tom pressed one of the keypad buttons and commanded, "Save Oracle scan."

A row of green lights flashed from left to right for several seconds before a female computer voice said, "Oracle saved. Enter when ready." The pocket door opened automatically to a dark room.

"This is your office, Angela."

She stepped past him. When she crossed the threshold, the lights illuminated the room. The large office was bland, furnished only with a desk, chair, a widescreen plasma monitor on the opposite wall, and the other three walls were blank. "Kind of boring, if I may say, sir," she said with a smile. "If this is the government's way to impress a girl, it's a huge fail."

Tom smiled back. "Actually, this will be equipped with whatever you say you need."

"And what exactly will I be doing?"

He leaned against the desk and said, "Computers can do whatever functions and calculations they're programmed to do. We get gigs of information streaming into all the federal departments every minute of every hour, day, week, month, and year. But the sheer volume then takes days to search if there's one good piece of Intel. We've been waiting for someone like you."

"Someone like me, what?"

"Someone who can look at streams of data and make fast and logical sense of it. Like Hephaestus of legend, your job is to take the raw data in all formats and algorithms and tell us how to build it into useful tools and techniques. Like an oracle of myth, you will see the information and translate it for us.

"Colonel?" she interrupted as she pointed to the door. "My nameplate is made of copper, a different material. And 'Oracle' or 'Hephaestus'? Well, other than he was a guy and modern mythology has him named as the Roman god Vulcan—um, do you think I have pointed ears, sir?"

Tom laughed. "Definitely no points on those ears with that military bun, Angela. As you were saying?"

"Right, the copper. It's a great conductor of heat and electricity. It's a binding medium between two metals that don't ordinarily adhere, but it's also non-magnetic." Angela grinned. "Dad always said I had a temper. But, like copper, I'm flexible, I can be shaped into things with great ease. I can be used for a wide-multitude of things." Angela had one hand on her hip and the other hand waved an index finger in the air to point out a revelation. "And if I remember from my chemistry classes, copper is in the same periodic table of elements section as gold and silver! To the point of being a semi-noble if not a true-noble metal. Well, Colonel Michelson, I'm honored."

Tom bowed his head, proud of Angela's observations. "If anyone else were to give that speech, I'd say he was bragging."

A soft knock came from the open door. "Hi!" Tom and Angela turned to see Proteus. "Angela, good to see you again! You look great in uniform!"

"Thanks, you always look good in yours as well."

The diminutive agent was dressed in her full black Task Force uniform, her cocoons hooked over her utility belt. "Yeah, but when you're my size the diet's gotta be maintained. This outfit is *so* unforgiving."

"Glad *I* don't have to wear one," said Angela. She turned to Tom. "Or do I?"

"Well, not as a standard, no, but we will have one designed for you anyway. No, you're remaining active duty, so you'll always report in your service uniform. Skirt or slacks, your choice. You'll be doing a lot of sitting. But we have ergonomic desks and workstations so you can stand, sit, walk on a treadmill, peddle a bicycle or move around the room as you want."

"Oh, you're working here now? Cool!" Proteus reached out and shook Angela's hand. "Well, I hate to shake and run, but I got a hacker to catch."

"Hacker?" Angela asked. "Who hacked into what?"

"A trap I set online, so to speak," Proteus replied. "Someone'd been breaking into bank computers and transferring small amounts out at a time so as not to be immediately noticed. Feds couldn't catch 'em. Took almost half a year but he fell into a trap I designed to attract him. Back-ran the IP through fourteen countries. I'm on my way now to take him down."

"Alone?" Angela looked back and forth between Proteus and Tom. "I thought this was a team-thing here."

"It is," said Tom. "Sometimes team, sometimes individuals. Depends on the needs of the mission."

"Anyways, gotta scoot!"

"She's entirely too happy to be a secret agent," said Angela…

CHAPTER 21

A TASKING MEETING

"Sir, WE HAVE UNAUTHORIZED PERSONNEL entering the complex," the guard said into his voice-activated communications unit. The receiving unit itself was clipped to his belt, retrofitted by JE to serve as more than a radio. The wireless earpiece was invisibly tucked behind and into his ear. The entire Task Force Division used the units, and more specialized ones as necessary.

Mark Jason activated the monitor in his office in the Task Force command center outside Washington, D.C. He saw the main gate and the guard keeping one of the field team's black sports cars from entering. He switched to a second monitor for a better look at both people in the front seat. Agent Seeker was driving, but the woman in the passenger seat, wearing a set of one-way cocoon glasses, was his FBI partner, Special Agent Stephanie Anderson. He responded to the communication, replying, "Tell him to take her to Debrief 1, I'll meet them there."

"Spy ordered you to Debrief 1, Agent Seeker."

Seeker smiled and jokingly gave the guard a sharp salute. "Kinda expected that. Thank you, sergeant." He rolled his car forward slowly. When he was about fifty feet away from the gate, he punched the accelerator to the floor, spinning tires to rocket to his destination.

"Stop doing that, dammit!" Stephanie yelled. "Can I take my glasses off yet? I hate not seeing anything, especially when you start drag racing like that."

"Sorry, beauty, not yet," Seeker replied. "I'm in enough caca for taking you to Argentina as it is. I don't want to add revealing our secret location to non-personnel on top of it."

"You don't sound worried."

"I'm not paid to worry."

"No, you're paid to drag me off to the Southern Hemisphere at the drop of a hat. And I never got to go to the beach to get a tan."

"Well, it's not like you had your bikini."

"Why would I want tan lines?"

Seeker had no comeback except the big smile she couldn't see.

The car came to a warehouse bay door which opened at its approach. Seeker slowed and gently coasted into the building. Once he brought the car to a stop and the bay door closed behind them, he said, "OK, beauty, you can take your blind off."

Anderson took off the glasses and looked around. There were three other cars identical to Seeker's parked in a row beside them. She noticed there were only the bay doors and a door leading into the building, no windows or other exits. Motion activated lights and cameras came on and a small hum could be heard from each as they rotated.

She opened the car door and stepped out, her pumps clicking on the cement deck. Her dark gray suit and white blouse was a contrast to Seeker's dark brown suit and green shirt, but his boots made no sound as he walked. "Come with me. Do what I say, and don't say a word, ok?"

"Hey, it's me, remember?"

Seeker sighed. "My point exactly. Not a word?"

She rolled her eyes and huffed. "Fine! Not a word."

He took her hand and led her to the solitary door. A section of the wall to the left of the door opened and a hydraulic drawer extended outward. "Put your weapons in the drawer." He removed his gun from his shoulder holster and laid it in the drawer, as well as the other weapons hidden within his suit. She removed her gun from her belt holster and laid it beside his. The drawer stayed open.

"The ankle holster," said Seeker. Anderson smiled as she lifted her leg and pant cuff to expose the holster around her right ankle and put the weapon in the drawer. The drawer still did not move. "And the small one clipped to your left bra cup."

"Well, damn, I didn't know you knew about that one!" she said as she reached under her blouse for her third gun and placed it in the drawer.

"There's scanners all over this room, Steph. They can detect weapons anywhere on your body, even, well—" He cleared his throat without saying the obvious.

"Well, that's a bit personal," she said.

The drawer retracted into the wall. The door clicked and opened on its own. Seeker stepped in first and motioned her to follow.

The door closed behind them automatically and locked. "Close your eyes and don't move," he said. They stood silently as laser lights played across their bodies, and a computerized female voice echoed through a speaker in the ceiling, "Recognize Seeker. Do not recognize female. Please identify."

"State your name and title," Seeker prompted.

"Anderson, Stephanie, Special Agent, Federal Bureau of Investigation, assigned Charleston, South Carolina."

"Stand by," said the disembodied voice. The two stood in silence for nearly a minute until the voice spoke again. "Anderson, Stephanie, confirmed. Does Agent Seeker wish to permanently log Agent Anderson, or allow single access?"

"Single-time," he said.

"'Single-time'?" she asked. "You don't plan to bring me back again?"

"Permanent log allowance is a shitload of paperwork," Seeker said.

"You Task Force people and your paperwork. And I thought the FBI went through trees!"

A drawer slid out of the wall to their right with their weapons. They retrieved them, putting all their guns back in place.

Seeker led her down the hallway to an intersection and guided her to the right. They passed a female staffer dressed similar in style to Seeker's Task Force uniform, except hers was a light gray. "Is she an agent?" she asked.

"Support," Seeker said.

"Oh."

They reached another intersection and turned left, nearly running into two men dressed in slacks and long-sleeve shirts. "IT guys," Seeker said without waiting for her to ask.

He led her to a door on the right. There was no doorknob, only a glass panel the size of a postcard at eye level on the wall. Seeker placed his face in front of the panel, activating the machine to scan his eyes. "Recognize, Agent Seeker," said another robotic voice. The door slid into the wall.

The room contained a conference table with a dozen chairs. Four of them were occupied by a man and three women, all in civilian clothes except for a woman in a navy uniform. She didn't recognize the blond woman, or the brunette woman with Polynesian features, but she had previously seen the man holding the electronic tablet. "I know you. You're Mark Jason, president of Jason Enterprises. You, and you two ladies, you're the rest of the Task Force?" she asked as the door slid closed behind them.

Hunter, a Hawaiian woman with long black hair said, "So, this is the legendary Stephanie Anderson."

"Hey, Seeker, she's gorgeous!" said Proteus. "You've been holding out on us." She glanced down at the engagement ring on Anderson's finger. "Check out that rock!" She stood to shake Stephanie's hand. "I'm Proteus, by the way."

Anderson stared at her left hand and the 2.5-carat marquise on her ring finger and couldn't help but smile.

Hunter gently grasped Anderson's left hand, admiring the engagement ring. "I'm Hunter," she said to Stephanie. She looked at Seeker and said, "You got some nice taste there, Seeker. You kinda left this big ol' ring part out when you were talking about this."

"You've been talking about me with your partners?" Anderson asked Seeker.

"Let's just say we're called 'gasoline and fire' amongst the bosses," Seeker said.

"Oh, really? And which one am I?" Stephanie looked away, pouting, until she saw the Navy Ensign. With a fresh smile she asked, "And you are?"

"Angela Jason, ma'am."

"'Jason'? Relation to Mark Jason?"

"He's my dad."

Mark stepped forward and extended his hand. "Yes, I'm Mark Jason, but around here I'm called Spy," he said as she shook his hand. "As you can see, we're quite the family here, very informal as you can tell. Please, everyone be seated."

"Mr. Jason," Anderson asked, "what's it like being the Task Force leader, if I may be so bold to ask?"

Seeker gently kicked Stephanie underneath the table. "I told you not to say anything," Seeker muttered.

"Seeker, it's okay. Miss Anderson, we're glad to have you here today but hold your questions for just a few minutes, if you don't mind. We're waiting on one more person to join us, any minute now. And it goes without saying that you did not see any of us here today."

"Of course, sir." Stephanie looked at Seeker, who stared back with an unflinching poker face. She looked at Mark. "Yes, sir, thank you, will do." She intertwined her fingers on the table and sat still.

The pocket door slid open and a rugged-looking older man stepped in. He stopped to hang his coat and a charcoal gray fedora on a rack near the door. The hat was outdated and well-worn, but it suited him. The gentleman was no taller than Anderson at five-foot-five, wearing a black suit and tie with a white shirt. He carried in his arm a black folio binder, placing it on the table as he sat. "Good morning, everyone," he said in a bass voice, fingering back his receding white hair. He was greeted with a round of "good morning" from the Task Force agents and Anderson. "So, Agent Anderson, it's a pleasure to finally meet you. I hope your reputation does you justice."

"Thank you," she said, "I think."

His voice was gravely, and he smiled. "Don't worry, Agent Anderson, you're always welcome here now. Your relationship with Seeker has provided us with some humor over the years. And, um, a few minor problems from time to time. But, congratulations on your engagement, by the way."

"Thank you, again," she said, unable to keep from smiling.

"Steph," Seeker said, "this is Tom Michelson, the head of Task Force Division." She nodded hello, as did Tom in return.

"Yes, Ms. Anderson, I'd served in the Marine Corp for many years. Close to retirement, but still in good shape. Then bam! The Pentagon repositions me to run this group of misfits," he said, winking at Mark. "I mean top of the line, best of the best agents you'll ever find in the world. So, first note is this." He opened a certificate folder from within the folio. "This is a letter of commendation from the President of The United States to Agent

Anderson for her capture of one of the world's most-wanted criminals."

"But, sir," Anderson interrupted, "I only helped Seeker."

"Yes, we all realize it, but no one else is publicly aware of our department's true existence. In light of that, we always let the FBI or other agencies take the credit for our work. So, you get full credit. If the media asks you about it, as it will, you can tell the story the way it happened. But you will not mention Seeker or Task Force in any fashion. You were on vacation in Charleston when you first came across him. You were given clearance to follow up on clues to chase and capture The Talon in Buenos Aires. All official records have been so modified to support your eventual press interviews."

"Have you set a date?" Proteus asked out of turn.

"Ah, no," said Anderson. "I only said yes yesterday."

"Back on track, people," Mark said politely. "We'll have the chit-chat later." He addressed Tom, "What've you got?" He handed the tablet to Tom, who keyed in a command code to activate a mission screen. Tom handed the already-active tablet to Mark, who scrolled through the preloaded list. "Bank robbery, hostage situation, jewelry theft, murder in a hotel room in North Carolina, art treasure theft in Makawao—" He stopped reading aloud and kept scrolling down the incident list. "Tom, I don't see anything in this briefing that requires our attention or involvement."

"That was my thought, too," Tom replied. "And intelligence reports that all is fairly quiet internationally as well. I'd say it's your call, Mark."

"Well, there's one off-book mission that requires all of us right now," said Mark, "and this is a dangerous one. We have a situation review in the training room. Let's adjourn to there in ten minutes. Seeker, why don't you take Agent Anderson to your office and pick up—" he looked at something on his tablet display "—artifact number E1621, bring it with you."

The team rose from the table and left the conference room, all scattering in different directions while Seeker took Stephanie to his office. He opened the door by another optical scanner beside it, which unlocked the door when it confirmed his identity. The door slid open and let Anderson and him enter; the overhead lights came on automatically.

"Ho-lee-shit," she said, her Southern accent tumbled out of her mouth in excitement. She looked around at the walls and the myriad shelves of artifacts from around the world. "You work in a museum!"

"Yeah, you could say that" said Seeker, looking up at the walls. "The majority of these are gifts from different countries and cultures from various missions over the last decade and a half. Some items are on loan from museums or collectors asking for my help with more history than their own resources could provide." He walked along the far wall from his desk and computer to an Egyptian statuette under a bell jar. "Item E1621, statue of Horus, one of the old deities worshipped in pre-dynastic Egypt, son of Osiris and Isis."

He put on a pair of white gloves before removing the bell jar and picked up the statuette to place it on a cushioned specimen tray. "Wonder what he wants with this?" he mused. He moved to a worktable with sample boxes underneath to pack it for transport. The door chime sounded. Seeker said aloud, "Open," and a male staffer in a gray uniform entered when the door receded.

"Sir, Spy says to disregard the specimen request and report to the training center immediately. You also, Agent Anderson."

"Thank you," said Seeker. He took a moment to return the artifact to its protective bell jar. "That's damn strange, very unlike him to change his mind like that. C'mon, Steph, let's see what's up."

They walked down the hall to the training room. Seeker looked into the optical reader, but it didn't activate. He knocked on the door, and it silently slid into the wall to reveal a darkened room. "Hello?" he said aloud.

The office lights suddenly flared to full brilliance. Colored streamers fell from the ceiling, balloons floated from tables covered in colorful cloths. Punch bowls, finger sandwiches and hors d'oeuvres lined one table. In one corner were several gifts stacked neatly. "SURPRISE! CONGRATULATIONS!" All the Task Force field team and support members yelled out in joy.

Mark came out of the crowd with Hunter at his side, both carrying two glasses of champagne. Hunter gave her second to Stephanie, and Mark gave his to Seeker.

"Oh, my God!" said Stephanie. "I never figured secret agents would put on a party like this!"

"Honey," said Hunter, "wait until the female staff gets you alone for your little, um, pantie party later!" She winked teasingly, taking Stephanie by the arm and pulling her into the huge throng of people.

"Congratulations," Mark said to Seeker, smiling. He raised his champagne glass in toast.

The two agents sipped their drinks at the same time. "You did it," Seeker said, shaking his head in disbelief. "You actually did it. You surprised me, you son-of-a-bitch. I'll get you for this!"

Mark took another sip of his champagne and placed a friendly hand on Seeker's shoulder. "You're welcome to try, my friend..."

CHAPTER 22

A GOLDEN CAGE

"JUNGEN, NIKLAS," SAID THE HEAD PRISON GUARD.

A tall, slender man in his early forties wearing an orange prisoner jumpsuit spoke in a German accent. "Ja." Niklas Jungen, also more commonly known as The Talon, was once on top of the world's most wanted list for terrorism, murder, kidnapping and extortion. He stood passively, his legs and arms shackled together.

The senior guard, an older, slightly overweight man with a perfect military crew cut, glared at him. "We don't speak anything here except American, you got it, asshole?"

"I do," Talon answered calmly.

"You may have been some hot shit out there, Mister '*Talon*', but in here you're just number 101561, no different than any other prisoner. You behave yourself until time for your transfer and you may arrive at your next cell intact."

"Understood," said Talon.

The guard pointed a finger at the cell block guard, "Take this shit-bag to his room. And Talon, there ain't no room service, so don't bother asking."

"I had no intention," Talon replied respectfully.

The cell block guard guided Talon through a series of transfer rooms until they arrived at Talon's cell. Inside was a small steel table bolted to the wall. On it was a plain white teapot with steam floating out its spigot, a teacup, and napkin, as well as a cushion on the steel seat bolted to the floor. "Wanted to make sure you had your afternoon tea on time, sir," the guard said.

"Thank you, Mr. Gamble," Talon said after glancing at the guard's nametag. "I could use a relaxing cup right now. I'm very pleased to have a friend in here."

"Everything's in place," Gamble said while taking the shackles off Talon's ankles.

"Excellent. Be a good man, and bring me a strudel? It's been a long day."

"Of course, sir," said Gamble. He locked the cell door after The Talon sat at the table and poured his first cup of tea for the afternoon. Smacking his lips together, his tongue searched for a familiar flavor. "Ah, Darjeeling, very impressive. Mr. Gamble did well." He took a second sip and looked out the cell door. "Very good to have friends everywhere. Yes, friends everywhere..."

CHAPTER 23

DISCOVERY

"**W**ELL, WUD'YA FIND, SAM?" Sheriff McCall asked, sitting down in an old-fashioned wingback leather chair. The chair was deep red with gold brads beading the seams from top to bottom. There was a matching chair beside it and a loveseat in a sitting area behind them. The sheriff stopped at the coroner's office after getting word that Jake's cause-of-death was determined. Coroner Ryan Trice knew the sheriff wasn't going to like his answer.

Coroner Trice's personal office held a mystery of wonders unto itself. Shelves of oddities lined the entire room, nothing at all personable about it. Jars of all sizes filled with formaldehyde held strange and distorted anomalies. He was a collector of eccentrics, always interested in the bizarre, strange, and weird world of science.

"Coffee, Max? Fresh brewed. I promise, there's no formaldehyde in it," he said, knowing the sheriff had been eye-balling the jars on the shelves.

"I like mine black, no additives."

The coroner chuckled, moving to the counter to prepare two cups of coffee.

"How the hell can you stand working in a place like this all day, Ryan? It gives me the creeps just walking in here. And the smell! Then there's the jars of frogs, two-headed mice, a cat with six legs, how'd you grow up to be so weird? We grew up together, and I sure didn't turn out like you."

"Science, my man, the wonderful, magnificent world of science. It gives us these strange things to study, experiment with, make us better at what we do." He handed the sheriff a Styrofoam cup of black coffee. "Max, there's some sick people in this world. There's a lot of psychology thrown in to help detect what's going on with them, but sometimes it still makes no sense." Coroner Trice took a seat in a comfortable brown chair; the old leather creaked as he settled. "I may be a little Podunk town coroner, but I went to the same schools and keep up with the same studies as those big shots in the big cities."

"That's great, Ryan. Why'd you call me here? You got something or not?"

Trice took a sip of coffee and picked up the folder containing the autopsy report from Raleigh. "Damnedest thing I've ever seen, Max. I'm used to seeing drug overdoses, bullets, knife wounds, even the occasional alcohol poisoning, but not this. Took the body up to Raleigh myself; watched the forensic pathologist do the autopsy."

"Will you get to the damned point?" McCall growled.

Trice sat forward, interlocking his fingers. "Okay, the blood tox report came back. Jake Collins was killed by a massive injection of Latrodectus venom."

"Latro-what?" McCall asked as he set his cup on the desk and stared at Trice.

"Latrodectus. It's the scientific name for the black widow."

"Black widow? So, what. We've had black widow bites here before. What's the big deal?"

Trice rotated the report in his hand so McCall could see where his finger pointed. "It says here the amount of venom in his system was equivalent to dozens of black widows."

"Ok, so he got into a black widow nest and got bit to death?"

"There was no evidence of any insect bites, widow or otherwise. There was one puncture spot on his hip where something was injected perimortem."

McCall squinted at Trice. "You saying some prostitute bitch killed this guy with spider venom?"

"That's the way it looks," said Trice. "And it's gotta be premeditated, 'cause there's no way outside a laboratory this much Latrodectus venom could be accumulated."

"Well, shit!" said McCall, sitting back in his chair, befuddled. "So, we're looking for a murderess?"

"If it was one of the women working at the motel, yes. But I dunno. Most likely no one local."

McCall looked at him. "How you figure it's not a local?"

"Anyone in this town with the smarts to make a serum like this?"

"Aside from you?"

"Ha, ha, smartass."

McCall stood to leave. "Keep this under your hat; tell no one about it, okay?"

"Well, the lab knows, and it's on their computers, and uploaded to the national database, but without any kinda match it's likely just gonna sit there. Officially, I have to rule the death due to anaphylactic shock from spider venom of unconfirmed origin."

"This fellow, this Jake, he was a local nobody—let's just hope he's not missed by no one. You got the body back there, just keep him on ice for as long as you're supposed to. We'll let the funeral home bury him as soon as the holding time is up. His truck can sit in the impound yard in the back corner 'til the weeds cover it."

"Whatever. You got it, Max."

McCall left the office without speaking. Trice sat, opened the bottom desk drawer, pulled out a silver flask, and leaned back in his chair. Taking a deep swig of whiskey, he sighed, "Never in all my days…"

CHAPTER 24

MARK OF THE BLACK WIDOW

"**H**OW'S THE TATTOO, LACY?"

Lacy struggled to put her hair in a ponytail. She wore only a long pajama top; her pubic hair was shaved off and her new black widow tattoo was where the hair used to be. "Sore," she emphasized. "But I can't stop looking at it. It's perfect, he did a great job! See how it's sort of sideways so you can see the red hourglass?" She ran her fingers across the tender area. "I kinda like being all shaved. Never did it before."

Lexi commented, "Yeah, I think I kind of like it too, Lacy," Lexi said, her fingers brushing Lacy's tender pubic flesh. The two stared at each other, realizing a new, strange sensation. They'd seen each other naked many times, like sisters, but now they were seeing each other in a new way.

Lacy squeezed Lexi's hand to keep them focused. "I got some good news—been dying to tell you. I found the next one today, on the Internet."

"You did? Which one?" Lexi asked as she leaned forward, eyes wide.

"Randy. I found him, Lexi. Found his social network page, and there he was—big as life. The son-of-a-bitch looks *happy*. He's turned off a lot of his personal info, but after scrolling down I read all his conversations. He lives somewhere in West Virginia, I'm searching online. You can find anyone nowadays it seems. After reading everything, I found out he's considering whether to go to our high school reunion."

Lexi looked at her, mouth half open. "I didn't realize there was a high school reunion, did you?"

"Yeah, I got an invitation in the mail today. It was a computer-generated form letter, not personalized beyond that. You should be getting yours anytime now, I'm sure. Not sure how they found our address."

Lexi knelt down in front of Lacy's chair, her eyes scrunched, contemplating the uneasy conversation. "Um, honey, we're listed in the phone book, not that hard to find us? C'mon, Lacy, you *really* wanna go through with this again? I mean, Jake was the biggie. He was the one who raped you first, stole your virginity. But don't you think the others may be on their guard now?"

Lacy snapped the recliner forward. "Dammit, Lexi, yes! Those bastards are still out there. I don't give a rat's ass if they know Jake's dead. They raped me, they hurt me! And yeah, all that stuff I went through in school because of them. They got away with it for so long. They need to pay for what they did, all four of them! They took away the life I could have had. They don't deserve to live theirs any longer! I have the perfect weapon to pay them back, and it can never be traced back to me!" Lacy stormed down the hall into the bathroom and slammed the door behind her.

"Damn her mood swings, they're getting worse. Okay," Lexi mumbled to herself. "Guess it's time to sit down and work out that plan, before she makes a mistake…"

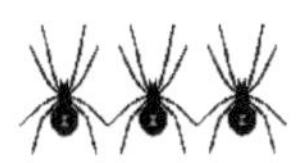

Lexi paced back and forth in front of Lacy. "Okay, this time *I* go with you, for protection. There's no need to go to a seedy motel like last time. Besides, it didn't work out the way you wanted anyway, remember? We have the money, let's do it up right this time, if you really have to do it. What if we lure him to a nice, posh hotel? Who's not gonna fall for two hot women, dressed to the nines? Get a room, do him, then hit him with the venom, and get out."

"No, not get out," Lacy interrupted, shaking her head. "I gotta watch. You're not understanding! You didn't see Jake after I stuck him. It was great! You sit and watch the venom do its work. It sets their nerves & muscles on fire, they can't breathe. That's the whole point, I need to see them suffer, like they made me suffer. I want them to know what true fear feels like." She shook her head, her brow furrowed, determination in her eyes. "It's about getting even, Lexi. Revenge. Taking it back. I can be in control this time. Don't you get it? We can find him, here on the computer. They've made it easy now."

"I get it, Lacy, I really do, and I love you. But, I've never seen you like this. In a million years, I'd never thought I'd go along with something like this. You've changed, something's snapped, and—and, you're actually starting to scare me."

Lacy looked up without expression, watching Lexi's eyes. She cupped Lexi's cheeks with her hands, drew her close, and kissed her on the lips. Both women's eyes welled with tears. Lacy rested her forehead on Lexi's forehead and replied, "You're probably right. But I finally have a chance to settle everything, Lexi. Maybe fate or destiny, or God, or the demons, put them all in my path for vengeance now. I have to follow through 'cause I may never get a second chance. And, I love you, too…"

CHAPTER 25

THE BLACK WIDOW BITES AGAIN

"Is THAT HIM, LACY, COMING IN THE DOOR?"

Lacy and Lexi took their time in preparing to meet Randy at the Seanbury Hotel and Suites in Huntington, West Virginia. They helped each other select short, seductive dresses, dark stockings, and black stilettos; apply their makeup, and work on each other's hair and nails. Lacy constantly wiggled in anticipation of the evening. She fidgeted during the drive, and even more in the hotel's lounge.

The two ladies sat at a table in a far corner of the luxurious lounge. A giant chandelier hung in the center of the room, and dimly lit sconces adorned the walls, producing an atmosphere of warmth and comfort. The carpeting was ornate, and tapestry inspired. Classical music hummed softly from speakers hidden throughout the room.

Lacy craned her head to see around other customers. "Yep, that's him," she said in a half-whisper. "The asshole. He looks so full of himself, doesn't he? You got the bag with the stuff in it, right? Auto-injector? Sheets? Washcloth?"

"Yes, for the hundredth time. I've got everything. Relax already, sweetie."

The man was tall, thin, and sported an expensive suit and tie, not bothering to remove his sunglasses once inside. He searched the room for the two women.

"Randy? Over here," Lacy waved.

He saw the two and waved back. "Ladies, hi!" He hugged Lacy then Lexi, removing his sunglasses as he sat at the table. "God, ten years, can you believe it? Seems like high school was just yesterday." He couldn't remember the two women. He had racked his brain all week trying to recall who they were, after their call to him.

"Randy, it's been so long!" Lacy was laying it on thick. "We got the high school invitation and decided to look up all our old classmates online. Everyone else looks older, but, geez, you've barely changed! You're as handsome as ever. I'm so glad you agreed to meet us to talk about going to the class reunion."

Randy looked down at the table and gave a small chuckle. His ears turned pink, embarrassed from the compliment. He still had no idea who they were. "Well, tell you what. You ladies have only gotten prettier over the years. I can't wait to hear about both of you, what you've been doin' these past ten years." *And hope I finally remember you,* he thought. "How about I order us some drinks, then we'll sit and chat as long as you want. I was even considering not going to the reunion, but I've changed my mind." Randy hailed a passing waiter and ordered their drinks.

Lacy and Lexi stood on either side of Randy in the elevator, giggling and laughing. All three stumbled onto the fifth-floor hallway. "Shhhh." Randy hushed them as he held a finger to his lips and whispered. "Gotta be quiet, at leas' until we get to the room. Lexi, lemme have that key card. I'm the gentleman here. Gotta open the door for the ladies, y'know."

Lacy smiled. He staggered slightly as they walked down the hall looking for the room number, with the two ladies following behind. Though not as intoxicated as Randy, they were a bit off-balance after several drinks. Lacy glanced down to Lexi's hand to make sure she still had their bag.

He found the door and slipped the key card in the slot above the door handle, and a red light appeared on the lock. He tried again, and the red light appeared a second time. "What the hell? Damn thing don't work."

Lexi took the card from him, turned it around, and slipped it in the slot in the correct direction. The green light appeared, and Lexi levered the handle with her elbow.

"Hey, you're one smart lady," Randy said laughing at his ineptness to open the door correctly.

The room was large, a suite with a bedroom, seating area, bathroom, and a small kitchenette. It was plush, elegant, and roomy. Lexi retrieved the washcloth from her bag. She slipped the room's 'Do Not Disturb' sign on the outside doorknob, and locked both inner locks, ensuring there were no fingerprints by using the cloth.

Randy asked, "So, we gonna do this thing?" He began unbuttoning his shirt, reveling in the opportunity to have easy sex with the two beautiful women.

Lacy pulled him toward her, kissing him, letting her tongue linger around his bottom lip for a few seconds.

Randy smiled. "Oh, yeah. Damn, it's my lucky day. Hey, but first I gotta pee. You two got to go to the bathroom downstairs but I can't wait anymore. I'll be right back." His words slightly slurred. He unzipped his pants before getting to the bathroom. "And don't you go anywhere. You get ready for the screwin' of your life!" He chuckled loudly, stumbled into the bathroom, and shut the door.

"Geez, Lacy. He's disgusting."

"He'll only be disgusting for a few more minutes. Now, get the silk sheets out of the bag and onto the bed. Get the injector ready."

The women heard the toilet flush. Their nerves were on edge; Lacy, from the excitement of what they were about to do, and Lexi because of the unknown and about taking a life. They jumped when the bathroom door handle clicked, and Randy came out. "Ah, much better." He rubbed his hands together. "Now, where do I start?"

"Uh, uh," said Lacy, in an enticing voice. "You come over here and lie down, we kinda got a big surprise for you." She unzipped the back of her dress and let it fall to the floor. She wore neither bra nor panties, only thigh high black stockings and stilettos.

Randy's mouth fell open, unable to speak at the sight of Lacy's gorgeous body. She was petite with small pert breasts, and hairless pubic area. "Man, my wife'd never shave hers for me! And she sure as hell'd never put a spider tattoo on her twat," he said with a big smile on his face, and a bulge growing in his pants. Lacy's long red hair rested in spiraled curls down her shoulders. She stepped out of the dress and walked over to him. Lacy kissed his neck and worked her way up to his mouth, awaking a lust in him that lingered beyond his inebriation. He fondled her breasts as they kissed, and his hands worked downward, her skin smooth and warm. Lexi approached the kissing couple and began undressing Randy and placed a condom on him. Within minutes, Randy was naked, his man-parts stabbed into Lacy's stomach as they clenched together.

"Damn, I'm in heaven," Randy muttered. Lacy placed both hands on Randy's chest and shoved hard, pushing him onto the silk sheets covering the bed. He toppled over with no problem, not fighting back. "Oh, like it a little rough, huh? Okay, come here, baby, lemme show you what I can do to you. Hey, Lexi, you gonna join us? I'll show you how a real man can do two girls at once."

Lacy climbed onto the bed, astride Randy while Lexi undressed. Lacy abruptly took his hands, pulled them up over his head, and held them down on the pillow. She was taking control, and he wasn't resisting. She leaned in and kissed him hard. She gyrated her hips against him, thinking all the while how the widow spider would react to the same situation, depending on how hungry she was. Lacy moved back and forth until he was able to enter her. He gave a long, low satisfied groan.

Lexi straddled Randy's chest face to face with Lacy. She kissed her hard, placing the injector in Lacy's right hand. Lacy was stunned by the kiss. "Like what you see back there?" Lexi asked Randy, still staring into Lacy's eyes. "It's gonna get better, you know." Lacy felt exhilarated; like nothing she'd felt before. Lexi slid off his chest, leaving Lacy to her job.

Lacy thrust hard, so much that he couldn't wait any longer. He grabbed her by the hips and with a final push upward, he moaned in mind-shattering ecstasy. Lacy held the injector tight and with a sideways swing jabbed the needle into his hip. The venom shot into his body while he continued to buck upward, pushing himself deeper inside Lacy, immersed in the euphoria of the moment, not feeling the needle.

Lexi took the injector from Lacy, being careful not to touch the tip or any of the liquid substance that might still be on it. She placed it in its case and slipped it back into her carryall bag.

Randy stopped, his body wilted, exhausted from the energetic romp on the bed. Lacy bent forward, placed her hands on the bed, and lingered above him. She spoke in a low, deliberate intonation. "Randy, oh, you were good, like you were in high school. Remember?"

"What? We never did this in high school."

"Yeah, we did. Remember the gym, on the stage, you four guys raped me and left me there. *I* remember it *too* well. Jake got his a few weeks ago; it's your turn now. It's time for you to pay. Give you what you gave me times ten years?" Her eyebrows rose in inquiry, waiting for his answer.

Randy sat up on his elbows. "Whoa, wait—what's goin' on here? *No, that was you?* You—you've got it all wrong! We didn't rape you, remember, we were all just having fun." A burning sensation began to surge through his body. Uncontrollably, his muscles jerked, his nerves were on fire; sweat beaded on his forehead, and nausea set in.

Still sitting on his groin, Lacy pulled back. She savored the fearful look in his eyes, reveling in what was going to be a grueling and painful death. Lexi sat on the second bed, watching. She realized she loathed seeing Lacy atop the naked man before handing over the injector. She began to recognize the deep romantic feelings she had for Lacy. Lexi now realized she wasn't just a roommate or best friend, but something more carnal, sexual. "Lacy, come on. Get away from him."

Lacy moved to the other bed as Randy's death throes continued; she sat and hugged Lexi. "It's ok, girlfriend, I'm getting what I need, and you're here to help me, protect me. It's wonderful!"

"Lacy, I just have—I need—damn. I don't know how, but this is really a—" she stumbled over her words, "a turn on. Things I've never felt." She reached over and delicately kissed Lacy on the lips, this time with emotion, not like the abrupt kiss minutes earlier. They parted and stared into each other's eyes. Lexi moved forward again, kissing Lacy, deliberately, passionately. She bent Lacy backwards, letting her tongue probe her mouth. Her hands explored Lacy's body, and Lacy didn't resist. A magnetic, sexual chemistry took over, neither wanting to stop.

The sounds from the other bed broke the spell, both sitting up to observe Randy's imminent demise. His body curled, cringing in searing pain. "Oh, God! Help me! Please! Call—"

Lacy stood, interrupting him. "You don't deserve help, you disgusting pig! You're getting what you deserve!" Lacy's personality changed in an instant, abruptly angered, losing control of her senses. Fist curled, she struck Randy on his cheek, throat, then two fists to the belly. Randy screamed out in pain. Lexi, nearly panicked, retrieved a towel from the bathroom. They tied it around Randy's mouth and head, knotting it in the back, so his screams couldn't alert anyone in the next room. "I hate you; I've always hated you! You and all the others! You use your strength, dominance to take advantage of people like me. Well, we're done taking it, *done*—you hear me? I'm gonna sit here and—" Lacy drug out the last few words "—watch—you—die. Just like I've died inside all these years."

Randy's eyes bulged, his face and neck turned a reddish-purple. He rolled back and forth on the silk sheets. Turning on his side, he vomited into the towel over his face. Liquid seeped through onto the sheets and backed up into his esophagus. Gurgling noises exuded behind the towel. Lexi said, "Lacy, I don't wanna watch. This is really nasty. I've never seen anyone die. I get it, for you, but damn!"

Lacy spoke calmly. "Go to the bathroom, Lexi." Lacy stroked Lexi's hair, pulling it back and tucking it behind her ears. "It's okay. I'll let you know when it's over. He can't hurt me now. I just gotta do this, okay?"

Lexi's emotions were broken. She spoke, her eyes tearing. "Yeah, I guess." Lexi gathered her clothes and moved to the bathroom, shutting the door. Lacy watched her best friend walk away, experiencing a new stirring inside. Lexi turned on the water in the sink and shower in an effort to not hear the noises from the bedroom. She sat on the toilet lid covering her ears, realizing there were two more deaths to come, knowing she'd have to get used to them.

Randy strained hard against the intense sweltering pain. Sweat ran down his face. He stared with pleading brown eyes at Lacy, and she simply sat and watched from the other bed. The venom infiltrated his internal organs, his brain, killing him from the inside out.

"Die, you monster, I need to see you suffer and die." It took minutes. Randy couldn't breathe. His bowels involuntarily let loose on the bed. He closed his eyes, giving in to the pain that coursed through his body. One last jerk, gasp, and he quit moving, his death finally achieved.

Lacy grinned. *Good. The second bastard is gone. This went perfectly, just as planned,* she thought. "Lexi, come out, sweetie. Let's get this over with and get out."

The two women wrapped Randy in the silk sheets, bundled smooth and neat, sealing him in with white lace strips on the top and bottom. "It's done. In a spider-like cocoon. The venom did its job. I killed him—just like a true black widow..."

CHAPTER 26

AW, SHEET!

THE HOTEL'S HOUSE CLEANING STAFF PASSED BY ROOM NUMBER 504, noticing the "Do Not Disturb" sign on the door handle at 10:00am. Checkout was at 11:00am. They kept going, making note to come back a while later.

At 11:15, the two housecleaners, Jean and Marguerite, came back to the room. The 'Do Not Disturb' sign was still on the handle, which wasn't that unusual. It was normal for people to forget to remove it before they left. Jean knocked on the door, announcing "Housekeeping" in a loud voice. No answer. She knocked and bellowed her greeting a second time, receiving the same silent answer. Jean shrugged her shoulders, "Guess they forgot." She opened the door with the master key and the two entered to carry on their cleaning duties. "You smell that? Damn, I hate it when they don't flush."

Jean entered the bathroom to clean, and Marguerite headed toward the beds. Marguerite gasped loudly when she saw a large mummy-shaped bundle on the bed wrapped in silk sheets. Jean said from the bathroom, "What's the matter, Margi?"

"Jean, come out here—come see what's on the bed!"

"Oh, Mother Mary, what did someone do now? I hate when they leave—oh my God, Margarite! What's that?" Jean covered her mouth with both hands.

"How the hell should I know?" Marguerite poked a finger at the bulky object. There was no movement. She gave a gentle push and it moved slightly. "Whatever it is, we're gonna need help moving it like this. Let's unwrap it and see if it's just trash or something."

"That's not trash, Margi; I'd bet a million if I had it."

Jean untied the ribbon holding the sheet corners together. The dead, naked man's folded-in limbs fell free, his arm struck Jean in the stomach.

Both women screamed...

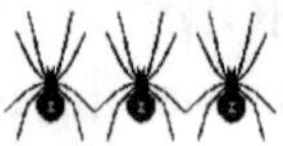

"Looks like we got a dead one here," the hotel manager said to the head of security.

"No shit, you think?" said the security chief. The manager's brow furrowed. "Sorry, sir—didn't mean for it to come out like that."

The manager nodded. "Yeah, I know, no problem. Let's keep everyone out until the cops get here. We just need to keep the guests happy and not make a scene..."

The local police department descended on the Seanbury Hotel and Suites, followed by the coroner, detectives, and their forensics team. The chief detective spoke with the hotel manager in the fifth-floor hallway. "Shit. I've never seen anything like this. It's a new one on me."

"Just tell me the media's *not* gonna get hold of this. We'll have people canceling rooms left and right."

"Don't worry, sir. Deaths in hotels aren't unusual, and we're trying to keep this as standard as possible. We'll do everything we can to keep it quiet, but there's no guarantee the media won't find out sooner or later."

"I know. Damn..."

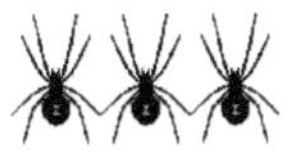

"And in tonight's breaking news, a man was found dead in a room on the fifth floor the Seanbury Hotel and Suites this morning. The identity has not been released pending notification of next of kin. Reliable sources on the scene speculate this was highly likely not a natural death. There are no suspects at this time..."

CHAPTER 27

THEME PARTY

The day-long annual Jason Enterprises picnic was the third-most anticipated event of the year for company employees, surpassed only by the New Year and Christmas parties. Company founder Zachary Jason began the annual tradition the first year the company made a profit, then continued the practice for over thirty years. When Mark took over, the first party under his leadership was changed to a themed event. Everyone wore the uniform of their favorite baseball player. At the time, Zachary wore a replica of the Yankee uniform of Babe Ruth. Mark wore a Washington Senators uniform with Frank Howard's number. Mark's mother and wife wore cheerleader outfits, and then-nine-year-old Angela sported an umpire's suit, complete with face mask and chest guard.

Jan worked with a catering company to create a Hawaiian Luau theme for this year's party, ensuring it would be lavish and flawless, especially with extra-special guests who were invited. Mark requested Mae-Lei Komala (Task Force agent Hunter) to help because of her personal knowledge of her home state to make the event as authentic as possible. The catering company and Mae-Lei managed to turn the front five acres of the hundred-acre Jason family property into the best re-creation of a Hawaiian Luau as possible.

The rest of the Task Force field team was invited, along with their personal guests: Calvin Geffers (Agent Seeker) brought his fiancée Stephanie, and Harri Lewis (Agent Proteus) brought Elise DeVeaux. Now good friends with Harri, Elise was the partially deaf sister of Richmond's late serial murderer, *The Biblical Bomber*, killed by the Task Force team several years earlier.

A contracted valet service took care of parking. Mark and Jan stood at the door to receive their guests and direct them to the expansive party around the corner of the house.

Mark wore light khaki slacks and brown loafers, and a blue-and-white flowered shirt. Jan wore a flowing flower-patterned white skirt that reached her ankles with thigh-high cuts on both sides, exhibiting her shapely porcelain-toned legs. She wore white sandals, and a white tube-top that bared her smooth abdomen. Her long flowing red hair ended in waves that gently brushed her back. As each guest approached, they were presented with a genuine flower lei.

Tom arrived unaccompanied. He walked past the attached multi-car garage and stopped at the front entrance of the mansion to shake hands with Mark, and hug Jan and Angela in turn. Angela snickered at Tom's attire. "Bermuda shorts, flowered shirt, sandals, and wide-brimmed hat. Sorry, Colonel Michelson, it's just, well, I can't picture you in anything but a suit."

Tom gave an exaggerated bow to Angela. "Thanks for having me over, Mark. Angela, enjoy the view—it's probably the last time you'll see me in such a get-up, unless next year's picnic is also a luau."

"Glad you could make it," Mark answered. "I figured it would be okay to mingle our two jobs for a day, since there's no one trying to take over the world at the moment."

"Well," said Tom, "we're keeping an eye on ISIS for potential terrorist acts, but yeah, all's quiet for now. So, getting right to the point, where's the bar?" he asked as he grinned and clapped his hands together.

Jan pointed past the garage. "To the end and turn right, you can't miss the tents and tables, but the bars don't open for just a few minutes. And don't step in the pig pits."

Tom tipped his hat brim and began to walk away when he came face-to-face with Harri and Elise.

"Oh, my God," said Harri when she saw her division boss. "Damn, sir, but you've got great legs!"

Tom smiled and took a second bow of the day. "This is the only time I won't bring you up on sexual harassment charges, agent," he replied, "only because you're absolutely correct!"

"So," said Harri, who was wearing a black bikini top and sarong, covering very little of her small frame, "can a couple of hot beach girls buy you a drink?"

Elise blushed. Months of concentrated voice therapy and implant surgeries for her hearing impairments had brought her voice to an almost normal tone. "Oh, Harri, I'm not hot!"

Tom looked at the girl, nearly forty years his junior. "Elise, if you don't leave here with a boyfriend tonight, I'll be greatly surprised."

"But I'm here with Harri to have fun, not to meet a guy."

"And we're gonna get a drink with the colonel to thank him for all the support we've gotten the last few years. Then we're gonna get those jeans and shirt off you and get wet in that big old pool!" Harri grabbed Elise' arm with one hand and Tom's with the other. Elise blushed again as they walked toward the bar.

Calvin wore a white T-shirt with gray shorts and black flip-flops. His flawless light-chocolate skin and brushed-back black hair accentuated the attire. Stephanie wore a small pink bikini under her translucent beach dress. Calvin spoke while he approached Mark and Jan. "Wow, nice spread you got here."

"Better than that private 747 of yours?"

"Hey, the advantage of a home with wings is a different front yard any night I want." Mark grinned in agreement.

Jan reached out and grabbed Calvin in a hug, then the same to Stephanie. "Congratulations on your engagement, you two! Hi, I'm Jan."

"I'm Stephanie," she replied. "Thanks for having us!"

Jan looked at Stephanie's engagement ring while their hands were still clasped. "Wow, that's magnificent! I can't wait to hear all about how you two got together! You just head on into *Hawaii* and start enjoying yourselves. Some of the company staff is already here. Mingle and meet them. Just remember, no business talk! Food, drinks, the pool and fun, that's all."

Mark greeted more guests as Calvin and Stephanie walked on. The grounds overflowed with Jason Enterprises employees and their families, as well as several special guests from the political arena, entertainment, and support companies.

When the last guests were greeted and made their way toward the party, Jan took Mark's arm in hers and guided him to the bar. "Y'know, I noticed *you-know-who* didn't make it here."

Mark chuckled. "Yeah, he's still busy at the big office keeping his campaign promises. Can't fault a guy for his dedication." Jan gave Mark a loving smack on the arm at his reply.

They arrived at the bamboo tiki-bar hut, which was covered in a traditional thatch roof. Inside, strings of lights hung in crisscross strips, giving off a warm orange glow despite the clear morning sunshine. Two flaming torches stood a few feet on either side of the structure. Resting his arms on the bar, Mark ordered a Bahama Mama. "Extra Bahama in that Mama, if you don't mind, Andy."

"Yes, sir, Mr. Jason, coming right up."

"And I'll have a Mai Tai, nothing extra in mine," said Jan.

Andy smiled, slid their drinks toward them, and presented both with their own, pink-flowered leis. Andy didn't officially open the bar to anyone other than the Jasons until Mark made his opening comments to the crowd.

The female wait staff wore grass skirts with colorful flowers woven into the waist, along with coconut or seashell tops. The male staff were bare-chested, wearing only warrior shorts and grass bands around their calves and biceps. Each wore a white shell necklace to complete the authenticity.

Hula dancers were setting up to perform on a stage. Tiki torches adorned the entire area, as well as more overhead tropical hanging lights. Mark and Jan admired all the decorations and activities that the theme company had provided, knowing it would look even more spectacular at night. "We did good, hon," Jan commented.

A limbo game was set up near the Hawaiian band. Face-painting chairs were scattered across the entire party grounds for the kids. Seating mats ensconced the large grassy yard. Multiple serving tables were covered with towering spires of food: meats, fruits, vegetables, breads. Tiki-hut bars festooned the property, including a swim-up pool bar in the shallow end of the Olympic-size pool. Horseshoe games were in a few locations, and a pony ride was in a portable fence enclosure for the children. Potted palm trees dotted the property, and a photography company had four locations for commemorative photos for the several hundred guests, all of whom were gently milling about, waiting for the party to begin.

Jan looked at Mark's bearded face and saw a slight grin. "Are you pleased, love?"

"Yup. Just one thing to do to get this thing started." He gave her a gentle kiss on the cheek, and an intimate nibble on the ear, then guided her to the hula stage. The scattered conversations stopped without prompting.

Sarge was standing on the stage, dressed in a light brown long-sleeve shirt, dark brown slacks, and loafers. He held a wireless microphone, looking very much out of place. He tapped the mike and unceremoniously spoke in his normal, gruff demeanor. "Everyone hear me okay?" Sarge had been assigned to provide security for the event, though his staff blended in so as not to be noticed, unlike him.

"Yes, sir!" someone yelled from the gathered throng.

"Now, dammit—" The entire guest company yelled in unison, "I AIN'T NO SIR!" Raucous, good natured laughter broke out along with loud applause. The burly security chief smiled and raised his right hand in a thumb's-up gesture. Sarge realized how predictable he'd become. He let the gaiety die down on its own before he continued. "Yeah, yeah. Same thing I always say. Well, there's only one man here worthy of being called 'sir', and that's this man here. Let's hear it for Mr. Mark Jason!"

Deafening applause and cheers broke out as Sarge passed the microphone to the company president. Mark raised a hand to gently urge the crowd to settle, but the applause didn't stop. Finally, he said into the microphone, "The sooner you settle down the sooner the bars open!" The applause and laughter increased. At long last, though, the crowd calmed. "Thank you all for coming today for the forty-fifth annual Jason Enterprises Picnic. I remember the first party Dad held here for the company, everyone was dressed in slacks, stuffy shirts, and dresses. I don't think Dad could have handled all the bikinis and biceps on display here today!" The crowd broke out into laughter again. "Well, first and last order of business. Jason Enterprises had record profits for the last fiscal year, and every employee will find a *generous* bonus in your next paycheck. And I believe that will be next Friday?" He turned to Jan for an answer.

"As long as you don't drink so much you forget to sign the vouchers tonight," Jan teased. Everyone laughed again.

"I'm sure there's a security chief around to protect me if I forget," Mark replied, pointing a thumb at Sarge. After more laughter, Mark continued. "Company, friends, family, invited guests, and anyone who was not invited who successfully snuck in, please enjoy yourselves. The party lasts until midnight. If you leave hungry it'll be your own fault. May God shine down on us today, keep us warm and safe! And, Mae-Lei, if I get this wrong you better yell real loud and quick—HIPAHIPA!"

At the Hawaiian word for *cheers,* the crowd applauded and shouted. The loud rhythmic drums and music started, the hula dancers began their first performance, and food and beverages were served.

Mark handed the microphone to one of the sound engineers and walked off the stage with Jan and Sarge. "So, big guy, who'd you come with this year?"

"Just me, sir," Sarge answered, as relaxed as he was able. "Keepin' my eyes on everything."

Mark stopped walking; a wrinkled expression of concern formed on his forehead. "Sarge, I've got over two dozen security guys and gals all across the property, from the valet parking, to the stables, to the mailbox. I think you've earned a day off. Now get over there and get your bourbon."

"It ain't noon yet, sir."

Mark sighed. "It may be ten in the morning here, but it's noon in Greenland, so get the hell over to the bar, and relax."

Sarge opened his mouth to protest, but Mark's scowl quieted him. The burly man turned and headed toward a tiki-hut.

Jan laughed, and the couple moved in to mingle with the crowds...

Sarge took a sip from his bourbon tumbler and savored the taste. He sucked in gently through puckered lips and said to the bartender, "Whoa! Hey, what is this?"

"Glen Garioch, 1958," the bartender replied. "Single-grain scotch whiskey."

Sarge smiled. "Nice. Gotta say, the boss has taste."

"Buy a girl a drink?" said a female voice from behind. Sarge turned to stare in surprise at Sandra Freeman, dressed in her usual work slacks, blouse, and flats.

"Freeman, I thought you pulled the skeleton duty for today."

"I was ordered to attend today."

"I didn't order you—"

"I was ordered by the one man in the company who doesn't take 'no' for an answer."

Sarge wanted to grumble but couldn't bring himself to do it. The bartender asked, "What'll it be?"

"I'll have what he's having," she told the bartender, and took a seat on a stool beside Sarge.

"Scotch neat, coming up."

"Um," said Sarge in as low a whisper as he was able, "remember what happened the last time you drank with me? Lord knows what the good stuff'll do to ya."

She took her glass from the bartender and raised it in toast to Sarge. "Why? Don't *you* remember?" She winked, taking a sip.

Sarge smiled, downing the drink in one swallow. "Okay, but this stuff's a whole lot stronger—you live a dangerous life, lady. Okay, you've been warned, Freeman..."

Calvin sat in a lawn chair, Stephanie on the grass beside him, both enjoying food and the summer sun. He began to tell her about one of his flamboyant adventures, then realized a group of children were sitting nearby, listening to the story. He winked at Stephanie; hopeful the kids would enjoy the tale. "So, there I was, hiding about twenty feet up inside of a baobab tree, watching this pride of lions. Musta been a good fifty of 'em easy, and the alpha male, he had to be three-hundred pounds if an ounce!"

The children scrambled one-by-one, scooting across the lawn toward Calvin to listen in on his travel stories. Curious adults began to mill closer as well, intrigued with what was bound to be an incredibly unbelievable story.

"Now the wind had been with me the whole day," he continued, smiling at every break in his tale. "Suddenly, the breeze shifted, and that big kitty's head went on alert trying to figure out where the new smell was coming from. His head pulled up; whiskers started to twitch—"

"What did he smell?" a little boy yelled, louder than intended, wide eyed and mouth hanging open in excited anticipation.

In an exaggerated voice, Calvin replied, "Well, *me*, of course! Even though he couldn't see me, he knew I was around, and let out the biggest, loudest roar in the world!" Calvin placed his paper plate on the grass and sat forward. More children gathered and he tempered his words, trying to excite the little ones even more. "Well, if I was gonna get a shot I had only one chance. So, I lifted up the viewfinder, focused the range and calculated the wind speed, then pulled in my finger just a little—"

"What did you *shoot* him with?" squealed a pre-teen girl, sitting by his right leg.

"I think it was an EOS 5D Mark III," he replied, rubbing his chin. "Very excellent camera for high-quality resolution and image capture." The adults laughed, some rolled their eyes, a few walked off still chuckling. Calvin retrieved a cell phone from his pocket and flipped through the digital library. "Ah, here it is—told you, he was a biggie!" He slowly waved the phone to the crowd, displaying a photo of the lion, its mouth wide open in mid-roar.

"How'd you get away?" another child shrieked, fascinated with the story.

"That was the scary part!" Calvin exclaimed. "When he finally saw me, he started whacking at the tree trunk with his huge paws, knocking chunks out with each swing!"

Children looked on in awe, some covering their mouths or eyes. "Aw, man, that's like in the cartoons," said another boy.

Calvin flipped to another image on his phone, this one showing the same lion scratching at the tree below Calvin's feet. "You were sayin', young fella?"

"Weren't you scared up there taking pictures while the lion was trying to get you? He could have eaten you alive!" the boy said in horror.

"Nope, I had a secret escape all set," said Calvin.

"What was it?" another girl yelled out.

"Yeah," said Stephanie, "how did you get out? I'd love to hear this one." She leaned backward onto her elbows and stared at her man with big teasing eyes.

"Well, I was in trouble, but a good adventurer is always prepared. So, what I did was put up a zip line *before* I got in the tree and attached it to the other end beside my safari truck. When that lion was just inches away from my legs, I got on that line and slid out of harm's way, faster than the lion could run!"

Stephanie's head fell backwards, and she groaned. "That is the *worst* escape story I've ever heard."

Calvin flipped to the video folder on his phone, and played the video of him sliding, from his perspective, camera around his neck, on a zip line from the large tree to his vehicle. His audience burst into laughter.

"I don't believe it," Stephanie said, shaking her head.

The crowd applauded and broke up to other parts of the party grounds. Children jumped up and scattered, sharing the story to anyone who wanted to listen.

Stephanie rose with Calvin and wrapped her arm around his left arm. "You sound more like an 'adventurer' than a 'seeker', big boy," she said. "Why isn't that your, um, business name?"

"Maybe it was too long for the business cards?" he said.

"You don't have business cards." Even though she was only a couple of inches shorter than he, Stephanie rose to her tiptoes and kissed him on the lips. "Well, Tarzan of the zip line jungle, I'm going for my first pool dip. Join me?"

"Thought you'd never ask." He smiled and watched Stephanie strip down to her bikini while he pulled off his shirt to join her in the water...

Tamara Jason was behind the counter of the pool bar. She wore a white Jason Enterprises Cut-off T-shirt and a white bikini underneath. Her long black hair skimmed the top of the water, floating like waves of dark silky seaweed. She volunteered to tend at the pool bar during the annual company picnics and had the biggest crowd during the event. While the drinks were free at all the bar stations on the grounds, TJ usually collected the most tips, all of which were donated to local children's charities.

She smiled as she watched Stephanie and Calvin dive into the deep end and swim underwater all the way to the bar. Breaking the surface cleanly and taking deep breaths, they walked the last few steps to her counter. "Nice entrance, folks," said TJ. "What'd you like to start the day?"

"Champagne, TJ," said Stephanie, looking at the nametag on the bartender's T-shirt.

"You do realize that drinking and diving don't mix?" TJ said.

Calvin groaned at the bad pun. "I think I know where I'm getting all my drinks today!"

"Well, the drinks may be free but the one-liners' gonna cost you," TJ replied, tapping the weighted TIPS jar on the left side of the counter.

"And, um, just why do you think I'd be carrying cash in a swimsuit?" Calvin asked.

"Just trade in some hard-earned cash for plastic tokens at the tiki-hut. They don't get ruined by the water."

"Would you take a rain check on the tokens then?"

"Trust me," Stephanie interrupted, "he's more than good for it." She raised her left hand and rubbed her fingers together.

TJ noticed the diamond engagement ring. "Wow, that's a pretty bauble. You guys engaged?"

"Just a few weeks ago," Stephanie said.

"I love to hear engagement stories," said TJ. "My cousin Mark took my cousin-in-law-to-be to an old Demi Moore movie and then an Italian restaurant to propose. How'd you two do it?"

Stephanie smiled and lowered her head, cocking to the side to look teasingly at Calvin. "Well, it all started with me ending up topless on a highway south of Charleston."

"Charleston, you say?" said a female voice. A tall dark-haired woman approached the bar. "Cosmo, please," she said to TJ. "That sounds like quite a story, indeed."

"It's not as bad as it sounds, ambassador," Stephanie replied. "But it certainly took enough years and wardrobe malfunctions, not to mention quite a few gunfights, to get this lunkhead to finally propose."

"Sounds like it was quite a challenge," said the ambassador. "Took a while to build your courage, sir?"

Calvin smiled. "Actually, I preferred to travel across the world doing my philanthropic work to popping the question to her. My only fear in the world was hearing her say 'no' when I asked."

"So, what finally made you ask?"

He rubbed his jaw. "She slugged me before the appetizer..."

"I love watching Washington and Atlanta play ball," said the senator to Tom Michelson at the bar near the hula stage. "But I'm certainly not doing another season bet with you again, not after last year. I'd swear you had some inside info."

"Who, me?" said Tom, feigning being insulted. "Just because I run an intelligence agency? 10K on Washington this season. Winner's choice of charities."

"You're on," the senator replied.

Tom said to the bartender, "You're my witness, Andy."

"And he leaned forward and kissed me!" Elise said to Harri.

"You're kidding me!" said Harri. "Wow, I'd no idea you'd gotten so chummy at therapy group!"

"Well, I don't think he meant anything, because he kissed *all* the girls on the cheeks," Elise stuttered and blushed as she spoke.

"But that was your first kiss from a boy! That's wonderful!" Harri wrapped her arms around Elise and hugged her tight.

"But, um, I, um—"

"Now, girlfriend," said Harri. "No stuttering, remember."

"Thank you, Harri. I couldn't do all this without you."

Harri gave her another hug. She picked up the full glass from the bar and gave it to Elise. "Now, this is blush wine. It's one of my favorites, a sweet one, you should like it."

◆◆◆

"All he did was whine and bitch," said Jan.

"Hito always whines and bitches," Mark replied. "But he's the best IT guy in the state."

"Problem is he knows it. Even in that wheelchair, he gets around with so much speed; nothing stops him."

"With what we're paying him to maintain our systems, I don't care if he comes to work in his pajamas and bunny slippers."

"I still can't believe he volunteered to cover the computer center on picnic day, *again!*"

"Well, love," Mark said taking Jan's hand while they strolled the grounds, "all I can say is he's our very own Mr. Scott from *Star Trek*; he's happiest when he has a technical manual or new hardware and software."

"True, but one request—please tell him to go home once in a while and shower."

"Genius knows no aromas."

Mark stopped their walk when he spotted an employee sitting alone at one of the picnic tables. He nodded at Jan for them to join her. "Chrystal, how are you doing?" Mark asked as they arrived at the table and sat across from her.

Chrystal Leigh smiled at the couple. "Mr. and Mrs. Jason. I'm, um, I'm fine, thank you. And thank you for inviting me here."

"We take care of our people," said Jan. "We push everyone to excel daily, and we like to show our appreciation and reward everyone for their hard work."

"That's really nice. You're so generous to everyone. I still can't believe I'm working for Jason Enterprises, and in such an important job," Chrystal said shyly. She glanced at the picnic grounds and the large mansion behind her. "You have a really nice home."

"Thank you, Chrystal," said Mark. "My dad built it a few years after starting the company. He wanted plenty of room for his brothers and sisters and their families to come visit without having to deal with hotel reservations." Mark looked up at one window in particular on the third floor. "They both passed away in the home they built."

"Oh, I'm so sorry!" said Chrystal.

Mark smiled back. "Thank you, but that was a long time ago. I just hope they're up there, approving of how we're keeping the company moving forward." Mark studied Chrystal, concerned, watchful of her wary responses, something he wasn't used to from his employees. He thought perhaps it was her youth and inexperience.

"Speaking of, may I ask—" Crystal began to say.

"No, you may not," Jan said gently. "There is no business discussed at the company party. No exceptions. You're supposed to be enjoying yourself and relaxing!" Jan looked at the empty bench area beside Chrystal. "Are you here alone?"

Chrystal's eyes widened. "No, ma'am, my roommate just went to the bathroom in the garage, one of the staff said it was the closest. Oh, there she is!" Jesse arrived with two cups of beer and set them on the table. "Mr. and Mrs. Jason, this is my roommate, Jesse Lexington."

"Welcome, Jesse," said Jan, shaking her hand, "I hope you're enjoying yourself today."

Jesse shook hands with Mark across the table. "Very pleased to meet you! Wow, can I say I love your cars? Especially the '69 Charger and the '57 Corvette! I see you've got the '57 open, doing some engine repair?"

"I am," Mark said, proudly. "Um, that was my dad's favorite car; would you believe it stopped working not long after he passed away? I just hadn't had time to fix it and really don't want any other mechanic working on it. Just been having some trouble with the engine, it's hard to find authentic original parts, and I don't always have the time to do the research."

"Mr. Jason," said Chrystal, "she's an expert on top-of-the-line cars and classic cars. Maybe she could help? She's got a degree in engineering, you see—even owns her own classic car repair business."

"Is that so?" Mark asked Jesse. "Would you like to take a closer look?"

Jesse's eyes widened. "Oh, may I? I'd love to!"

Mark glanced at Jan, got up and rounded the table to take Jesse by the arm. As they walked back toward the garage, Jan and Chrystal heard Mark say, "My dad loved that car, he spent so many evenings and weekends fiddling with it. I'd sit in the passenger seat and he'd always remind me, 'you can look at it but I'm the one who drives it.'"

Jan and Chrystal laughed. "Mark and his cars. Well, he could have worse hobbies."

"I don't know much about cars except what she shows me," said Chrystal. "I just turn it on and drive."

Jan changed the subject. "So, Chrystal, are you two—?"

Chrystal narrowed her eyes for a moment trying to understand Jan's unfinished question. "Oh! No, not like that. We've been best friends since we were in grade school, it's just financially better for us to share an apartment."

"You have a boyfriend then?"

"No, ma'am," Chrystal replied. "Can't say I've had much success with men so far. I'm simply happy to concentrate on my job."

Jan stood. "You sound a lot like Mark. Well, Chrystal, since my husband has run off with your roommate to show off his prize convertible, how about you join me so I can introduce you to some people?"

"Um, I, uh—"

"Consider it the only business order I'll give you today." Jan held out her hand and smiled warmly. Chrystal smiled, taking her hand for a moment until they started walking. "I wonder if the Jurgens boy made it here today..."

"He wanted to tell you himself," Rachel Jurgens told Angela as they sat on a picnic mat, "but was afraid of what you'd say."

"As long as he's happy, that's all that matters," Angela replied.

"Your mom always thought you two would make a great couple," Rachel continued. "He was immensely proud to hear you got accepted into the navy, just like your daddy. What do you do, dear?"

Angela lowered her head in apology. "I'm sorry, Mrs. Jurgens, I'm just not able to talk about my posting."

"Oh, that's ok, dear, I understand! The world being the way it is today and all, I'm sure all our military is on alert at all times."

Angela smiled. "You could say that, yes."

Jan and Chrystal approached them, Jan smiling and reached out to Rachel. "Rachel! So, glad you could make it!" The women hugged and Jan introduced Chrystal. "So, Angel, you seen Brandon around?"

"He's here," said Rachel. "Just not sure where that boy is."

"Oh, look, there he is," Angela said, pointing past the hula stage.

Jan, Rachel, and Chrystal looked to where she pointed. Jan said, "Now's your chance to show him how good a lady the navy's turned you into."

"Mom, please!" Angela replied, rolling her eyes.

Brandon Jurgens and another young man joined the three women. Brandon and Angela had been schoolmates since kindergarten. She didn't know the other man. Angela gave Brandon a big hug. "So good to see you!" she said happily.

"Same here," Brandon replied. "Hey, Angela, this is my friend, Theo."

"Hi," said Theo, extending his hand.

Angela shook his hand, as did Jan.

Jan said, "So, Brandon, Angela's home for a while before her next posting, maybe a chance for you two to finally go out?"

Angela smiled and shook her head. "Not happening, Mom."

"Well, why not?" Jan asked. "You don't have a boyfriend that you haven't told me about, do you?"

"I'm not the one with a *boyfriend*, Mom."

Jan and her daughter exchanged glances, then Jan looked at Brandon who was holding Theo's hand. "Oh, well, now I understand..."

"Oh, my, that's nice," TJ said stepping from the deep end of the pool into the shallow.

"I'll say," said a young man, watching her walk toward the steps to get out.

TJ winked at him and smiled. She saw Sarge and Freeman approaching the pool. "Hiya, Sarge," she said in her perfect friendly bartender voice.

"Hiya yerself, TJ," Sarge replied. "Lookin' good there, kiddo."

At the top of the steps TJ reached for a towel on the service table. "Gotta, if I want those tips."

Freeman whispered to Sarge as they walked past TJ and alongside the pool. "Isn't she the girl from that bar?"

"She's the bartender at the Recovery Room, and always has a bourbon ready for me when I go in!"

"Ah."

"And she's Mr. Jason's cousin."

"Yep, I remember now."

Mark and Jesse arrived at their sides, still talking about the cars in the garage. "Sarge, Freeman, I'd like you to meet an incredible young lady. Jesse, this is Sarge Brunson and Sandra

Freeman, they work in my security department. This is Jesse Lexington, probably the youngest car expert I have ever met. You need work done on your wheels; I'd say give this lady a shot at it first."

"Mr. Jason, you're too kind," said Jesse, smiling.

"He's a good judge of people, Miss Lexington," said Sarge. "Mark Jason doesn't recommend anyone lightly…"

CHAPTER 28

TO VISIT OR NOT TO VISIT, THAT IS THE QUESTION

MARK AND TOM WERE DISCUSSING TASK FORCE DIVISION REPORTS in Tom's office, one of the necessary boring details of a government agency, especially one which operated basically off-book from the Federal budget. Ever since Mark joined, his business acumen helped make budget control within the department better than ever.

"This is such a pain in the ass," Tom said under his breath. "Every year it gets more and more complicated."

"Sounds like someone is starting to consider retiring," Mark said just as quietly.

"Yeah, right, and just who would want my job? You?"

"Nah, I've already got several thousand people on one payroll, I don't need to add more."

"It would be a perfect fit, though," said Tom, "considering just how much your company has been tied to this department over the years."

Mark removed his bifocals, set his papers in his lap, and looked at Tom. "I've been noticing that for some time now, Tom. Just how long has my company been linked so close to Task Force?"

Tom's assistant entered without knocking and handed him a report folder. Tom opened the report and smiled. "Ah, thank you, Barbara—just what I've been waiting for." She left as silently as she entered.

"Mark, that's actually a story for another time. I've been waiting for this report to be finalized and it's a little more urgent." Tom handed Mark the folder. "Your ol' pal, President Komiani of Ollistan."

Mark took the folder and opened it. "Of course, an old friend. We were both fighting on the same side in the mid-east a long time ago, but what now?" Mark put his glasses on again and read aloud parts of the document. "Allegedly associated with al-Qaida— purportedly a bankroller and arms supplier—no solid evidence to support the accusations—never left his country since becoming its president." Mark looked up at Tom. "What the hell? How did all these reports come about? He's been a friend—people change, but it's really hard to believe *he* would, Tom. Not like this. I've been friends with him for years."

"He's leaving his country for the first time since becoming president, Mark. If you're a president of a country, you make plans way in advance; six months to a year even. When we were informed, we started looking into things. This is what we found."

"So, probably got tired of the heat and the sand—needed to get away for a while."

Tom leaned back in his chair. "Our Chief Executive agreed to have him come here, in a display of mutual cooperation, to talk about combatting terrorism."

"So, what does this have to do with us?"

"President Komiani has requested extremely *advanced* technical advice and assistance with his government's security systems and such. He specifically requested *you*, it seems."

"Very nice," Mark said dryly. He sat back, not happy with the conversation that was to follow. "And as much as I would love to crack a bottle with an old comrade, why would I?" Mark tossed the folder back onto Tom's desk, papers spilling from the folder. "I, the president of a well-respected international corporation, meet with your so-called suspected *terrorist sympathizer*? Really, Tom? Come on."

"Because the meeting will be in his embassy compound, here outside Washington in a week. If anyone can find out where to get the proof in his compound, and what he's up to, it would be the man who killed the enemy with him on the front lines. FBI, Secret Service, all the others, they got their orders today, too, and they're working to get ready for the visit. Trust me, the State Department is *not* happy with his plan to visit with you before he manages to fit the White House into his busy schedule…"

CHAPTER 29

THE SECRET OF THE SPY

Al was closing the Recovery Room for the night. TJ and the staff had already departed, and he sat alone in his office preparing the bank deposit for the next morning. Friday nights were always the best financially, thanks to Sarge Brunson and Roger "Dodger" Ahrens and their weekly drink fest.

He sensed he was not alone. Without looking up from his desk, Al spoke gently, "Been wondering when you'd show up."

The Spy stepped from the shadows of the hallway and into the office. "You still got it," said the electronically altered voice. "No one else could have heard me."

"As one special agent to another, I can't figure out how you just appear and disappear like that. Trade secrets, I understand." He looked at Spy's holster. "Ah, that's the new quick-release I've heard about. What's your draw speed?"

"One second."

"And fire precision?"

"100% on first-fire."

"May I?" Al asked, extending one hand. "And take that damned black computer mask off, it gives me the creeps. You look like an evil Spider-Man or something. And what are you doing out dressed like that anyway?"

"Oh, you know me, I have missions. I just finished one and thought I'd stop by." Spy detached the mask from his head before reaching for his belt buckle. He released the locks and handed over his utility belt. Al looked at the .45 held securely by the steel spring clips. "And what's the new gizmo that keeps someone from removing the gun from the slat? Is it what I'm hoping it is?"

"Go ahead, try to remove it."

Al tugged at the gun, yet the weapon stayed rigidly attached. Mark stepped forward, waved his gloved hand over the weapon and the springs clicked open. "Biometric sensors. The slat is programmed to recognize the owner only. Same goes with all the equipment pouches along the circumference, for either opening or removing them."

"Glad I was able to pass on useful suggestions."

"To ignore wisdom breeds ignorance," Mark said. "Our tech department just needed to work out the sensor system."

Al smiled wide returning the gun and belt back to its owner. "All the surveillance equipment you had installed still working okay?"

"Yeah, IT stuff's working fine. We've picked up a terrorist and al-Qaida sympathizer or two, thanks to your cooperation." Mark sat in the second chair in the small office. "Just wanna chat about something in your area of expertise. What do you know about Komiani?"

Al sat back in his chair and took a deep breath. "Since he became president of his country? Well, in this business you hear all sorts of things." Al reached behind him and retrieved two beers from the small refrigerator he kept in the office, handing one to Mark. "I hear he's different from the guy you fought alongside in the Far East years ago. Yet, very much the same in many respects. He seems solid with honor, whether he's dealing with freedom fighters or terrorists. If he's treated with respect and honor, he reciprocates fully in kind. Cross him in the slightest, and he'll destroy you completely. Then go after everyone you know. Not so bad in my opinion. But his son, on the other hand, is a true sexual deviant. Hates the women in his own country, wants only western women because of our sexual freedoms in films and society."

"How about something that's *not* in the official records."

"Well, there was an old rumor of an upcoming coup, first by cyber means, then by armed or military forces. If his opponents can hack his systems and take away control of his armaments, the revolutionary forces can take over his capitol without resistance. But, I dunno, his opponent's a dangerous man. Give him a nuke and he'll use it. Komiani, on the other hand, is at least the devil you know. As long as it's in his best interest, he won't press his 'red button'."

There was a light crash of glass from the bar area. Both men sat straight and listened. "Hum, sounds like someone's trying to break in," said Al calmly. He reached into his desk drawer and retrieved a 9mm Sig Sauer. "Not a problem."

Mark grabbed his gun belt and clipped it around his waist, then placed the hood over his head, attaching the collar. "I'll take a look. Stay here, Al." Spy disappeared into the shadows outside Al's office.

Al spoke aloud. "That person has no idea the ass-whooping he's about to get…"

The young thief reached in through the broken glass to unlock the door. He tiptoed behind the bar to the cash register but found it open and empty. "Well, damn," he said.

A large, black-gloved hand grabbed the young man's shirt front and spun him around. The thief stared at the ebony mask; his pulse quickened at being caught. His deep voice spoke, "You picked the wrong place to rob." Spy lifted the man into the air and slammed him onto the countertop, then stepped out to the sidewalk, still holding the would-be thief by one hand. The thief's eyes darted to the side, noticing a man on the sidewalk. "Help!"

The agent gazed in the same direction, in time to see a large fist rocketing toward his face. He ducked, his movement causing him to release the thief. Spy instinctively backed away.

It was Sarge Brunson. Both hands rolled into massive fists. The thief was already on his feet and starting to run. Spy raised a forefinger to Sarge, "Hold off pummeling me for just one moment, if you don't mind."

Sarge, caught off-guard at his masked opponent's polite request, stopped in mid-swing. Spy reached into a pouch on his belt, removed its contents, and flung his arm tennis-backhand style toward the escaping thief. The pouch content hit the man in the back, exploded, and covered him in a rapidly expanding plastic that solidified within seconds. It rendered the man into a near human statue before he reached the end of the block. Falling to the ground, he was unable to fight against the coagulating substance, with only his head and uncovered arms free of the element.

Spy turned to Sarge, "Special expanding mixture that solidifies on clothing but not human tissue. Now, where were we? Oh, right. Your turn."

"I dunno who you are or what this is all 'bout, but you ain't goin' nowhere until the cops get here." Sarge lunged at the agent.

Spy, as Mark Jason, had sparred enough with Sarge in the Jason Enterprises gym that he knew almost every defensive move the retired army sergeant would make. Spy also knew Sarge would recognize any move Mark had ever made. He needed to react completely different in order to not be recognized.

Sarge swung his arms down for a double-shoulder crush. Spy dropped into a deep crouch and rolled under Sarge's feet; the momentum sent him into a collision with the frame of the bar's window. The sergeant quickly recovered, and the black figure was ready.

Sarge armed himself, pulling a military .45 automatic from a belt holster at the small of his back.

"SARGE! STOP!" a voice yelled.

Spy turned his head toward the voice. Sarge took the opportunity to slam his huge fist into the back of Spy's head.

Sometime later Spy opened his eyes, realizing he wasn't looking through the black, computerized lenses of his mask. His vision blurred in and out. Sarge was bent forward above him, hands on his knees. Al was standing beside him, next to the bar.

"Mr. Jason, just what the hell are you doing dressed like that?" Sarge asked.

Mark held the icepack to the back of his head, finishing his tale to Sarge of how he was recruited to take over the Task Force field team. He explained the murder of his predecessor, taken out by Richmond's Biblical Bomber, years earlier.

"Well, most of that long story now explains why you had your balcony turned into a private computerized office."

Mark grimaced in pain, trying to sit forward, "Well, so now you know the secret of my frequent international trips. I could order you to keep silent—"

Sarge stood at attention and saluted, almost comically. "I will never compromise my commanding officer, sir!"

Mark smiled, shaking his head. "As you were, Sergeant. We're not active duty anymore, you know."

"It's only that I want to say you can count on me any time, sir."

Mark stood and extended his hand, which Sarge accepted. "Glad to have you on my side, Sarge."

"Just one thing sir," Sarge said as his face scrunched into a scowl, "I don't have to wear one of those sissy black outfits, do I?"

Al burst out laughing. Mark and Sarge stared at him. "Sorry boys, just the thought of Sarge Brunson *squeezing* himself into a Task Force uniform—oh, I'd pay to see that!" He poured three shots of bourbon and set them on the bar.

Sarge growled, quickly downing his shot…

CHAPTER 30

SMILE, YOU'RE ON CANDID CAMERA

Negotiations for the visit had only been a few weeks in the making. White House and State Department staff, even the president, tried in vain to persuade Komiani to stay at the White House. In fact, President Komiani wanted nothing to do with the American president. He did, however, stay firm in his wish to see his old comrade-in-arms, Mark Jason.

Mark's limousine came to a stop near the main entrance of the Ollistani Embassy in Richmond. A line was painted on the concrete entrance with the words *STOP HERE*. Freeman stopped precisely on the line a few yards from the embassy guard post. Two guards stepped out, suspicious of the large limo with blackened windows.

"Stay calm," Mark said to those in the vehicle. Jan, Sarge, and Freeman accompanied him, both for security and a proper appearance. "No one moves unless I order it, understood? And remember what I told you to say?" Everyone nodded. "Besides, we don't want to alert all the Secret Service and FBI agents hiding around the neighborhood." He pressed the button on his armrest and the darkened window lowered.

One of the uniformed guards stopped at the window, his AK-47 pointed at Mark while he surveyed the other occupants. In a Middle Eastern accent, the guard spoke. "Open your vehicle doors to be searched, everyone out, now!"

"Mark," Jan whispered, "they were supposed to be aware we were coming. Why are they acting like this?"

Mark opened the car door and stepped out. At six feet tall, Mark towered over the shorter embassy guard. His black Dolce & Gabbana suit helped hide his muscular frame and the black sunglasses hid his eyes. The guard took a few steps backward, his weapon still pointed at Mark but within arm's reach. The guard was young and wiry, in his mid-twenties.

"We're here at the invitation of your president. So, you care to try that greeting again?" Mark took one step forward in a willful act of defiance.

The guard growled, "American! You dare speak to me that way?" he said, raised his gun as if readying to fire.

The second guard watched as Mark disarmed the first guard with lightning speed. He flung the weapon into the bushes while forcing the guard to the ground with his free hand, applying pressure to his neck. Sarge and Freeman itched to jump out of the car, but Mark had ordered them to remain in place unless called.

The second guard grabbed his own AK-47 from the guard shack, but Mark was gone. Surprised, the guard made his way to the rear of the limousine, then stopped when the cold steel of a gun touched the back of his neck. The guard closed his eyes, knowing he'd been duped.

Mark had a mini revolver 22LR pointed at the guard's neck. The hidden miniature gun was spring-loaded so it could vault from his sleeve into Mark's hand. It wasn't effective in a gunfight, but handy to prevent one. "Consider your next action carefully, son."

The guard dropped his weapon and raised his arms into the air. Mark backed away, the right-hand 22LR sprang back into place.

"Slowly turn around, go call your boss and tell him Mark Jason is here for our appointment, the one for which I'm now ten minutes late."

The guard looked up at Mark, then down at his unconscious partner, knowing he'd be punished for failing to carry out his duties. He began to step into the guard shack to call inside the embassy, but stopped short when he saw President Komiani standing a few feet away, along with the Ollistani ambassador.

Komiani began to applaud and grinned. "Mark Jason! Nice to see you haven't lost your touch!" He stepped forward to shake Mark's hand.

"I promote physical fitness for all JE employees. But you might teach your boys a little international courtesy. And, um," he said as he pointed to the now-wobbly guard, "he may need a little help." He removed his sunglasses and tucked them in his breast pocket.

"I observed," said Komiani. "You *did* warn him, and they had been advised of your visit. They have learned a valuable lesson, yes?" The Ollistani president stood in sharp contrast to Mark, with his thick black hair brushed across his forehead, hawk nose, tan skin, and thick black eyebrows. He was slender but fit, and wore a dark gray Armani suit. "I should hire you to train all my staff."

"You can't afford me," Mark replied, absolutely straight-faced.

"Indeed!" Komiani said. He motioned for Mark to walk beside him to the gate. "Well, obviously, your military training has not diminished since becoming an office worker." When they entered the gate, several loud alarms sounded. The two guards had not silenced them. A dozen guards ran forward and surrounded the men, weapons drawn. Komiani whispered, "Now, time for a moment of formality if you don't mind, my old friend." He took a deep breath and squared his shoulders to produce his best presidential pose. "You have those trick guns up your sleeves. Any other items you wish to declare, Mister Jason?"

Mark flexed his shoulder and torso muscles and looked at Komiani with a cold stare. "Sir, I have 22LRs up both sleeves, a Beretta in a shoulder holster, and a Ka-bar in my right boot. I carry a GPS tracker on my belt, and my company cell phone. I either walk in like this or I walk out, makes no difference. If anyone tries to disarm me, well, I hope you have a large infirmary, or morgue."

Komiani gave Mark a serious stare for several seconds. A small grin formed on his face, followed by boisterous laughter. "You still have balls, Jason! I love it! You stand your ground like a true soldier as always, not some pompous politician who wants to kiss my ass. You would just as soon try to kick my ass anyway, for the fun of it. Come!" He turned to his staff. "This man is a friend of Ollistan and my personal friend. He will be treated as Ollistani royalty!" He took Mark's right hand and shook it vigorously.

Mark looked back at his car, "Um, you probably don't want my limo blocking your embassy entrance," he said.

"Your driver may park to the left of the guard house and wait in our guest lounge while we conduct our business. My promise, he will be treated as a guest."

"Actually, it's a 'she', and I've brought a few special guests. Hope you don't mind." Mark turned to the limo and motioned them where to park. The passengers lined up beside the car as Mark led Komiani forward for introductions.

"May I introduce Ollistan President Moham Komiani." As one, Mark's staff politely nodded in acknowledgement. "Mr. President, may I present three of my most important employees." Mark waved to Jan, the first in line. "This is my wife, Janice Churchill Jason. She is the mother of my warrior daughter and Executive Vice-President of my company."

"'Warrior daughter', Mark?"

"Yes, sir, Navy."

The President shook his head in disbelief. "A woman, in the military. And your wife, so high in your administration. That is unheard of in my country. Hum, please continue, Mark, but let us be informal here today. I'm happy to see you again, and I welcome your staff." Komiani watched Jan's waist-length red hair drift about in the light breeze. "You are as beautiful as Mark has described," he said. "How did you come to be so prominent at Jason Enterprises?"

Jan smiled as she replied, "I obeyed my husband's every instruction, of course, Mister President." Mark grinned.

Komiani stared at her for a moment in mock indignation, before laughing. "He always told me you were an ice-breaker!" He held his arms out, inviting her for an embrace. "You are always as welcome here as your husband."

Jan accepted his invitation and they hugged. "And you're even more handsome than Mark told me you were. I see why he kept that secret from me," she teased.

"That's Mark for you, never wants to admit anyone is more handsome than he!" Komiani released his hold on her, and Jan stepped back into line.

Mark took two steps. "This is Sergeant Brunson, my personal bodyguard and Chief of Security."

Komiani looked up into Sarge's eyes. "That Mark Jason would ever need a bodyguard surprises me. At least he has someone like you to protect him. Tell me, Sergeant, how many have you killed?"

Sarge looked down at Komiani. "What date, sir?"

Komiani laughed again, then slapped Mark's back. "Quick on their feet, aren't they?"

"That's the way I like them," Mark said. "This is Sandra Freeman, Chief of International Information and Analysis and second in charge of security."

Komiani looked at the tall slender Freeman. "You don't strike me as a warrior, you're such a tiny thing," he mused.

Freeman said, "I'm free to demonstrate, anytime you want, sir."

Komiani chuckled. He said to Mark, "You always said you were bringing in the best people when you took over your father's company. I never thought they'd be comedians."

"I permit an atmosphere of levity as long as the work gets done."

"You are a work, Jason," said Komiani. "Come, you and your lovely wife may join me. The others will be escorted to our lounge. They will be safe; you have my guarantee."

Mark walked beside Komiani, with Jan following. The Ollistani president guided them through the embassy's main hallway, showing off pictures of his country, paintings, sculptures, and tapestries, until they reached his private office at the far end.

Along the way, Mark noted each security camera, armed guard station, infrared motion detectors, taking in their locations as he made a pretense of studying the artwork. The hidden camera in the hinge of his exposed eyeglass wing recorded everything in sight as he walked, and his computerized contact lenses recorded everything in viewing range as a backup. He also noted one door with a guard standing in front of it, rather than beside it, located across the hall from Komiani's office.

The President's office was richly decorated, with adorned sculptures containing precious metals and jewels. Italian hand-carved furniture covered in expensive crushed velvets, and an Alabaster chandelier hung in the middle of the room. Guards stood at each corner of the overly grand office. Female servants were dressed in beautiful sheer, ornate floor-length dresses that did little to hide their bodies. Scarves covered their heads. They stood ready at the bar and buffet. When they all sat, Komiani snapped his fingers at the bar staff. "Jason, you're still a bourbon man, yes?"

"Good memory. A gin and tonic for my wife, please."

The servants nodded and prepared the drinks, as well as one for Komiani. "My wives, always concerned about my health, told me to add wheat to my diet, so I found your Bernheim whiskey. I love it!"

"Somehow, I don't think that's exactly the wheat they had in mind," Mark said.

"They weren't more specific!" Komiani replied, laughing.

The servants approached with drinks for the trio. A short female handed Mark his drink and whispered, "Do you know how hard it is to hide weapons in an outfit like this? Never mind the full-body makeup." Proteus bowed to Mark and returned to her position at the bar.

"So, Jason, there is a reason I wanted to meet with you. What can you do for my country's security systems, and such, to make them impenetrable? There's more than just security, mind you. Not just here, but back in my homeland as well. My palace, and all my outposts, places throughout my lands."

Mark rubbed his beard as if searching for an answer. "First, you read The Washington Post every day, correct? This morning you had a classic southern American breakfast of scrambled eggs, wheat toast, and grits. You really should try the bacon one day." Komiani's mouth dropped in surprise. Mark gave Proteus an imperceptible nod for the information.

Komiani roared in surprise, his hands slapping his legs. "Jason, how in hell did you know that?"

"Just showing you're not secure at all. You made it all the way here for your first visit, checked in and got settled into your embassy. Your son and his staff flew to the Richmond embassy before continuing on to Charleston. You left Washington at 4:37 a.m. and arrived here at 6:02 a.m. with CIA and FBI escorts, as well as your own staff." Mark took a sip of his bourbon before continuing. "You took a shower and changed suits, had a cup of your own country's wonderful coffee before ordering breakfast. One of your guards was caught fondling a servant half an hour before we arrived."

"Amazing," Komiani said as he sat back in his chair. "It was as though you had a spy in here behind my back!" He looked at all his guards and his ambassador, wondering if any of them were traitors.

"Oh, I can promise you, old friend, you definitely don't have a Spy behind you," Mark said. He noticed Jan trying not to smile. "But, I wanted to show just how easy it is for someone to get all the intel they want on you, if they tried."

"So how did you do it?" Komiani asked.

"Ancient Chinese Secret," Mark replied. Komiani's brow furrowed in confusion. "Sorry, old American joke. It's like this, if you want me to fix your problem, I have to show you how big your problem is. Now, it's a problem if the government did what I did, it's another thing between friends, especially one who saved your life on the battlefield."

Komiani nodded. "This is true, Jason. And you did say if I ever needed your help to just ask. Thank you for demonstrating the flaws in our security. I realized it was bad, but not this bad. Name your price, I'll pay it."

Mark said, "That's why Jan's here. She's also my Chief Financial Officer. She speaks for me in these matters." The ambassador's expression showed he was insulted that he would be negotiating with a female. "I trust my condition is accepted, Mister President? Jan will consult with you on this?"

"But of course, Mark," said Komiani. He said to his men, "Janice Jason has my permission to speak freely. No one will interrupt. Understand?

Everyone nodded in agreement. The Ambassador muttered something, eliciting harsh stares from both Komiani and Mark.

Komiani rose from his chair and offered his hand to Jan. "Now, shall we begin negotiations?"

"I'd be honored, Mister President," Jan said, accepting his hand.

"And *I* will invite myself to more of your bourbon," Mark said. He rose and stepped to the bar while Komiani and Jan moved to a conference table on the other side of the buffet. "You," he said to the disguised Proteus, "attend me."

"Yes, Mr. Jason."

Servants began plating fruits and vegetables for the conference and the second bar server approached the table to freshen Komiani and Jan's drinks. "Good job, Pro," Mark said softly to the Task Force agent.

"I'll be glad when this job is over," Proteus whispered, helping him with a fresh drink. "I've only been in here two days with these guys. All they've been doing is ogling or pinching my ass. It's all I've been able to do to stop them from full-out molesting me. And you, sir, sounded just like an Ollistani."

"Thank you, I think. Any of them succeed?" he asked, deeply concerned.

"No, the other women help me out. I'm new here and I look young. The men tell me I'll have a long line waiting when the time is right. Pigs. They're even accustomed to being serviced by children in their country."

She used tongs to put ice cubes in his drink, and a fresh napkin under the glass, placing it in his open hand. "The roof key is in the napkin. I'll wait for your signal. When do you move?"

"Tomorrow night."

"Okay, boss, one more night of fondling for the country and that's it." Proteus bowed to Mark and turned back to her servant-waiting stance.

"Thank you," he said loud enough to be heard before joining Jan and Komiani at the conference table. "What I'd love now is popcorn while my wife makes the mighty President Komiani empty his bank account for her..."

CHAPTER 31

DESSERT FOR LUNCH

IT WAS AN UNUSUAL DAY WHEN SARGE WASN'T in his office at Jason Enterprises, let alone stop by the Recovery Room any day besides Friday. However, now he was part of Mark's inner circle of Task Force confidants. His newest duty was to check in with Al on a weekly basis to pass on confidential information or surveillance and do routine systems checks on the bar's security system.

The bar was empty of any patrons. Sarge sat in his usual seat at the bar, sipping a cup of coffee. "Got a good one last night," Al said, handing Sarge a flash drive. "Two non-regulars stopped in. They took a corner table, right under a camera, and talked about what sounded like plans for a shooting spree."

"They say when?" Sarge asked.

"Friday," Al replied. "Details are in the video. Ya think this one's worth the team's time?"

"Nah, I'll send it on through my new channels to the Feds. Let 'em get some good press for stopping one of these dirt bags in advance for a change." He inserted the drive into a port on a newly developed Task Force phone, and uploaded the file to the Task Force

Division, with instructions for the security team. When finished, he returned the drive to Al.

Al smiled. "Otherwise, been kinda quiet. That Komiani kid though, he was a piece of work when he came in here. Tried hitting up all my staff, and when that didn't work, he tried some of the lady patrons. If looks could've killed, that kid'd be twenty feet under today." He chuckled. "It was all everyone could do to keep their seats. And his bodyguards were more than obvious. Hear tell he took off for someplace in South Carolina; wonder how their Southern Hospitality will put up with him there!"

"So, you've known the boss for a while, Al. How long've you known he dressed up like a crazy ass secret agent with this Task Force group?"

Al took the towel from over his shoulder and began polishing a bar glass. "Oh, it was before the Biblical Bomber case came to an end, he came in here afterward. He had some personal issues about killing that psycho and his brother, leaving their handicapped sister all alone. It's hard takin' out a kid. And besides, you can talk to your bartender about anything."

"Didn't think you were a shrink, too, Al."

"There's a lot you don't know about me, Sarge," Al replied with a big smile, his large bushy moustache spread wide. "He'd been okay with it for a while, but it ate at him a little. Jan told him to talk to someone about it, though I'm sure she meant someone at T.F. medical. Nope, when ya gotta talk, ya talk to the man who fills your glass!" He leaned over the bar at Sarge. "But I already knew."

"Ya' did?"

"Yeah. Black suit types interviewed me and TJ about his personality and stuff long before he was selected and recruited. Never said why they were asking, but guys like me, we know what's up."

"What ya mean, 'guys like you'?"

Al stopped wiping down the glasses and looked at Sarge. "What security level are you in Task Force?"

Sarge thought for a second. "Five, I think."

"When you reach nine, ask me again." Al winked and stepped away to place the glass on its shelf. Sarge stared at him, baffled.

His surprise increased when Freeman entered the bar. "Isn't it a little early to be hitting the sauce, sir?" she teased.

"I ain't no—"

"'Sir', I got it." She sat on a stool beside him.

"Wow, must be a light day at the Jason building. What'll it be, Freeman?" TJ asked.

"Coffee, black," she replied. TJ poured a cup and stepped away to do other work. "What are you doing down here?"

Sarge squinted at her and grumbled something inaudible. "My job, Freeman. Doing my job." He took a sip of coffee. "How'd you find me?"

"Your phone GPS." She took a sip of her own coffee. "So, what aspect of your job are you doing, sir?"

"Security. As always." He looked at her, then stared down at the coffee cup. *Dammit, forgot to adjust the location function on the phone after that upload,* he thought.

"This place needs Jason Enterprises security?"

"Somethin' like that."

"Ah."

They sat in awkward silence.

TJ came back to them. "Doin' ok, guys?"

"Yup," Sarge said.

"Okay, love, just tell me if you need anything."

A man in his early to-mid-thirties entered the bar, a guitar case in one hand and a large canvas bag in the other. Al called from the other side of the room. "Hey, Jimbo, you giving us some background today?"

"Yeah," said the young man. "Got a few new numbers I wanna try. I hope it will be a good night for it."

"It'll start to pick up around one or so. I'll get TJ to get a couple meals together for ya today."

"Yer on," said Jimbo. He moved a table and chair set away from the front window to begin making his stage for his performance later in the day.

"Got anything romantic, Jim?" Sarge growled, looking at the musician's reflection in the large wall mirror behind the bar. Freeman raised an eyebrow at him.

"You?" said the musician with a slight chuckle. "Romantic?"

"'S'what I said, Jim."

"Don't call me 'Jim', sir," Jimbo deadpanned. Freeman realized this was another one of Sarge's conversational routines.

"Is there anyone who doesn't know your hang-up about being called 'sir'?" Freeman asked.

"I got something good for ya, pal," said Jimbo. He stopped setting up his impromptu stage, took the guitar out of its case, and began playing *I Only Have Eyes for You.*

Freeman looked at Sarge. "Don't get any ideas, mister. We're on the clock."

Sarge looked at his watch. The time was 12:15. "TJ, a couple bourbons in a hurry?" The young bartender came back and poured the couple a tumbler of bourbon each. Sarge raised his drink to Freeman. "Cheers, Freeman."

She picked up her glass and clinked it against his. "Cheers, Sarge."

They again sat in silence.

"So, you guys busy today?" he asked.

"Just S.O.P., nothing special. Even the 14th floor is quiet today." She lifted her glass, contemplating taking another sip.

Sarge downed his drink. "Hey Freeman, did you know Al's got a small apartment with a bed upstairs?"

She sprayed out a sip of her drink in surprise. "No, I didn't know. Why would I want to?"

"He sometimes rents it out to guys just coming back from overseas. It's empty right now. All clean and tidy, just like home."

The bourbon was calming, as were her inhibitions. "So?"

Without any inflection in his voice, he replied, "So ya wanna go have an afternoon quickie?"

She looked at him wide-eyed, smiled, and drank down the rest of her drink. "Lead the way, *sir*…"

CHAPTER 32

THE BLACK WIDOW LURE

THE DUAL-LEVEL BAR AND LOUNGE WAS comfortable and elegant. The main area contained a large extravagant dark walnut bar, curved in a U-shape, and polished to a mirror shine. The room allowed for private seating and several round swivel-stools, which made for easy conversation. The upstairs offered a more private seating area with a balcony, a smaller bar also made of walnut. It was furnished with cool-gray cushioned leather chairs and drink table combinations in the center. There were recessed natural-gas fireplaces, used more for ambiance than heat. The walls were covered in dark blue-gray fabric, topped by light-blue track lighting along the ceiling's edge. Canned lights glowed dim on both levels, creating a relaxed and serene atmosphere.

Two women, dressed in stunning black attire, sat at the bar. Lexi sipped happily on a Bloody Mary, Lacy had a Black Widow. "Tell me again," said Lacy, "about this 'aressess' thing that led you to him."

"That's RSS," Lexi smiled at Lacy's lack of computer terminology. "It's a simple way to find information online without spending hours and days doing manual searching. Richard doesn't seem to have an online presence of any kind, but I managed to get a hit on him and that's how I got his phone number. I gave him the class reunion story and he said he'd be glad to meet us here. Sounded almost, well, peaceful on the phone." She took a sip of her drink. "It's unusual for someone to have almost no online footprint somewhere."

"Is that a bad thing?" Lacy asked.

"Not really. It means he's got better things to do with his life besides talk about what he had for dinner on all the social network pages. There's a lot of people who aren't online these days."

Lacy took a drink of her Black Widow. "Frankly, I couldn't care less. If you found him and he agreed to come, that's all that matters. Tonight's his last night on earth anyway. If he's not online, fewer people will miss his pathetic ass." Lacy lifted her glass to Lexi in a toast. "I'm halfway to vengeance, love."

"Yep, I guess you are," Lexi hesitantly toasted back, dreading another death. She didn't like the killings, but she'd been with Lacy so long and loved her to the point where she'd do anything for her, even murder.

An hour passed, and both of them ordered another drink. From her angle, Lexi stared at a well-dressed man, middle eastern in appearance, who entered the room. Several similar-looking men trailed behind and walked to the upper level. A waitress followed to take their orders. The waitress watched in surprise as the men separated, taking seats in different places. Yursi Komiani, who looked like a perfect youthful version of his father, sat near the balcony so he could look down to watch women as they came and went. He spotted the two women at the bar.

Lacy looked at her watch. "Where is he? He's late, dammit."

"I dunno, honey, maybe caught in traffic," said Lexi.

Lexi looked at her phone. "Well, shit, I had my sound off and missed a text from him." She showed Lacy the screen on her smartphone: "Sorry. Can't make it 2 night. Have rites 2 do. Another night?"

"Son-of-a-bitch!" Lacy said, a little louder than was appropriate. Lexi motioned to keep her voice down. "What's he mean 'have rites 2 do'? What kind of text is that? He's going to do some writing tonight instead of coming to get killed?"

Lexi saw the bartender glance at them. She said with a big smile, "We're actors, just trying some character dialogue—don't mind us! How 'bout a couple more?" She lifted her glass and rocked it like a bell, then turned to Lacy when he began preparing two more drinks. She whispered angrily, "Will you keep your freekin' voice down? Get a grip on yourself before your mouth gets us arrested!"

Lacy glared at Lexi. In an instant, her anger subsided. "You're right, hon. I'm just—I'm so pumped to do him my way this time and end him." She lowered her head in resignation.

"It's been all these years; he can wait a little longer. And, we can reach him, again?"

"Well, duh, I got his phone number, didn't I?"

"I need more. Find out what he writes about—maybe he's a murder-mystery writer and we can use his own ideas against him."

Lexi smiled. "That almost sounds like fun. And, the Widow Web I built for you is already upstairs, waiting for a victim who's not coming'." Lexi's eyes followed two of the dark-skinned men descending the stairs, taking a seat at the far end of the curved bar. "Hey, babe, check out the hotties who just sat down," she whispered.

"Pfff, not interested."

"Sweetie, one day you're gonna want a man to truly love you."

"Not while I have you."

Lexi blushed. "And I love you back."

Someone touched their shoulders lightly. "Ladies," said an exotic voice from behind. "May I make an order to freshen your drinks?" They swiveled around to face a handsome man, the one who led his followers into the bar earlier.

"Thanks, we already have 'em ordered," Lexi said, before Lacy could say a word.

"Bartender?" Yursi said loudly. Lexi shivered at the sound of his accent, enjoying it tremendously. "Put their drinks on my tab for the night. And bring one each of whatever they're drinking."

"Thank you, but—" Lacy objected.

"No, I insist. Two such beautiful visions alone on a lovely night? I don't know about the rest of the world, but I still believe in chivalry."

Lexi smiled, attentive and stimulated by the stranger. "Um, thank you—?"

"Yursi," he said, smiling. His teeth were straight and bright, enhanced by his tan-colored skin. The uninvited touch on their shoulders caught them both by surprise, and his hands began to slide up and down the women's arms. "Yursi Komiani. My friends call me Yursi. You may call me," he said as he leaned close to Lexi's face, "anything you'd like."

"Hum—" Lexi blushed.

Lacy gulped the last of her drink. She shouted at the bartender, "Hurry with that refill! I'm needing a big one! Hey, Lexi, you two wanna take this conversation upstairs? You're making me wanna yack."

"Don't mind my girlfriend," Lexi said to Yursi. "She got stood up tonight."

"And," Yursi said as he gently advanced his hands up to the back of their necks, giving a gentle massage, "were you stood up, too?"

Lexi smiled. The effects of the alcohol had kicked in. "We were gonna be a threesome. I was supposed to be, um, the dessert." Her eyes widened, embarrassed, and spun away from Yursi. "Oh crap, I can't believe I said that! How many drinks have I had?"

Lacy said softly, with a hint of irritation, "Either too many or not enough, depending on how froggy you are." She took a large swig of her new drink.

Yursi turned his attention to the cold and indifferent Lacy, sliding his hand down her back, all the way to her butt. "That is a magnificent drink, my lovely. I've never seen one red on the bottom and black on top. What's it called?"

Lacy fumed at the man's arrogance, feeling him squeeze her left butt cheek. She gave him a pretentious, but polite smile. "Well, you see this red layer?" She asked, pointing a red fingernail at the bottom of the glass. "This is cranberry juice. This black layer on top is Blavod vodka. The vodka floats on top of the cranberry juice. Together, they're called a Black Widow."

Yursi laughed. "'Black Widow', you say? Are you telling me you bite like your drink? What about you, sexy lady," he said to Lexi, "what are you drinking?"

"A Bloody Mary?" Lexi said, not meaning to make it sound like a question, her voice raspy with excitement.

"Oh, my," he said excitedly, "you two have the most dangerous-sounding drinks! Would you care to join me and my fellows upstairs for some delicious conversation, and perhaps some, um, tasty dessert?"

Lacy looked at him with narrowed eyes. "Thanks, but we're gonna have a girl-on-girl night, if that's all the same to you."

"Oh, I would love to watch."

"Yeah, no," said Lacy. "She's the only one who gets to see my stuff tonight."

"What a shame," Yursi said in mock displeasure. "I would truly love to see you together. You are two magnificent creatures!"

"Flattery isn't getting you into my panties," Lacy said, tipsy herself, but trying to remain polite. "But I really appreciate the effort."

Yursi gave a dramatic sigh. "Well, you can't blame a guy for trying. Nonetheless, please allow me to pay for all your drinks this evening, for having a fun conversation."

Lexi grabbed his jacket lapel and pulled him to her, giving him a gentle kiss on his cheek. "Thank you for being so…chivalrous. Have a nice evening."

He nodded in genuine disappointment, then headed upstairs to rejoin his friends.

"What the hell is your problem?" Lacy hissed at Lexi. "You're acting like you want him!"

"Well, right now I actually *do* want someone!" Lexi said, downing her Bloody Mary. "Oh, my God, I've never met a man who made me feel like that. He oozed sex appeal! Don't you get it?"

"No. I'm just nauseous, watching you fawn over him like a whore," Lacy huffed.

"I gotta see what he's all about," Lexi said. She attempted to search for anything about him in the browser on her phone. "How the hell do you spell his name?"

"And I would know that how?" Lacy retorted sarcastically.

"Yeah, right." Lexi pressed the audio control on her phone. "Find 'Yer-see Comb-ee-ahn-nee." She waited while her phone's search engine translated her voice command into text and searched.

"He's probably another guy looking for a Friday night screw while his wife thinks he's bowling or some such shit," Lacy said, irritated.

A minute later Lexi gasped, "Oh, my God."

"Look, if you wanna get laid by him, go right ahead."

"No, look!" Lexi showed her the search results on her phone and smiled as Lacy's eyes widened and her mouth opened in surprise.

"Lexi—yes, he'd be a perfect Widow candidate! But, wait, he didn't do anything to me. No, he's *just* like all the others. But I'm really only after the four who raped me, I think, maybe not."

"Yeah," Lexi muttered. "And, he's most likely the same kinda guy as all your other bastard boyfriends. And here we are, all dressed to kill. Wait, no. I didn't say that."

Lacy raised her glass for another sip. "Dressed to kill. Yes! Dressed to kill! And you did build that Widow Web for tonight. No reason it couldn't be field-tested with someone who's as disgusting as Richard. Maybe it's the booze talking."

"Maybe it's the booze talking, and—?"

"You don't get what you really said? He's the perfect candidate to test the Widow Web. And, after all, the venom won't last forever." Lacy patted her handbag. She downed the last of her drink and took Lexi by the hand, leading her to the upper level.

Yursi saw them approach and stood, adjusted his suit coat, and smiled. "Did you change your minds, my lovelies? Come, join us!"

"Actually," Lacy cooed, feigning her seduction as much as possible. "We talked about it, and decided we wanted you to join us." She advanced, her body almost touching his. She didn't notice his men adjust their postures, placing hands on guns hidden under their jackets. "If you think you can handle two at once."

Yursi lifted his hands up to her shoulders and grasped them hard, pulling her to his chest. "I can handle you easily, 'Black Widow'. Do you think you can handle me?"

"My money's on Yursi," said one of the men at the back of the room.

Lacy gave Yursi a big smile, rubbing her leg against his. She noticed Lexi had found one of Yursi's men, and leisurely sat on a chair arm beside him. Lacy's hand reached for Yursi's groin and squeezed. "I think you're ready to show us what you got. Come up to room 308 in a few minutes. Give your big cannon a little time to settle down." She reached a hand around his neck and forced him down as she planted a hot, wet kiss on his lips. His security staff quietly laughed. She pulled back, looking down at the growing bulge in his pants, "We'll see *you* upstairs in a few minutes, Yursi. You better be ready for the best night you'll *never* have again." Lacy put her hand out to Lexi, and the two walked out of the lounge area.

"Yursi," asked one of his men, "how do you do that?"

"How about that, two American women at once!" He grabbed his groin area and smiled. "And yes, they are going to have the best sex play of their life. Don't wait up, this will be a long night."

Waiting for the elevator, Lexi said to Lacy, "Wow, you had me believing you really wanted him!"

Lacy smiled. "I want him, yes. We do need to test the Widow Web, after all. Why waste the opportunity? Just a quick word of advice. Be ready for a *big* time!

CHAPTER 33

THE BLACK WIDOW SPINS HER WEB

Yursi STEPPED OUT OF THE ELEVATOR, checked the long hotel corridor for other guests, then turned right and walked to room 308. He was thankful no one was out late as he wasn't comfortable without his security entourage.

He stood at the door, hesitating to knock. His normal demeanor was brash. Now, however, the excitement and adventure of two partners made him relax and let his guard down.

He tapped the door lightly. There was light movement in the peephole, then the door opened as far as the security chain would allow. Yursi looked inside and gave a confident half-smile. "Hello, it is I," he whispered in a calm, low accent.

The red-haired woman behind the door eyed him, saying nothing. She unlatched the chain and opened the door wide, gesturing for him to enter.

Yursi stepped into the room and stared at the beautiful nude redhead, who wore only black silk gloves, black stilettos, and a derisive smile. She placed the room's "Do Not Disturb" sign on the outside doorknob, closed the door, and secured the two locks.

In a deep baritone voice, he said happily, "I *do* like American women..."

"I definitely like American men better than European," Freeman said, running her fingers over Sarge's crew cut hair. "Especially American military men."

"Hum. I didn't think you were the kinda gal to have been around that much."

She kissed him gently; their energetic sexual romp had done an excellent job of purging the bourbon's effect on her mind. "What did you think 'undercover agent' means, anyway?"

He reached up and put his massive hand on the back of her head and pulled her face to his, kissing her hard and deep. Her hand moved down his torso. "Ready for another 'undercover mission', Miss Former Agent?"

CHAPTER 34

GUY TALK

Yursi's private security detail gathered in the hotel lounge while he was upstairs. "Did you see him? Shit, two women at the same time! How does he do that?"

"Haqqan, really!" another guard answered. "He's done it before. He says he's never been with two, but he has. Oh, you weren't with us then." The agent kicked back the last of his self-imposed drink limit. "The American women, they know he's aristocratic, exotic and rich. Someone of great importance. They like to believe his lies and he'll spend a lot of money on them. They don't care who he really is, and we keep it that way. He's *not* the president's son; he's simply a very wealthy businessman. If anything happened to Yursi, we'll be the ones without sons one day. If we even get another day!" They all nodded in agreement.

"Security detail for an over-active Romeo. Oh, well, one must take any job that comes along, right?"

A middle-aged, nicely dressed man approached. The security staff remained tentative. "Good evening gentlemen," the man started, one hand in the other. In a low voice he spoke, "Gentlemen, as you can see, we're getting ready to close, it's pretty late. It's way past closing time and I must allow my staff to leave.

But, under the circumstances, I can get the hotel manager's approval to stay open a little longer."

The lead security agent reached into his pocket and withdrew five one-hundred-dollar bills. He folded them twice, stuffed them into the nightclub manager's shirt pocket and patted it with his hand. "Yes, of course, we understand fully. Men, let us take our leave. We've over-extended our stay. Sir, thank you for your hospitality. We appreciate your kindness."

The group stood, taking a final sip from their drinks…

CHAPTER 35

RUB-A-DUB-DUB, A BLACK WIDOW IN THE TUB

YURSI STOOD STILL, taking in the beauty of the curvaceous young woman, alluring surroundings, fragrances; it was intoxicating. A hot tub in the corner of the room, jets bubbling, contained the other woman he'd met in the lobby. She, too, was nude, her creamy-white breasts visible amongst the bubbles.

Lexi sipped red wine while she sat in the bubbling water. She raised it toward him in a wordless, non-expressive salutation. She tried in vain to not let his exotic appearance make her heart flutter. Lexi looked forward to the next hour of being in his company.

Pillar candles were placed around the hot tub, the countertops, and bedside tables. There was no need for other lighting, and incense provided a relaxing scent.

"You both, you are too quiet, no? You do not speak? You chatted away downstairs."

Lacy chuckled, "No, Yursi, we definitely speak." He sensed a change in their attitude. Not the assertiveness he'd first seen in the lounge. He also wasn't accustomed to being referred to by his given name; such boldness wasn't allowed in his country. He felt a sudden aggressive bias toward the women. However, he remembered they were American, beautiful, and willing and needed to play along.

Yursi admired Lacy's nude body, watching her walk to the bar in the extravagant room. She removed one of many champagne bottles chilling in ice and held it up for her guest to see. "Bollinger, Blanc de Noirs?" Her gesture seemed kindly malevolent.

"Yes, I am familiar. France, about three-hundred and fifty dollars, American." He said, stepping closer to the seductive woman. "I own a vineyard there. Mine, however, costs one-thousand dollars a bottle."

Lacy stared into the man's eyes, never blinking. "It's not just what you drink, it's also about the glass from which you drink."

He cocked his head sideways, staring curiously at the hourglass symbol etched into the flutes. "Interesting. You are full of surprises, are you not?" He placed a tanned index finger on her neck and deliberately traced it downward between her breasts, onto her stomach, then stopped just below her navel. His brow creased, realizing there was a small tattoo above her shaved pubic area. "Now, why would a beautiful woman have a tattoo of a spider right there?" He looked up, staring into her deep green eyes.

She gave him a mischievous glance. "Mr. Yursi, if that's your real name, would you do the honors?" She handed him the champagne bottle, as one would a servant. "We've many things to celebrate this evening." She nodded her head toward the hot tub. "My girlfriend is waiting for us, and she's the first thing to celebrate..."

CHAPTER 36

THE SPY IN THE EMBASSY

SEEKER SAT IN HIS BLACK TASK FORCE CAR with the engine and exterior lights off and the liquid-crystal windows set at opaque. No one could see inside. The digital dashboard displays were active, but dim and viewable. One screen showed a map of the streets surrounding the embassy while a second display showed an internal layout of the embassy and grounds.

"Proteus, Seeker,"

"Proteus, go ahead, Seeker."

"Are you in position?"

"Confirmed. You showing all channels encoded and scrambled still?"

"Yep. You gave Spy his access, did he say how long it would take him?"

"Negative, as usual. But front, east, west are all set with our special surprises if needed," she said.

"So, where the hell is he?"

"Only *he* can answer that," Proteus said sarcastically.

The distance from the wall to the main building was almost two hundred feet with few plants or structures to give a hiding place for possible intruders. With full floodlights illuminating the open grounds, no one would be able to skulk around without being seen.

Seeker's eyes widened when he heard Spy's voice.

"I'm in place." He could only imagine Proteus' reaction.

How the hell does he do that? Just gone into thin air and appearing outta nowhere? Seeker asked himself for the thousandth time. Ever since the Biblical Bomber case, he'd experienced The Spy's talent for appearing and disappearing. *Probably something new he invented and won't share with us*, he thought.

"Status?" Spy ordered from the rooftop.

"Seeker, wheels ready, and we got lotsa eyes watching the target." While the Secret Service, FBI, and CIA were fully aware of the Task Force Division, they weren't aware of the agents' identities or their special capabilities. Task Force and the Pentagon preferred to keep it that way.

"Proteus, evac routes one and two secure," said Proteus. "Interruptions are in place just in case."

"Frequency confirm protocol Echo Tango?" Spy asked.

"Affirmative." Seeker said. "GPS tracker active on the dashboard LCD." Intercepted feeds kept other surveillance teams from listening in. A small four-sided-diamond-shaped icon flashed on the screen, showing Spy's location. Proteus' icon of three upside-down triangles was close to Spy's. "Tied in. No one outside Task Force is listening. I read Proteus is also in the group." He chuckled as a frequency scanner showed hits across its display. "I'm also seeing the other agents are searching frequencies to find us. Good luck with that."

"Seeker, don't react when I go off-grid," Spy ordered. "Wait for the signal."

"Oh, crap, you're gonna do it again," Seeker said, groaning. "You're gonna have to teach me how the hell you do that."

"Patience, grasshopper," came the reply. The diamond icon abruptly vanished from the screen.

"I see you on the screen, Pro, but where are you?"

"Inside his entry point."

"Did you see him come in?"

"Negative," she said.

"Tactical, Seeker."

"Seeker, Tactical Two," said a male voice.

"Confirm satellite image. Is Spy on target roof?"

A few seconds passed. "Negative. Spy is not visual."

"Son of a bitch. I'll learn how he does that if it's the last thing I do!"

Proteus chuckled.

The Ollistani Embassy was fully lit inside, although the intensity was lowered to a pleasant soft glow for night-time hours. Guards walked methodically through the halls, weapons always at the ready. The empty halls echoed every sound and footstep.

"Proteus, position?" Spy's voice sounded in her ear. The unexpected sound caused the hidden agent to jump.

"Proteus, east stairwell, using a refraction screen." Proteus, now dressed in her standard black uniform, held her weapon in one hand and the screen in the other. The screen aided in making her location invisible, camouflaged so she looked like the surrounding wall. Feeling a presence, she rotated, raising her gun intending to fire when Spy snatched it from her with lightning speed. "How the hell did you get here?" she whispered in surprise, her heart pounding in her chest. She grabbed her gun back from him, scowling.

He ignored the question. "This is Tactical. He just came back on grid in the east stairwell,"

"Duh," said Proteus.

Spy replied, "The guards are keeping to their third standard patrol routine. Good work, Proteus."

"Orders?" she asked.

"Since they're on Pattern Three, set the evac-two decoys to go off after I've completed the mission."

"Got it, boss." Proteus took a remote-control device from her belt pouch, pressing a button on the top edge. "Two is on remote activation, one on standby," she said, then looked to her leader...

...who was gone.

"Dammit!" she whispered.

"No cussing on the job," Seeker chided in her ear. "Don't worry over it, he does that all the time. He's disappeared from my grid, too. *Again...*"

A uniformed guard passed the President's office. He nodded at another guard who stood directly in front of another office door on the opposite side of the hall.

The hallway abruptly dropped into darkness. The air-conditioning system and other nearby equipment snapped off and wound down to a stop. Backup generators for the embassy didn't come on as programmed. One guard was about to speak when a gloved hand covered his mouth and nose. Another arm covered his free hand and gripped the man's weapon slung across his chest. Seconds later he sagged to the floor, unconscious.

The Spy's automated hood gave him the advantage of seeing in the dark. It also received computer generated feedback which helped with heat seeking capabilities, observing radiation, EMP, hazardous materials, and other dangerous weapons.

An unexpected sensor code appeared in the corner of one lens. The code indicated each door on the corridor was set with an alarm. He wasn't surprised. He'd deduced every door in the Embassy was most likely installed with an alarm, battery operated if there was no electric power. A code punched into the keypad would allow safe access. He needed to find the room containing all the servers and security panels. Disabling all security features, including motion detectors, was a priority for this operation. Most all Task Force uniforms were designed as their own radar reflectors, rendering the agents' invisible to common monitoring systems.

Near the end of the long hallway he observed a distinctive door to his right, not like the others. It opened outward rather than inward. Two signs were on the front of the door, one similar to Arabic, the second sign was in English: PROCESSOR ROOM. *Processor room, exactly what I need. Could I be any luckier?* Spy thought.

Instead of a keypad, the door needed a card to unlock it. Spy was about to use the electronic card reader from his belt to hack into the lock when he noticed a security card clipped to the guards' shirt pocket.

He retrieved the card from the guard's pocket hoping he wouldn't set off alarms. He speculated the card could open any "swipe-card" lock in the building, so he swiped the card. A green dot appeared on the card-swipe box.

"Twenty seconds until light restore," Proteus' voice crackled.

Spy didn't reply. He dragged the unconscious guard in with him and shut the door. "Activate!" Spy ordered.

From her hidden position, Proteus pressed a pre-set program on her tactical wrist display. The hall lights resumed night-time illumination.

Spy electronically scanned the unconscious guard, then relayed the information to the Task Force Division. Once activated, it projected a "twin" to a series of sophisticated holographic projectors aimed at the door. Over the last several hours Proteus, disguised as embassy staff, managed to retrieve a variety of equipment which Spy planted on the roof. She installed them as opportunity provided. She called her operation the 'PMS' – 'Proteus' Mobile Substitute'".

"Two minutes until next rotation, at 2215 hours," Proteus reported.

"Copy," Spy replied. "Turn on your PMS."

Seeker chucked, heard by all.

A hologram of the displaced guard took its position outside the secure hallway door.

The processor room was firewalled, and a secret door led to a library. The library contained floor-to-ceiling shelves lined with books from around the globe. Some were extremely old and valuable, others were new. The room was dark except for small LED ceiling lights. A single-seat recliner and side-table sat near the back of the room. A large computer station and desk chair were set forward a few feet. There were no other furnishings. Spy noticed a second door on the opposite wall, not remembering it from the schematics of the embassy. He crossed his arms and cradled his chin in a thumb and forefinger. *Now if I were a terrorist, where would I hide incriminating evidence in here?* he thought to himself…

CHAPTER 37

YURSI COME, YURSI GO

Yursi's security staff left the lounge looking for another place to sit and talk about their bosses' lengthy retreat with the two American women. A small seating area at the side of the main lobby seemed to be the perfect place. "Alim," said one of the men, glancing at his watch. "He's been gone too long. Almost three hours now. How much sex can you have in two hours?"

The leader responded. "You don't know Yursi, he can do much sex. But, yes, you're right. His little escapade is going to get all of us into trouble. Jabbar, you and I will go check on him, and his prostitutes. The rest of you, wait here."

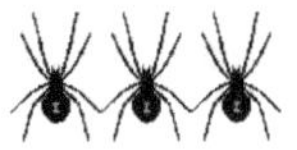

Yursi spoke in a broken Arabian dialect. "You see, the amateurs always let the bottle cork fly off to hit the ceiling, for a laugh. No, my charming ladies, you have sophistication, an eye for luxury, and apparently—" he looked at the women who had moved to sit on the couch "—a very exciting love life." He took the champagne bottle in both hands, expelled the cork, his thumb keeping it from becoming airborne. He began to pour the cold champagne into a flute, then stopped when he noticed the hourglass etching again. "An hourglass means we have all the time in the world, yes?" He finished filling one glass for himself, only.

"Like what you see, Yursi?" Lacy asked as she stood.

He gazed at Lacy. She pressed her naked body against him, and he smiled widely.

"Oh, yes, you women, I love what you do. And I now understand what you mean about it being the glass you pour it into." Yursi turned his attention to Lexi entering the hot tub again. He followed, drink in hand, unbuttoning his shirt.

Lacy stepped to the bar to finish pouring the bubbly into the other flutes for Lexi and herself. *Arrogant ass didn't even bother pouring us any,* she thought. She took both glasses and the bottle back to the hot tub. He'd already downed most of his drink, so Lacy took his glass and refilled it. Yursi realized that both women were wearing black silk gloves and black stilettos, even in the hot tub.

"Well, you both are full of surprises. Come, everybody in, and see what we can find to do." Once they were all in the water, he raised his glass in a toast. "To my new American beauties! Um, what did you say your names were again?

The redhead replied, "I'm Lacy. And my special friend here is Lexi. We plan to relax and wrap you up in passion tonight!"

The bottles of champagne seemed to appear out of nowhere. Yursi, Lacy, and Lexi frolicked and drank in the hot tub. The women took turns giving him a massage above and below the water, and he returned the action in kind. Laughter and giggles continued.

Yursi was getting woozy but gave it no thought. *I've never had as much joy and fun as with these two American women,* he thought. One of them grabbed him under the water and squeezed hard. Had he not already been in the mood, the pressure may have hurt. Instead, he was stirred by the bold advancement and wanted one of them at once, he didn't care which. "You," he growled at Lexi, "stand up and bend over the side. I have something to give you."

Lexi narrowed her eyes at his sudden outburst, but remembered the game.

"No, Lacy wants to go first. You can play with me soon." Lexi raised her glass in one last salute to the yearning foreign man.

Lacy smiled, setting her glass on the floor. She stood, water dripping down her stomach and legs. She bent over at the waist, her torso on the floor, legs in the water revealing her tub-soaked treasures. Yursi used Lacy as a support until he could stand near the steps of the tub, then forced himself on her.

Abrupt rage built inside Lacy, and she opened her mouth in a soundless gasp. His unexpected energy and size was painful. A lifetime of memories flooded back, bringing anger, pain, and perfect focus for her hatred. Her sudden new goal was revenge on every abuser who took what they wanted without regard.

Lexi eased herself out of the tub, retrieved the injector from its box in her carryall bag and returned, placing it in Lacy's right hand. Yursi was oblivious to what she was doing.

The sensation of her wet body against his was overpowering, and the constant impact of the hot bubbles around his legs forced him to plunge harder. A rumbled whisper escaped from his mouth, "You like it, woman—don't you?" He looked at his reflection in a wall mirror as he thrust back and forth, enjoying the image.

How long is he gonna hold out? He's taking forever! Lacy thought. The man's breathing quickened, and his movement slowed.

His eyes squeezed tight, and a low exhilarated growl began in his throat...

CHAPTER 38

ALAS, POOR YURSI, I KNEW HIM

LACY HELD THE INJECTOR IN HER HAND, ARCHED herself slightly, and plunged it into his hip. His eyes were closed tight, and he felt nothing but the overwhelming electric sexual surge that shook his body. Lexi quickly retrieved the injector, placed it in its case and shoved it in her bag.

Exhausted, Yursi withdrew and stepped backward in the hot tub. He then sat on the steps as dizziness rapidly took over.

"Oh, no, you don't, stud," Lacy said as she tugged at Yursi's arm to get him to stand, Lexi taking the other arm. "We've laid out some nice, comfy silk sheets for you." Climbing out of the tub, they walked unsteadily toward the bed. "We can finish playing over here, okay?"

Yursi's head pounded, and the thought of playing anymore wasn't at all appealing. "Ladies, I believe you've worn me out. Perhaps I've had too much champagne. Let me lie down a few minutes to rest. Then I'll give you even more pleasure."

Lacy gave him a hard shove. Weakened by the venom that pumped rapidly through his system, he had no resistance and landed face down on the mattress. He bounced comically; arms and legs flopping up and down. Lexi's bag flew off the bed onto the floor and the injector case popped open, allowing the auto-injector to tumble under the dresser. Yursi moaned as the effects of the venom increased. Confusion struck when his heart rate increased, and nausea began to take over. His esophagus began to close, leaving him gasping for air.

"Come on, Lexi, let's get that contraption of yours set up quick. This was an awesome idea you had; I hope it holds his weight."

"Hey, I'm not just another pretty face, okay?" Lexi said with a proud smiled. "Of course, it'll hold. I can design and build anything!"

Yursi turned over in the bed, facing the two nude women. "Something, it's bad!" He reached an arm out for help. "Go, get the men who were with me, my security."

"Security?" Lacy laughed. "What are you, a prince, or something?" She spat on his open hand. "You're just a piece of garbage, just like all the rest. We came here looking for someone else, then came across the likes of you, Mister Hot Shit, ogling us, feeling us up in the lounge. Throwing your money around like you were God's gift to the world."

"What? I do not understand," Yursi croaked out the words. "I did nothing! What did you do to me? Did you poison me, yes? In my drink, maybe? You bitches will die for this! I'll have you beheaded!" Yursi leaned over the edge of the bed and vomited onto the floor, the contents splattering on the women's feet and legs.

"You son-of-a-bitch!" Anger fired in Lacy's eyes. She grabbed a decorative sculpture from the dresser and pounded him in the back of the neck as hard as she was able. They heard a distinct snap, and Yursi's body convulsed. His eyes rolled back into his head and only the whites were exposed.

"Lacy, damn! I think you broke his neck. Did you hear that loud crack?"

"Yeah. And you know what? It felt good, too. Let's get the rig up quick. It's not gonna take long now. We gotta get him in it and get the hell out of here."

Lexi watched Lacy bend over to start positioning Yursi's body and realized they both need to clean up. "We got his stuff all over us. We gotta clean up."

"Good idea. Just give me a minute to get his grungy crap off me." She went to the bathroom to clean up, leaving Lexi to assemble her new *Black Widow Cocoon*. "When we're done, Lexi, we leave separately. People saw us come up the elevator together, they shouldn't notice us leaving alone."

Minutes later Lacy and Lexi left, using separate stairwells, just missing Yursi's security team exiting the elevator…

Spy was using the computer wireless interface in his hood to search through the Ollistani embassy database. He was so intent in his search, that he was surprised when the room burst into full light. He looked around as alarms blared in ear-deafening volume. "What the hell happened?" he whispered angrily to his team.

"The guards just went on full alert," Proteus reported.

"The compound's entrances just tripled in guards," Seeker added.

"Proteus, to the roof," Spy ordered. "Seeker, pick her up when she's clear."

"What about you?"

"Follow my orders," Spy said.

The hallway door opened swiftly, and several Ollistani guards burst in, weapons pointed at the agent, itching to take a shot at the black clad stranger. President Komiani stepped in as well, dressed in pajamas and a silk housecoat. His guards parted as he walked forward. Komiani spoke in a tone that Mark Jason had never heard before, "I don't know how you got in, but you're not getting out." Though Komiani's skin was a light brown, anger seethed inside, and his ears and neck turn a dark shade of red. He looked Spy over from head to toe. "That is, you're not getting out—alive…"

CHAPTER 39

NOW YOU DON'T SEE HIM...

KOMIANAI SAT IN A RECLINER, LEGS CROSSED, smoking an Arturo Fuente cigar, better known for its nickname "BBMF" *(Big Bad Mother Fucker)*, a brand intended to spark controversies. He was in a bad mood, stewing over what he thought was the audacity of the American Government to invade Ollistani territory. "So, I did have a spy in my midst," he surmised, blowing a puff of smoke toward the ceiling.

Six Ollistani guards encircled the intruder. He lowered his arms, his open palms rested akimbo-style on the pouch-laden utility belt and stood in a defiant pose.

Komiani rose and approached the man, noting how close the agent's hand was to the .45 automatic on its clip. "Well, you are impressive. I think a man trying to disarm you would experience great pain. So, let's agree for now that you don't move, and my men don't shoot you." Komiani nodded the order to his men. "Now, you didn't set off a single alarm breaking in here. But, if you wanted a book, isn't an American library much easier to access?" Komiani smiled at his own sarcasm. "You did very well, too, I must admit, except your special-effects fake guard outside vanished in front of me when I made an unscheduled visit to my office."

The agent merely tilted his head in acknowledgement as he heard Proteus whisper in his ear, "Son of a bitch!"

"So, you're looking for something in here," Komiani said. He waved his arms around the room. "What do you possibly hope to find in here? Moby Dick, perhaps?"

Abruptly, an aide burst into the room. "Sir, I have terrible news—your son, he has been murdered!"

Both Seeker and Proteus said, "What the hell?" in Spy's ear.

Komiani's eyes widened, and his mouth opened to speak, but no words came forth. He looked to his aide, disheartened. "Murdered? No, it cannot be! How dare you burst in and tell me that in front of everyone?" He grasped the edge of his desk with both hands, suddenly fragile in his stature but growing rage in his mind and heart.

The aide lowered his head in embarrassment. "But, sir, I am sorry. It is true, I am certain. I received word from Yursi's guards just now when they discovered his body."

Komiani's knees buckled, and he quickly sat in his recliner to keep from collapsing and losing face in front of his mysterious captive. An abrupt sadness coupled with anger took over, tears welled in his eyes. He felt as if he'd been punched in the gut. The guards wondered what would happen next. He looked back at the intruder. "You! You were part of this! Why did you kill my son?" He shook his finger violently at the agent.

For the first time, Spy spoke calmly. The electronic vocal enhancers lowered Mark's natural baritone into a filtered deep bass, leaving Komiani hearing an unrecognized voice. "Your son is dead?"

"Of course, you would say that! You're obviously a distraction so his killers could get away!"

Spy listened to a voice in his comm unit, "Spy, Seeker. Proteus is with me; we're waiting for you. What's going on in there? Did we hear that right? Yursi Komiani is dead?"

"I am going to unmask you and learn who you really are, so I can prove to the world what happens to invaders of my country. Show me his face!" Komiani ordered one of his guards. A guard stepped forward cautiously. He studied the suit, trying to find the hood release, baffled at its complexity and lack of visible seams. He instead tried to remove Agent Spy's belt, attempting to find its clasp in the buckle. "Don't move a muscle, whoever you are," Komiani ordered.

The guard fumbled with the flat metal buckle but couldn't release the lock. "Would you like some help?" Spy asked calmly. "Watch carefully, it's tricky." He brought his left hand slowly forward to the metal buckle. No one moved. Spy's hand balled into a fist and flew up into the guard's jaw, snapping his head back and sending him off his feet. His sudden attack allowed him the second of surprise to pull the barrel of the other guard's rifle to his side, bringing that guard close enough for a quick chop to the base of his neck. Next, Spy's right hand opened a belt pouch and flicked off a small smoke grenade, which burst into a thick cloud when it hit the floor.

"Don't fire!" one of the guards ordered. "You could hit the president!"

Within seconds the gray smoke dissipated. President Komiani and the mysterious intruder were gone…

CHAPTER 40

NOW YOU DO

"**H**OLY SHIT!" SEEKER SAID FROM THE DRIVER'S seat of his car.

"'Holy shit' is right," Proteus agreed.

The two agents watched the embassy floodlights flare to full intensity, searchlights playing along the walls separating the sovereign foreign soil inside from the American ground outside. Alarms shattered the quiet of the night.

Seeker studied the scene, casting glances at the Secret Service and FBI cars he'd spotted while on stake out. "I'll assume that since we haven't heard from him that Spy has created a scene."

Proteus held the remote-control device in her gloved hands. "Should I fire the decoys?" she asked.

"Not just yet, but keep your finger on the button."

Abruptly they both heard in their comm-units, "Open the back door." They whipped their heads around to see Spy jogging out of the shadows to the rear of the car. Seeker pressed the unlock button and Spy tossed in a hooded body followed by his own. "Seeker, get us the hell out of here and don't spare the horses. Proteus, blow your surprises now and don't forget any."

"Aye, aye, boss," said Seeker, bringing the LCD dashboard displays to full intensity. The windshield's computerized tinting changed for better visibility to green-hued enhanced night vision. Explosions sent smoke and flashes of light above the compound walls. "No one will see us until we're already past them," he said. The car rocketed into the dark streets, far ahead of the federal agents who might be in pursuit.

Proteus smiled. "I love it when I get to blow things up with absolutely no damage! I use this technique in my movie gags!" She checked the readout on her control. "All charges show activated. No evidence left behind, and my bed exploded, so hot that there's no body to find." She turned and smiled at her leader. "I die well, too."

"Get us to Langley," Spy ordered.

Seeker gave a voice command to the dashboard GPS, which lined the fastest route to the military airport. "Six minutes if we don't stop." Seeker also contacted his crew to ready the plane.

"Control, Spy."

"Spy, Tactical 4," he heard in his ear.

"Tactical 4, make sure every traffic light on our route is green."

"Copy, Spy. You are green."

"Roger. Leader, this is Spy," he said to Tom Michelson, also on the channel. "I'm borderline creating an international incident, so cover our asses as you can, please. I was seen but not identified, escaped but not followed." Without waiting for Tom's reply, he spoke again, "Proteus, get a round trip flight plan filed for *The Adventure*. Just in case we picked up a tail, either Ollistani or American... and just in case our friend here has an embedded tracker we don't know about yet. I want to be out of their reach as soon as possible."

"Destination?" she asked.

"How about Bermuda?"

"Nice," said Seeker. "I maintain favored status there."

"Is there any place that doesn't like you?" Proteus asked.

"I'm betting right now that'd be Charleston, seeing as how I blew up one of their docks."

"Have you ever considered just staying home for vacation?" she asked Seeker.

"As much as I love living in my own flying armory and three-story home, a vacation in a 747 on a parking ramp isn't that exciting."

"Boys and girls, now's not the time," said Spy. "I want us to be over international waters when I wake our friend here. Proteus, tell me your bugs are still in his office and can project as well as transmit."

"Yeah, I didn't blow them with everything else, they're on one of our special passive frequencies and impossible to detect. They're so well-hidden that even if they emptied the entire building and moved, our bugs will go right along."

"Good," said Spy, "here's what I want you to do..."

The Ollistani Embassy was a scene of smoke, confusion, and yelling, both inside and outside the main building. Guards searched for the president and the black-clad intruder. One guard tried to open the presidential office, but the door was locked from the inside. He pounded on the door, "Mr. President! Are you in there?"

From the other side of the door came, "I am fine, you damn fool, find that damned spy and kill him! I am safe in here! Go!"

The guard yelled back, "Yes, sir!" He instructed other guards with the orders.

Proteus muted her headset microphone. "Spy, as far as they're concerned, President Komiani has barricaded himself in his office while they're looking for you. We can keep the connection intact no matter where you take us through our satellite network's encoded frequencies. I've heard him enough to know what he'd say in almost any situation and recorded enough that the vocal modifier can sound just like him."

"Nice. Glad our company geeks keep making everything better and better." Spy looked forward as they slowed at the rear of *The Adventure*, Seeker's private jetliner, and drove up the rear ramp into the bottom level of the 747. The aircraft's engines were already turning, and the ramp door closed as their car came to a stop.

Seeker didn't wait to get out of the car. He started a comm link to Lee, the plane's captain, from his driver's seat. "Lee, get this bird up, now!"

"Roger that. Langley ground, *Adventure* ready to taxi," said the pilot's voice in his ear.

Within moments the rear hatch was up and locked, the automatic chocks secured the car in place so it couldn't move when the plane was in flight.

Komiani gradually opened his eyes and saw only darkness. A familiar voice filled his ears, but he couldn't immediately place it.

"Good, you're awake," said a deep voice.

"Wh-where am I?" Komiani asked. The room came into focus, what he could see of it. It was dark, with dim track lighting along the wall at the ceiling. His arms were strapped to the chair in which he sat. In front of him was the masked man, and a similarly dressed man to the side, wearing black glasses to hide his eyes. "Who are you?" he demanded.

Spy answered, "Right now, I'm the one who holds your life in his hands. Whether your life continues after our conversation depends on your answers."

"I will not answer questions from idiot spies!" Komiani growled. "I am President Komiani of the holy country of Ollistan!"

"Oh, I've heard it before." Spy interrupted. "Let me save time, Mister President. No one knows you're gone, and we found your GPS tracker in your thigh, so no one knows where you are aside from believing you're still in your office, thanks to some electronics that still work there. My partner and I are the only ones aware of your exact location, so just skip all the political bluster. Tell me about your ISIS connection."

Komiani laughed defiantly. "How dare you insult the integrity of the Royal President of Ollistan. There is no connection, you fool. I am connected to no terrorist group!"

Spy leaned in closer. "That's not what I hear—*fool*."

"Then perhaps you should take off that mask and let your ears listen unimpeded!" Komiani sneered, sitting back in his chair.

Spy calmly turned to Seeker and said, "Leave. Seal the room."

Seeker nodded and left.

When they were alone, Spy turned back to Komiani. He drew his .45 and brought it up to the president's nose. He gradually lowered it until it was pressed firmly against the president's groin. "You will die at my hand, you arrogant piece of royal crap. The only choice you have now is whether you will have the tool for your seventy-two virgins when you join them."

Spy left the room, locking the door behind him. Seeker stood in the hallway, leaning against the wall, his arms crossed. Seeker chided, "Where was the kaboom? There was supposed to be an earth-shattering kaboom.!" he said, mimicking Marvin the Martian as best he could.

Spy released the seam of his uniform collar to unhook the hood and pulled it off his head. "I gave him a choice, 'Marvin'. He chose wisely. He said he has no such connections, but his interior minister has had some questionable contacts recently. He gave me the access to his minister's email and database. I didn't think he was connected, but I never thought about the people who work for him—neither did anyone else. But, we now have a nice new contact in the heart of the Middle East."

"Good job!"

They walked down the hall to a conference room where computer stations were lined against the walls. Mark tossed his mask onto the table, removed his utility belt, and placed it on the table beside the hood, and sat down. His place at the table allowed him to look out the cabin windows at fluffy white clouds. Seeker sat opposite him. Proteus joined them a minute later, still wearing her specialized headset to provide Komiani's voice in his embassy office hundreds of miles away. She and Seeker sat patiently waiting for Mark to speak.

"Boss," said Proteus, "what set off the alarms? We had everything planned out perfectly. Simple in-and-out."

Mark continued to stare out the window. "The two things we couldn't expect: Komiani wandering the halls at night and your holographic guard fritzing out, and someone killing his kid." He turned to his teammates. "We're gonna find the killer. That'll be the only way to prevent an international war with a country that will only get obliterated and create a bigger Middle East conflict. Seeker, ask Lee to turn back and head for home. Proteus, hack into all the records, find out where it happened. Keep Komiani's office electronically locked until I can get him back in."

"How—" Proteus began.

"Don't," Seeker interrupted her. "Some things Spy does are just better left unknown…"

The Ollistani guards and staff had the embassy cleaned up and under control again. President Komiani's voice continued to give orders from behind his locked door, and everyone obeyed without question…

Komiani opened his eyes. His mind was still foggy from the second tranquilizer the masked man had given him. When he was able to focus on his surroundings once more, he was back in his embassy office, sitting at his desk, dressed in one of his normal business suits. "How—?"

"Good morning," said a voice from behind him. Komiani turned to face his kidnapper. "Mister President, before you say anything, let me tell you about one of our arrangement's extra details. While you were asleep, we implanted one of our special little explosives into your scrotum, so if you step out of line, even a little—then, boom! No more Komiani, no enjoying your afterlife. And if I call you for anything—"

"I will comply, yes, always!" Komiani replied quickly, nodding his head rapidly, placing a hand to his groin, rotating to look at where Spy was pointing at his desk. "Yes, yes, of course!" He noticed a cell phone placed before him on his desk; it was specialized with no way to dial out, only an answer button, and a digital display showing the local time. He looked up to ask a question, but the black figure was gone…

CHAPTER 41

TWO PRESIDENTS IN TWO DAYS

"**I** MUST REMIND YOU HOW IMPORTANT THIS IS, Mark."

"Piece of cake, Mr. President," Mark said sarcastically.

"Mark, be serious. This could be a *huge* incident."

Mark glanced at the face of the President of the United States on the video screen imbedded in the dashboard. "Not to worry, sir. It's not like I haven't stopped a war before."

"Fine, fine," the president said, lowering his eyes to his desk. "Just remember, if this goes south, it's your ass on the line along with mine, and I have enough problems right now as it is."

"Tut, tut, Mister President—such language." The President was about to respond when Mark continued, "Sir, with all due respect, I'll stop the war before it begins. And don't forget about our little waiver agreement." The president nodded and disconnected call. Mark couldn't help but crack a smile.

Mark drove his Mercedes convertible through the Ollistani Embassy gate without challenge by the guards, who didn't relish a second ass-whipping by their president's favorite American. He parked in a guest slot, stepping out under watchful eyes. He deliberately took a few seconds to smooth the jacket of his dark blue suit, and then adjusted the black tie over his crisp white shirt. The gold cuff links on his sleeves glistened in the noon-time sun.

He entered the building without concern, ignoring the alarms which went off when his concealed weapons activated the metal detectors. Though angered, the guards kept their weapons pointed down as he passed them. Mark was stopped by the guard at the president's office. "Tell him I'm here," Mark said, without emotion.

The guard pressed the intercom button, announcing the visitor. Komiani's voice came from the speaker, "Send him in, alone."

The guard opened the door and stepped aside to allow Mark to pass, closing the door behind him. President Komiani was seated at his desk, his head in his hands. He looked up as Mark approached. "Mark," Komiani said rising to his feet, offering Mark his hand. "Thank you for coming to see me again on such short notice."

"Of course," Mark replied. "My condolences for the loss of your son." Mark could tell the President had been crying. Though his eyes were dry, they were red and puffy. A stab of compassion washed over Mark, thinking what it would be like to lose his own daughter.

Komiani did his best to hold back anger and tears. "He may have been a foolish immature dog, but he was *my* foolish immature dog of a son. You have a child; you should know how I feel. You realize this is an act of war, Jason." He looked at Mark, his black bushy brows furrowed with hurt and anger. "Find out who killed my son, Jason. Or Washington will experience my wrath!

Mark sat and crossed his legs. "Listen to yourself, do you hear what you're saying? Besides, I'm not law enforcement. I have no authority in such matters."

"You pointed out how lax my so-called modern security really is. Your country's Secret Service and security were supposed to keep my son safe while we were here."

"As I hear it, the FBI was close by and saw no threats."

"*They* obviously can't do the job of finding who did it any better than they could protecting him."

"And, I also learned your son's own security detail was downstairs drinking while he was being murdered."

"Yes, they were, and they have been permanently—well, we'll not speak of their fate." Komiani made an obvious cautious adjustment in his seat. "You made fools of my best guards without wrinkling your expensive suit, and you have a powerful staff at your command. I fought beside you and trusted you, Mark Jason. I have kept up with you over the years, old friend, and other people of power in your country respect you, and many fear you. That is why I want *you* to find out who did this."

Mark smiled. "Your words do me honor, old friend. And it is to my old friend, not the president of a Middle Eastern country, that I say, yes, I'll get my people to see what they can find."

"Thank you." Komiani stood, indicating their meeting was concluding. "Join me. I want to go where he was killed, to see for myself. I want you to bring your security people to do the investigation, not your incompetent government. Give me a name, or I swear *there will be war*."

Mark stood still, momentarily seething at the comment before looking at Komiani eye-to-eye. "Let's get one thing clear, *Mister President*! Stop the damned war threats! I'm here as a courtesy to both you and my president, and I have offered you my help as a friend. Politically both of you seem to think I'm the key to stopping a war neither of you wants and you know you damn well no one can win. You and I both know that it would lead to the immediate decimation of Ollistan, military and civilian alike." He pointed his finger at Komiani's nose. "*NO more threats!* Do I make myself clear, *old friend?*"

Upon hearing the heated argument within the office, the guard opened the President's office door, and entered with his rifle pointed at Mark.

"I would kill you where you stand for such impudence, Jason," said the president.

"You're welcome to try," Mark replied, with a deliberately delayed, "SIR."

Komiani studied Mark's unwavering, unblinking glare. He watched Mark's eyes glance at the guard, ready to kill without hesitation. He also knew from personal experience that Mark could quickly and permanently carry out his threat before the guard could lift a finger. His instinct told him to tread cautiously, however. "My apologies, Mister Jason. I fear my emotions have gotten the better of me." Mark's furrowed brow relaxed only slightly. Komiani noted the massive muscular shoulders move into a less attack-ready posture. "Guard, leave us. Everything is fine." The guard lowered his weapon and left. He extended his right hand. "Please help find my son's murderer."

Mark didn't move for several seconds, which prompted Komiani to wonder if he'd crossed the line and was now nervous for his own life. Finally, Mark shook his hand. "Very well, I will gather the best people I have, and we'll find the truth." Mark turned to leave, then stopped at the office door. He turned back to Komiani. "I hope this will show that you can trust us when it counts."

"I understand," said the president. "You were an honorable warrior and a friend to my family. And you don't cower under threats. Your politicians are the ones I don't trust."

"It's okay, most of America doesn't trust our politicians, either."

Mark drove his car out of the Ollistani Embassy and pressed a virtual comm button on the LCD screen. "Seeker, Spy. You, Hunter, and Proteus load up everything you need for an on-site murder investigation. Civilian clothes, fully armed as always." He waited for confirmation from Seeker before disconnecting. "Couldn't have worked out better if I'd tried."

President Komiani's armored limousine came to a stop at the entrance to the hotel in Charleston, with Mark's black SUV parked behind. When FBI agents stepped forward to tell them to move their vehicles, a sun-glassed Mark flashed his Task Force badge without Komiani noticing. "Please go ahead, sir."

Mark's staff gathered their equipment and waited at the hotel's entrance. "President Komiani, you are asked not to interfere with my staff as they work. If they give you instructions, you will follow them without question. And don't be deceived because I have ladies on my staff; the three of them are the best at what they do."

"Indeed?" the president asked.

"Just treat them respectfully, Mister President," Mark replied.

"I am so grateful you agreed to investigate this horrible scene. I don't trust your government to tell me what happened truthfully, but I trust Jason's people, even his women." He looked at Harri. "No offense meant, miss."

"None taken," said Harri, carrying heavy plastic containers in both hands. "Our cultures are different, but you'll only get my best efforts on your behalf."

He looked at her a little closer. "Have we met?"

"I don't believe we've been introduced, no," she answered honestly. "I have one of those common American faces, sir."

"Ah, must be. Very well then. Jason, let us get started."

Mark said to Mae-Lei, "You stay here in the lobby, interview the staff and any guests who may have seen anything the night of the murder. I know the FBI has already done all that, but I need *your* perspective." Mark pointed a finger at Komiani's armed guards. "They're not following us upstairs."

"They are here to protect me. And while you are helping me, they are protecting you as well."

Mark smiled and nodded. "I am quite capable of protecting you myself."

Komiani looked at Mark and his team. "Yes, that is more than true. But, protocol dictates that my men accompany, but they will remain outside the crime scene. Let us proceed."

FBI and Ollistani guards blocked the door to the suite where Komiani's son was murdered. With his back to the Ollistanis, Mark opened his coat to flash his Task Force badge at the FBI agent guarding the door as Anderson flashed her own FBI badge. The agent stood aside and whispered orders into his wrist comm. Mark, Calvin, Harri, and Stephanie, with Komiani following behind, entering the suite.

The rooms were filled with FBI and Secret Service agents, with Ollistani observers watching their every move. They all stopped when Mark's team entered. "Please clear the suite," Stephanie ordered. "No one is to remain, except my team and President Komiani."

"Everyone, you heard the lady," said one of the lead agents. "And forget you saw any of these people, by presidential order. They were never here."

No one disputed or grumbled at the order but packed up their equipment and left.

Komiani gave the same order to his men. Within moments the suite was evacuated. The foreign president looked around the room, considering the crime scene. The silence echoed deftly in his ears; a nightmare come true. Sadness pierced his heart, knowing this was where his only son had last been. He turned to Mark. "Jason, you appear to have even more influence than I thought. 'You were never here'? Impressive."

Mark smiled and replied, "We'll do our best, old friend, and you have my word. Okay, people, do what you do."

Komiani stood near the door while the Task Force agents put on blue gloves and began setting up their equipment. The president stared in awe at the rapidly assembled computer equipment, scanners and processors, the likes of which he'd never seen. He was particularly intrigued by the device Harri was assembling. "Jason, what is that device?" he asked Mark.

Mark said to Harri, "Would you care to do the honors? It's your baby, after all."

Harri smiled and stood face to face with the president. "Well, Mister President, this device I call 'REDS': The Residual Epidermal Detection System. She motioned toward a foot-long cylinder protruding from the computer base. "This part will send out impulses in a 360-degree arc and get back reflections anywhere organic tissue still resides. Works just like radar, except what gets bounced back are reflections of only those cells containing human-genetic material, so things like pets and such are ignored. What we'll get is a 'radar' image of where people spent any periods of time greater than a minute or two during the past couple days. The strength of the reflectivity will also tell which reflections are more recent than others. Any reflection image in the red-range will be more recent, and the older the image the deeper into the blue reflection."

Komiani looked at Mark. "What did she say?"

Mark smiled. "Just watch. It's still in beta."

Harri continued setting up her equipment, while Calvin placed a steel headband over his forehead to which one magnifying lens hung over his right eye. Electrode wires ran from the back of the headband to a receiver on his belt beside the Sig Sauer 45 in its holster. He was checking the settings on a palm-sized device shaped like a gun grip with a probe-like cylindrical extension off the top, tipped with a tiny glass ball. "And what is he doing?" Komiani asked Mark.

"What Harri finds in the broad sweep, Calvin will check in detail. Also, still in beta."

"Mr. Jason," said Stephanie, pointing at her ear comm, "I'm being asked how much longer we'll be."

"When we're finished, agent. We do it right, not fast."

"Almost ready," said Harri. She attached a flat-tipped probe and plugged it into her laptop. "I need to take a quick epidermal scan of each of us to remove our individual signatures from the imaging. Just having us here these few minutes has already left a lot of cells in places." She placed the probe on her left hand and pressed the single button on the grip. A red light came on, then off. On her keyboard, she typed in her name. "Who's next?"

"Ladies first," Mark said to Stephanie. The FBI agent extended her left hand to Harri. Mark said, "Calvin," then, "Mister President."

A moment later Harri was finished with both Komiani and Mark.

"Now if everyone will gather in one spot, preferably there." She pointed at the wall beside the door. After the group was where she directed Harri activated the device and stood beside them. "Now, nobody move until the cycle is finished."

For several minutes, the cylindrical extension sent out barely perceptible beams of light, slowly turning clockwise until nearly every bit of the room was scanned. As the scanner approached them, Harri said, "OK, everyone move left." Everyone complied, and the scanner completed its circuit of the room.

"Why did you make us move?" Komiani asked. "You said we wouldn't be seen by your machine."

"We would be ignored, yes, but we're not transparent. I still needed to get the wall behind us scanned."

"Now what, Harri?" Mark asked.

"Just wait for the processor to render a panoramic reflected image of the room."

"Wait and wait," Komiani grumbled. "All this waiting and no answers."

Mark looked at Komiani, glaring anger. "Answers take time. If you want guesses, bring the others back. If you want answers, be patient." He paused before adding for emphasis, "Sir."

Komiani glared back, but couldn't stop himself from smiling. "By Allah, Jason, you have balls! No one else would ever talk to me that way! Proceed, Miss Harri."

"Yes, sir," she said, still running the decryption and analysis programs on her computer.

Calvin whispered to Mark, "Is he always like this?"

"Nah, he's a saint right now. Just keep him away from the wheat bourbon…"

"Analysis complete," Harri announced. "And wow."

"That was a sedate 'wow'," Mark said, "coming from the most excitable member of the team. So, what's the 'WOW'?"

"Well, I wasn't expecting this." She laid out the printed panoramic image of the hotel room on the table. Several areas of bright red inched across the image. "Starting from here," pointing at the hot tub, "I make out that someone sat here, there was a head here, someone different sat beside the first."

"How do you know it's someone different?" Mark asked.

"Slight variation in the red hue, indicates a different body," Harri answered. "And the head is different altogether. If I were to speculate just from this, I'd say we had a threesome in the hot tub.

Since the victim is male, and based on all the postures I see here, I'm guessing the other two were female, and here's why." She pointed to the couch area. "Two people recently sat on the couch. This one is male by the outline of the body. This one is female on the front of the couch; there's her breasts. Betcha our male someone was getting some, a, special attention." Suddenly realizing her blunt remark, "Oh, sorry, Mr. President, but the readings are the readings. Now here," she said, pointing at the tripod holding the torn-open sack which once held the body, "are two definite sets of hands. But it doesn't tell me if the third is male or female." She scanned the printout to its right. "Looks like the male sat here in the armchair." She indicated further to the right, on the bed. "Okay, the male was laid out spread-eagle on the bed. Two figures beside him." She looked closer at the bed section. "Ah. Definitely two females and the male." She stopped at the bathroom door on the printout. "I'd have to do a separate scan for the bathroom, but I'd say at this point we're looking for two women."

"Calvin, you're up," Mark said.

Calvin reached into one of his bags and pulled out several Task Force cocoon glasses, handing one set to each person. Stephanie and Komiani's glasses were regular commercial glasses, while the three agents wore the standard computerized units. "These glasses are to protect your eyes while I run infrared scans of Harri's hot spots," he announced.

With all the eyewear in place, Calvin began to run detailed examinations of the bed first. Komiani made a dramatic sigh and fought to keep himself calm…

CHAPTER 42

CONNECTING THE WEB
SEVERAL DAYS LATER

MARK ENTERED HARRI'S OFFICE IN THE TASK Force Division's administrative wing. "Tell me you have something."

Harri was at her desk computer. She wore faded jeans, flip-flops, her toenails painted bright red, and a white T-shirt with the Washington Nationals baseball team logo emblazoned on the front. "I do. A possible serial killer using—spider venom."

Mark's eyebrows rose in surprise. "Really? Enlighten me." Mark flipped a chair around, its back to his front. He sat in front of her desk, his chin resting on his muscled forearms on the back of the chair.

Harri wasn't used to the more relaxed side of Mark. "Ah, why don't you have a seat, sir, make yourself comfortable," she chided.

"Thanks," he said, smiling.

"Well, this is one I'll bet you've never seen. Spider venom, lots and lots of spider venom," she said, rotating the plasma-screen to show her team leader. "Latrodectus Mactan." The screen showed a photo of a common black widow spider with a red hourglass on its underside. Beside it was a photo of the venomous neurotoxins through a microscope lens, blown up large enough to see the liquid.

"Okay, why do you think Yursi Komiani was murdered by a serial killer?" Mark asked. "You think there's been others killed by this woman? Who's working on the profile now? Why is this the first we've heard of this? Why aren't we further—"

Proteus put a hand up, "Okay, boss, hang on, slow down with the questions. I'm getting to all that, just listen. You've been way busy keeping two nations away from war, and, truthfully sometimes we really need more staff and profilers who can do this kinda stuff. But, okay, here goes: our intel department learned of an earlier killing as part of a routine event review. You and Tom passed on it because it didn't qualify as a Task Force matter, since it didn't fit our protocol at the time." She clicked a window on the screen, bringing up cascading photos of a crime scene and the dead body of Jake Collins. "We think he was the first victim in a spree of serial murders, killed with black widow venom. When we first got this, and began a base line profile, we thought the murderer was disorganized and unprofessional because of the horrific mess throughout the motel room crime scene. And, there was female DNA behind. Yet, she seems educated enough or connected enough to obtain great quantities of venom. Though the victims were beaten badly she didn't seem to take any obvious trophies with her—you know, like body parts and stuff. Disorganized serial murderers are, well, just that—pretty disorganized. They leave evidence, fingerprints, take trophies, many are just opportunists. We're getting into specific sciences now, however, since she's using this venom."

Mark lowered his head, shaking it back and forth, envisioning jars of body parts lined up on a shelf. "Yeah, a real creep chill here."

"What? Oh, cheap thrill—word play, boss. Not your best. Anyway, then there was another gruesome murder in a nice hotel a few hours away in West Virginia, just over one month ago. Good timing for a second hit. Cooling off periods go in cycles with serials. Sometimes once a year, sometimes one every month or two."

"Yeah, just like our Biblical Bomber case: three sets of murders every two years."

"Exactly. Just depends on your psycho. It hit our database because of the specifics of the murder scene. But since the FBI was already looking at it, you and Tom relegated it to stay with the local authorities and the FBI. Looking back now, it seems she upped her game by adding silk sheets to the scene. He was tied up nice and snug on the bed, not hanging on that contraption thing like in the third murder, Yursi's. She changed from a small trashy motel to a high-quality hotel. These are indications of growing confidence in her killing ability". She flipped the computer screen around again, showing more photos of the second crime scene.

"God, Proteus, I don't have a weak stomach for any murder, but that's gross."

"Yeah. All are signs of acting out something, a trauma or abuse, a fantasy most likely. But at the time, it was just another murder we wouldn't get involved with. And again, he, too, was killed with widow venom, but a *second* species of widow."

"Second species?" Mark asked.

"Yeah, boss. There're thirty-two species worldwide. Anyway—"

"Thirty-two?" Mark interrupted. "I thought a widow was a widow."

"Wow, so the mighty Spy doesn't know everything after all!" Snickering, she punched his arm. "I was researching the nature of black widow venom and found both of these murders in the national unsolved cases database. The first with one species, the second murder with a second species of Latrodectus. The second crime scene was a mess as well, but more confined. Then," she said, maximizing another window on her computer terminal, "this is Yursi's crime scene. See the difference? Higher quality hotel, hot tub in the floor, champagne glasses with hourglass shapes on them, DNA from two females, not one, and now a *third* species of spider. Again, the victim is tied up in silk sheets, most likely an homage gesture to mimic a spider spinning its victim into a silk cocoon to eat later. Then, it seems they hoisted the *cocoon* onto this tall metal tripod, probably using it as a make-believe spider web or something. More indications of confidence and progression."

"Good job. So, to digest it, no pun intended, this killer woman is more like the spider itself? Copulate, then kill the mate, if you will."

"Yes, and unfortunately, I can't find any direct connections to the three victims, yet. DNA testing of the female will take a while, but my gut says I will. Two guys from two different states, and an international playboy, the son of a mid-eastern president. Yeah. Three victims in three months with the same MO, and that's, well, all I have for now. Aside from the fact that the killer is getting more *professional* on how she picks up the murder scene after she's done."

The addendum told Mark that Harri was only just beginning her scientific investigations, and on the right trail. "But, Harri, how much venom? Because even I realize that someone doesn't usually die from a single widow bite."

"No, sir, our black widow lady used huge amounts of venom on each victim, deadly enough to kill an elephant on the spot."

"Geez, she, or they, are just whacked out. And how would one get that much venom?"

"Oh, they milk them."

Mark tilted his head. "Say again? They milk them?"

Harri laughed. "It's a very lengthy process. They use electrodes to help extract the venom, only getting a tiny drop per day. It would take hundreds of spiders being milked daily to get this much venom. From different species. That's why this shows we have an extremely smart killer, one who's had time on her hands and knows what she's doing."

"I'll say. So, if the timeline holds, that gives us about three weeks to figure out who the next victim might be." He stood, flipping the chair back into place. "I have some investigating to do."

Mark's cell phone rang in his jacket pocket. He looked at the display before answering. It was Stephanie Anderson's number. "Go, Stephanie, what's up?

"Where are you?" Stephanie asked impudently.

"In Washington. And why do you ask?"

"I'm in Washington, so I assume you're at your other office. I'm on my way. Be there in ten minutes." She abruptly ended the call.

"Steph—shit," he stared at the phone. "She hung up on me! Remind me to discuss protocol with her, Harri. I guess I'm not leaving just yet," Mark said.

About fifteen minutes later Stephanie walked down the Task Force hallway, stopping when she found Mark and Harri. "I gotta tell you," she said, "the best thing you ever did was give me Task Force status, because I never would've gotten access to this." She handed Mark a folder.

He opened the cover and looked at the report pages clipped inside. His forehead wrinkled in concern. "Why didn't we find this when we were there?" he asked Stephanie.

"The FBI had already tagged and processed it before we got there. And we didn't *ask* if they had already found anything. Our bust."

"Hum, true. Good point, Stephanie, well done."

"Thank you, sir."

"What is it?" Harri asked. Mark handed her the folder, and she quickly read the evidence analysis. "Holy shit. Are you certain?"

"Cross-checked three ways to Sunday," the FBI agent replied. "The microscopic ID chip is unmistakable. That's a Jason Enterprises auto-injector..."

Crystal was working late in her private lab/office on the 14th floor of the Jason Enterprises building, the highest-security floor of the entire complex, studying cultures with both an electron microscope and special magnifying goggles over her eyes.

Only the employees assigned to work on that floor had direct access via an elevator behind the security desk in the lobby. Stepping into or off the elevator required retinal and fingerprint-scan verification before entrance or exit, within the bulletproof glass enclosure. Once the door opened, gentle tones rang to announce someone was on the floor. Newer employees still had to check in with the guard team outside the elevator door. The hallway area beyond the glass wall was darkened, with only dim red tracer lights along the wall and ceiling joints to indicate how far the hall went.

"Chrystal?" a male's voice said behind her.

Deep in concentration, she was startled and nearly spilled her water glass on her desk papers and keyboard. "Y-yes, sir, Mr. Jason!" she replied, lifting the safety glasses onto the top of her head. "H-how did you get in? The alarms didn't go off to announce someone was on the floor."

"It's *my* building, last time I checked," he said. Changing the subject, he continued, "I have a special job for you."

"Me? Why me?"

"Calm down, Chrystal. Take a breath and relax, you're such a skittish little thing."

She did as she was instructed until her racing heart slowed. "I'm ready, sir."

Mark looked around at her work area. There were test tubes containing fluids in a tube rack, additional microscopes of various sizes and functions, folders containing chemical reports for review and analysis. He handed her a folder. "We're tasked by a special investigative team to study this. There's a serial killer—"

"Serial killer?" she interrupted.

"Yes. This killer is using concentrated Latrodectus venom to kill her victims."

"It's a 'her'?"

He ignored her question. "If you'll let me finish, please. The only connection so far between three separate murders is the use of concentrated venom from the Latrodectus. And, as our new resident bug expert, you're the best qualified to answer questions."

"But, I—"

He held his hand to stop her constant interruptions. "I need proof of how such a concentration could be developed, and how it could get out of a laboratory without the CDC or anyone else knowing about it? Also, can this new antivenin of yours be effective against someone injected with the venom? Get on it, Crystal. This task supersedes anything else you're working on until further notice."

She glanced at the folder in her hands and opened the cover. "I—I'll have to study it for a while before I start, sir," she said, then looked up to an empty office.

"Guess he knows exits no one else does," she said to herself. Chrystal stared at the open report and single paper she held. "Well, now, let's see what Mr. Jason wants..."

Connie Park was an intern in the Inventory Control department of Jason Enterprises, brought on after college, when she earned the Zachary Jason Award. The daughter of Korean immigrants, she had been well-trained by her parents to be a hard worker. After Mark reviewed her aptitude for statistical analysis, he placed her in his company's inventory department and challenged her to design a new algorithm for improved data recording.

She liked to work late into the evening alone at her desk in the cubicle area of her department. "Miss Park?" She gasped at the sudden inquiry and spun around in her chair to face the voice behind her.

"Easy does it," said the company president. "Everyone's so jittery around here." Mark figured he better make a little more noise around his employees so as not to give anyone a heart attack.

"Mister Jason, sir," Connie stammered regaining her composure. "W-what are you doing here this late?"

"It *is* my building," he replied, smiling, recalling saying the same words minutes earlier. "I keep getting asked that question. Maybe I better start pulling more evening and overnight shifts," he openly mused. "Anyway, I wanted to see how you were doing. I've been getting commendable reports about you."

"Thank you, sir," she said. She felt her face blush.

He pulled a folded paper from his inside jacket pocket and handed it to her. "What can you tell me about this item?"

Connie took the paper and began to read. "Standard auto-injector. Manufactured for commercial distribution, based on the number." She looked up at him; his gaze said he wanted more information. She rotated her chair back to her computer, keyed in the auto-injector number and waited for the inventory software to finish its search and display the results. "Sir, this was, well, part of a lot that was discarded due to a production defect. It was sent to the disposal center across the city."

Mark leaned forward beside Connie and studied the screen. "Twelve cases of 1cc auto-injectors failed inspection and sent for recycling. How many cases were actually received at the disposal site, Connie, if you don't mind checking?"

Connie keyed another command. "Yes, sir, again, shipping invoice says they received twelve cases."

"Was there visual verification?" he asked.

Connie's eyes widened, realizing the revelation on the computer screen. "Um, no sir. There's no record of visual verification because there's no signature."

Mark stood erect, crossing his arms, and thought aloud. "Not a surprise, really. Trucks back right up to the bins and unload. Check to see if that truck stopped anywhere along the way."

"Yes, sir." She changed screens and looked for the truck assigned to carry the cases. "Yes, sir, stopped once for refueling. Seven minutes."

"Location?"

"Carron Brothers on James."

"Thank you, Connie." He patted her shoulder.

She closed her eyes and took a deep breath. "Thank you, Mister Jason." She opened her eyes to ask a question, but she was now alone in the cubicle farm. "Mister Jason?"

The Carron Brothers station was a small family-owned convenience store which also had an exclusive contract with Jason Enterprises for fueling its fleet. The Spy brought his black Task Force car to a stop on the side of the station away from the road. It was night, and no one should have been inside. He activated the heat-resolution sensors on his dashboard and confirmed no one was in or near the building.

He pulled his black hood over his head and sealed its seam with the matching uniform collar before getting out of the car. The door closed silently on its own as he moved toward the back entrance of the store.

Locks were no challenge to him. He was inside within seconds, and in the interior office even faster. As a Jason contractor the station was equipped with better than state-of-the-market surveillance equipment. Mark knew he shouldn't look at the footage from his office, as the inquiry would leave access footprints, which would take more time to remove than he desired. Retrieving the recordings from the source was faster, easier, and non-traceable if he used the owner's login to check the records.

Within seconds he was reviewing footage of the day his truck with two crewmen stopped for gas. It was a standard company box truck without markings. One man went to the restroom inside while the other gassed. Mark watched, noticing that neither man noticed a car that pulled up close behind the truck. A woman got out, went to the back of the truck, and unlocked the padlock. She opened the rear doors and removed a small box. She closed everything and put the box in her passenger seat, then calmly started pumping gas using a cash card.

She was a long-haired redhead who wore a baggy blouse and loose-fitting jeans, with black glasses and a large-billed hat to cover her face. *Smart girl,* he thought. *She knew there was a camera somewhere. Very interesting.*

He tried to see the car tags of the otherwise nondescript light blue sedan, but the truck blocked the view. When she completed filling her tank, she got back in her car and backed up, revealing no license plate. *Very, very smart.*

Spy reset everything, returned to his car, and sped off into the night.

The Drop Inn Bar and Motel was functioning as usual. Lots of drinking going on in the bar, and a steady stream of people coming and going from the motel.

A shadowy figure watched as one room was vacated by a couple. Once they returned to the bar, the figure approached the motel room door.

Spy placed an override card in the door's keycard slot, and the lock tumbler released.

The room was in decent condition, though it had just been used for a quick rendezvous. As expected, the bed sheets were tossed about. There was an empty bottle of Jack Daniels on the dresser.

In the official report, the first black widow venom murder was treated as a homicide. It was later determined the victim was injected with a Latrodectus venom, but the case was left unsolved and officially closed. The local sheriff was not interested in pursuing the case any further. He, with his brothers who owned the bar and motel, let the murder die quietly.

After the scene had been investigated, the live-in cleaning lady did an excellent job of making the room usable again. But, he knew no amount of cleaning could get rid of all the evidence.

Spy adjusted the operational settings in his hood's lenses and removed a special blue-light emitter / receiver, connected by Bluetooth to his hood's electronics. It glowed slowly along the baseboards first.

As the wide-beam light played along the floor, the sensors in his lenses compared the readings of the residue to a known chemical data base. The readings however, only showed gastric and stomach acids, along with proteins and alcohol. *No surprises here*, he thought.

He recalled from the murder scene reports that the victim was found in the tub, with digestive contents spilled across the floor. He turned his attention to the carpeting in the front area bordering the bathroom tile.

The sensor readings showed great amounts of both fresh and long-dried DNA, but none of the residue matched the specific composition he sought.

The door lock clicked. He drew his .45 and aimed at the door as it swung open.

Gail was surprised to see the masked man in a semi-crouch between the bed and dresser, but not scared. "Oh, please, tell me there's not supposed to be a kinky play-act thing in here tonight. That's reserved for the rooms at the other end. Nice-looking prop, though, I'll give you that."

Spy tilted his head, surprised. *This is a first, I usually scare the shit out of people dressed like this,* he thought. The moment was unusual. He stood and clipped his gun back in place. In his electronically altered bass he asked, "Who are you?"

"You must be new, if you gotta ask," she replied. "I'm Gail, 'round-the-clock housekeeper. This room is supposed to be empty right now. I got about a half hour to ready it for the next booking, and if you're it, you're way too early." She looked at her activity register.

He looked at the cleaning cart outside the door and the baby in its seat on the bottom shelf. "Yours?"

"Yeah, that's my little Virginia, she helps me." Gail smiled at her daughter, sound asleep in her carrier. "So, what are you supposed t' be?"

Quickly Spy composed a hopeful-believable answer, based on what she was saying. "I'm playing super-hero of course, waiting for my girlfriend to be rescued," he said. He took a relaxed stance by crossing his arms and leaning against the wall. "But, I heard there was a murder here a couple months ago, so I wanted to search for evidence. Got a super-villain to catch, you know."

"Mister, aint'cha kinda big to be playin' make-believe cop like a little kid? Although I love the outfit, looks lots more realistic than all the other crazy getups I've seen since I been here." She gave him two thumbs up. "Okay, so interview me like a super-hero would."

The Spy nodded. "How long have you been here, Gail?"

"Oh, about a year. Mister Jim lets me live in the last room in exchange for keeping everything tidy. The ladies leave me cash from their fellas so I can get food for me and Ginny, and clothes and stuff. Tonight's a real busy night, that's why Ginny 'n me's working so late."

"So, you were here when that man was killed in the tub?"

"Oh, yeah, that scared the shit outa me! Made poor Ginny scream, too, 'cause o' me. Man, I never seen a dead guy before, that was scary weird, y'know?"

"I can imagine. So, you saw everything here? Did you see who was in the room?"

"Nah, I found him during my morning cleanup. The room was checked out to a lady named 'Lacy'. I don't know who the guy was."

"Did you see this 'Lacy'?"

"Nah," said Gail. Virginia moved in her carrier and Gail knelt down to adjust her baby blanket. "Just the name on the register." She stood to face him. "You're good, you sound like a real cop. So, you doing some kinda cop-and-robber game tonight?"

"Something like that." He watched her park her cart all the way in the room and began stripping the bed of its sheets.

"Why do you live here? Shouldn't you be home?"

"This is my home, like I told you," Gail said, matter of fact. "My folks kicked my ass out when I told 'em I was pregnant. All I had was the clothes on my back. Mister Jim is the only family I got now. I can't get another job around here where I can keep Ginny with me, and there's no money for daycare."

"Is there anything else about that night you can recall?"

"Aside from all the mess I had to clean up once the cops were gone? No—oh, wait. I remember Mister Alex telling someone that this guy left the bar with a pretty redhead, dressed all in black. Not like you, in a costume, she was dressed to kill, all fancy an' all."

"Did she come with the victim, or did she drive herself?"

"Folks saw her walk into the bar. They said she ordered a fancy drink called a 'Black Widow'. No one had ever seen her before, ain't seen her since."

Hum, seems she already gave herself a villain name, he thought. He stepped toward her, his right hand opening a zipper in the inside of his left glove and removed a plastic pouch. He extended his right hand to her. "Thank you, Gail, you've been a great deal of help. You're a brave young lady, and obviously a good mother. Little Virginia will grow up to be very proud of you."

She accepted his gloved hand. "Wow, mister, that's some grip ya got!"

"Sorry, hope I didn't hurt you."

"Nah, I'm good. Well, hope you had fun playing detective, but I gotta get my work done. I don't have much time before the next lady gets here. Ginny, baby, say bye-bye to the nice man in his great costume." Gail looked down as Virginia barely opened her eyes and cooed before going back to sleep, warm and comfortable in her carrier. As she turned back to her guest she said, "Thanks for letting me be part of your game, I don't get to do—"

The man in the black costume had vanished. On the floor where he had been standing was the plastic pouch he removed from the secret pocket in his glove. She knelt down and picked it up.

She looked at the pouch and found its seal, and gently opened it.

Gail's eyes widened when she removed ten one-hundred-dollar bills. "Holy shit, Ginny! We're rich!" She stood and looked around the room. She looked in the bathroom and, in the closet, but the man in black had disappeared. "Wonder who that was Ginny, and how'd he disappear like that?..."

CHAPTER 43

AN EYE FOR AN EYE

"Lexi, I'VE BEEN LOOKING FOR THIS GUY FOR TWO WEEKS, and I can't find him!" She pounded her fist on the desk then stood in anger, abruptly forcing her chair to roll backwards. Her neck and ears turned a light shade of red. Lexi realized another outburst was beginning.

"Look, it's Saturday, Lacy. You go down to the basement and work with the spiders. I'll keep looking for him." Lexi was holding a dishtowel after washing dishes in the kitchen. She wadded it into a ball and threw it into the kitchen, not caring where it landed. She hugged Lacy around the waist. "I was damn lucky to find him the first time around, even if it was just a phone number. He's not an easy guy to find. So, I bought a program online yesterday. It's called 'I-Search', a program bounty hunters or detectives use to find people. You pay for the service; it downloads to your computer. You can find their name, address, how many people live in the house, where they work, average income, where they went to school, just everything. There's even satellite imagery."

Lacy was amazed with the technology, but not surprised that people could have such access. "But why, Lexi? Why would you do that, buy that?"

Lexi cupped her hands on Lacy's cheeks, staring into her eyes. "Because I love you, hon, and I want to help." She gave Lacy a quick kiss on the lips and walked her to the door of the basement. She pointed downward with an index finger. "Go. You do what you need to down there, that's why we moved into this place, and I'll start working with this program. I haven't even studied it yet; it may take a little time."

Lacy offered a small grin, and descended the creaky stairs of the hundred-year-old house in the rural area west of Richmond.

Lacy spent most of the weekend in the basement working with the black widows. She fed them, separating the newborn spiders to their own plastic cages, carefully weaving her way through the strong silk webs. She contemplated how useful the spider venom would be, thinking about how to use it in different ways. The basement was musty, dank, and chilly. There were no windows, just old incandescent lighting. Stainless steel tables lined each wall, the working space for Lacy to milk the spiders, which was an extremely delicate and precise process. She didn't want to kill any of what she called "her babies." There she also worked on cages, used laboratory microscopes, electrodes, magnifying goggles, tools, vials, refrigerators…everything she needed to work with thirty-two species of black widows. The new guns they had recently purchased after the Yursi killing were beside their black travel bags on another counter. She was tired, the work was delicate and time consuming. It could be dangerous to someone who was fatigued. Too tired to work anymore, she headed upstairs. About halfway up, she smelled something delicious. "Garlic bread!"

Lexi replied from the kitchen, "With spaghetti and my secret sauce recipe. Oh, and a bottle of Pinot Grigio."

"Oh man, I love your spaghetti. And the Pinot is great with it!" Lacy strolled into the kitchen, placed her elbows on the counter, resting her chin in her hands. "Okay, what's the special occasion?"

Lexi stirred the pot of sauce with a wooden spoon. She shook her head, her blonde ponytail swayed back and forth. "No occasion. Just thought I'd cook a meal for once. Besides, you've been down in the dumps and I wanna cheer you up."

Lacy frowned at the revelation. "Yeah." She sauntered to the refrigerator, retrieved the bottle of wine, and poured its contents into two extra-large glasses. "I've been a real bitch lately. I'm sorry. I just can't get *him* out of my head. I wanna rip his—"

"Stop right there." Lexi held her hand in the air. "Set the table. I have good news for you."

Seated at the table, Lexi raised her wine glass. "A toast to me, the internet geek. Cheers, honey, I found what you've been looking for."

Lacy cocked her head, narrowed her eyes, a small grin forming on her face. She clinked her wine glass with Lexi's. "You what?"

"Yep, found him a little while ago, while you were isolated from the world downstairs." Lexi took a sip of wine. Lacy took a huge gulp of wine, and set her glass on the table

"Are you sure? How do you know? Where is he? What's he—"

"Hold on, girlfriend, I'm getting to it. Now that's the good news." Lacy steadied herself for what might be the inevitable bad news. "He's, well—different now. He's not the monster he used to be; I think."

"Whoa, wait, uh-uh. I don't care if he's turned into a chimpanzee. You found him, we're gonna take care of his sorry ass."

"Lacy, he goes by two different names. That's why I've had such a hard time finding information on him. The reason is, he's some sort of minister now."

Lacy almost choked. "What? A preacher? How in the hell did that son-of-a-bitch get to be one of those?" She leaned over her plate and spoke in a low, deliberate monotone. "I don't care if he's the freekin' Pope."

Lexi placed a hand atop Lacy's. With a resigned sigh, she replied, "Okay, sweetheart, I get it. Luckily, we don't *have* to go to Rome. He's about nine hours away, a long trip, but we can make it work. Now, eat your dinner..."

Once the table and dishes were cleaned, the two retired to the living room couch with a laptop computer. "So, which venom you gonna use this time? Not that I really care."

Lacy thought a few seconds, drumming her fingers on her chin. "If he's a holy guy, I think perhaps it would be a significant irony to use the European Black Widow. Don't you?"

Lexi shrugged her shoulders. "Not sure what you're getting at, love. But, I dunno, you're the doctor, I'm just the hired help." Lexi laid her head on Lacy's shoulder while they both scanned the information about the man. "If we leave late on a Friday night or early on a Saturday morning, considering he agrees to meet with us, we could get to Charlotte, North Carolina, and check-in. We'd have to take him to a nice hotel restaurant, like the others. But, to get him up to the room, that'll be the hard part. Then take turns driving back to get here Sunday before anyone knows we were gone."

"Yeah, there's more than one way to skin a cat, Lexi. We're good; we can manage getting him up to the room with no problem. Might take a little coaxing, but we can do it. I'm so looking forward to this one. Repentant of his sins? Yeah, right. I'll teach him repentance."

"I guess an eye for an eye," Lexi said…

CHAPTER 44

"HOLY BLACK WIDOW"

Rᴇᴠᴇʀᴇɴᴅ ᴜɴᴅᴇʀᴡᴏᴏᴅ ʜᴜɴɢ ᴜᴘ ᴛʜᴇ ᴘʜᴏɴᴇ, placing it delicately into its cradle. He sat at his desk for several minutes, perplexed by the call. Thinking again about the girl he and the others had raped years ago. He felt as if a knife had been plunged into his heart, and he hung his head and cried. "I must pray," he whispered aloud, and proceeded to the sanctuary. He stood before the dais and stared at the statue of St. Peter, its eyes looking heavenward. St. Peter was a harsh reminder of the minister's youth, and his past personal denial of The Savior. On the right was an ornately painted lifelike statue of Jesus. Its hands and feet were nailed to a cypress wood cross, eyes closed, and head hanging low, lifeless.

He fell to his knees, grieved, and prayed for guidance. Though long absolved of all sins, he couldn't help but feel sorrow and regret. *She said she wanted to make amends, to meet in person and talk about it,* he thought. "Father, guide me, give me the wisdom and strength to handle this. I'm forgiven in your eyes, but the pain and shame has always remained."

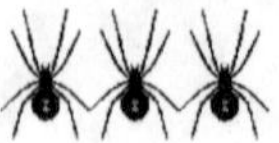

Lexi and Lacy readied to leave the house, anxious to meet the reverend later in the day. Lacy had instructed Jesse to 'dress it down' a bit. They needed to look more attractive than seductive, showing less skin. "I dunno, Lacy, this whole thing about killing a man of the cloth, it bothers me. I gotta be honest with you."

Something in Lacy's brain snapped when Lexi spoke. *"For God's sake, Lexi, we've been arguing over this all week!"* Lacy, sick of the constant bickering, slammed Lexi against the wall, hard. "You listen to me," Lacy said through gritted teeth, her hand closing around Lexi's throat. "I have a goal, a mission, a task, whatever the hell you wanna call it. Have you ever been raped by four sickos? Your mom and dad hate you? The whole town hates you? Every relationship abusive? Look at how they *all* treated me, *took away my life*? They got to live theirs. It's not fair! And it's time to make the last one pay! I'll never be the same, Lexi. My mind is all over the place and it's getting worse. The nightmares are always there, I can never love a man, I'm afraid of what's around every corner!"

Lexi pushed her away and walked a few feet toward the bathroom. She turned and stared into Lacy's eyes. They were cold, defiant. Lexi said nothing. There was nothing left to say. She walked into the bathroom to finish getting ready, slamming the door behind her.

Lexi and Lacy arrived at the Reed Memorial Hotel earlier than expected. After freshening up, they took the elevator to the first-floor restaurant. When they walked in, they were taken aback at the spectacular view. The lighting was dim. The entire restaurant was decorated in a sophisticated jungle motif, adorned by tropical trees, plants, flowers, and ponds with fish. "Wow, this place is beautiful, Lexi!"

A waitress greeted the two and showed them to a table in the back, as Lexi had requested when she made reservations. "Lacy, I had no idea it was this kind of restaurant when I called. I hope this guy isn't intimidated by it."

"Na, I'm sure he's been around. Doesn't just sit in a church all day. He'll probably enjoy it, despite the discussion we're gonna have."

After a few minutes, the waitress escorted a man to their table. He wore a conservative blue pin-striped suit, and white shirt. His blue tie held a gold cross tiepin. They awkwardly shook hands, and all introduced themselves. He sat, smiling, but with concern in his eyes. They made small talk for a while, then decided to order drinks. They perused the menu offering pricey tropical delicacies. Everyone's appetite seemed diminutive, nervous about the meeting. They chatted as they ate, not going into great detail, since nearby patrons could hear their conversation.

"Ladies, this dinner is on me and I'd love to buy another round of drinks. If you don't mind."

Lexi raised a finger. "I was just thinking. I didn't realize that reverends were allowed to drink." Lexi said.

"Well, don't confuse me with some of the other, stricter orders," he said with a gentle smile.

Both women nodded, knowing they could both use another drink or two. Lacy spoke, "Reverend, when we're done, would you consider coming up to our room to talk about this further? As you can see, they've seated us close to other people and, um, well, it's hard to talk about the past with so many people around."

He looked down, staring at the white cloth napkin in his lap, considering the request. "Yes, now that you say that, I think that's a good idea. We've not been able to speak frankly with each other this evening, or since that unforgiveable time."

"—it was because of that terrible moment," he continued with his story, "that I sought forgiveness from my pastor. I was drunk, not in control of myself. I was not like that before that night, Lacy. Jake just had this bullying way over the rest of us, whatever he wanted, we did. When I sobered up and remembered, I tried to find you, but you weren't around. My pastor told me to turn myself in, but I just couldn't do it. I deserved punishment, so the only way was to forsake my original plans in life and devote myself to only serving others. I hoped one day you could forgive me as the Lord has forgiven me." He placed his hands in his lap. "It's obvious that God finally sent you to me so I can ask you personally for your forgiveness."

Lacy sat opposite him in the hotel room seating area; she was transfixed, confused, and angered. A confession was the last thing she expected. Lexi picked up on her bafflement and took Lacy by the hand and urged her toward the bathroom. "Excuse us for just a minute, Reverend Underwood," Lexi offered. Alone in the bathroom with the door closed, Lexi whispered, "Will you freekin' cry or react or something? The man just laid out his soul to you for forgiveness! He's not the same man or personality as the kid who was part of that gang-rape."

Lacy stared at her friend, confused.

"Dammit, Lacy, go forgive him! We can't kill that man!"

Lacy's expression hardened. "He—*cannot*—leave alive. He stole my life, along with the rest of them.

"He lost his life, too!" Lexi interrupted. "His life changed because of that night!"

Lacy leaned against the bathroom counter, near their bag, still containing their guns, a venom-filled auto-injector, the tripod and silk sheet sack. "I—he can't—"

"No, you can't, and you don't have to kill him. He died a decade ago, the same time you did."

Lacy stared into Lexi's eyes, her fury unmasked. She growled, "No, dammit, he did not die the same time I did. He's a liar. He's the same person, hiding behind a bible. No telling how many women he's abused. He's rich, probably has women on their knees every night, and not for prayers!"

"Lacy! That's a horrible thing to say! You really *don't* have a conscious, do you?"

"No, Lexi, I don't. It died when I died! When those four killed my soul while they raped and killed me!"

The reverend knocked on the bathroom door. "Lacy, are you alright? I heard you yelling." He opened the door.

Lacy reached for a gun inside the bag, pointing it at him. He simply stood at the door, calm and unmoving. "Why don't you finish your story. That forgiveness you spoke of? Why don't you start begging for it now?"

His hands were placed on either side of the doorframe and hung his head low. He cried. Not sobs, no sound at all, only tears, falling to the floor. He moved back to the sitting area, and sat, expressionless. The two women followed.

"You want me to beg? Then I beg of you, Lacy, I ask for your forgiveness."

"I—I—don't—"

"You don't what, Lacy?" he asked. "You don't want to kill anyone, do you?"

"YES!" she shouted back. "I want you all to die for what you did to me! For all the other people just like me. You're the same as you were when you raped me. Two of the others already got theirs. They're dead and gone. I finally have the means to kill you, too, and you're some sort of freekin' minister? Why, why did you do that? Hiding behind your mask? A little wuss, still getting his way!" The gun shook in Lacy's hand.

"I told you," he said calmly, "this was my penance."

"Do you see this?" She showed him the auto-injector box in her other hand. She placed the gun on the bed, opened the box and showed him the auto-injector filled with concentrated venom. "This is black widow venom. Remember what happens after the male spider mates with the female spider? Yeah, she kills him. So, we're gonna do just that, rev. Stand up, take your clothes off. I'm gonna do what you did to me, but a hundred times worse. Payback's a bitch, and I'm the bitch who's gonna make you pay for what you did to me!"

He sat, listening. Tears continued to run down his face.

He stood. "Lacy, your heart is cold. I understand that. But *you* don't have to do this." He dropped to his knees. His face was serene, staring up at her. His large brown eyes emoted a deep sadness.

"Get up! Do what I told you. Plead for your life! Because of you, and those others just like you, I'm dead inside. I'll never be normal. I'll never have anyone who can love me. And I *don't* want to love them."

"Lacy, *please*." Lexi begged.

"She's right, Lexi. I guess it was stupid of me to think God or anyone else could forgive me. And Lacy, I will not have your soul tainted twice because of me."

Before she could react, he snatched the auto-injector box from her hand, removed the auto-injector, and stabbed himself in his leg. He grimaced at the pain. "I accept my punishment for my actions, but at my hand, not yours. You were innocent a decade ago when I was part of stealing your innocence then, I will not allow you to be guilty of my punishment now."

"No!" Lacy screamed. "No! That's not the way it's supposed to be!" She dropped to the floor and pulled the empty auto-injector from his leg. "*No! Why did you do that?*" She threw the auto-injector off to the side. She shook his shoulders violently. "You can't take this away from me, it's mine! MINE!"

Lexi was transfixed, hands over her mouth.

"Forgive—me." He wasn't able to say anymore. The powerful venom was already doing its work on his body. He made no sound when he fell over, curling into a fetal position.

Lexi pulled Lacy upward and away from him, forcing her to sit on the bed.

The man suffered the same as the others. The violent convulsions, vomit, and more. The women sat and watched. Within minutes, it was over. "It's done, sweetie. Doesn't matter how, even if he did it to himself."

Lacy seared inside, but when she spoke it was in a weak whisper. "It was mine, and he took it. Now, everyone will pay."

"What, everyone who?"

"I don't know yet, but all of them."

"You're not making sense, hon."

"Get the web Lex." She stared angrily at the reverend while she spoke. "Let's put this son of a bitch in his cocoon and hang him in the web for all to see. I can already see the looks on the faces of the cops." She turned to look at Lexi. "This is just the beginning…"

A national television station aired a report the following morning. "We have a breaking news alert about an ongoing hunt for a possible serial killer, who could still be in the Charlotte area. The body of Reverend Richard Underwood from the Charlotte/Mecklenburg Church of Renewal was found murdered in a room in the Reed Memorial Hotel in Charlotte, North Carolina. According to sources, the crime scene is a near duplicate to that of another murder last month in Charleston, South Carolina. Yursi Komiani, son of Ollistani President Komiani, was killed in the same, gruesome manner. One other similar case is still under investigation from three months ago in a motel off Interstate 95 in North Carolina. More updates as we receive them…"

CHAPTER 45

A HUNGRY WIDOW

Lacy and Lexi always slept in the same BED. They were used to sleeping close to each other for comfort and safety. Lacy despised being alone, anywhere. They'd lived together since college, whether it was a rented house or apartment, or now in their new home.

Lexi woke with a start, hearing a noise. She propped herself on her elbows and called out Lacy's name, thinking she may be in the bathroom down the hall. There was no answer.

She stepped into the hallway; the wooden floors creaked with each step. Lexi realized the house was colder than normal and saw a light on downstairs. She grabbed a housecoat from the back of the door, deciding to join her girlfriend. She heard the floorboards creaking and moaning to a back-and-forth rhythm beneath her bare feet. She clicked the iridescent green light on her watch: it read two a.m.

She crept down the thin staircase, pulling the housecoat tight around her body. The stairs led into the living room where Lacy had apparently disappeared to in the middle of the night. The computer was on. Lacy was pacing back and forth in front of the desk, oblivious to Lexi's presence. The window by the desk was half open, the cool night air flowed in. Lacy was wearing only a pair of thong panties and a cutoff tee-shirt.

Lexi leaned against the wall and crossed her arms. "That's a pretty sexy outfit, but the mood and atmosphere is all wrong."

Lacy jumped at the voice, not realizing she was being watched. "Not now, Lexi, I'm thinking. It's been two months and nothing. Just damned nothing."

"Not everyone gets on those social networks. They like their privacy. Do you realize it's two in the morning? You're prancing around half naked with the window open? Not that I'm complaining, mind you." Lexi closed and locked the window, pulling the curtains together. "Some people would label you a sociopath and a psychopath, never mind an exhibitionist!"

"What do you know about it? You're no freekin' psychiatrist! So, I couldn't sleep, I came down and opened the window for fresh air to help me think!" She advanced on Lexi, inches from her face. Lacy's eyes were crazed, like a caged animal. "I've gone two months, *two months*! Do you know what that means?"

Lexi replied, irritated, "No, Lacy. I *don't* know what that means, except you're turning into the *bad mood from hell!* Every day you get more weirded out. You're losing your mind! And by the way, I have a minor in psychology, remember?"

Lacy pounded the edge of the wall. "I—I, shit, I *need* it, dammit! I have a minor in psychology, too, Lexi, *if you remember, too*." Lacy took a deep breath. "After all these years, after they took away my future, I was given the opportunity for revenge. I need my vengeance, I've always known it, and they all need to pay. He's the last one. The last one of those four damn animals! No, I can't get rid of all the jerks I've had in my life, the old boyfriends, my parents, and those abusers. But I can get rid of *him*. Then, at least these four will get the justice they long deserved, and I can *try* to be normal for once."

"I get it, honey, I have from the beginning, not that I like it. I'd do anything for you, you know that." Lexi stepped forward, wrapping her arms around Lacy from behind, and kissed her shoulder. "I've fallen in love with you. I guess somehow, it's always been this way. Watching you the last couple months, so desperate. You're raw and vulnerable. And at the same time, strong. I wanna get on with our life. I want to go places, go out to dinner, get ice-cream downtown, just sit together in the damned park. We can't do that right now. Not until your, whatever, is finished."

Lacy turned herself around inside Lexi's hug and kissed her passionately. Lacy pulled back, a rare smile on her face.

Lexi smiled in return. Stepping to the old piano, Lexi pulled out a pack of cigarettes and a lighter hidden in the piano bench. Lighting one, she took a deep puff and exhaled, blowing smoke toward the ceiling. "So, we're officially lesbians I guess, huh?" Lexi sat on the antique bench, taking another puff. "Wanna come back to bed and snuggle? I'm freezing. From the looks of things, you are too."

Lacy crossed her arms in defiance, covering her chest. "I thought you quit smoking. For me."

"Well, when I get *you* back from your sacred mission, maybe I'll quit again. "You used all the features of that program I bought, love? It's pretty damned thorough. You can find just about anyone in there."

"Yeah, I've searched it backward and forward, there's nothing."

"And, you've tried the high school reunion page? That's where we found the last one."

Lacy's face went pale; she sat in the chair at the desk. "Lexi, my God. It was right in front of my face the whole time." She smacked her forehead. "That's the *first* place I should have looked. *Damn!*"

"I assumed you looked there. Fire up the computer again. We'll find this son-of-a-bitch."

Within a few minutes, they found his picture and profile on the reunion page. Over the years, he had posted photos of himself, and dialog about his life. Then, it suddenly stopped. No posts in over two years. "Lex, this makes no sense. Yeah, we found him and his address and all. But someone who's this egotistical wouldn't just stop posting. He'd continue on with his bullshit, but he didn't. It just simply stopped."

Lexi responded, "Maybe something happened to him. Jeez, what if he died? That'd piss you off more, I'm sure. Well, we got all his info, let's work on it tomorrow. You need sleep. You haven't been sleeping right for a long time. You know what happens when a person is sleep dep—"

"I know, Lex! I know what sleep deprivation does to people," Lacy snapped.

Lexi finally scowled back, but not as loudly. "Okay, okay, let's just go get a few hours of sleep and we'll start looking for him." Lexi held her hand out to Lacy. Lacy looked up, seeing the sweetness in Lexi's eyes…

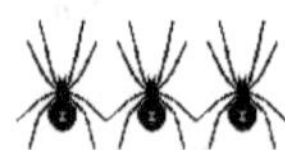

"He doesn't live there anymore, Lexi. I called the number and there's a new couple living there. He sold the house to them and moved to California two years ago. Of all places, California."

Lexi sat on the couch still in her pajamas. Her hair was in disarray. She sipped her coffee in between yawns. "Okay, let's think this through logically. He graduates, buys a house, lives, and works in that city for several years, posts crap on the high school page. Then suddenly he stops posting, sells his house, and moves. California, the big city. Something must have happened, compelled him to move on. Didn't want to be found maybe? So, we find his friends or co-workers. They'd know where he went, and why. Hell, my new program should have picked him up. I don't know why it wouldn't."

"Yes, yes, co-workers. He worked at that fancy men's clothing store." Lacy leapt from her chair, heading toward the stairs.

"Where ya going?"

Lacy grinned and looked back from the bottom step. "I'm going out to look for a pretty suit for my man. I'll make sure the vest is made of silk…"

CHAPTER 46

A KILLER IN SHE-EP'S CLOTHING

IT WAS SATURDAY. LEXI WAS LOUNGING ON THE couch, reading a book, when she heard the front door slam. "I got it, Lexi! Where are you? I got his address!"

"In the living room." Lexi sat upright and hopped off the couch, meeting Lacy halfway around the corner at the foyer. The two hugged and kissed.

"How in the world did you get them to give you his address?"

"Easy! I said I was on the high school reunion committee, then talked with one of the guys who knew him pretty well. He had his new address and phone number. I told him I was trying to find the guy so the committee could mail him an invitation to the reunion. The man didn't hesitate, just opened the contact list on his cell and gave me everything I needed. So naïve!"

Lexi hesitated, thinking back on the grisly murders, knowing she'd have to go through it one more time. "That's great, Lacy," she said, not sounding at all enthused. "I'm glad you found him. It'll be the last one, right?" She forced herself to smile at Lacy.

Lacy saw the reluctance and hugged her. "Yeah, baby, it's the last one," she answered. "I won't put you through any more of this."

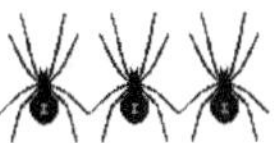

Lacy had gone out for a few groceries, leaving Lexi in a perpetual online search mode.

Lexi slammed a fist on the desk. She'd tried calling Alexander Weathers all week, but the man never answered his phone. He had no voice mail, which made Lexi even more frustrated. She lit a cigarette and leaned back in the chair. "Can't get him at his apartment, can't find his work, no social networks. Is this guy a freekin' ghost? Dammit, why am I even doing this for Lacy?" She spoke aloud, talking out her frustrations. *Wait, what if I called the apartment building manager?* she thought.

The apartment manager spoke with a heavy Boston accent, a deep voice made rougher by years of heavy smoking. "Yeah, yeah, you got the right place, sweets. Alexia lives up in three oh one. Been here a while now. Nevah late on rent, real quiet like, keeps to herself mostly."

"No, ma'am. I'm looking for an Alexander Weathers. A man, not a woman. We need to confirm his address for our high school reunion."

The manager cackled on the other end of the phone. The laughter sent her into a rage of coughing. "Sorry 'bout dat, the old lungs aren't what they used to be. Didn't mean to laugh at yah's, dear, but I'm guessing you're the last one to know. Alexander is no longer a 'he'. He's now a 'she'! Had da operation and all. It took a while for the transformation and stuff but yeah, she's a knockout now." Lexi heard more cackling and coughing. "You send your invitation in the mail. She'll get it. Just address it to Alexia, not Alexander. Doubt she'll go, though. Her kind of life is normal here, but probably not where you're from."

Lexi tapped "end" on her phone, stymied at the conversation. "Oh, God, what's Lacy gonna think?" She headed to the kitchen to pour a large glass of wine. She needed to calm her nerves before Lacy got home.

Lexi met Lacy at the door when she returned from grocery shopping. She had been lounging in a bathrobe which hung loose, exposing most of the front of her body. She handed Lacy a glass of wine and took the grocery bags. "Well, this is an unexpected surprise. My woman half-naked, serving me wine when I come home and taking on domestic duties at the same time. Couldn't get much better!" She smiled, sipping the wine, and followed Lexi into the kitchen. She noticed Lexi's ashtray where three cigarette butts lay dead, and also noticed Lexi had downed most of a glass of wine. "Okay, what's the matter?"

"Nothing, nothing's wrong," Lexi replied, placing a bottle of orange juice in the refrigerator.

"Lexi, I'm no therapist but it's obvious you're worried. The wine, the cigarettes, the extra attention, you're dreading something."

Lexi put a finger to Lacy's lips. "Shush. Drink your wine, then we'll go sit and talk."

A second glass of wine later, the two women sat on the couch. "You found him, didn't you, Lex?" Lexi's eyes lowered to the couch. "That's what it was, you found him! This is the last one, I promise." Lacy lifted Lexi's chin with a forefinger and kissed her lightly. "You did a great detective job. I'll take care of everything from here, okay?"

Lexi wrapped her arms around Lacy's neck, rested her head on her shoulder and wept into her hair. Lacy reached inside Lexi's bathrobe. Her skin was soft and warm, and rubbed a comforting hand in circles on her back. Lexi dreaded telling her the last of her gang-rapists was no longer a "he" but now a "she". She shook at the thought of Lacy's rage. It would be just like the reverend who took away Lacy's control and her revenge.

"You found him, right?" She wiped the tears from Lexi's face. Lexi nodded in affirmation.

"*He's* not a *he* anymore."

"Say what?"

"He had a sex-change operation a couple years back. He's transformed his entire persona into that of a woman, even—" she threw her head back and stared at the ceiling. "—even his body parts are female now."

Lacy closed her eyes, her hand on Lexi's shoulder, trying to stay calm. "That's okay, Lexi, we'll overcome the obstacles. If Ms. Alex wants to be a woman, then she's in for a rude awakening. I have the perfect plan. The double entendre of this one will make it a great finale. I think I'm really looking forward to it."

"Okay, all packed up?" Lacy stood at the door, dangling the car keys. "Don't wanna miss the train. Got the rig packed nice and snug? Thank goodness they don't x-ray your bags at the train station; I'd hate to have to explain that thing."

Lexi's suitcase clunked down the stairs. "Sure glad this thing has wheels. I packed light, like you said, and even got the web in the suitcase, too. I'm glad we got a couple vacation days added to the long weekend."

"It won't be so bad. Got my book, the auto-injector in the bag and my girl to talk with. There's a bar on the train, did you know? All's good. We've been wanting to take a train ride for a long time!"

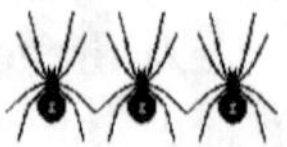

The two checked into the station, then waited outside for the train to arrive. "Lacy, I thought you said there was no security. Look at all of 'em. They're gonna go through all our stuff and they're wearing vests that say, 'Homeland Security'."

Lacy looked around and watched the passengers. Most were boarding the train with luggage or carry-ons in hand. "Lexi, I think all's okay. See, people are getting on board with no problem. I think they're here just to scope out stuff in case something looks hinky. We're just two cute chicks with suitcases. No need to profile us, now is there?" Lacy gave Lexi a mischievous grin. "Not like we're terrorists or anything."

Lexi mumbled, "No, but just as deadly."

It was an uneventful train ride, and both looked forward to the comfort of their hotel room. Once at the station they rented a car, programmed the GPS on Lexi's cell phone, and drove to the hotel with no problems. "Wow, this is a huge city! Cool."

"Lexi, you're acting like a kid on vacation," Lacy chuckled. "Look, when we get to the hotel, let's just relax, we'll climb in the shower, have some long-needed chill time and order food to be brought up. We'll laze around, watch some TV. How's that sound?"

"Yeah, sounds great."

"Then tomorrow we'll meet with him. No, her. Shit, we'll meet *it* for breakfast like we planned out over the phone."

"Think she'll even show up, Lacy? You were really insistent. I hope you didn't scare her away."

"Naw, she'll be there. I mean, yeah, she was hesitant at first, but after that long talk, she calmed down and sounded like she looked forward to seeing us. We know what we're doing, kiddo. No worries..."

CHAPTER 47

THE LAST SUPPER

"**O**KAY, EVERYTHING'S READY, LEX. DON'T FORGET to put the 'Do Not Disturb' sign on the door. A place this nice, they'll disturb no one if that sign's out. I'm glad we could find some of those old yearbooks. The bitch will never know." Lacy wore a short denim skirt and a button-down blue cotton shirt which left little to the imagination. Lexi dressed conservatively, wearing khaki slacks with a tucked-in white-collared shirt. "See, Lexi, one little hottie and one sophisticated butch, not knowing which the lady would like more, if at all. She might totally be into men now, but we'll try it."

The two waited in the downstairs restaurant. Lacy was antsy. She wondered if the ploy to get Alexia to the room would work. Anything that messed with her method made her angry. Once Lacy had a plan, she wanted to stick with it. *I'll still get my satisfaction. Watching her die. And now as a side plan, she'll get what it's like to really, really hurt,* Lacy thought.

A tall, thin, short-haired blonde woman entered the restaurant. It was obvious that she was looking for someone. "I bet that's her, Lacy. Wow, if it is, they did a great job. She's beautiful."

Lacy glared at Lexi. "She's a snake, Lexi, she's not pretty. She deserves what she's gonna get." Lacy leaned forward and spoke quietly. "They all deserve it. They all need to be punished, to die. There's a million of 'em out there and I wish I could take care of all of them."

Lexi said nothing, thinking Lacy looked and sounded like a snake. There was little doubt her friend had taken her vengeance to a whole new level.

The waitress escorted the woman to their table. "Coffee, black please," Alexia said to the waitress. She extended her hand. "Good to meet you both, Lacy and Lexi. I'm Alexia."

They exchanged niceties and pleasant chitchat. "So, you two are in town for a vacation? This is a wonderful city. I was hesitant on the phone. It's just, this change and all. I didn't think anyone from the old days would understand."

Lacy spoke sympathetically, placing a hand atop Alexia's. "No, we understand completely. The good thing is we're on this reunion committee. And now, after talking on the phone and here in the restaurant, I think we're becoming fairly good friends. You think?"

Alexia grinned, "Yeah, I was thinking the same thing. How nice it is that you understand. And having someone from the past who saw both sides of me really helps. You get where I'm coming from."

Lacy thought to herself in response, "*Yeah, where you came from. And, where you're going next...*"

After breakfast, Lexi grabbed the check from the waitress. "Nope, my treat ladies. This one's on me."

Alexia replied, "Well, okay, thank you so much. That breakfast was big, I don't know where I stuffed it all!"

Lacy clucked her tongue and grinned. "Yeah, that might be the last meal you'll need for a while, right? Oh, yeah, like I said, I brought some old yearbooks and pictures from school. You still wanna see 'em? Remember Eviland Stork? Her nose looked like a real stork's beak?" Everyone laughed. "Oh, I got some funny ones of the class clown, Chip Andrews!"

Alexia's eyebrows rose. "You have pics of Chip? I had such a crush on Chip back then. Coming out of the closet wasn't easy."

"Alexia, we've got some fixins for Mimosas up in the room. You wanna come up for a few drinks and look through some of these? Have some good old laughs. You'll love the pic of Steve mooning us out of his car window!"

"Well, sure. Hell, I don't have to be anywhere. Let's go…"

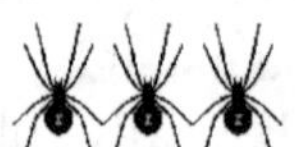

Lexi opened the door to their room. Everything looked fine, just as they'd left it. Alexia was still laughing at some of Lacy's real and 'made-up' school remembrances. "Come on in, kick your shoes off, Alexia. Make yourself at home. Look at the space in here, like a condo or something back home."

Alexia agreed and took her shoes off, choosing the chaise lounge to sit in. "Ah, if it's all the same by you, I'm gonna stretch out right here. And I apologize, I still don't remember you from high school. Funny how we all change, especially me."

The bar area was already set up with the auto-injector in its box, the drugs, and the drink glasses. Lacy handed some photo albums and yearbooks to Alexia to flip through. "Here, you start looking through some of these. I'll start mixing mimosas, okay?"

"Oh, yeah, can't wait to get my hands on these babies, especially those old ones of Chip."

Within a few minutes, Lacy came back with three drink glasses, handing the "special" one with the drug in it to Alexia. "Thank you, love," Alexia said, taking the drink. "Oh, look at this gorgeous crystal! These are beautiful. And what's this thing on the glass? An hourglass! Very clever. Almost reminds me of that shape that black widows have. Kind of unsettling if you're afraid of spiders, but I love it."

The three sat for a couple hours looking at old photos, drinking one mimosa after another. Alexia stopped chattering in mid-sentence, and sat up. "I think I may have had more than my share of mimosas. I'll be back in a minute." Lacy and Lexi watched as Alexia staggered to the bathroom, knowing the drug was kicking in.

"How you want to do this, Lacy? Let's just be quick and get it over with. Not like you can screw her or anything. She doesn't even have an interest in women, that's for sure."

"Lex, just give me the injector and follow along. I don't have much control over this one either and it pisses me off. But, I will have my say-so before she's gone."

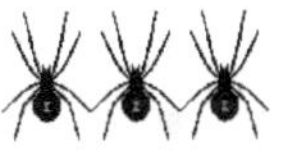

"You ladies make some strong mimosas; I'll give you that!" Alexia pushed her blonde hair back behind her ears and made waving motions at her neck. "It's a little warm in here. Mind lowing the A/C a bit?"

"I got it," Lexi said.

"Alexia," Lacy said as she sat hunched forward in her chair. "There's one funny incident I remember from high school." Lacy chuckled. "I bet you don't even remember. There was one day I was late for a class, and I tried to take a shortcut through the gym to get to my class faster. When I passed by the stage, I heard voices behind the curtain. Remember that stage?"

Alexia's eyes darted around the room. "Ah, yeah. Seems I do remember that stage. Used to play basketball in that gym all the time. I was rather good for a girl," she deadpanned.

"Yeah, well, I remember it vividly. Probably more than you. Like I said, I was walking by that stage and as I remember, there was a boy named Alexander who ran down the stage steps and grabbed me from behind. Can you believe that? He clamped a hand over my mouth and pulled me back up and behind the stage." Alexia's ears began to turn red. She set her glass on the coffee table. "There were three other boys back there. Jake was their leader, I think. They'd been drinking. I remember it like yesterday. They had their *way* with me. Threatened to kill me and my family if I ever told the police, or anyone."

Alexia wanted to bolt out of her seat. Too woozy, she couldn't move. "No! That wasn't me, Lacy. I'd never, I couldn't do that. I mean, I was gay! If that's what you're getting to, accusing me of raping you?" Alexia finally stood; hands balled into fists. "I couldn't have done what I think you're about to say."

Lacy stood. "Yeah, Alexia, it is what I mean. It was you, Alexander. Mr. Big Dick. I've traced it all the way back to you, to this moment. I've looked for you for a long time. And guess what? I don't give a shit about your trans-whatever lifestyle. Who you're trying to be, what you think you are now, how you think you've changed! All that makes *no* difference!" Lacy moved forward, nearly nose to nose with Alexia. "I remember *you* throwing me down on those pillows. It was *you* raping me from behind, gay, or not. It didn't seem to matter to you then!" Lacy poked at Alexia's chest each time she spoke a sentence, harder with each enunciation. Alexia staggered back onto the chaise lounge. "You don't have the right to speak now, or say you're sorry, or plead your case, or say it wasn't you, because I have the truth! I got the dickless wonder right here in front of me. I'm in his face and he has nowhere to go. He can't fight the big boys fight anymore. He's a little sissy girl, now!"

Alexia thrusted forward, wrapping both hands around Lacy's throat, squeezing, knocking over the coffee table with her sudden movement. Lacy fought back, trying her best to push back. It wasn't working. Alexia was bigger and stronger.

"Lexi! Where's the auto-injector? Let me have it!" The words squeaked out of Lacy's constricted throat. Nervous, Lexi couldn't find the auto-injector at first. Finally, she found the box on the bar. Running toward the fighting women, she plunged the auto-injector into Alexia's neck.

"What the hell!" Alexia let go of Lacy. A burning sensation spread through her body. Her eyes widened. "What did you do to me? *What the hell!"* Lacy and Lexi watched as the venom took effect.

"Lexi, you did good. You saved me again. You need to get the silk sheets and web. It's about time to wrap up our new girlfriend, for her final bye-bye..."

POP!
The champagne bottle cork flew out of Lexi's grasp. A small stream of bubbles flowed out. She and Lacy smiled and giggled, sitting on the couch in the hotel room. The bubbly was poured into both glasses. "To justice!" Lacy said, clinking her glass against Lexi's. She looked at the silk sheet cocoon holding Alexia's body hanging from the metal tripod. "Revenge is, *sa-weet!"*

"To justice," Lexi replied. "And thank God this shit is finally over." She leaned over and kissed Lacy hard, but quick. "You got what you wanted with no one the wiser!"

Lacy took another sip, still smiling. "Because we did it right. We were smart, and careful. And I couldn't have done any of it without your help. And no one will ever figure it was us. Because those bastards scared me so much as a girl, I never reported it. Oh, they'll figure out the four were high school friends, but they'll never connect it to me. It's impossible." She sipped again. "But it was fun, wasn't it? They call me 'The Black Widow' now! In the news and on the internet. Guess that makes me an actual desperado."

A frown formed on Lexi's forehead. "Yeah. It does, doesn't it?"

CHAPTER 48

A VERY FRUSTRATED SPY

THE SPY STOOD IN THE HOTEL ROOM LOOKING AT the fifth victim of the so-called 'Black Widow Killer'. When the body was discovered, local police were ordered to notify the FBI before any investigation began. This allowed the agent to study a pristine murder scene.

Her body was suspended in white silk sheets. The tripod holding the body-cocoon was made of standard piping and metal pieces. There were no fingerprints or DNA residue visible through his hood's computerized lenses. The crystal drinking glasses were also commercial grade.

"Control, Spy"

"Control."

"Patch me through to Michelson."

There were two clicks as he was relayed to the Task Force Division leader. "Michelson. Talk to me, Spy."

"It pisses me off to say it," the agent replied, "but we're dealing with the perfect serial killer..."

CHAPTER 49

THE BLACK WIDOW RETURNS
WEEKS LATER

Lacy SAT IN A CHAIR, looking through her high school yearbook. "Hey, Lacy, whatcha doin'?" Lexi asked.

"Just wondering, Lex."

Lexi pulled a chair over and sat beside her. "Wondering what?"

"Y'know, it was exciting, getting revenge." Lacy looked at Lexi. "It was sort of fun. It was a *rush!*"

"You sound like you want to do it again."

Lacy looked at her yearbook, pointing a finger at her photo. "Those four, they killed me that day. And with all the other shit in my past, it's taken me all these years to become this 'Black Widow' thing that's all over the news. And now, it's over. I had my vengeance. I'm not the *thing* anymore, The Black Widow." She chuckled. "I'm missing it, actually."

Lexi placed a newspaper atop the yearbook and pointed at one particular article. "What if there is a need?"

Lacy read the article, then looked up at her girlfriend. "I love you, Lexi! This is a fantastic idea! You're learning to like this after all."

Lexi smirked. "I don't think I'm learning to *like* it, no. But maybe The Black Widow really does have a place in society..."

A couple weeks later, sitting on the couch next to Lexi, Lacy read parts of the newspaper article aloud. "—Herman Salzer—accused rapist, released because of a mistrial—found dead in a hotel room this morning—according to sources at the scene, Salzer is the latest victim of the so-called 'Black Widow Killer'—for the sixth time, she continues her string of murders—FBI spokesmen state that the scene is a near duplicate of her previous killings…"

CHAPTER 50

CLUELESS

"THIS IS GETTING OUT OF HAND," MARK SAID TO the assembled Task Force field team. "Once the media gets hold of something that it helps with ratings, they run with it and keep on going."

"Naming a woman killer, a 'black widow' is definitely good for ratings," Mae-Lei confirmed. "Look at how well that appellate worked for the female suicide bomber threat for the Moscow Olympics."

"Yeah, but that interest died down fairly quick," Calvin added. "They're hot on this 'Widow' because she's not the traditional brand of 'Black Widow' serial killer. This one's not a woman killing husband after husband for their money." He keyed a command on his tablet, and a display flared to life on the conference room's Smart-TV. "Of the first five victims, four of them were found to be a group of high school best friends with a reputation for promiscuity. Yursi Komiani had no connection to any of these men, except that he was most likely the right kind of target in the wrong place at the right time." He keyed another command on his tablet and the reverend's profile filled the screen. "According to his calendar, the reverend who was murdered was supposed to be at that hotel, but canceled at the last minute because of a medical emergency with a parishioner. Our murderess," he said as he keyed another virtual button, "was stood up. See the video there." He pointed at the smart TV's display of the hotel bar security video. "See where she gets a text and she's obviously upset. Her partner is trying to console or calm her. And here's Yursi. He kept hitting on women in the bar while his guards laughed at his failures, until he hit on the Widow."

"She was all dressed and prepped to kill," Stephanie mused. "And rather than call it off she took the closest personality to her intended victim, and Yursi fit the bill. A smug sexual deviant who got off on using women like toys. She profiles out perfectly."

"Exactly." Mark said.

Harri chimed in. "What's frustrating is the complete lack of a suspect now. We've checked every known acquaintance of all four high school buddies. Everyone, without exception, has solid alibis for all the murders."

"And with not one clear view of their faces." said Mae-Lei. "We can't construct a facial recognition Trojan for our software. They're always wearing large sunglasses or wearing their hair in such a way that we can't lock in a complete facial image with any known female criminal."

"Stephanie, the auto-injector the FBI found," said Mark, "was a commercial-grade JE product sent for destruction because of a production flaw. Our murderess managed to steal a case when the truck stopped for gas. It could be a coincidence, or it could have been planned. If it was planned, then it would have to be one of *my* employees who had access to that transport's cargo."

"That's a big leap, Mark, but you have a valid point," said Stephanie.

"But your employees have some of the tightest security conditions in the world," said Mae-Lei.

"And thousands of people across the world, and a number of the people from the Richmond office attended the same high school as those four men. There's no criminal record on any of them, aside from the first one, Jake, being a basic asshole to everyone he knew," said Mark.

"Now the pattern is broken," Mae-Lei continued. "Before, she was meticulous in her timing. Once per month, almost to the day. The fifth victim was two months after the fourth. Now this sixth victim several weeks later. The style was exactly the same, including info not released to the media."

"And now there's this." Harri tapped at her own tablet and the Smart-TV image changed. "It's a 'Black Widow Fan Club' social network page. It's already getting posts from anonymous women, and some not-so anonymous. About men who got away with rape, physical abuse, and such, and are asking for revenge or justice."

"Well, that's just lovely," Mark said. "Okay, Oracle," he said to his daughter, "now's your chance to shine. Have you found anything in your matrix?"

"No, sir. I'm sorry, not yet." Angela said, sounding dejected. It was the first time she was asked for her knowledge in a Task Force meeting, and she had nothing to offer.

"Don't take it personally," said Harri. "You're here because you're the best at what you do." She looked at everyone around the table. "Right now, this Widow bitch is even better at what she does. She fits all the profiles for a serial murderer. Probably a long history of physical and mental abuse which may have even started in childhood. She's getting back, getting even. People like this stew on it for years. Fantasize about killing, then one day. *Snap!* Something goes off and they do it. The not so smart ones want to keep trophies. The smart ones don't. But she's methodical, I'll give her that. She's progressing nicely as a serial killer." Everyone in the room looked at her, faces scrunched. "What? Don't look so incredulous. We've all been to the same profiling schools."

"Yeah, we know Harri. You almost seemed a little too happy about it," Mark chided.

"I pose that the first four, not including Yursi, were indeed revenge killings, because they were meticulous in timing and gradual execution, and they did have at least one connection: they went to high school together," Mark announced. "But this last one is a break from that timing, which tells me she's changed her pattern for a new reason. I'd wager that because she perfected her method and completed her revenge, she can't stop and has to continue. I also think she may now go after sexual predators who have escaped justice. Since she's broken her original pattern of monthly cycles she's turned from revenge to justice, as she sees it. And I agree, Harri. There's a piece of the puzzle missing here; something from her childhood. And let's not forget she's probably working with a partner who may also have revenge issues."

"Mark, do you know what you're suggesting?" Stephanie asked. "There's thousands of men across the country who've committed sexual crimes of some kind. Either they were accused and got off or were found guilty, did their time, and released. There's no way all the police forces across the country can watch every one of them in case they become her target."

"No, of course. We may not have to go *that* far," he replied. "Her victims have all been from the mid-Atlantic states area, from West Virginia to South Carolina, aside from that west coast victim, but he's originally from Virginia. So, concentrate our efforts on those states. Other than the one who moved to California, of course. Probably even Virginia, North Carolina, Maryland, Delaware, New Jersey. I'd even add Kentucky, Georgia, and Tennessee as far as that goes." He fixed his gaze on Harri and his expression changed.

Harri looked at him quizzically. "What?"

Angela laughed.

"What's so funny?" Harri asked her.

"You've been around him for how many years now? And you don't know *'The Look'*?"

"Huh? What look?"

Angela pointed at her dad. "You see the way he's looking at you? He's not looking *at* you. He's looking *past* you. He always does that when he's looking down the highway at the answer. Except—"

"Except what?" Mark interrupted, confused at his daughter's remark.

"Except," Angela said, "you don't see the answer yet. Only the road to it."

"All right, smartass," he said to his daughter, smiling. "Get back in your matrix and get me an exit number from 'Interstate Answer'." Everyone chuckled. "Okay, suit up and pack up. We each take an area and wait. She's got a mileage radius she needs to stay in. Probably because of her regular job, whatever that might be. Stephanie, you have your home state of South Carolina and Georgia. Mae-Lei, North Carolina, and Kentucky. Harri, the Delmarva Peninsula and New Jersey. Calvin, West Virginia, and western Maryland. I have Virginia and D.C. Everybody in a TF transport with cars loaded for the road. All the appropriate equipment you'll need for this kind of mission."

Angela's tablet beeped. She looked down for a second, then gave a forlorn view to the team. "She's struck again."

"Um, Lacy, sweetie," Lexi said, her voice shaky. "You remember saying something about there being no one who could chase you?"

"Yeah, why?"

"Well, remember you said you wanted to watch how the cops investigate us? I snuck one of those tiny camera devices in the last place. Look at who's there now."

"You did *what*? Why didn't you tell me? What if it has fingerprints on it? Or trace it back?"

"Relax, Lacy. You forget how tech savvy I am. The feed is scrambled, they can't trace it back to us."

Lacy sat beside Lexi at the desk in their hotel room and watched the video feed. A large muscular man dressed in black was accompanied by a similarly dressed short blonde woman. They stood in the middle of their latest victim's house.

"Look at them, the way they move." Lacy crossed her arms on the table and rested her chin on her forearms. "So slow, methodical, calm. Can you pick up what they're saying?"

"The volume's up to high, I don't think they're talking at all," Lexi said.

The agents touched nothing, but obviously studied everything in sight. The man stopped, turned his head, and looked up at the camera. "Oh, shit, he found the camera!" Lacy exclaimed.

"How?" said Lexi in disbelief. "They're not using any kind of detection equipment."

"Wanna bet? Disconnect the feed, quick! And we gotta get outta here before they trace the signal back to us!"

Lexi began uninstalling the video software from her computer. She cleaned out the cookies and did a hard shutdown of her computer. "It must be some kind of tech-field-team. If so, they *may* be able to find us. I shouldn't have planted that camera after all!"

Lacy sat back in her chair. "Well, it's a good thing we wiped down the room, Lexi! What the hell? Now we know someone outside the normal police is looking for us. We have to be more careful. We can't let them stop our mission."

Proteus held the deactivated camera in her hand. "Standard home security model, commercial grade, we can trace it to its store but if it was paid for by cash and no extended warranty, it won't help."

"Not even the IP that thing transmitted to?" Spy inquired.

"Nope. Part of the whole 'security' thing, sir. In the current world of hackers coming out of the woodwork, these home security systems are actually decent."

"So, you're telling me you can't hack it yourself?"

"Don't be insulting, sir, of course I can. Just not fast enough before the killer is long gone. They already know that we know they've seen us. They had enough time to uninstall the software and delete all connection to the camera IP. I'm pretty sure they're in a temporary location nearby, like another hotel maybe. I'm sure under assumed names, too. Fake ID's and all. At least, I'd have fake ID's if I were them."

Spy crossed his arms and looked down. "Well, shit. This bitch is starting to really piss me off…"

CHAPTER 51

**THE LATRODECTUS LESSON
ONE WEEK LATER**

"HOW ARE YOU GETTING THESE SAMPLES, MISTER JASON?" Chrystal asked when Mark handed her another sample.

"My friends have access to the evidence retrieved from the growing number of victims and crime scenes," he said coldly. She had never seen such a grim look on his face before. "This Black Widow is making headaches for them, and they want something—anything—that will put them on the track to catch her before she kills again. And they're pushing me for answers since I said we could help."

"Well," she replied, "the one thing that jumps out, so far, is she's using a different strain of Latrodectus venom."

Mark looked at her. "Come again?" he asked, despite already knowing the answer.

"There are thirty-two species of black widow across the world," Chrystal explained, "and each time she's used a different one. You haven't brought me one duplicate sample from your friends."

"So," he said, cocking his head sideways, more contemplative in tone than before, "she used, what, ten by now? You're saying she could kill twenty-two more times before she finally stops? If that's her process?"

"If she stops at the end of that group, I suppose it's probable, sir." Chrystal replied. She shuffled through a stack of folders on her desk. "There are countless labs across the world where someone like her could get her hands on that many different varieties of Latrodectus venom—including us, sir."

And I'm sure our inventory is spot-on, Miss Leigh?"

"Absolutely, sir."

Mark narrowed his eyes at her for a moment and then offered a small smile. "I'm very impressed, Chrystal—you're much more confident of yourself now than you were prior to the beginning of this whole 'Black Widow' affair."

She smiled back, nodding gently. "You gave me an important job, over many others whom I'm sure were more qualified to do the work. I'm proud of my work, sir, and immensely proud to be working for you. You put a lot of trust in me, and I will *never* betray that trust."

Mark chuckled. "Sounds a little rehearsed, Chrystal."

She laughed back. "Well, yes, sir, I suppose, a little," she said, her eyes now staring at the floor.

"I'll leave you to your research then," he said. He turned to leave her office on the highly secretive 14th floor, but stopped at her doorway. "Chrystal, come to my office in one hour." He left without waiting for a response.

Chrystal sat at her desk, her mouth readied to respond, but he was gone. Baffled, all her recently accrued confidence seemed to fly out her office door.

"Miss Leigh is here," Eleanor said at the entrance to Mark's office on the 20th floor. She stepped aside to allow Chrystal to enter, then closed the door and walked to the office's wet bar, leaving Chrystal standing alone.

Mark Jason was not sitting at his desk; rather, he was seated in one of the plush chairs in his office's conversation area. His wife Jan was seated on the couch, both of them sipping on their usual end-of-day martinis. Mark rose to his feet and stepped to Chrystal, hand extended. "Chrystal, welcome. Would you care for a martini?"

Chrystal blushed, as the end of her day was going nowhere as predicted. Her confidence willowed again. "Um, perhaps, sir?"

Mark turned to Eleanor and nodded, and as Eleanor prepared Chrystal's drink he escorted her to the couch seat beside Jan. Eleanor presented her with a martini and returned to the bar area. Chrystal took a careful sip, never dropping eye contact with the company president, and coughed gently when the gin hit the back of her throat. "Um, I forgot to say to not to make it a double like mine, Eleanor, my bad."

"Quite alright, and sorry, sir." Eleanor replied in her crisp British accent. Jan laughed and Mark smiled. Chrystal had no idea what was to take place.

Jan reached over and grasped Chrystal's hand gently. "I've been hearing wonderful things about you, Chrystal," she said. "And you've been impressing the hell out of my husband. And let me tell you," she added as she leaned over in a confidential posture, "Mark Jason is never easily impressed."

"Thank you," she replied modestly.

"Your insight and specific knowledge of the Latrodectus genus did it," Jan continued. "We had no idea we had such a jewel in our intern corps when this whole 'Black Widow' event happened."

"I understand you've made a personal goal of developing that universal Latrodectus anti-venin," Mark said. "The tests you've performed, and replicated by other JE scientists, the CDC and other health departments, have put your name at the top of many powerful people's lists." He reached over his head and without hesitation Eleanor placed a folder in his hand, opening it. "Would you care to guess just how much I've been offered to sell your contract from JE?"

Chrystal's eyes widened, afraid to answer. Fearful that she may end up with another company other than Jason Enterprises.

Mark saw the concern in her eyes. "Don't worry, you're not being sold to the highest bidder. But, it tells me you've become extremely valuable to this company."

"It's okay, I guess, sir," she said.

Mark said, "So, this will come as no surprise to anyone around here."

Jan continued, "We will immediately promote you from your lengthy intern status to regular status, with permanent assignment to the major research projects as they are assigned and deemed necessary for your participation. At your rate of efficiency, you could be a permanent project leader in less than three years." Mark handed her a piece of paper from the folder, and Jan showed the number written on the employment form. "This is your new salary effective tomorrow. I do believe it will exceed any other offers you'll receive any time in the near future, should a competitor want to steal you away."

Chrystal nearly dropped her drink, had Jan not reached forward and grabbed it and set it on the coffee table.

"W-when do you need an answer?" Chrystal asked.

Mark's cell phone buzzed in his jacket pocket. He looked at the phone number and pressed 'answer,' but didn't speak into the phone. "I usually like answers as soon as the questions are asked," Mark said, deadpanned. He rose to his feet, held up an index finger to the women, returning the folder to Eleanor. He took his drink to his desk, sat, and keyed commands into his computer. "You and Jan can talk for a bit while I get some essential work done, it won't take long."

"Um," Chrystal started to say, "I, um—"

"Chrystal," said Jan, "you can speak freely."

"I—really need to use the restroom."

Jan smiled and pointed to the door at the far corner of the office suite. "Go right ahead. Not everyone gets to see inside that particular door!"

Mark watched as Chrystal rose and entered his private bathroom. He brought the cell phone to his ear. "What?"

Calvin's voice was on the other end. "We've got another one, boss."

It was all Mark could do not to punch his desk. "Son of a bitch! Where?"

"Luray Caverns, sometime last night."

"Okay, I'll be on my way. Who else is close?"

"Actually, that'll be me. I'm already here. Police have the area cordoned off. The FBI is doing preliminary casing and removing the body. All notes are being done on tablets and forwarded to one of my email addresses to transfer to our database. I can save you the trip, boss, there's nothing here."

"There's always something," he said, "sometimes it's not always in plain sight."

"The Black Widow has been really careful," Calvin replied. "She hasn't left one damn clue to her identity or her next target. She's making a fool out of all of us."

"She will not be a serial killer version of D.B. Cooper," Mark said. "We're going to find her if it's the last thing we do…"

CHAPTER 52

A FRIENDLY REMINDER

"I'M VERY DISAPPOINTED IN YOU, JASON," President Komiani said to Mark. "You promised me results, and it has been far too many weeks since you and your staff investigated my son's murder scene!"

Mark calmly sat back in his office chair, looking at the Ollistani leader. "The only time murders are solved in 40 minutes is on TV, Mister President," he replied. "And as I have come to learn, this particular murderess is beyond very good. My investigative team is impressed with how well this 'Black Widow' is evading identification, let alone capture, and it's pissing the shit out of them."

Komiani set his drink down on its coaster and took a deep breath. "My friend, I have withheld any reprisals against your country solely because of you, but my people are not so easily forgiving. Their favorite son was murdered here, and by not only by *one* woman but by *two* women! There are demands to enact our own vengeance. You've seen it on television, the news. The pleas from my country are overwhelming."

"You really don't want to allow that," said Mark. "This special team I mentioned has the ability to wipe any existence of you off the planet in no time at all. I have no idea how they'd do it, but I suggest you don't press them."

Komiani swiftly crossed his legs at the knees tightly, remembering the 'implant'. "I—um, agree," he replied. "I only humbly ask that you pass on my concerns and return any information you get."

"Count on it. Truly, they are moving as fast as we can. This murderer, she's good; way too good. But my team is better, and while they enjoy a challenge, they are professionals and are following every lead, no matter how obscure. It just takes time." Mark stood and extended his hand, which Komiani accepted as he stood in reply. Komiani nodded without a word and left the office through the open connecting door to Eleanor's office and his waiting personal security team.

After Komiani left, Eleanor approached her boss. She saw the seething expression in his eyes, and asked, "If I may, sir?"

He looked at her and smiled. "Always, Ellie. What's on your mind?" he asked as he motioned for her to sit in one of the chairs across from him.

"This 'Black Widow'," she began, "is making you miserable."

"Is it that obvious?"

"Actually, she's pissing you off in a big way."

Mark laughed. "Thanks, Ellie, I needed that from you. But tell me something I don't already know."

"Your frustration is because you're always a couple steps behind her, and aside from the standard victim discovery setup she has not established any pattern."

"Yep. And there's this series of social network pages praising her, with more and more women asking her to dispatch their own 'sex enemies'. The ones she's been picking, they're all too random. I figured she would stay in the mid-Atlantic states, but she's gone as far as New York and Florida. She's definitely an East Coast entity, but still not enough to narrow her down anywhere."

"So, treat her like the spider she emulates."

Mark looked at his assistant, his eyes crinkling as he smiled. "Offer her food?"

"Plant bait, Mark," she said in a crisp British tone.

"And it has to be a very delicious bait, doesn't it, Ellie?"

"And," Eleanor said slowly, "one willing to be sacrificed. A male black widow to mate with our Black Widow…and die for the cause."

Mark looked at her with narrowed eyes. "That'd be asking a lot from someone."

"My job is to offer assistance. Yours is to stop the villains any way you can, sir." She nodded and left the office, leaving Mark to ponder her incredibly perceptive words…

CHAPTER 53

TABLE FOR ONE, PLEASE

Prisoner 101561, THE TALON, WAS RETURNED TO his cell by Guard Gamble. On the cell's table was a covered dinner dish. "Vaht is tonight's fare?"

Gamble said, "Pheasant, sir."

"Acceptable, thank you," Talon said with a nod.

"The kidnapping trial is set to begin this week," Gamble informed him.

Talon lifted the dinner cover and lightly breathed in the aroma. "Of course," he said softly. "And I should be concerned, why?"

"The prosecution appears to be loading its case against you, sir."

Talon cut off a piece of the pheasant meat, savoring it as he ate. "Magnificent. Please tell the cook to expect a bonus this month." He dabbed the corners of his mouth with his napkin, then turned to face Gamble. "Please contact your friends; I'm finished with my vacation."

"Yes, sir," Gamble said, then turned and left the cell, leaving the cell door open, same as all the others on block.

A few minutes later a couple of other prisoners came to his open cell door. "Well," said the larger of the two, a bald muscular man with tattoos on his upper arms. "Lookee there. The child kidnapper gets dinner in his hotel suite."

Talon looked up at them.

"Yeah," said the other, an even stronger-looking man. He held onto the bars and leaned forward. "We don't take kind to guys who do things to young girls."

Talon crossed his legs. "I have no idea vaht you're talking about."

The two men looked at each other, then back at Talon. "You took a girl from her daddy. We might all be in here for doin' shit, but we don't touch kids," said Tattoos.

Muscles added, "We gonna teach you a lesson 'bout kids." He stepped into Talon's cell.

Talon reached into his jumpsuit pocket and withdrew a small pistol with a silencer on the barrel. He rapidly fired two muffled shots, sending the men to the floor, both dead. From the other pocket, he took out a cell phone and pressed one number. "Mr. Gamble, it is time to get me out now. Oh, and I believe you need to bring a cleanup crew with you."

CHAPTER 54

CHECKING OUT, PLEASE

GUARD GAMBLE RETURNED PRISONER 101561 to his cell, after the prisoner's shower. The Talon, infamous for his international crimes and assassinations, was in confinement and under extra guard after murdering two other prisoners.

Talon noticed a pile of fresh clothes on his bed, but not the normal prison orange he wore daily. They were, in fact, the same colors as Gamble's uniform. "Lights out in five," Gamble barked at the other prisoners. He was standing by The Talon's cell, and added a whisper to him, "Your route is ready, sir, as is everything you need for tonight. The camera is already on a loop, so the security office will see nothing." Gamble nodded at the clothes pile on the bed.

Talon nodded in acknowledgement. In his soft German accent, he responded. "I shall remember you, Mister Gamble. I appreciate the loyal kindness that you've provided me. Good-bye, sir, and may I suggest—you enjoy your financial retirement immediately, which I already have in the making."

"Thank you, sir. It's been a pleasure to assist you, now, and hopefully in the future." Gamble closed the cell door. Talon sat on his bunk, in his robe, waiting for the lights to go out on time, watching closely for any other guards who passed by.

A few minutes later, the prison's lights faded to a dim gray in the high-security hallway. His day had been uninterrupted as hoped and was ready to carry out his evening plans. His vision adjusted in the lighting, and he searched through the clothes on his bunk for the magnetic override to his cell door's electronic lock.

The morning guards began their shift, checking the prisoners in the high-security hall. One stopped at Talon's cell door and peered through the small window. "Up," he ordered after he pressed the intercom next to the door. "Up!" he repeated when he saw no movement. "Dammit all. What's up with this guy?" He motioned for a backup to step beside him while he unlocked Talon's door with his keycard.

He swung the door outward, advancing to the still form in the bunk, partially covered. "Get up, Jergen," barked the guard, "time for chow." He saw no movement, looking to his fellow guard, suspicious. He pulled the sheets back, revealing a blow-up doll in a wig matching Talon's hair. A note was taped to the doll's chest: CHECKING OUT. MANY THANKS FOR THE WONDERFUL SERVICE.

"SHIT!" the guard roared. He keyed his lapel mic. "Alert! We have a prisoner attempting to escape!..."

CHAPTER 55

CATCHING THE BAIT

JACKSON BERNARD WAS SERVING MULTIPLE lifetime sentences for a rape and a murder.

He also had stage four cancer. The prison doctors speculated he only had a few couple months to live.

At his diagnosis, he told his wife to stop visiting, and said goodbye to his young daughter. He didn't want them to see him rapidly worsen physically as his end neared. His physical appearance had already begun to deteriorate, and he refused all treatment. "Hell, after what I did to that woman, this is justice, ain't it?" he confided in his doctor.

He was confused when guards came to his cell in the state prison in Columbia, South Carolina. They instructed him to pack his belongings, few that they were, and accompany them to a waiting unmarked white panel van. The guards opened one of the back doors and told him to step in. Halfway inside a black curtain hung from the ceiling of the van, obscuring the forward half from view. Crouched, he stopped and turned back to the guards as they closed the windowless door, leaving him in complete darkness.

"Sit down," said a deep voice in the blackness.

"Wanna tell me where?" said Jackson.

Someone grabbed him by the upper arm and guided him to a seat. He expected to be chained and cuffed, but that didn't happen. The van began rolling forward. "Don't bother thinking about escape," said the voice. "You'll be dead before you touch the curtain."

"I'm freakin' dead anyway," said Jackson. "It'd only speed up the process by a couple weeks." When he heard no reply, he looked around, hoping his eyes would finally adjust to the darkness, but to no avail.

"Nice tattoo," said a higher female voice to his right.

"How many of you are in here?" Jackson asked. A dim light snapped on directly above his head. He saw what he thought was a solid black male figure sitting across from him, with a pistol pointed at him. "Okay, what's the hell's going on?" he demanded.

Another arm appeared in the cone of light, obviously female because of her long-polished nails, clad in a dark jacket. In her hand, she held what looked like a check, blank side up. The deep voice said, "We know you're dying, Jackson. We're giving you an offer to let you go out in style." The female's hand flipped over, revealing a check from the U.S. Treasury made out to his wife for one million dollars. "Holy shit," Jackson said. "Who do I gotta kill?"

The dark figure across from him leaned forward, revealing a man's head wearing a black hood with black lenses hiding the eyes. "Not funny," he said.

"Sorry," said Jackson. "But I don't understand."

"You don't have to," said the dark figure. "Your wife will get this check. An additional stipend of one million dollars will be given to your victim's family. All you have to do is meet two women, have your way with them however you want…then let them kill you…"

CHAPTER 56

TAKING THE BAIT
THE NEXT DAY

"**O**H, MY GOD, I FOUND A GOOD ONE!"

"What is it?" Lexi asked.

Lacy pointed at a news article on their laptop. "This guy here, this Jackson Bernard. He just got released from prison in Columbia, South Carolina. Where is that, anyway? After his sentence for rape and murder was thrown out by some judge, some technicality." Lacy smiled. "This is one who really deserves justice, seeing as how the judicial system just screwed his victim and their families."

"But, Lacy, that's a long trip. That place is in the middle of South Carolina. We don't have time to go that far right now."

"Sweetie, it's ok. I've learned this RSS thing so we can follow any time he's mentioned online." She looked at the screen again. "I think this one deserves a quadruple-dose of Latrodectus venom. He didn't just rape her, he killed her. Get our travel bags packed, girlfriend, so we can go at a moment's notice."

A WEEK LATER

"Ha! And he's off and running. Yeah, I've been watching your every move, scumbag!" Lacy exclaimed. Lexi joined her at the computer. "His wife just posted she's meeting him at some hotel in Charleston today."

"Get the keys, hon, we're hittin' the road now!"

"He just contacted his wife to meet him in a public place, and it's already posted on the Black Widow's page," Harri reported to Mark on the phone. "Are you really sure this is the one that'll bring her to us, boss?"

"It's a calculated gamble, Harri," Mark interrupted. He pressed a number on his phone. "This is Spy. All Task Force field agents report to Charleston, South Carolina, as fast as you can get there. I'll provide target info en route." He disconnected the phone just as Jan entered his office. "I'm on my way to South Carolina, love," he said as he met her halfway to the door and kissed her. "Hope to catch a killer by tomorrow morning."

She kissed him back. "Good hunting and be careful. I'm only glad our headstrong daughter isn't going with you."

CHAPTER 57

WALKING INTO THE WEB

JACKSON BERNARD WALKED THROUGH THE FRONT door of the Francis Marion Hotel in Charleston, South Carolina, and met his wife Judy in the lobby. She wore a flower-print sundress and white sandals, and her pageboy-style brown hair glistened from the overhead lighting. Her eyes sparkled at seeing her husband again, but her face also showed the confusion on his sudden release and his open presence in public. She was surprised that there were no protesters or anyone disputing his freedom. She was more confused than she was happy.

"You didn't want to see me again," she said, squeezing his hand after a long kiss, "and now you do. I don't understand."

He nodded gently. "I'm still dying, J-Belle, you know that. But I got a chance to help someone make a right thing happen, and set you up for life by doing it." He took both her hands in his. "I'm so sorry, J-Belle, I really screwed everything up back then. I still don't remember anything from that night, but the evidence showed I did it and all I could do was accept my punishment. Kinda figured that I'd see our little girl grow up, even from behind bars."

Judy started to cry. "I still—"

"Let me finish, J-Belle." Jackson took a deep breath and gave Judy a moment to calm herself. "All I'm allowed to say is that the Feds gave me a mission to do for them, and in return you and our baby's gonna be set for life. I'm kinda like a soldier goin' on a suicide mission, sweetie, and I ain't comin' back. Not that I was ever really comin' back anyways."

Judy's eyes widened in horror and she scooted across the lobby couch and held him tight. "No!" she said in a loud whisper. "I can't lose you again, I just got you back!"

"J-Belle, you're lucky you got to see me outta there at all. They said I could see you for a little bit. You didn't tell Missy anything, did ya?"

"No, she's in school, and my folks'll pick her up after school." She kissed him again on the lips. "When—when do you have to go?"

"I dunno. I'm to look for two women in black, one's a redhead, that's it. Been out a couple hours now, hadn't seen anything like 'em."

She sat back and looked in his eyes, her mouth open in surprise. "I saw them."

"Where?" he asked quietly.

"They came in a while ago. I saw them check in while I waited for you." She glanced around cautiously. "I don't see them now, though."

Jackson remembered his instructions from the man in black, and took Judy in his arms. "You have to go now, J-Belle. Just remember that I love you, and I love our Missy. You tell her I made a mistake, a bad mistake, but I made it good today. I can't tell you what now, but you'll find out later. And you'll understand what I did and why." He gently grabbed her head with both hands and guided her crying face to his. He kissed her tenderly on the lips, then touched his forehead to hers. He whispered, "Now, J-Belle, I want you to get mad at me. I want you to yell hateful things, hit me, and make a damn huge scene and run the hell outta here."

Horrified, she shook her head, trying to pull back. But he held her head to his. "You want me to do what?"

"Please, J-Belle, those are my instructions, and you *gotta* do 'em. You *gotta* do what I tell you. Get mad at me, hit me, and get the hell outta here and never look back. I love you, baby, but you gotta go! NOW."

"I love you, J.B.!"

"Damn it, woman, hit me and RUN."

Judy's tears flowed, and she stood up and began yelling. "You bastard! After everything you did, and you want to get back together!" She swung her hand and slapped him on his face, hard. She covered her mouth in shock as he looked up at her; to everyone else he looked surprised, but she only saw love in his eyes. She burst into sobs, grabbed her purse, and ran for the door. She couldn't look back.

At the entrance to the bar, Lexi sat on a stool and casually watched the exchange. After the wife ran out of the hotel lobby, she reached into her purse and pressed one number on her smartphone. "Hey, sweetie, guess who's all alone now and probably ready for a good time?"

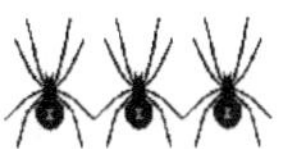

Jackson ordered a whiskey at the bar, and when he was sure no one was looking popped one of the pills the mystery man gave him in the van. It masked the pain his cancer was causing inside his body. It worked so well that it seemed like he was on another marijuana or cocaine high from high school. The man also told him it would ease the pain from when he was injected with the "Latro-something" venom, although it wouldn't ease the physical reactions. Jackson didn't care because his J-Belle would live without another worry. And his little Missy would hopefully remember that her daddy died to help catch a serial killer.

"Hi, handsome," said a female from behind him.

He managed to put on a fake smile before rotating on his stool. The woman was medium height, in a black pantsuit, black stilettos, and large black glasses to hide her eyes. The only color on her was her bright red hair. *It's her!* he thought. *The Black Widow! They weren't kidding!* "Hi, yourself," he said gently.

"Buy a girl a drink?" she asked in a soft seductive voice.

"Sure," he replied, "have yerself a seat." He motioned to the bartender. "Give the lady whatever she wants, on me."

"What'll you have, ma'am?" the female bartender asked.

"Let's make it a—" she glanced up at the TV over the bar with a news discussion about The Black Widow, "—Scotch and soda, please."

"Comin' right up."

"So, what's a handsome gentleman like you doing in a bar this early in the day?"

Jackson smiled politely. "Just doin' some private celebratin'."

The bartender set the cocktail tumbler on a napkin. Lacy swirled the straw around the ice cubes, then clinked her glass against his. "Congratulations in order then?"

He returned the gesture by raising his glass. "You could say that."

She took a gentle sip and licked her lips, a bit of her drink dropped from her red-tinted mouth to her exposed cleavage. "Do tell."

"You may not want to stick around if I tell ya."

"Oh, give a girl a chance, handsome."

He looked down at the drink in his hand. "Just got outta the clink."

"Sorry?"

"Prison. Just got released from prison."

She smiled at him. "Should I run away from you? Is my life in terrible danger?"

Jackson looked at her. "What's yer name, anyway?"

"Lacy," she replied. "You didn't answer me. Should I be scared?"

"That depends," he said calmly. "Do I threaten you just 'cause I been in prison?"

Lacy slowly traced her fingernails along his forearm. "How long's it been?"

"How long's what been?"

"Since you been with a girl. I figure you mighta had other men behind bars—"

"Nope, never did that," cutting her sentence short. The only thing I believe is men and women together."

She smiled at him. "Just the way I like it, too." She slid off the stool and leaned inward against his back. "Have you ever had two women at the same time?"

He turned his body around and wrapped one arm around her back. "Why you comin' on to me like this? You don't know me. Hey, maybe you're a cop trying to catch me soliciting or some shit like that and throw me right back in prison."

"Hey, easy, handsome," Lacy said, stopping her inducements. "I'm no cop." She looked around to make sure they were still alone in the hotel bar. She placed her sunglasses atop her head. "Tell you a secret?"

"Help yerself."

"Cops would be interested in me, too." She dipped her forefinger in her drink and rubbed it against her exposed inner breasts. "Come on, all I'm offering is the best fun you'll ever have the rest of your life, and all it'll cost you is time. That's not prostitution, just an invitation to a very private party."

Jackson looked around the bar, wondering if anyone was watching. "Private party, huh?" he said, a bigger smile formed on his face. "What kinda party?"

She stepped back and took his hand. "The most killer party you'll ever have."

A beeping alarm came from one of his belt pouches. Mark pulled the tracking device from its container and turned off the alarm. It was Jackson Bernard, using the cell phone he was given in the van. It was a message that he was in the hotel room with The Black Widow. He turned around to the computer console in the aircraft's lounge. "Dammit, he's too soon! We're not in place yet. Captain, how long until we land?" he said aloud to the voice-activated communications system.

"Ten minutes, sir," came the reply.

"Get us down fast as you can, hot if you have to. Air traffic is usually light in Charleston; maybe you can get us a straight approach to the runway." He pulled on his black hood and fastened it to his uniform collar. He ran to the bottom deck to his waiting Task Force car, then tapped the right side of his hood to activate the satellite feed to his team. "I have Bernard's signal; you have the coordinates. He's in the room with The Widow. Let's hope he lives long enough for us to get there and finally capture her."

He rammed Lacy from behind so hard her face hit the headboard, leaving a small cut on her forehead. It was all over-emphasized, as Mark had instructed he should do. Without warning he threw Lacy to the side. He pulled Lexi over, turned her over onto her stomach, lifted her by the hips and forced himself into her. Lexi screamed in surprise by the sudden penetration. Lacy held a hand to her forehead while she tried to get off the bed to get the auto-injector, until she was stopped by his grasp. "Oh, you're right, sugar, I love this party! Get down there." Jackson could hold out a little longer, but not much longer.

"You son of a bitch," Lacy said as she pulled away. "What the hell do you think you're doing?"

"I'm having a party, like you said! Ain't been with a woman in a long while, never mind two. I plan to enjoy every inch of both ya! Now get back down here." Lexi tried to move away but her legs ached too much to propel herself. He reached down, pulling her back. "Uh, uh, little girl, not done with you yet."

He was enjoying himself despite his 'mission.' He briefly pondered if he'd been like this the night he drank too much, when he raped and killed a woman.

The urge was getting too strong to hold back any longer. He rolled himself onto his back and forced Lacy atop him. Her makeup was smudged, and a small trickle of blood rolled down her forehead and left cheek. Her hair was wild, as was the look in her eyes. She said breathlessly, "You finally ready to finish, mister?"

He said, "Oh, yeah. You ready?"

"Bring it, baby, show me what you got!"

He closed his eyes, knowing that any second a needle would hit him somewhere, filling him with the venom and opening the door to his rapid death. He never felt the needle that was plunged into his hip.

Lacy slowly slid off him, auto-injector in hand. "For your crimes against women, The Black Widow has passed judgment on her latest mate and found you guilty on all charges. The penalty is death," she pronounced.

The venom was already working on his body. Cramps and spasms began, but not the intense pain he thought he'd have, thanks to the narcotics given to him earlier.

"Any last words, from the man with the 'get out of jail free card,' if you can still talk?" Lacy asked.

"F— for—Jay—Bell," was all he could get out before his esophagus began to close.

"Jay Bell?" Lexi asked. "He have a gay lover in that jail?"

"No idea," said Lacy. "And, shit, I'm too sore and tired to kick his ass around this room right now. Damn him—"

They watched as his convulsions continued for several minutes until he moved no more. "Time to wrap it up."

"And do some cleaning up," said Lexi. "No telling what we gagged out because of him. Wow, he really got down to business after being in the slammer."

"I'm not worried," Lacy assured her. "They have our DNA and never anything to match to. You're right, we got a lot of scrubbing to do. But, yeah," she said as she rubbed her tender vagina gingerly, "I think the next one can wait a few weeks..."

CHAPTER 58

SAW THE TALON FLY THE COOP

ANGELA JASON WAS HAPPIER THAN SHE'D EVER dreamed possible. While being the daughter and only child of Mark Jason afforded her many benefits, she'd been instructed her entire life not to rely on the family wealth for a lifestyle, but rather it was better to engage in productive work to help others.

Her office in the Task Force Division was furnished with half a dozen separate computers, each receiving never-ending data streams from innumerable government security agencies worldwide. Four large plasma screens, two on top and on bottom, were built over her horseshoe-shaped desk, displayed text-rendered readable columns of information which flowed upward on each screen. It had taken her several weeks working with the Task Force tech staff to determine the optimal speed and number of screens for Angela to efficiently scan for intel, both real-time and in review, when keywords were found in computer software programs. Her office was miniscule in scale to a second similar division on the other side of the building harboring ears and eyes 24/7. Hers was more structured for cryptology, her special talents, hidden information that others would likely miss.

She proved her value within the first week when she detected transmission data indicating a possible terrorist attack on Washington, D.C. Seeker was the agent dispatched to investigate and found a pair of American al-Qaida sympathizers planting explosives around the Lincoln Memorial during the night. They were timed to go off the following day when tourists were viewing the memorial and the grounds. By the time Homeland Security realized what they had in their own data collections Seeker had already captured the would-be terrorists, defused the bomb, and disappeared, leaving the terrorists bound hand-and-foot on the scene.

Over the next several weeks she discovered more terror plots in the United States and in Europe, keeping the Task Force field team, CIA, and FBI constantly moving to stop and capture the terrorists. Major bank crimes, kidnappings, and other planned activities were halted or stopped while in-progress, thanks to her spatial deductive talent. Unfortunately, some crimes could not be thwarted if there was no electronic data connected to them.

The frequency of major criminal or terrorist activities ebbed and flowed. In the quieter hours and days Angela continued her regular studies, as required by the Navy in order to eventually advance in rank over her career.

Like her father, she took correspondence college classes in business and psychology for a planned double major, with political science as a minor. After her workday at the Task Force Division, she went home to her apartment in Alexandria, Virginia, and spent her evenings studying with news channels playing on the TV. On weekends, she went home to the family estate in Richmond.

Friday morning found Angela reporting for work as usual, getting her glass of orange juice from the lunchroom, and settling at her desk to run the system review before turning on monitors to begin a day of live monitoring. With nothing noteworthy in the overnight data, she activated her monitors and hoped for a normal day with nothing critical in the streams before the weekend.

The bottom left terminal began blinking a red border around the edges of the screen. This was the computer which monitored activity related to any past or present Task Force mission. Angela turned her full attention to it and reversed the data scroll until she found the keywords that set off the alert.

"'Talon'?" she said aloud. She turned on the voice interface for that server. "Access files containing all references to 'Talon'," she ordered the computer.

Seconds later the data stream shrunk to the left side of the wide-screen terminal and a computer folder filled the blank right side. "Open folder," she ordered. The virtual folder opened displaying the digitized report filed by Seeker, detailing his pursuit of the international extortionist from Charleston, South Carolina, to Buenos Aires, Argentina, where he had captured Talon. He had involved FBI Special Agent Stephanie Anderson in the case to initially rescue a kidnapped teenage girl in Charleston before realizing The Talon was behind the kidnapping. The Talon was transferred back to Charleston to face the kidnapping charges.

The data stream showed he had broken out of prison just an hour earlier.

Angela searched the overnight stream for more details, hoping to find anything that might have more information of the planning for the escape. There was nothing aside from the official prison report. "Oh, man, Seeker's gonna have a cow. And how the hell did it take so long for this report to work its way through the system? Gotta remember to ask some questions to someone later."

She tried to contact Tom Michelson, but his line was blocked, which meant he was following an active field team mission. She tried to send messages to her father and Seeker, but both messages were bounced back as blocked; they were both silent to all but current mission-critical communications. She tried contacting Proteus and Hunter as well, with the same blocked responses.

Angela returned her attention to the Task Force data screen. As she read further, she found coding to indicate that known Talon associates had booked a room at the Francis Marion hotel in Charleston, where The Talon was going, and what his plan was: escape the country.

She was in a quandary. At Task Force, her single line of command was to her father then to Tom; she did not have a Navy liaison in her assigned capacity. She thought through her options and could think of nothing satisfactory.

"What would Dad do?" she asked aloud. Immediately the answer came to her. She picked up her desk phone and called another office in the Task Force complex. "This is Lieutenant Angela Jason. I need transportation to Charleston, South Carolina, and I need a weapon, mission ID 'Talon'."

"Yes, ma'am," said the male voice on the other end. "Report in ten minutes, we'll have you ready to go."

She hung up the phone and sat back in her desk chair. "Wow, that was too easy. No wonder Dad loves it here, saving the world with no paperwork!" She looked at her white uniform skirt and blouse. "I think I'll need a change of uniform first." She rose and went to her office closet and pulled out a Navy operation uniform better suited for criminal pursuit. "Dad's gonna kill me, after Tom kills me, if I don't get myself killed first. Oh, computer," she said as an afterthought, "connect me to Agent Stephanie Anderson."

CHAPTER 59

CLOSE ENCOUNTER OF THE FATAL KIND

"**O**KAY, DID WE GET EVERYTHING CLEANED UP? We didn't touch anything without gloves and shoes on, so we're good. All we had was our twats getting banged to hell, and our heads against the walls; we cleaned up everywhere we touched, right? Then let's get outta here," Lacy said, walking toward the beds. Lexi was already bending down to pick up their clothing from the floor.

"It's getting easier to kill these guys, especially with what I just went through with this one," she said, getting dressed. "I mean, I don't *like* it, just getting used to it is all."

Lacy pulled on her black pantsuit, an outfit far more reserved than Lexi's, or even what she traditionally wore after a Black Widow killing. She reached for both .380 autos from their equipment bag. Lexi placed hers in a holster clipped to her belt at the small of her back, concealed by her untucked blouse. Lacy placed hers in an elastic underarm strap under her jacket.

"Remember, as always," said Lacy, "separate exits, separate routes." She pulled Lexi close and kissed her. Turning to the metal tripod holding the white silk sheet cocoon hanging underneath, she gave it a poke with one finger. "Bye-bye, Jackson." She blew a quick kiss toward him.

They both put on sunglasses, Lacy turned out the lights and slowly opened the hotel room door. There was no activity when she checked the hallway. "You go right, take the stairwell at the end, I'll go left and do the same," she whispered.

"See you at the car, okay?" Lexi asked, needing reassurance, still anxious whenever leaving a kill.

"Yeah, hon, we'll be fine, you always worry." Lacy hugged her before heading for the stairwell.

Lexi placed the "Do Not Disturb" sign on the door handle, walked toward the opposite stairwell, and began her journey down eight floors. The stairs would eventually exit into the lobby and out into the predawn darkness.

Angela met Stephanie outside the hotel. "Are you sure he's up there?" the FBI agent asked.

"As of a couple minutes ago," Angela answered. "Figured since you were credited with the first capture, you'd like a chance at a second credit."

"You've no idea," Stephanie said. "Asshole caused me to walk on Highway 17 with my tits exposed for every driver to see."

"I guess I really don't want to know."

"I'm sure it'll come up at the wedding party," Stephanie chuckled. "So, it's just you and me, no time for backup with everyone else on presidential detail across town. What's your plan?"

"You think he'd take the stairs or the elevator to get out?" Angela asked.

"Talon doesn't like routes where he's closed in. I'd bet on the stairs."

"So, two stairwells, two of us. You go right, I'll go left."

"Sounds like a plan, Lieutenant."

Angela smiled and nodded as the two women entered the hotel lobby and separated to the opposite stairwells. As soon as she went to her stairwell, Stephanie got a cell phone call. "Anderson," she said into her phone's speaker.

"Hey, Anderson," said the voice of her easily pissed boss in the Charleston office. "Your bigwig friends in Washington want you to help 'em on another fancy case. So, drop whatever you're doin' at the Francis Marion and meet with those guys at the front door onna double."

"The front door?" she replied, looking back at the stairwell door to the main lobby.

"You heard me, now drop what yer doin' and meet 'em out front and save their butts again like you did in Argentiner. I'm ready for another commendation for my office, y'know."

Stephanie shook her head. "Roger," she replied. She quickly dialed Angela's number, but it went to voicemail. "Dammit," she said, "get this message quick. The whole damn Task Force is about to get here, so watch who you shoot at, and be careful." She hung up and went back through the lobby to the front entrance to wait on the Task Force…

Spy couldn't help but relish the irony of finding The Black Widow, thanks to something as simple as social networking, and a big reward to a dying man. He pulled his black Task Force car to a stop in the hotel parking lot. "Command, any change in target's status?"

The voice in his ear said, "She hasn't exited the hotel yet, sir. We're tapped into all hotel surveillance cameras."

Spy surveyed the grounds; the only light came from the street and walkway lights. There was the faintest glow of dawn on the eastern horizon. He wanted to get in and out as fast as possible without being seen. "I'm going in through a service entrance. Override the cameras and security system until I'm in and keep me hidden from them."

"Copy, Spy."

He made a quick physical check of the equipment and weapon pouches on his belt while moving into the shadows toward the service entrance. "We have eyes and ears on the complex," the voice of the tactical contact said. "Enter at your discretion."

"Are there eyes opposite this door?"

"Negative, Spy."

He tried to open the door, not surprised it was locked. Using a small metal tool from his utility belt, he had the lock picked in no time.

Spy smiled under his mask. "Status of inbound team?" he asked, entering the empty hallway.

"Proteus is seven minutes, Seeker is four minutes, Hunter is also four minutes. Agent Anderson has been ordered to meet agents in front as she is already onsite."

"She is? How did she know to come here?"

"Apparently she is on another case that is coincidentally at your location."

Spy shook his head in disbelief. "I don't believe in coincidences, Tactical. Regardless, override the traffic lights, green-light them all the way."

"Copy, Spy."

He tapped a button on his hood, adding his teammates to a secure, encrypted comm channel. "I'm inside. Secure all entrances on your arrival and move in."

"Boss, what's the exposure risk?" Seeker asked.

"Pretty damn high. No doubt we'll be exposed to morning guests on their way to breakfast or checking out. Do your best to stay dark."

"Says the man in the mask," said Seeker.

"You're a riot, Seeker. Command, monitor and reroute audio and video as I move."

"Spy, you tend to disappear in the field. How will I know where you are?"

Spy couldn't help but sigh. "I'm in the hotel kitchen, and everything is lit up. I'm gonna have to scare the staff into silence." He opened the front panel of his diamond-engraved metal belt buckle and removed a palm-size Federal badge. He attached it to his upper left chest Velcro strip. "Team, shield-up before moving in. There's no way we won't be seen. Let's minimize it as best we can. I'm going silent, maintain connection and advise."

He closed the buckle panel and moved forward through the utility hallway, weapon in hand.

I'm so gonna get sent to the brig, Angela thought as she moved up her stairwell, one slow step at a time. She listened for any activity, holding her military-issue .45 auto in a two-hand grip. *I'm not supposed to be in the field, so why the hell am I here? Because Intel said this "Talon" guy is here, and none of the field team agents are available, that's why. I'm talking to myself, geez. And then answering myself!* she thought.

While she was still active-duty Navy, Angela was also a member of the elite Task Force Division, which gave her the same credentials as an NCIS agent. She was warm under her tactical vest. The stairwell wasn't overly hot itself, but she chalked it up to being anxious on her first hunt in a Task Force situation. Sweat rolled down her temples and the back of her neck. She pushed her cap back to clear her field of vision.

An echoing sound clicked above, sounding much like a door shutting. She steadied the grip on her weapon. Adrenaline pumped and her pulse quickened. Gun pointed upward, she peered up the next two levels of stairwell in her line of sight. She heard the distinctive sound of footsteps descending.

Steady, girl, she thought. *You'll have only a second to react if it's him.*

She glimpsed a pair of black dress boots and legs in black stockings leading up to a black blouse and skirt. She lowered her firearm. *Okay, NOT the guy I was looking for,* she thought.

Lexi rounded the level above Angela and looked down into the eyes of a woman wearing tactical clothing. She panicked at the sight of Angela's weapon. Lexi drew the pistol from her holster. Angela had only a second to realize what was happening. She threw herself to the side and bolted down the steps to the prior level, losing her hat but keeping hold of her weapon. Three gunshots echoed in the stairwell as bullets traced her path down the stairs. She rolled onto her back and returned fire up the stairwell.

The clickity-click of boots resonated in the stairwell as the shooter ran up and away. Angela scrambled to her feet, back in the chase. "Shit! Now who was *that*? Maybe one of Talon's lookouts?"

"Spy, we have target in sight, red hair, black glasses and black pantsuit."

"Direct me."

"Turn 180 degrees and go ahead to the last door on the left, which is the stairwell. I'm switching to the next internal camera to continue guidance."

Gunshots came from the far end of the hallway. "Control?"

"Gunshots in the opposite stairwell, Spy."

"Who's over there?"

"Stand by, switching camera feed. We see one Navy personnel and one blonde-haired woman in a black dress. The woman is running up the stairs with the Navy following."

"What the hell?" Spy said aloud. "Where are you, Proteus, Seeker and Hunter?"

"Pulling into the parking lot," Hunter said.

"I'm right behind you," said Seeker.

She ran up two steps at a time, pulling on the handrail for support and extra thrust, pausing at each level to look up. When the path was clear, she'd run to the next level, quickly reaching the eighth and highest floor of the hotel. There was no sign of her new quarry. *Damn, she must've ditched out a door on one of the floors.* Angela knew the sound of the gunfire would draw attention. It was likely that hotel security was on the way and had already called the police. She bolted down the carpeted hallway, taking the other stairwell back down. She didn't see or hear the woman she assumed was in league with her target as she descended, not that she expected to. She did expect to meet up with Stephanie in the other stairwell, but the FBI agent was not there. Angela holstered her weapon and exited into a dining area at the lobby level.

Less than a minute later, Seeker entered the hallway and joined Spy at the stairwell entrance. Hunter went in the opposite direction, hoping to head off anyone trying to escape.

"It seems we have two Widows on opposite sides of the building." One is a red-head, one is blonde," Command said. "Both dressed in black. Each in opposite stairwells of the building. Hunter, you go that way, toward the shots. I'll go to the other. Command, get me an ID on the sailor. Tell me why an armed sailor is here." Mark took off at a full run down the long empty hallway. In seconds, he ducked through a side door and out of Seeker's view.

"Tactical Seven, status of target in my stairwell," Seeker ordered.

"She departed the stairwell on the second floor," the voice replied.

"Son of a bitch," Seeker said. "She must've heard us down here and detoured. Tactical, what's on the second?"

"Guest rooms, offices, conference rooms."

"Where'd she go?"

"Conference two, but we lost her, Seeker."

"*What?*"

"She stepped into a camera blind spot and hasn't reappeared."

"Dammit," Seeker growled. He bolted up the stairwell to the second floor, and rushed toward Conference Room Two.

Seeker approached the closed doors with caution. He removed a motion resonance sensor and placed it on the door surface. The display read "NONE". *Damn, she either got out or she's as still as a statue inside.* Thinking the room would be dark at this early hour, he reached up to his cocoons and activated the infrared spectrum in his lenses, then opened the door inward.

He felt an instant unease. He turned toward the hallway just as the red-haired woman fired, a bullet hitting him in the neck. He fell to the floor, hand against his neck, in a futile attempt to stop the blood flow. His dropped weapon lay four feet away.

The redhead stepped into his field of vision and knelt beside him. His cocoon lenses showed a fuzzy female shape in the green toned screen. She leaned forward. "I'm very sorry, whoever you are. You're following me, and I can't have that." Her voice was soft, almost sensuous. The words echoed in his ears, fading in and out. Something stabbed him on the other side of his neck.

His world went black…

Spy arrived at the far stairwell and opened the access door quietly, listening. He heard distant footsteps and a faint closing-door sound. "Tactical, status of Navy."

"Eighth floor, running for opposite stairwell."

"And the opponent?"

"Already in opposite stairwell, departing at seventh floor, heading for the elevator."

"Will the sailor intercept in time?"

"Negative, Spy."

"Where will that elevator let out?"

"Suspect has selected the first floor, there are no stops selected on any of the other floors. Car will open near the first-floor ballrooms."

"Status of ballrooms."

"Stand by, Spy." There were a few seconds of silence. Then he heard in his audio feed, "There are no feeds to tap into the ballrooms. Continue at your discretion, we have advised hotel security to keep all staff and guests away from the ballrooms."

Angela surveyed the small crowd that had gathered for breakfast, looking for the stairwell shooter. She never saw the face, so she looked for the clothing instead.

The lieutenant promptly found her. Lexi was fast stepping it out of the dining area and down the main hall toward the ballrooms past the dining rooms. She hurried through the small crowd, bumping into people as she went. In the hallway, she picked up her pace to a jog. She stopped long enough to quickly look in each ballroom along the way. In the next-to-the-last room she saw a red-haired woman in a black pants suit. She was walking toward a stage which had large plasma screens above it. Angela continued on.

At the last ballroom, she stopped and looked in. Lexi was walking through the middle aisle of hundreds of chairs that faced the stage and podium. Angela drew her weapon and announced loudly, "Stop! Drop your weapon, now!"

Lexi turned, bent at the knees, and fired twice at Angela. Angela fired at the same time. Lexi's aim was off, but Angela's was closer to target. The .45 slug grazed Lexi's left shoulder, sending her toppling backward against the stage with a painful scream. She managed to right herself and return fire. Angela dove into a row of seats for protection. Rising slowly, she saw the woman was gone, but the door to the kitchen was gently swinging back and forth.

"Tactical, tell them to evacuate the damn first floor! Advise when completed." Spy closed the stairwell door and started back down the service hallway until, checking the doorways one by one, he saw one leading to a ballroom. He exited into one that was lit only with electric wall sconces and was completely empty.

Angela ran into the kitchen behind the ballroom. It was easier to track her this time, by following the drops of blood on the tile floor. She didn't have to tell anyone to get out of the way; they already stepped to the side because of the fleeing Lexi.

The trail led to another door, which opened into the ballroom where the red-haired woman was located. Angela followed carefully. The large plasma screens blocked her view of the rest of the room. Pointing her weapon forward, she stepped slowly to the edge of the stage. Peering around the screens, she heard someone say, "What are you doing here? My God, you've been shot!"

Her quarry's attention was not toward her now, and Angela stepped out from behind the stage and yelled again, "Stop! I said drop the weapon!"

Spy stopped in the middle of the room and holstered his weapon on its clip and removed a pouch from the belt's left side. He opened magnetic flaps and exposed a miniature heat-resonance scanner. Spy activated the device and faced it toward one side wall then the opposite. Through the second wall the scanner showed a human figure walking through the ballroom. He drew his weapon and went out the main entrance and immediately to the next ballroom entrance.

Lexi turned and looked at Angela, raising her gun to fire again. Angela knew her opponent's gun only had one bullet left, provided she didn't reload when out of sight. Angela fired, hitting Lexi dead center in the chest.

Spy entered the room as Lacy watched Lexi drop lifelessly to the carpet and scream, "NO!"…

CHAPTER 60

FINAL SHOWDOWN

SPY NOTED THE SAILOR AT THE EDGE OF THE HUGE electronic stage, standing in a firing stance and the red-haired woman in a black pantsuit dropping to her knees beside the dead woman in a black blouse, skirt, and boots. The voice modulator in his mask's electronics altered his voice into its deeper baritone as he ran forward yelling, "Nobody move!"

"Dad?" said Angela softly.

Spy stopped in his tracks, gun pointed on the women in black, then looked over at the source of his identification. *Angela*? He held back the urge to ask his daughter why she was there.

The Black Widow looked up at the mysterious masked man in black in the middle of the room, then over at the young naval woman. "Angela?" Then she looked back at the solid black muscular figure pointing a .45 automatic at her. "She said 'Dad'? Mr. Jason? Is that you?"

He didn't move but kept his gaze on The Black Widow through his non-reflective mask lenses.

"Miss Leigh?" Angela asked, recognizing the voice. "What the hell is going on here?"

Her *Lacy* identity blown, Chrystal Leigh reached up and removed the large black sunglasses and red wig. Tears flowed from her eyes as she looked at Angela, then at the unmoving body of her beloved Jesse. "Why?" she whispered aloud through her sobs. "Why did you have to kill her?"

"I told her to drop her weapon, she chose to aim at me," Angela answered, angered and still shaken herself from her first kill. She held her stance like the professionally trained sailor she was.

Chrystal's torso heaved from her grief and sobs, tears flowing from her eyes, mixing with spittle from her grimacing lips. "You killed my Jesse, *damn* you! YOU KILLED MY JESSE!"

With impressive speed, she rose from her knees, pulled the .380 from its holster, aiming it at Angela in mid-rise. A blast of thunder echoed in the ballroom, and her gun exploded in her hand. In reflex Chrystal dropped what was left of her gun, grabbed her bloody injured hand, and fell once again to her knees beside Jesse's body.

Angela was confused but impressed, observing her father working in the role of "The Spy" for the first time. Her eyes followed his massive form as he advanced on Chrystal's shaking body. His left hand grabbed at the front of her clothing, pointing his gun at her head with his right hand. He lifted her off her feet effortlessly, gun barrel following her forehead smoothly upward.

Her face was a combination of grief and fear, makeup-smeared tears streaked her cheeks. "Are—are you Mark Jason? What are you doing? She's the one who killed Jesse! You should be killing her!" She pointed a finger at Angela.

Security personnel and guests who had not evacuated began to fill the ballroom. They knew special forces were in the building and assumed they were looking at one of them. One began taking photos with his cell phone as others recorded video of the event.

Proteus, Hunter, and Stephanie pushed their way into the ballroom. Anderson said, "Oh, son of a bitch…"

CHAPTER 61

CHECKING OUT, PLEASE, TEIL ZWEI

"Sir, THERE'S A PROBLEM."

The Talon finished brushing his hair and straightened his tie without reacting to the announcement. He turned and held his arms backwards while the valet helped him get into his suit jacket. "How can there be a problem in a hotel at six in the morning?" he asked in his soft German accent.

"Our lobby lookout reports gunshots in the eastern stairwell."

Talon remained unfazed. "And is it something I should be concerned about?" He smoothed his suit coat lapels gently. "Ah, so much better than prison orange, yes. I'm so glad, Mr. Gamble, for the very satisfying accommodations and wardrobe. So, let us be on our way."

"Sir," said George, "it may not be safe." Talon stared at George; his gaze caused his aide to lower his head. "Yes, sir, we will remain on schedule."

"Sehr gut," Talon said, in a heavier than normal German accent. His half-dozen-strong security staff escorted him to the elevator.

George held his hand to his ear and said, "Repeat." He nodded his head as he listened to their lookout in the lobby in his Bluetooth. "Sir, our lookout reports a female sailor chasing a blonde woman into one of the ballrooms."

"Sounds like an interesting start to the morning, but it is also a fortuitous distraction. We proceed."

The elevator opened, offering an empty car to Talon and his staff, and they began their descent to the lobby.

George said, "When the door opens, we'll take a right, sir. Our driver will have the car outside the service entrance."

One of the other guards spoke. "Negative. Plan two. The gunfight has moved to the service hall."

"Out the front door we go, sir." George handed Talon a pair of black sunglasses. "Like a Hollywood star, sir."

"Hollywood star indeed," Talon huffed. "And just what Hollywood star would I be recognized for?"

George looked at him seriously. "Dolph Lundgren perhaps?"

"Never heard of him."

"He beat up Sylvester Stallone in one of the 'Rocky' movies."

"He was German?"

"No, sir. He was a Swede who played a Russian boxer."

Talon smiled. "I like him already."

The elevator doors opened, and they watched as people ran through the lobby in a panic. There was a gunshot, and his security staff reached for their guns under their coats. "No, hold your positions until I verify," said George. He stepped out and looked both ways. He saw a man in a black body suit and hood, holding a gun, entering a ballroom. "There's something going on, but it's not with us. To the front entrance, nice and slow." He and his men led Talon forward calmly.

Two black cars screeched to a stop outside the entrance. A short blonde woman and tall brunette in matching black body suits ran toward the building, their weapons drawn. George stopped and turned gently toward Talon. "Authorities of some type, sir. I don't recognize the uniform or badges, but there's something big going on here."

"You may not recognize them," said Talon as his eyes followed the agents' movement behind his glasses, "but I do. So, Monsieur Chercheur, where might you be?"

"Who, sir?" George asked.

"I suspected the man who caught me was some kind of policeman or agent, but I could never confirm it before now. Do you see their belt insignia?"

One of his guards said, "Looks like X's or triangles, but they're moving too fast."

"Not a bull's eye target?" said Talon. "Interesting." He moved to one of the seating areas and lowered himself into an armchair. He picked up one of the free copies of USA Today from the coffee table and opened the front section. "Sit down, gentlemen," he said softly, "I suspect there will be company directly."

Almost on cue Stephanie Anderson burst into the lobby, following the agents' path to the ballrooms. "FBI!" she announced to everyone in the lobby. "For your safety, everyone move outside, and I mean NOW!"

Talon lowered his newspaper at the sound of her voice. He said in a soft tone to his staff, "Agent Anderson. Very interesting, and confirms my theory. We wait for Checheur any moment now."

"Who is this 'Cheshire' person, sir?" asked one of the guards.

Talon looked at him. "He is not the fictional cat. Although, he is like a panther." He smiled. "A black panther? Yes." He glanced at his watch and sighed. "But, we must keep our schedule. Make sure the entrance is clear before we depart. Keep your eyes out for a light-skinned black man in one of those black uniforms. We *do not* want to run into him. At least…not today."

One of his staff walked unhurriedly to the front entrance, verified that all was clear, and signaled to The Talon to exit.

Talon was seated in the rear of a non-descript sedan, watching local police descend on the hotel's entrance. His car slowly rolled out of the parking lot. "Gentlemen, I believe I'm now indebted to someone who has let me leave unnoticed. Find out who it is, so I may repay them accordingly…"

CHAPTER 62

OVER-EXPOSURE
A FEW HOURS LATER

*"**D**O YOU SEE THIS SHIT?"*

Tom turned up the volume of the newscast so Mark, still wearing his uniform but without the hood, could hear clearly. The network on-scene female reporter spoke. "Here, outside the Francis Marion Hotel in Charleston, South Carolina, the vigilante killer renowned as The Black Widow was taken into custody just a few hours ago. It was reported that an unknown SWAT-like team captured The Widow inside and removed her from the premises. We speculate they used a back entrance where vehicles awaited. Hotel personnel have confirmed the discovery of a Black Widow victim on one of the upper floors. A growing crowd of what would be considered as *her fans* have converged on the grounds to shout for her release. For months, the Black Widow has garnered the interest of followers supporting her efforts, believing her killing spree against purported sexual predators was justice and not murder. As you can see—" the cameraman panned the crowd "—they're all wearing black T-shirts with a red hourglass emblem on the front." Shouts and chanting emanated from the crowd. "We're also getting unconfirmed reports that The Black Widow had a partner, who was killed by the unidentified police agents. Mike, back to you—"

"Thank you, Andrea. If you're just joining us, the hero-vigilante-serial killer nicknamed 'The Black Widow' was captured by a team of police agents, who disappeared with her following her capture. There's no additional information at this time, however, watch as we show you the cell phone video feed just provided to us from an eyewitness—"

Tom and Mark took in every detail from the television in the Task Force Office in Washington. Mark sat, irritated, while Tom paced around his office. Mike, the Anchor, continued. "This cell phone video from a hotel security officer shows the red-headed Black Widow taken down by a man dressed in all-black. Here, another cell phone feed shows a woman in a navy uniform helping. Anna," said Mike, "I understand you're on the scene, also." Mike spoke to someone off screen. "Can we get Anna's feed? I understand she has some new information."

A camera video feed flared to life behind Mike, the image righting itself as the cameraman focused the image while Anna adjusted a two-way audio feed into her ear. Anna, a short brunette woman with stunning blue eyes, stared into the camera. "Mike, yes, we're here—and we're going to make our way as close as we can to the front entrance of the hotel." Anna's voice joggled as she and the cameraman bolted toward the hotel. The cameraman caught up to her, stopping to steady his focus. "As you know Mike, although it's unconfirmed, witnesses report that a team of some sort of secret or special agents took down The Black Widow this morning at the Francis Marion Hotel here in downtown Charleston. We've made inquiries to the FBI, CIA and the local Charleston officials, all of which have no comment at this time."

A large man with curly black hair stood in front of the hotel, his blonde-haired wife clung to his arm. They stood, gazing up at the hotel. Anna interrupted the couples' hypnotic stares to ask a few questions.

"Yes, ma'am," the man said in a thick southern drawl, "we saw it all. This man, he was huge, muscles like a wrestler, dressed in black from head to toe. Weirdest get-up I've ever seen, with that black mask and all."

"Yeah," said the woman, "he *was* big! Whatever uniform he was wearing, we've never seen the likes. Had a badge, too, but couldn't tell what department. He had a gun pointed at a woman. There was another woman lying on the floor, she mighta been dead from the looks of it." The man's wife began to sob. "I saw another woman in a navy uniform, I think she had a gun, too."

Tom clicked off the television with the remote control and sat at the desk, angered. He looked at Mark seated on the other side. "Our invisibility is shot to shit!"

Mark sat silently; his impassive cold eyes fixed on Tom.

"You made the best call you could, but this event may have cost us our anonymity, Mark."

Mark nodded his head in agreement. "I told everyone…EVERYONE…before I entered the building that this was not going to be an anonymous takedown. What were my exact words? Oh, yeah: 'Team, shield-up before moving in. There's no way we won't be seen. Let's minimize it as best we can.' So, it was exposure or lose The Black Widow."

Tom went on without acknowledging Mark. "The oh-eight election, the Saddam affair, the end of the Jong Il—Marshall kept us secret like he was supposed to."

Mark bolted from his chair and leaned forward, slamming his fists on the desk, glaring at Tom. "I am NOT Marshall Gray. Remember, *Colonel* Michelson," he growled loudly, in a voice that shook even the retired marine, "YOU came to ME. I never asked for this job, you offered it to me. I saw this as an opportunity to finish serving my country, because I couldn't finish my original tour thanks to Dad getting mortally ill. And you gave me the autonomy to run Task Force as I saw fit, and unfortunately this time we had witnesses. I wear this stupid-ass mask and uniform to protect the connection between Jason Enterprises and The Task Force—which I *still* haven't completely figured out, by the way, and you still won't tell me! Just what the hell did you expect, us tracing our suspect to a packed hotel? That we'd let her walk out into a public parking lot and then chase her through the city? And why the hell was Angela there? She's not supposed to be in the field."

Tom took a deep breath. "Sit down, Mark," he asked politely. "She took it upon herself to track down The Talon because all of us were incommunicado on the Widow issue. Mark, I'm sorry. You're right. It is your team, your decisions in the field, and it's my job to support you and cover as necessary. It's also your job to deal with your daughter's actions, as she is, despite her actions today and technical assignment, a member of Task Force Division's Field Team. You should have provided her with a backup plan."

Mark stood erect, mask dangling from one hand. "You're kidding me," said Mark. "Provide a backup plan to a plan that shouldn't have even been, for a team member—my daughter or not—who wasn't even supposed to leave this damn building on a freelance mission of her own design? The mission was The Black Widow, not The Talon. And you can't tell me that in a dozen years, no one has ever seen a past or present member of this team anywhere in public?"

Tom stared at Mark; his brow furrowed. "Well, of course they've been seen. But it was always just eye contact, or special inter-department contacts, nothing reproducible in the media." Tom squinted an eye at him. "And don't you get holier-than-thou about this subject on me, Mark Jason. I've heard all about your own information-persuasion techniques on the street."

Mark turned around, walking to the office door. "Don't even bring up my 'street techniques', Colonel, or do you not track your agents' other independent activities? Surely you don't know about Proteus' secret partnership with her police connection back home, or Seeker's worldwide financial resources, or Hunter's—"

"I get the point," Tom interrupted. He lowered his head and took a deep breath. "Mark, you have my apologies. I was way out of line." He looked at Mark eye-to-eye. "Oh, I'm quite aware of what every one of you do as parts of your individual lives. You each have built your own information networks very efficiently and have usually avoided any local media reveals on your own personal jobs as Task Force agents. It's just that this one is causing hellfire raining on my neck from those above who finance us."

Mark smiled. "Just say the word, Colonel, and I can make some very special visits to some very particular politicians to convince them to—behave and shut up." He wiggled his black hood in emphasis. "On a more serious topic, however; Special Agent Anderson is telling the press that we were part of some special team of agents assigned to track down and capture The Black Widow. Not like there haven't been videos of SWAT teams or other black-suited police forces before." He put his fists on his hips and lowered his head. "Here's what we do. The field team is ordered to lay low until further notice. All major ops suspended unless the President so orders." He turned to face Tom. "And Seeker gets transferred to Walter Reed as soon as he's stable. No one goes in his room without Task Force clearance; medical or visitors. Set him up in a room with a magnetic lock and retinal scanner access. And all medical personnel will sign NDAs, and if they talk to the media—they'll answer to me."

"Will do. That's fair enough, Mark, we can make it happen. But when do you think the public will forget about you?"

Mark deadpanned, "When the next X-Men movie comes out." He pulled his mask back on over his head and sealed it to his uniform's collar. "Meantime, I have to go do one of those 'information-persuasion *techniques*' you mentioned, with a very special technique employed…"

CHAPTER 63

THE INTERROGATION

Chrystal SAT ALONE IN THE DARK, COLD interrogation room. The only light was a dim lamp that hung directly overhead, creating a cone of light surrounding her and part of the table before her.

It was an old-fashioned form of interrogation that seemed to work well for Task Force. The air conditioning was dropped a few degrees every so often, a means of physical discomfort to the perpetrator, an attempt to assuage her into talking. Aside from one escorted trip to the ladies' room down a darkened hall, four walls were all she had seen in hours. Chrystal noticed the cameras affixed to the ceilings, in the hallway, the lady's room, and in the interrogation room. She was well aware that someone was watching her the entire time. However, no one had asked her any questions. To Chrystal, it seemed like days had passed. She assumed it was a scheme used by her captors to break her down as much as possible, to retrieve information.

She was physically and emotionally exhausted, brokenhearted that her best friend was dead, murdered before her eyes. Mixed emotions played havoc with her mind, thinking of the long night with her latest victim. Her groin ached from his abuse, and she hurt all over from being banged and bruised, both by her victim and the struggle with the agents, especially the big black hooded one. At the same time, however, she reveled in the joy of retribution, giving the dead man his due justice. She stared off at a distant wall, reliving, recreating the scene in her head.

Chrystal finally placed her head on the stainless-steel table, hands shackled to the ring on the tabletop, scratching at her disheveled, tangled hair, minus the red wig. Her face was streaked with makeup from hours of crying fits. The air was getting colder, and she shivered, and cried some more.

Chrystal sat up, now angry, yelling as loud as possible, "Where the hell am I? Somebody talk to me! What are you doing with me?" Her voice echoed slightly against the close walls, resonating back to her, no one else hearing, except maybe the ones watching through the cameras. She contemplated her arrest and custody, and her future. She perceived that she was undoubtedly in an FBI office somewhere.

She contemplated her capture, and the last minutes before her arrest. Her hand hurt under the bandages, with traces of blood still working their way through the cotton strips. Chrystal's own weapon had been shot out of her hand, leaving a skewed bullet trail along the side of her hand between the thumb and forefinger. *Angela Jason called him "Dad",* Chrystal thought. *Why was Mr. Jason dressed like that? There's got be some SEC rules or something he broke to be running around like some vigilante—shit, like me?*

She heard a click-click sound at the room's door, then the metallic sound of the heavy door being opened, then closed, and finally locked. Chrystal dreaded facing whoever it was.

There was a soft sliding sound on the tabletop to which she was handcuffed; she smelled food, and realized she was extremely hungry.

Chrystal's head felt heavy. A paper plate was placed in front of her. On it was a sandwich cut into two triangular slices. Beside it was a large Styrofoam cup of water with ice.

She looked up even further, seeing two large forearms and hands wearing black leather gloves. She gazed at the shapeless masked face of the man from the hotel ballroom. Chrystal stared at the severe-angle cuts of the strange black lenses where the eyes should be, no doubt designed to help give the appearance of an angry and dangerous man. *Mr. Jason is not at all treacherous, but Angela called him "Dad".* Her eyes squinted and forehead wrinkled involuntarily.

The masked man intertwined his gloved fingers on the table as he sat opposite her.

Her stomach growled, yet she hesitated to reach for the sandwich. The temperature had dropped a few more degrees, and she was shivering. Her eyes went from the plate to his hidden eyes.

"It's safe to eat," said the man's deep, electronically filtered voice. "Miss Black Widow."

"What? Why should I trust you?" she snarled at the man.

He leaned forward into the light cone, his posture and the cock of his head actually produced a bit of the sudden fright that he needed to see from her. "If I wanted you dead, you wouldn't be here now."

She narrowed her eyes again, scrutinizing him, but couldn't help agreeing with his reason. He sat back into the shadows and she reached for the plate, dragging it close to pick up the sandwich. With her hands shackled to the table, she had to drop her head to take a large bite and chewed as if starved. She stared at the black-clad man the whole time, as if waiting for him to pluck the food from her hands. When she'd finished the sandwich, she picked up the water and drank nearly all the water.

He sat patiently, waiting. She ran her tongue along her teeth, searching for any morsels caught in between, and then across her lips, hoping for leftover mayonnaise or breadcrumbs. Satiated for the moment, she spoke insincerely, "Thank you, mister—?"

"My name isn't important," he replied.

"Oh, but I *do* know your name…Mr. Jason." She gave a smug grin.

She heard the unlocking of the door again, the lights came up bright suddenly, momentarily blinding her, and Mark Jason stepped inside. "Did someone call me?" he asked.

Chrystal's eyes widened with surprise, turning her head back and forth, looking at the two men she thought was one person. Angela Jason, dressed in her dress white Navy uniform, entered behind her father. Distressed, she looked at the mysterious man in front of her, then to the people at the open door. "But, I heard you call him 'Dad'!"

Angela smiled as she shook her head. "No, ma'am, you heard me say 'DAT', as in 'Department of Anti-Terrorism'. I was unaware they were on-scene. I was there on other business. You and your compatriot got involved in my mission all by yourself."

Chrystal shook her head in disbelief, then her face reddened in anger. "Why did you kill my Jesse?" she demanded, slamming a fist on the table, a tear rolling from one eye.

The masked man growled in his deep animated baritone, "She moved to fire first, after refusing to drop her weapon as ordered. Lieutenant Jason defended herself. All the video recordings from the hotel confirm it. In fact, she refused twice." He leaned forward into the light and said coldly, "I wouldn't have asked the first time."

Chrystal wanted to cry. *This is the right time to cry,* she thought. No tears would flow now. Her love of Jesse and hatred of the agents provided a conflict that she couldn't break.

"Miss Leigh," said Mark, "despite what you've done, sorry, 'are accused of doing,' Jason Enterprises still has you on its payroll, and you will be provided the best defense possible. If you want to call it a defense."

Chrystal looked at the unmoving masked man, then Angela and Mark. "What? Why would you still help me? That makes no sense! Quit playing with my head!" Chrystal was unnerved, confused at how calm everyone had become. "And why is it so freekin' cold in here?"

"Because, it's the right thing to do," Mark said mockingly. He and Angela nodded at the man in black, and stepped out of the interrogation room.

"Now what?" Chrystal demanded, wiping sandwich crumbs from her chin.

The masked man rose from his seat, the chair screeched across the concrete floor. For the first-time Chrystal observed him closely, from the form-fitting uniform to the leather utility belt with all the matching pouches and .45 automatic on its clip-holster. Her eyes fell on the diamond engraving on the belt buckle. "Who are you?" she asked, looking up to his face. *My God, you're huge,* she thought.

"Right now, I am your entire world, little girl!" He pointed a gloved forefinger at her. "You need to sit here, be uncomfortable, freeze to death for all I care. But you *will* talk, and you *will* confess every single detail. These few hours, they're nothing. They're NOTHING compared to what's about to happen if you don't open up and sing like a little bird." He left the room, flipping off the one lone light, and closed the door behind him.

Chrystal sat alone in the pitch-black room, with only the light cone over her and the table, tugging at her handcuffs chained to the metal table. It began to dawn on her that she now had no one to blame for the new direction her life was about to take, except herself. Her career at Jason Enterprises was over forever, her beloved Jesse was taken from her. She probably would never see sunlight again, and she was still sitting in soiled pants from her last victim. While she'd been allowed to use the restroom, she'd been denied the opportunity to clean anything from her skin or clothing. *I wasn't even able to tell Jesse goodbye*, she thought. Chrystal began to cry again, in the dark and cold.

Mark, Angela, and Proteus waited in the hallway. "Have a seat, big fella," she said to man in black, motioning to the folding chair beside her. He sat and watched as she opened her black bag and removed a few items. "So, how'd it go, boss?" Proteus asked, looking over at Mark.

"Perfectly," said Mark. "Left no doubt in her mind that Mark Jason and The Spy are two different men."

Proteus lifted the black computerized mask off, revealing the grizzled face of Sarge Brunson. She sprayed a light mist of antibacterial where the mask had chafed his neck. Sarge was larger than Mark, and the black outfit, despite its flexibility, was more than uncomfortable for him.

"Shit, that hurts!"

"Well, big fellow, how 'about losing a few pounds?"

Sarge only grunted a reply.

"Stand up. Let's pull the top of this suit down and get to what's really bothering you," she smiled a knowing smile.

He pulled the top of the uniform down to his waist to reveal what kept his extra stomach pounds held inward. "Get this freekin' girdle off me! Damn, I could barely breathe in there. Don't know how you women do it, wearing this kind of crap."

Proteus began unhooking the girdle that had forced Sarge to look smaller, more well-proportioned. He breathed a sigh of relief once the contraption was off, and his overweight belly pooched out again.

Proteus smacked him on the belly, teasing, "Looks like you need to hit the gym more often, Sarge. Maybe lay off the bourbon and chips for a while."

Sarge's face reddened, and opened his mouth to rebuke to the master-of-disguise, but noticed Mark had his hand over his mouth, trying to stifle a laugh.

"Yeah, yeah, funny, boss. So, I've put on a few pounds. Didn't stop me from taking *you* out recently, did it?" The chiding words popped out before he had time to think. "Um, sorry, boss—didn't mean to insult you. But, yeah, maybe I need to lose a pound or two. You satisfied?"

"Or five or ten," Proteus mumbled, bent over as she sprayed more antibacterial around his abdomen, rubbing it in where the girdle device had chafed his belly and back. She stood in front of him, looked down at his feet, then up to his crotch. "Anywhere else you'd like me to rub this in? Sir?" she said, smiling as she shook the bottle.

"You wish, little girl. Nothin' there you need to see." He snatched the bottle from her hand.

She whispered in his ear, "That's not what Freeman says. Hear tell you gave her a new appreciation for baseball."

Mark couldn't hold it in any longer, he laughed out loud and Sarge blushed.

Proteus began to pack her equipment when Angela asked, "What now?"

"Now," said Mark, "there will be answers before I decide what to do with her."

Angela looked at Proteus and Sarge. "What do you mean, 'I'? You'll be deciding her fate alone?"

He stepped to his daughter, gently but firmly grasping her upper arms. Her eyes were drawn to his eyes, fairly confused. "This is a specialized Task Force unit, Angel. We enforce the law, we make the law, we are outside the law, all at the same time. The White House and Pentagon made that an essential part of the Task Force Division charter. Every member of this team is exempt from all punishable laws in this country as long as they remain active members. And that includes that little gunfight you had back there in Charleston." He released her arms and wrapped his powerful arms around her. "Go home to your mother, tell her everything you did, tell her I'm up here in D.C and that I'll be there in a few hours."

She hugged him back as hard as she could. "I love you, Daddy."

"I love you, too, Angel. I don't know how you pulled that off, that whole gunfight. Which we'll have a long talk about later, but I do love you. And…I am so very proud of you."

Proteus mumbled to Sarge, "That's just not right, The Spy being all mushy like that."

"If he hugs me like that I'll kill him myself," said the burly security chief.

Angela released her father and joined Proteus and Sarge to leave the basement wing of the Task Force Division. "Respectfully, sir?" Sarge asked.

"Yes, Sarge?"

"You still look like a sissy in this outfit, sir," he said with a grin. "Not that I have any room to talk, that is."

Mark patted him on the shoulder. "With what I'm paid, I'd wear a white suit and say, 'Welcome to Fantasy Island' and mean it."

Angela said, "Huh, I don't get it?"

Mark and Sarge chuckled. "Before your time."

Hunter approached from the opposite direction. "How's Seeker?" he asked her.

"No change," she replied.

Spy nodded. "Yeah, kind of thought that would be the case." He began to dress in his uniform and mask. "You ready?"

"Not really."

"I know." He unlocked and opened the door for Hunter to precede him into the interrogation room...

CHAPTER 64

ONCE UPON A TIME SHE LIVED FOREVER AFTER

CHRYSTAL LOOKED AT THE MASKED MAN AS HE re-entered with a similarly dressed woman, except she wore large cocoon-style black glasses instead of a head mask. They sat opposite her at the table, staying in the shadows. They said nothing.

She sat in her cone of light, just as silent.

Time passed. Chrystal had no idea how long.

Finally, exasperated and exhausted, she said, "What do you want? You're not scaring me with your stupid mask and sunglasses. You both look like idiots."

Hunter leaned forward slightly into the light. "You put our friend in the hospital. He's in critical condition. So, we're a little on the *pissed off* side right now."

"You can't do anything to me, I have my rights," Chrystal said, fighting to remember her legal options, hoping for anything that would set her free.

"You have nothing," said Spy. "All you are right now is a discussion on the news channels, with all those so-called experts arguing about your motivation. Making you a celebrity." He leaned forward also. "You don't deserve to be a celebrity. You deserve to die. And if our friend dies from your venom, I'll kill you myself.

Yes, we found the injection site in his neck, so don't bother denying it. So, why'd you do it, Chrystal? Why all the murders?"

"They DESERVED to die!" Chrystal shrieked without thinking first. Tears formed in the corners of her eyes. "What the hell, it's out now. Wanna hear my sad story, my tale of woe? Fine. They stole my virginity, over and over again! They *fucked* me and left me like a used paper towel on that stage, and all the others after them! Those four, they left me naked, bleeding. They threatened to kill my parents if I told anyone about it!"

"You still should have told someone," Hunter said gently.

"I couldn't take the chance!" she yelled back. "I'd already killed my brother! I didn't want to kill my mom or dad, no matter how much they hated me after Jeffy—" she stopped, recalling the image of her little brother's lifeless body under the house.

"Wait, what? You killed your little brother? When?" asked Hunter, arms crossed, staring over at Spy.

Chrystal hesitated, not really realizing she'd said her brother's name. "We were little kids. My baby brother. I killed him."

"You killed him?" Hunter asked incredulously. "And just how did you kill him?"

"I locked him under the house with those stupid black widows."

Hunter looked over at Spy again, who sat back in the shadows. "A black widow killed your brother?"

"We didn't realize we had black widows under the house, lots of them. I thought I was teaching him a lesson because he wouldn't listen to me. Instead, I executed him. He died alone, scared. He was only five. I didn't know the spiders were there." Chrystal began to cry. "He never got to play with his friends again, never got to open Christmas presents again. Mom and dad never stopped blaming me. They eventually divorced because of me." She sat back and crossed her arms, sobbing heavily. After a minute, she continued. "I had, um, issues, lotsa issues after that. I was sent off to a hospital for a while. I couldn't, well, function. The whole town hated me. The kids at school bullied me after that. The police and doctors said it was an accident, and I got off free, it wasn't right. I wanted to make up for it, so I worked for my Ph.D. in entomology so I could one day find a cure."

"That's why you became an expert on black widows?" Hunter asked.

Chrystal dropped her head. "Yeah. Thought I'd try to find a perfect anti-venin. Make a universal treatment. By working for Mister Jason, that dream finally became a reality."

Spy steamed inside, angered at himself that he'd not seen any of the signs of Chrystal going downhill, or even that she had been using his company to further her murderous plots. He sat composed, however.

"But what was this whole 'Black Widow' killer thing about? You had a good thing going with Mark Jason. Why blow it?"

"I didn't blow it! I—I got—revenge!"

"Explain," Spy demanded.

Chrystal took a deep breath, then sighed. Her brow furrowed as she recalled her rapists again. "The first four, not that foreigner, they were the gang-rapists. I hated them. For years I hated them, dreamed of them dying at my hand. I hated them so much I started thinking about *how* to kill them. It ate away at me, it got worse and worse, all I thought about was getting even, with them, and even the ones I didn't know. At Jason Enterprises, I discovered I had the means to make my toxins and anti-venin. Finding them gave me a chance for vengeance. I didn't make it at the office though. Everything I did at Jason was legitimate, even when I was ordered to help find…me, as The Black Widow. I snuck baby spiders out every day and took them home to my basement. In the house we bought, after Mister Jason gave me that great promotion. That's where I took care of them, milked them. Finally getting enough venom that I needed."

Spy sat forward, into the light. "So, you planned to kill them the *whole time* you worked for him?" he asked.

"No," she replied softly. "At least not at first, I tried not to. I'd finally pushed them from my mind as far as I could. I had my Jesse, we loved each other. I should never have let her be part of it." She began crying again. "Can I have some more water? Please?"

"Why did you then?" Hunter countered, ignoring her plea.

"Jesse didn't want me to do them alone." Chrystal wiped away a tear. "She was there for me when Jeffy died, and after those bastards' gang-raped me in college. She was there for me in college, when I'd go on dates, picking the wrong guys. I'd come home beat up and bruised. She always cleaned me up, told me it was okay, encouraged me to keep studying. When I won that Zachary Jason prize and internship, it was like the world was finally turning around for me. I got the resources to work on the Latrodectus antivenin on my own while building a new career for myself—"

"So, what happened to TURN YOU?" Hunter slammed her fist on the table.

Chrystal jumped. "Don't you GET IT? Like I said, I had the means to *do* something about it, finally. Not just make the antivenin, but I was given the power to do something. I fantasized about killing them for a long time! I never expected that I'd actually get the chance to do it. So, I buried myself in the antivenin work. Then I saw Jake at a gas station. He was the gangbang leader, the first one to rape me, he stole my virginity. He didn't recognize me, after all, why would he? I followed him, learned where he lived and where he went. I finally had the means to kill him as painfully as he killed me on that stage."

"Where did you get the auto-injectors?" the masked man demanded.

She picked up the Styrofoam cup and looked in it, saw the water from the melting ice, and sipped at it. "Can I have some more water please? My throat's really dry."

"NO!" Spy yelled. "You don't *deserve* to be comfortable! Talk!"

Chrystal shook, surprised by his angry demand, and exhaled loudly. "One of the test group injectors on the 14th floor was being sent for discard and melting. They had a tiny glitch in them; they still worked but had to be destroyed anyway. Annette showed me how to verify the manifests, and that's when I saw the case of bad injectors." She took another deep breath. "I followed the van, and when it stopped for gas, I took a chance. I figured anywhere a Jason vehicle was going to travel there would be cameras. So, I borrowed Jesse's car, instead of mine. Because mine had the Jason parking garage sticker in the window. I followed until it stopped. I stole the case at that station."

"Why didn't you stop after the last gang-rapist?" he asked.

She looked at the black lenses hiding his eyes. "Why the hell are you dressed like that? Both of you. Especially you, mister. Your whole team, like in some stupid ass Spiderman movie. You go out in public like that, why?"

Hunter answered, "Because that's what we do! It's none of your damn business! Keep talking, or do I have to pull it out of you somehow?"

"You'd like that, wouldn't you? Kill the killer. Force me to talk? Well, no problem! I gotta story for the whole freekin' world to hear!" Chrystal sat back and smiled at them. "Did you see all those women joining that Black Widow fan page? No, we didn't create it; those *other* women did. They're just as guilty as me, since you're looking to blame someone. All I did was do them a favor, one they wanted, needed. Those raping bastards created me. The media named me. And all those other sex crime victims worshipped me. They wanted my help. I couldn't say no. I'd do it all again, if I had a chance!" Chrystal stood, as best she could, pulling at the shackles. "And again! And again! And again!"

Spy stood. "Well, tell you what, *Miss Latrodectus*, you'll never have another chance. It wasn't your decision to make to kill those men. Any of them."

"Whose decision was it to *kill my Jesse*? Why isn't the almighty Angela Jason in here, too?"

He put his face nose-to-nose with Chrystal. "Your Jesse tried to kill a Federal agent." He turned to leave, Hunter joining him. He opened the door and stopped, turning back to Chrystal. "And she lost."

"Wait! I have a right to a lawyer! When do I see my lawyer?" Chrystal demanded.

"There's no lawyer for you. You'll spend the rest of your life in isolation from the rest of the world."

"But Mr. Jason said he'd get me a lawyer; my mom, my dad—"

He stepped back to her slowly, barely an inch from her and looked down into her eyes. He cocked his head, privately reveling in what he was about to tell her. "They've been notified you died in a fiery car wreck; barely enough body left to make a dental ID. Your Jesse died with you, as her parents were notified. Just like your victims, you are *dead* to everyone! As far as the world is concerned, The Black Widow is dead and buried forever. By the way, thank you for developing that antivenin. Our doctors have examined it and are going to test it on our friend. Fortunately, when you injected him it was with a very small dose, guess that's all you had left after your last murder. Just pray that he survives. If he doesn't—"

"Boss," Hunter interrupted. "She's a psychopath. A sociopath. You can't reason with a serial killer. She'll just make everything go in circles."

He turned back and led Hunter out, allowing the door to close behind them.

Alone in the room, Chrystal pulled at the handcuffs, but the floor-bolted table wouldn't budge. She pulled at the table until her wrists began to bleed, to no avail. She screamed for help, to be released from the solitude of the small dark room. Chrystal sobbed loudly; with what energy she had left. She dropped to her knees, her shackled hands keeping her from falling all the way to the floor. She looked through the table legs to the door.

...just like her little brother looked through the crawlspace grate with his final breath...

...Chrystal's world was fading to black. She cried hard and loud, tears running down her cheeks, mucus dripping out her nostrils. "Jeffy, I'm sorry. Mommy? I need help, I can't—get—out..."

EPILOGUE 1

MY JUSTICE HAS BEEN SERVED

PRESIDENT KOMIANI WAS COMPLETING REPORTS at his desk for his diplomatic pouch to his home country. He felt an uneasiness in the air, and the hairs on his neck stood on end. He grabbed a pistol from its hidden holder under a desk drawer and rotated, to face The Spy standing behind him. Spy's sidearm was already pointed at his head. "I suggest you put that away very slowly," said the deep voice in the black uniform.

"I—agree," said Komiani, placing the pistol in its holder. He turned to face his intruder, who was no longer there.

Spy's voice came from the front of the desk next, making Komiani nearly jump out of his desk chair. "I'm here as a courtesy."

"You have a very strange way of doing so, mystery man," the president replied. "Would you care to take a seat?"

"As I said, I'm here as a courtesy, not for a social event." Spy moved his gun back to the holster slat and pressed it against the metal plate. The biosensor powered clips snapped into place to secure the weapon. "Your son's killer has been captured and locked away."

For the first time in weeks Komiani was joyous. He stood from his chair and rounded his massive desk, extending his hand to the agent. He grabbed the gloved hand and shook it energetically. "Jason said he had friends who could find her! Thank you! You must bring her to me immediately, so I may take her home to face Ollistani justice!"

Spy gently withdrew his hand and crossed his arms. "That won't be possible."

Komiani's smile disappeared just as rapidly as it had formed moments earlier. "No. It is possible. You will make it happen."

Spy glanced down at Komiani's crotch, and the president followed the stare downward. "I suggest you remember who gives the orders between the two of us, sir," said the agent.

"Yes, the implant you put down there. I remember."

"The Black Widow has been captured and essentially 'buried alive' if you will. She will never see sunlight again. Her accomplice, on the other hand, met a much less pleasant end."

"You dishonor me, and my son, by denying me—no, denying the people of *my* country, Ollistan. We must execute that murderous bitch!" His fury was exemplified by his reddening face and bulging neck veins.

"You don't seem to understand, she committed numerous murders besides Yursi's, and every one of them, including Yursi's, took place on American soil," Spy replied. "If she had killed him on Ollistani ground, I'd be the first one to hand her over."

"I don't care where she killed anyone! *She killed my son!* I want justice, I need to show *my* people justice!" he yelled, spittle flying from his mouth.

"You'll just have to accept that I did what Mark Jason, my country, and my president ordered me to do, and that was to catch his killer." He stepped closer to Komiani, nearly nose-to-nose. "I was never ordered to deliver her to you." He moved toward the spot where he arrived, behind the desk. "She'll not be given to the American court system either. She will not be put on trial, where she could live in freedom awaiting her verdict. You, your country, my president, and my country will simply have to accept that where I've put her is the best for all. She will soon fade from everyone's memory. Or, boom." He nodded at Komiani's crotch again, where the make-believe 'implant' resided. "I foresee needing your services again in the future, and you *will* freely accept our request for help."

The president rounded his desk and stood defiantly in front of the uninvited guest. "You have balls, you and your country. You will regret what you did to me. You both will pay dearly for it one day. I will get this device removed from *my* balls somehow, without you knowing. And on the eve of war, I will capture you and unmask you before I kill you myself."

Komiani's view turned from that of the masked man's head to the barrel of his automatic pointed between his eyes. "If you think you can capture and kill me, you're welcome to try. And if somehow you manage to succeed, I have my own personal warriors who will avenge my death. And they won't stop at a simple 'boom'."

Agent Spy pulled his trigger, and his gun clicked.

Komiani involuntarily closed his eyes at the sound, expecting that he would suddenly be dead. Instead, when he opened his eyes, he found himself alone in his office.

"There will be payment for your slander, masked one!" he bellowed as he leaned against his fists on the desk. "*DO YOU HEAR ME?* As Allah is my witness, I will have revenge on you and your damned United States!" …

EPILOGUE 2

REPORT FOR DUTY

THE HOSPITAL ROOM WAS MOSTLY DARKENED. Lights from the various medical monitors and dim overhead track lighting gave the room an ethereal atmosphere.

Stephanie sat in a chair next to the bed, holding Calvin's hand in hers. Her cheeks were streaked with dried tears; too tired to cry anymore.

A large hand gently grasped her shoulder, and instinct kicked in. Stephanie bolted from the chair, reaching for her holster. "It's just me," Mark said softly, his hand gripping hers before she could take aim.

Stephanie exhaled and relaxed. "Now I know why he keeps asking how you do things," she sighed. "I never heard the door open." She looked at the door and saw the guard through a small glass window, still standing outside. "He's supposed to come in with all visitors, your own orders. Is he even aware that you're in here?"

Mark simply smiled. "Ancient Chinese Secret," he replied.

"You and your freekin' 'Ancient Chinese Secret'," Stephanie said, unable to refrain a small chuckle.

"Did the Doc's say if the antivenin is working?"

"Yeah, there wasn't enough left in the Widow's auto-injector to kill him, but more than enough to put him right on the edge. They had to guess at how much to give him, since it's not been used on a human before. Seems awfully slow to work though, I hope they gave him enough. Thank God you guys found the injection site on his neck, and got the antivenin in time. I just don't know, Mark."

He looked at the monitors and studied the digital readings, then put his face next to the ashen face of his teammate. "Agent Seeker, you've got the most important mission of your life awaiting your attention," he said in his best unaltered Spy-voice. He turned to Stephanie and continued, "Special Agent Anderson has all the information for your briefing. Time to finish your vacation and report for duty."

Stephanie smiled. "Appeal to basal response, nice," she said. "Wish I'd thought of that."

"From you? That line wouldn't've worked. Unless you were standing over him naked, maybe holding a gun to his chest."

"No, we already did that." She looked at him. "Wait! How did you know that?"

Mark chuckled. "Ancient—"

"Chinese Secret, I got it," she finished for him. She sat again and interlaced her fingers with Calvin's. "I wish I could tell what those machines are saying."

Mark chose not to reply. He understood what the readings indicated. Instead, he said, "I may have only known him for a few years, far less time than you've known him, but Calvin Geffers is one of the strongest men I know. I've seen him injured worse than this. He'll be back on his feet in no time. He's got you as the best incentive he's ever had."

She smiled. "Is that how all you secret super-hero agent types pick up us damsels in distress?"

"It's a standard contract clause, yes."

She laughed, then looked at him solemnly. "Mark, can you make him retire? Make him quit? Hasn't he done enough?"

He placed his hand on her shoulder again. "If you were in that bed and he were sitting here, would you expect him to ask that question and you say "yes" when you woke up?"

A single tear rolled down her cheek. "Well, when you put it that way."

"You did a great job on this case. A special commendation has been sent to your supervisor. Tom wants to recruit you into the Task Force Division, full time, when you get tired of the FBI."

"Thanks, Mark, but I don't have the legs for your very unforgiving uniforms." Stephanie turned around to face her unmoving fiancé.

"Well, if you ever change your mind, or think your legs look good in tight black—"

"Only one guy's ever gonna see my legs, Mark." She turned around to an empty room. "Damn. How did he do that?"

ONE MONTH LATER

Calvin sat in his desk chair at Task Force Division, looking at Stephanie as she modeled her new Task Force uniform. "Yep, yep. I jus' love how that uniform hugs your ass and legs!"

She closed her eyes and shook her head. "I still can't believe I let you talk me into this. I'm so embarrassed."

He rose from his chair and walked around to her. By contrast, he was dressed in jeans and a white dress shirt with the sleeves rolled up. "Until I'm fully cleared by medical, you've been given provisional assignment to the field team to help out on missions. And you should be honored."

"Well, I am, Calvin. But aren't there people already here to move up to an opening?"

"This isn't like pro sports. You don't expect to get called up unless it's going to be permanent. With you in my place, everyone knows it's temporary. For now, that is."

She draped her arms around his neck. "Does that mean I get the 747 all to myself, too?"

"Yeah, no," he replied with a smile.

"Daddy, are all missions like this?"

Mark, Jan, and Angela were sitting in the family mansion's den, where the ladies had convinced Mark to accept the Task Force's invitation to join and lead the field team. "More or less," he said before he sipped his Glenlivet.

"'More or less'?" she asked back.

"Meaning," Jan interrupted, "that the more you get involved the less you'll stop expecting the usual."

"All of this ruckus because a girl was gangraped in high school and threatened into silence," Mark added. "All the lives lost because four boys took away a life of happiness. The worst of it is, she had it buried so deep I never saw it at work, and it surprised the hell out of me to find out she was The Black Widow."

"You can't see through everyone, Mark," Jan said.

"Yup. Shows I'm not perfect, just like everyone else…well, maybe not like one other person, that is."

"What do you mean, Daddy?"

He pointed at a folded newspaper on the coffee table between them. "Have you read this month's Navy Times yet, young lady?"

"No," she admitted. "Been kinda busy.

"Good." He set down his glass and stood. "Come in please, gentleman."

Tom and the Navy admiral chief of staff opened the far door and entered. Tom was dressed in his colonel's dress uniform and the admiral, carrying a brief case, in his. Jan and Angela stood to welcome them. "Angela," greeted Tom.

"Lieutenant Junior Grade," said the admiral.

"Sirs," she answered.

"JG Jason, your performance in this crisis was of the highest caliber of study, planning, action, reaction, and conclusion. I have rarely read a report of others about you, considering you downplayed yourself quite a bit in your own report."

"Family tradition, sir," whispered Mark.

"Ah, yes," said the admiral as Angela flushed slightly. "JG, because you are also one of the hardest people to surprise, according to your father, we are here today to do what you have yet to read: by the authority vested in me by the Congress of the United States, you are hereby promoted to the rank of full lieutenant with all the duties and privileges accompanying." He presented her with a black jewel box, which he opened to present a pair of shiny new double-silver bars. "Congratulations, Lieutenant." The admiral extended his hand to shake Angela's as she accepted her new rank.

"Th-thank you, sir! I-I don't know what to say!"

"You will remain on detached duty with Task Force Division until further notice. Your father, here, is reputed to be one of the toughest bosses in the world. He'll teach you well."

"Lieutenant," Mark said, and Angela turned to him at attention. "Congratulations. And you are officially off duty until Monday."

"Um, that's tomorrow?"

"Don't bother me with details, just be there on time…"

ABOUT THE AUTHORS

Jack Gannon and Cyndi Williams-Barnier are authors from Beaufort and Ridgeland, South Carolina, respectively.

They met at Beaufort High School, discovering a shared interest in writing and graphic arts. The two friends talked of graduating high school, going off to college, and eventually writing the next Great American Novel. But, as it happens so many times, *life* got in the way. The two lost each other after high school, not to meet again until over three decades later.

Jack's career was in journalism/news, and Cyndi's was with local government. By happenstance (*or perhaps divine intervention*), the two bumped into each other on Facebook as they both entered retirement.

After writing several books together (with more in the works) and being asked regularly to help other authors get their books published, they founded YBR Publishing, a services publisher based in Ridgeland, SC. While they focus on helping South Carolina Lowcountry authors achieve published status, they have also helped authors in other states and even one in London, England!

Jack and Cyndi can be found on their author page:

www.facebook.com/jackandcyndiauthors

YBR Publishing can be reached or contacted as follows:

www.ybrpub.com
contact@ybrpub.com
www.facebook.com/ybrpublishing

REVIEWS

5-Star Review from Readers' Favorite LLC

This is an absorbing story, dark and oddly seductive. The darkness and the sheer violence in it could be repulsive to some readers, but it is hard to stop reading because of the author's storytelling skills, unveiling the dark world of a psychotic killer. The story has a strong psychological depth and explores how deep abuse and betrayal can sink a human soul. The writing is excellent, and it features wonderful descriptions, great diction, and engaging dialogues. Jack Gannon and Cyndi Williams-Barnier show great skill in character, setting, and plot. Yes, the characters are well-developed, and readers will find great interest in following the psychological contours of their minds. Bite of the Black Widow has a lot of surprises in plot development and the reader has to guess their way through the gripping plot till they turn the final page. It's a delightful and entertaining read.

~Romuald Dzemo, Readers' Favorite LLC

5-Star Review from Southern Owl Publications and Promotions

…a scientifically diabolical story of one woman and her need for revenge…well developed characters and a story line to die for ~ literally…I will never look at a spider the same way again. The authors have grabbed onto and held my interest in their shimmering web…an absolutely terrifying read.

~Crystal Gauthier, Author